HIGH

FINALIST

"*Wolf's Gam*... a sequel that not only surpasses the power of the original, but turns your expectations against you at every turn. His writing has never been crisper, his suspense never more nerve-wracking, and his dry humor so consistently refreshing. Gagliani is fashioning an epic werewolf cycle here, one filled with terror, passion, violence, surprisingly affecting sensuality, and enough fantastical twists and turns to satisfy even the most jaded horror reader."

—Five-time Bram Stoker Award–winner
Gary A. Braunbeck, author of *Far Dark Fields*

"A great big bloody beast of a book that enthralls the reader on multiple levels. Vicious, gory, sexy, fascinating—part supernatural thriller, part police procedural, pure dynamite!"

—Edward Lee, author of *The Golem*

"*Wolf's Gambit* is the equivalent of a North Woods rollercoaster—with each brutal twist the body count rises, but you never want the ride to end! This one goes for the throat over and over again, and as you slip through the slayings with Detective Lupo in a desperate race against time, the pages seem to turn themselves! I couldn't put it down!"

—John Everson, author of *Sacrifice*

"If you're looking for the same-ol'-same-ol' werewolf story, W. D. Gagliani's *Wolf's Gambit* is definitely not for you. Gagliani takes a rehashed theme and breathes new life into it with a cast of memorable characters and relentless suspense. *Wolf's Gambit* is one book you won't put down, and it's a story you'll never forget."

—Deborah LeBlanc, bestselling author of *Water Witch*

PRAISE FOR *WOLF'S TRAP*!

"Gagliani knows horror fiction and he has supplied us with a skillfully crafted piece of dark literature."

—*Midwest Book Review*

"Gagliani has brought bite back to the werewolf novel. . . . *Wolf's Trap* is a hirsute werewolf story that will grab you by the reading jugular and keep you clawing the pages until the story's exciting conclusion."

—CNN.com Headline News Book Lizard review
by James Argendeli

"This novel is by turns tough, suspenseful, poignant, surprisingly erotic, and, finally, beautifully measured. It can rightfully take its place alongside Harry Shannon's *Night of the Werewolf* and P. D. Cacek's *Canyons* as one of the best werewolf novels of the last ten years."

—Gary A. Braunbeck, author of *Far Dark Fields*

"Simply put, this book rocks. It's fun, exciting, gritty, sexy, and nasty, and I recommend it to anyone looking for a great read."

—HorrorWorld.org

"Gagliani . . . proves himself as a powerful new talent."

—The Horror Channel Web site

"W. D. Gagliani writes with the precision of a vivisectionist, pulling just the right nerve endings to make your skin crawl and your pulse race. *Wolf's Trap* catches you by the throat and shakes your senses hard. Highly recommended."

—James A. Moore, author of *Under the Overtree*

THEIR TERRIFIED PREY

He barely felt the deep scratches that lined his face and arms, smearing blood down his shirtfront. His jacket was gone, lost somewhere behind him. Where they were. He didn't care.

He crashed through a thick screen of bushes, tripped on an uprooted pine sapling and found himself facedown on the dirt road, grasping handfuls of red mud.

He heard bodies hurtling through the brush behind him.

Up and running, his fancy shoes slipping in the mud, he hurtled down the wet dirt road, barely aware of the rain and the receding thunder.

Howling came from inside the woods, where the dark shapes were pacing him from the side. Something crashed onto the road and he heard the scrabbling paws of some kind of beast.

He screamed loudly.

Something snagged his right ankle and he went flying through the air and face-first into the mud. Then the pain began. . . .

Other *Leisure* books by W. D. Gagliani:

WOLF'S TRAP

WOLF'S GAMBIT

W. D. GAGLIANI

LEISURE BOOKS

NEW YORK CITY

For my Mom and Janis, always loving and always supportive.
And once again, in memory of my Dad . . .

A LEISURE BOOK®

September 2009

Published by

Dorchester Publishing Co., Inc.
200 Madison Avenue
New York, NY 10016

ISBN 10: 0-8439-6249-6
ISBN 13: 978-0-8439-6249-9
E-ISBN: 978-1-4285-0730-2

Printed in the United States of America.

10 9 8 7 6 5 4 3 2 1

ACKNOWLEDGMENTS

Thanks are due to many people, among them my editor Don D'Auria and everyone at Leisure, my agent Jack Byrne, and my fellow writers David Benton, Jay Bonansinga, Gary Braunbeck, Judy Bridges, John Everson, J. A. Konrath, Richard Laymon (I miss you, my friend), Deborah LeBlanc, Edward Lee, Tom Piccirilli, Brian Pinkerton, Harry Shannon, Michael Slade, Tamara Thorne, Robert W. Walker, Christopher Welch, and Mark Zirbel. You guys are truly inspirational in many ways.

AUTHOR'S NOTE

The real Eagle River is located in the southern part of Vilas County, in northern Wisconsin. Once again I have altered it geographically, socially, and with regard to local city and county organization to suit my purposes. All characters in this alternate Eagle River and vicinity are either fictional or used fictitiously, and should in no way resemble their real-world counterparts. However, some things are unalterably true. If you drive up Highway 45 from Milwaukee, and find yourself in the North Woods just past dusk, you might notice shadows keeping pace with you from the undergrowth crowding the side of the road. The pines are set claustrophobically close together, but these shadows seem to move effortlessly among the trunks. If you look up, the moon's silvery sheen might be filtering through the treetops. If you roll down your windows, you might hear the howling.

Don't roll down your windows.

WOLF'S GAMBIT

PRELUDE

Five miles from Eagle River
May 17

He is running for his life.

Jimmy Blackthorn's Gucci shoes make sucking sounds in the mud, but he barely notices.

His ears are hypertuned for the sounds of pursuit. From behind and beside him, he can sense something—more than *one* something—is pacing him, remaining invisible.

A fast glance over his shoulder nets him a fleeting gray shadow.

He hasn't panicked yet, but he's about to.

When he hears the growls, the blood freezes in his veins.

When the howling begins, his thoughts degenerate into a cloud of primitive terror.

The dirt road is now mud that reaches up and snags his feet, slowing his headlong rush away . . . away from . . .

His mouth is open in a soundless scream.

Behind and beside him, the pursuit closes in.

When he arrived, the storm was rolling in, the sound of distant thunder echoing through the pines. Lightning flashed a glow over the treetops, off to the west. The strobe effect increased in frequency, and the thunder grew louder by the minute, a rumble you could feel down in your shoes.

Jimmy Blackthorn took only partial note of the approaching storm. He was fuming. He kicked a piece of sawed two-by-four out of his way and felt satisfaction. He rolled his eyes, stomped a step or two, then continued toward his car, parked near a large unfinished sign.

His anger was boiling inside, building like a locomotive's head of steam, threatening to set him off. He shook his head for the tenth or twentieth time. They had promised. There had been communication, and he'd been convinced they finally understood his position in this matter. The construction site would be humming the next time he stopped in, they'd said. There would be progress. Things would be moving, wheels rolling.

Blackthorn had liked what he heard. He'd agreed that this effort would stave off problems with the investors. He nodded and smiled, but then he came out to check the site, telling himself he was wasting his time.

When he arrived, the site was deserted. No humming. No wheels doing anything. Nothing moved at all.

"Jesus Christ," he'd shouted, after looking at the three big holes in the ground that would, with an inordinate amount of luck, become the Great Northern Casino & Entertainment complex. Casino, 400-room hotel, and adjoining theater for intimate performances by A-list celebs and bands gone C-list (but still willing to pretend if their fans were). He'd stared into the wide holes and felt the money sucked out of his pockets. Heard the sound of it clinking like casino change into the one-armed bandits.

Ha, they don't even bother with cash anymore, he reminded himself.

He had stomped all over the site, looking for Sabin, the head security guard. Hadn't found him at his trailer, in his car, or anywhere else. Nope, Jimmy Blackthorn was alone. The site was deserted. The workers were . . . just not there.

He had tried making a call, but he couldn't get a signal on his cell.

Damn woods. Too many trees.

He made a note to raise the topic of cell-phone repeater towers at the next meeting.

Still grasping the useless cell phone, he had headed over to the future parking lot back to his car.

He tried again to make a call, this time seeing the LCD bar that told him he was picking up a signal, then dialing, then seeing the bar disappear even as he started shouting into the phone.

Jimmy stood behind his Beamer, a silver rag-top roadster, and smacked the hood in frustration. Once, twice, three times.

Now he became aware of the rolling thunder that signaled the storm's arrival. The tall stands of pines all around the clearing couldn't muffle the thunderclaps any longer, and the lightning was beginning to filter through the thick tree line more insistently.

He climbed into his car. He'd have to go out of his way to report the site was abandoned.

Again.

This was the third time workers had walked off, and after he had been assured the head of security would make it his business to keep "accidents" and slowdowns to a minimum. Yes, there had been opposition to the casino being built, but it was a done deal now.

Thunder crashed almost overhead. Not more than a couple miles away.

Better get moving, he thought. *Beat the storm.*

He turned the ignition and pressed the starter.

Nothing. Not even a click.

What the fuck!

He repeated the procedure a half dozen times. Nothing.

A fat droplet exploded on his head.

Damn it. Rain. What else could go wrong?

And he couldn't put up the top without the engine on. Could he? He'd have to check the manual. But he didn't have it with him. He'd never had the car not start. He tried his phone again and saw the teasing bars, but when he dialed they disappeared.

Fuck fuck fuck.

Jimmy slammed the wheel repeatedly. More rain plopped into the car and on the upholstery. Would rain ruin the leather? Damn it, he was really pissed now. He would have Sabin fired first, and then he'd set about getting the workers—most of them local—replaced. They were under contract, and it was his job to make sure the construction was on time and under budget.

Fat chance.

He heaved himself out of the driver's seat and stood trying to orient himself. The dirt road was behind him, but it snaked and curled through the woods. If he wanted to reach US 45 and the series of filling stations he remembered spotting every day, then he'd have to cut through the woods at an angle. The rain was beginning to intensify, splattering all around him.

He took a last look at his car, almost crying to see the rain pelting the interior. Then he set off into the woods, heading approximately due southwest, where he estimated he could find a tow truck, a mechanic, a phone.

Something.

Soon he was surrounded by thick undergrowth and tightly packed pine trunks. Both made progress slow and draining. Jimmy Blackthorn was a city Indian, more accustomed to fancy bars and high-class restaurants. Any woodcraft he'd learned as a boy had long ago dissipated. And he'd never missed it.

Darkness settled on him, the only exception provided by the lightning, which cracked the sky overhead. Though he couldn't see the sky—the pines were too thick. Thunder followed each flash, loud booming gunshot crashes that took his breath away.

The storm seemed to have settled overhead by now.

But Jimmy Blackthorn was completely turned around. He realized that if he had any hopes of finding his way back to the highway it was going to be on the dirt road. But which way was the road?

Now and again a drop of rain penetrated the trees' deep cover and caught him in the face, but so far the storm was wimpier than he had expected. Lots of noise and flash, little substance.

He tried to determine the way he'd come, but all the pine trunks looked the same. Behind them there was only black. He turned 360 degrees. *It all looked the same.*

How could he get so lost in five minutes?

Jimmy was pragmatic. First, he tried retracing his recent steps. Five minutes later, he might as well have been in the same spot. He tried a tilt to his left. Same result.

Sweat now poured down his back, so he stripped off his leather jacket.

He was going to get some people fired, big-time!

He had to be a stone's throw from the site, yet he seemed hopelessly lost.

Something rustled in the undergrowth to his right.

Jesus, now what?

Jimmy Blackthorn had never been afraid of anything. But for the first time since leaving his car he wondered if he shouldn't have stayed until after the storm.

The rustling came closer, became louder.

Jimmy turned his back on the sounds and started to run.

The undergrowth reached out like clawing hands to grab his ankles and trip him.

He ran, and the rustling ran with him.

He stopped, and the rustling stopped.

Then he heard the same sounds on his left.

Christ, what—?

He turned right and crashed through the brush. Whatever it was, it kept pace with him, behind him now.

Wait, now there was rustling and . . .

Panting. Was that *his* breathing or someone else's?

Blind panic blanketed his mind.

The lightning and thunder seemed to be moving away,

but whatever was in the woods with him was infinitely more frightening.

Rustling and panting came together behind him, and he launched himself through the whipping branches in the opposite direction, desperate to put distance between himself and . . . and whatever that was.

Suddenly he heard more rustling to his left and he corrected his course toward the right, still lost but determined to outrun whatever toyed with him.

He barely felt the deep scratches that lined his face and arms, smearing blood down his shirtfront. His jacket was gone, lost somewhere behind him. Where *they* were. He didn't care.

Jesus, he prayed for the first time since he'd been a kid in the rez orphanage, *Please Jesus just get me out of here and back to the car.*

He crashed through a thick screen of bushes, tripped on an uprooted pine sapling, and found himself facedown on the dirt road, grasping handfuls of red mud.

He heard bodies hurtling through the brush behind him.

His fancy shoes slipping in the mud, he ran down the road, barely aware of the rain and the receding thunder.

Howling came from within the woods, where dark shapes were pacing him from the side. Something crashed onto the road, and he heard the scrabbling paws of some kind of beast—

He screamed, no longer owned by his outsized pride.

Something snagged his right ankle. He went flying through the air and fell face-first into the mud. Then the pain began.

All he could feel was the agony, not knowing that his ankle was broken and his tendons torn through by a mouthful of long fangs in a snout that was now grasping thigh meat.

Ripping thigh meat.

Jimmy Blackthorn screamed as the muscular gray wolf that had hold of him shook him like a rag doll.

Two more dark shapes burst out of the woods on both sides of him. They lunged, landing on his thrashing body.

Jimmy's voice turned into a gurgle as one of the wolves went for his throat, and the other sank its teeth into his stomach.

Jimmy Blackthorn's mewling was replaced by the sound of the wolves.

Feeding.

Part One

Andante

Chapter One

Lupo

The light was strange, seeming to squeeze through a yellow filter. Tornado weather, the sky brushed liberally with sickly color, the air still—all portents of bad things to come.

The house didn't feel right. The door, ajar. Inside, the yellowish light leaned toward green. The curtains hung limply in the bedroom window. Every piece of furniture was tainted with the unpleasant hue, but the light was sufficient for him to make out the figure under the bedsheets, curled like an oversized infant.

Heart beating more rapidly now, a shiver down the spine and a low growl building deep in the throat. Other changes beginning, minutely traversing paths unseen and unimaginable.

His voice came as a hoarse whisper.

"Jessie?" He swallowed through his tightening throat. Saliva tasted of rotted trash. He stared at the covered figure. It trembled gently.

The light seemed to separate into green and yellow bands. He squinted, approaching.

"Jessie, what's wrong?"

His voice sounded all wrong. The whole thing was wrong. He saw feet protruding from behind the bed. *Jessie's feet.*

The figure under the bedclothes reared up like a sheet-covered ghost from some video game.

But when the sheet slid off, it was Martin Stewart, brandishing a blood-slick scalpel.

Nick Lupo leaped backward, but he was too off balance to completely evade the attack.

The scalpel *swished* through the skin just below his chest. Lupo saw blood fly in a straight line from the long, clean incision. He barely felt the pain as the adrenaline kicked in, and he was able to avoid the return slice. The scalpel split air where Lupo's right side would have been.

Martin snarled rabidly.

His face was made up almost to clown level. Eyes circled in black and gold glitter. Lips swelled to triple their size by deep violet gloss outlined in thick black lines. Cheeks painted with huge red spots. His teeth bared, he was simultaneously clown and angry gorilla, standing on the ruined bed and lunging again.

Lupo's thoughts of Jessie slowed him, but he still sidestepped awkwardly out of the way and suddenly became aware of the intense burning that had enveloped his chest, raging now through his bloodstream and to his pain sensors.

Silver.

Martin's scalpel must have had silver smelted to the blade.

Lupo's sidestep turned into a fall.

Jessie!

Her dead body, mutilated by the freak, was sprawled beside the bed.

And Lupo landed on top of her, his open chest wound afire and his mind clouding in grief and unbearable pain.

Above him, Martin came in for the final stroke, scalpel raised high. The blade paused for a second, then flashed downward.

Lupo struggled to wake himself.

Jesus.

His body bathed in sweat, he slowly let his muscles relax, his fists unclench to reveal bloody gashes from his fingernails. He forced his breathing to become regular.

Another goddamned Martin nightmare.

This has got to stop.

Just for the hell of it, he checked his chest. No burning wound, no sizzling blood.

No murdered Jessie. This was his apartment in the city. She was still safe in her bed in Eagle River, up in Vilas County, a six-hour drive away. He had no reason to think she was in any danger. It was just his mind playing its tricks on him.

Six hours. He would break every speed limit to get to her later today. His lower belly tingled. Or something tingled. He wished he could snap his fingers and zoom past this day.

Short of sleep again, his heart still racing, Lupo rolled over and stared at his ceiling. He closed his eyes and could still see the vivid dream scene and feel the pain, the sadness.

Christ.

He knew he was supposed to talk about these dreams, but he was damned if that crone at the department would hear this one. Or any of the others he'd suffered through lately.

He sighed and rolled out of bed unwillingly. The sense of dread raised in the nightmare continued to flow through his nerves, making them twang with repressed energy. His hands shook slightly. The itch was coming back, and he fought the urge to scratch himself bloody.

It was going to be one of those days.

Arnow

They'd done it again. The three coffee mugs lined up on the utility counter did not include his. He scanned the room, didn't see it, and walked past the reception and dispatch station. It was unmanned because Rita had the flu, or a sinus infection, or one of her kids did. Arnow wasn't sure because halfway through her phone call he had shut her out—her droning voice was bad enough coming out of his radio, he didn't feel like listening to her on the phone, too.

"Thanks for calling, Rita," he had said, interrupting the stream. "Feel better!"

"It's not—" He had hung up before hearing any more.

But now that Rita wasn't here, no one would bother to get him coffee. No one had bothered to scoop up his mug, wash it, and line it up with the others to be filled.

He sighed.

It was always tough being *the new guy.* He should know. He'd been the new guy a half dozen times, though one was by default. He had started big, rising to detective in Chicago, but a smaller town had beckoned, and he'd found a niche in Daytona Beach. Couldn't fault the weather or "the view," especially during spring break. But you *could* fault the weather when you became aware of hurricane season. Daytona lay mostly off hurricane alley, but a few close calls had soured him on all the good stuff. Even when the hurricane was a bust, like 1999's Floyd, that bounced northward along the coast and never made landfall in Florida, the evacuations took a lot out of him—criminal activity always seemed to increase during bad weather, or the potential for bad weather.

Naked bank robbers, mummified corpses, buried body parts, alligator attacks and criminal use of alligators, homicidal relatives, kidnapped children, abused children, abused babies, crackhead babysitters—it was uncanny, but Arnow had seen more in his three years in Daytona than in all the previous years in Chi-town.

Becoming the new sheriff in sleepy Eagle River was possibly the best thing to have happened to him. In life. Well, as a bachelor he had to list some of the sex he'd had, too. But professionally, this was a superb gig, and he liked it even when they didn't get him coffee.

Arnow washed out his mug and dried it absentmindedly, then filled it from the pot. It wasn't as hot as when Rita made it fresh, but a spoonful of sugar and four ice cubes from the tiny refrigerator under the counter turned it into quite acceptable iced coffee. He returned to his office and sat behind his desk, sipping.

Technically, somebody should have been at the dispatch

station, manning radio and telephones. And e-mail. But Rita was sick, and Jerry Faber was out on a call. The other full-time deputies were either on their daytime patrols or not yet on shift. Hal Halloran, Jonston, Arrales, and Morton. He was still a bit unsure of his night cops because he didn't see them very often.

Arnow grimaced. He knew he was running his department still mostly shorthanded. Bunche, his predecessor, had six more full-timers and a couple more part-timers on the job patrolling Vilas County than Arnow did. But how much had it helped when the shit hit the fan a couple years back? That so-called homegrown terrorist cell had exploded into action and shot the hell out of Bunche and a deputy. Other local folks had been killed or wounded, including the reservation doctor, Jessie Hawkins, and that cop from downstate. That cop, what was his name? *Lupo.* Who was maybe turning out to be Jessie's boyfriend.

He'd wondered more than once what the Milwaukee homicide detective was doing in Eagle River. What exactly had been his involvement in the so-called terrorist plot? The whole thing stank to high heaven. Arnow wasn't born yesterday, dammit, and that was a load of crap they'd unloaded in front of the news media and even the feds.

He swiveled his chair and stared at the file cabinets. Nah, most of these files had been converted to the newer, more modern computer and server system that had been part of the upgrades done by Sheriff Bunche. The county supervisor and town council had spent considerable money just before and just after the whole terrorist thing. Arnow was still charged with hiring more deputies to fill the schedule.

He called up a master list of old case files and clicked his way to the appropriate folders. Nodding with satisfaction, he found brief descriptions of what had happened, links to news stories, and a dozen PDFs of reports filed since then, some of them by the feds.

He was about to click on a report of all the involved parties when his dispatcher's phone rang. He almost ignored it, having called up in his mind a picture of Jessie Hawkins that he would like to have had time to linger on.

She was something, the good doctor.

Pretty. Better than that—beautiful. Cover-model beautiful. And feisty as hell. She'd killed one of the terrorist idiots herself with a goddamn crossbow, no less. *Damn.*

The insistent phone broke through his pleasant memory of his last meeting with Dr. Hawkins, and finally he stood and stalked out to the abandoned station and snatched the receiver in midring.

"Sheriff's office."

There was shocked silence on the other end of the line. Then: "Is that Sheriff Arnow?"

"Yup. Rita's got the flu."

"Sheriff, it's Bob Anderson over at the Mobil station on Route QQ. I've got one of your deputies here . . ."

"What's that?"

"Huh, yeah. Jerry Faber's here. That is, why don't you talk to him just as soon as he gets done heavin' his breakfast all over my concrete?"

There was commotion at the other end. Arnow squinted as if he could see through the phone line. Why wasn't his deputy calling in on his radio?

Finally, a tremulous voice came on the line.

"Sheriff?"

"Jerry, what's going on?" Keeping it neutral. Lectures could come later. Lesson on protocol. More training.

"You'd best get down here, Sheriff. To the station, and then down to the casino from there. There's a service road—"

"Service road? Yeah? Jerry?"

He heard coughing, gasping. Retching?

"It's bad, Sheriff. Real bad." Jerry panted as if he'd run five miles before gagging up his guts.

"Do you need backup? Do *I* need backup?"

"Best bring Ted and anyone else. Lots of crime-scene tape."

"A body?"

"What's left of it . . ."

"Shit. Don't leave. On my way—I'll be there shortly."

It sounded as though Jerry had another case of the heaves.

Arnow hung up, then lifted the receiver again. Let it hang in the air.

He felt the familiar surge of adrenaline. Excitement, sure, but also a heavy dose of despair. You hated to have violent crime on your beat, on your watch. Now his idyllic paradise had just changed. He wondered if Bunche had felt this way just before the terrorist thing literally exploded. He shivered a little. *Someone walking on my grave*, his grandmother would have said, and for once it didn't seem so far-fetched.

What could be so bad Jerry had hightailed it away from his patrol car, away from the crime scene, making a call from a civilian phone? Why had he abandoned his cruiser?

Before he realized it, Arnow was dialing. Got her machine or voice mail, whatever it was.

"Uh, this is an emergency. It's Sheriff Arnow . . ."

"Dr. Hawkins." She'd picked up, interrupting his rambling. The voice was smooth yet very sultry. He pictured her face, wondering if she'd been asleep.

"Hello, Jessie," he blurted out. "I think I have a homicide on my hands. Can you get away?"

"Tom?" She hesitated, clearly a bit puzzled, as if not tracking. "Sheriff Arnow?"

Had he forgotten to identify himself? Jesus, he was rattled.

"Uh, yes, sorry about that, Doc."

"It's okay." She breathed audibly, a bit of a pant, as if she'd run to the phone. "A homicide?"

"A bad one, sounds like, really spooked my deputy." He told her what he knew.

"I'll meet you there."

He heard a half sigh in her voice. He sympathized. Things were going to get messy. He knew that now, without a doubt.

At least he'd get to see Jessie.

Sam Waters

The day began as they all did lately. His first awareness included pain.

Pain in his back. Pain in his knees. And, when he awkwardly rolled himself out of bed, pain in his legs and pelvis. He stood up, none too steadily, and let the tingly jabs dissipate a little. They would, eventually, after a steady diet of Tylenol, muscle relaxants, and whatever else the doc had prescribed. Oh, and exercise. Moving around would settle the pain down some, but moving around also caused pain, so the trade-off sometimes amused him. His wife, Sarah, often accused him of being the cynical sort. But now she was gone, and he let his cynicism run rampant.

He stood in his pajama bottoms and slippers, waiting for his feet to be ready, and then he tottered off to the bathroom with a sigh. Hold off too much in that department and he'd pay for that, too.

Shit. Aging sucks.

Sam Waters was seventy-five and had looked not a day over sixty until a few days two years before, when he'd aged much too quickly. The gunshot wound hadn't helped. Now he thought he looked his age and more, even if people never said so. Well, except for the younger members of the council. *They* thought he was too old to sit on the council in the first place.

He shuffled into the warm kitchen of his farmhouse and slowly made himself tea. It was his favorite time of day. He peered outside and said hello, glancing at his wife's grave. How many years had it been? He never thought he could survive her leaving him so suddenly, but he'd been driven then. He had still burned with the intensity of a quest that had robbed him of his youth. And robbed him of his son. His only son.

Then when his quest was fulfilled, he did not find it fulfilling because he learned he had been wrong all those years. His sense of justice was shaken on that day the Stewart gang had shot him.

The Stewart gang was his own shorthand. They weren't much of a gang really, despite what CNN had made of them with some careful prompting.

A serial killer, Martin Stewart, thrown in with three local thugs led by the sociopath Wilbur Klug. Not much of a gang at all, but they'd wiped out the sheriff and almost a dozen others.

Sam drank his tea after letting it cool. It took the edge off some of his aches and pains.

Sometimes he couldn't help thinking about that day. The gunfight. How his grip on reality at first seemed to have slipped—but then how his reality had been altered, forever upset like a cosmic apple cart.

You think you can count on some things, but then you learn you're wrong.

Even though he had always been prepared to experience the uncanny, thanks to what had happened to his son, that day he'd had one strange belief proved and another disproved, and the collision had almost cost his sanity.

At least for a while.

Sam Waters was a practical man and quick to bring his cynicism to bear. Along with that came an open-mindedness born of various cultures at war within him. As a Native American, he understood natural magic most non-Indians simply glossed over. As a modern practical man, he placed trust in science.

So when a stranger named Dominic Lupo had entered his life, a confluence of cultural, religious, and scientific streams proved to him without a doubt that Shakespeare had been right—there were indeed more things in heaven and earth, etcetera. He thought of it that way, with the *etcetera.* Maybe rendered in Yul Brynner's timeless inflection.

Sometimes Sam thought he was too tied to the movies.

Then again, the best movies reflected life and the human condition. So why not be tied to the movies?

He shook his head. It felt as if he were trying to shake off something, a dark thing that wanted into his head. There was a fuzzy feeling in his ears, almost as if they were submerged. Sounds were muffled.

What now?

He'd been healthy as a horse before being shot, but now new aches and pains crept in almost daily, announcing themselves with a sharp jab here and a dull throb there.

The telephone rang, and Sam's ears popped as if he'd been on an airplane.

He looked at the phone and felt a physical temptation to ignore it. No explanation for it, but he knew whoever was on the other end, the call would change his life again.

The device continued to squall, and he reached for it.

Lupo

His partner waited behind the wheel of an unmarked detective's car.

Lupo left his building's lobby and headed for the nondescript Impala. He hated driving—he was the only cop he knew who hated it with a passion—but if it had been his turn, he would have preferred his own well-worn Maxima. Given it was his partner, Rich DiSanto's week to drive, Lupo climbed into the passenger seat and buckled up with a greeting grunt.

"Hey, Nick," DiSanto said. "Hope you don't mind I'm early."

"Nah, what else is there to do?"

Lupo didn't have to think very hard at all to come up with something, anything he'd rather do than go to work. He let the lie fester. No point in whining every week about how much he hated the gang task force assignment.

Lupo looked at DiSanto surreptitiously as he drove. A small smile played on his thin lips. DiSanto really did enjoy his task force assignment, Lupo decided. He wasn't faking. Lupo couldn't help thinking about Ben Sabatini, his former partner, who had succumbed to Martin Stewart's ferocious attack while Lupo frittered away his time in Eagle River.

Sabatini had been seasoned, a veteran cop from the old school who had taught Lupo much over the years. But he had forgotten one of his own lessons when it counted most and let down his guard at the worst possible time. Still, Lupo felt the guilt of having been too far away to prevent Ben's murder. Sometimes it almost crippled him, the guilt. But then, he had plenty of guilt already, and his conscience overflowed.

"Have a good weekend?" DiSanto was all about clichés.

"The best," Lupo said with a smirk his partner didn't see or hear. He played along, most days.

"Me too! Too short, though."

Lupo grinned without mirth. DiSanto annoyed him to no end, but he seemed like a solid partner most of the time. On the force ten years, plenty of street experience. His love of clichés was forgivable, if just. His shooting was among the best in the detective squad—he had plenty of department championship trophies to prove it. Lupo had been paired with the younger cop when reassigned to the gang task force—officially until he could recover from his injuries at the hands of the Martin gang.

Lupo smiled to himself. The Martin gang had certainly helped cause the injury, but technically Jessie Hawkins had inflicted the awful wound itself, severing his foot at the ankle to free him from the implacable jaws of the trap that held him prisoner. And that would have kept him from saving them both.

Thankfully Jessie was a doctor. She'd known how to perform the surgery (if wielding an axe could be considered surgery), and how to take care of him after—

After. Even after the foot regenerated itself. Though Lupo had to keep that fact hidden with a false artificial foot. There was no way he could explain how his foot regrew without admitting to the world what he was.

Lupo still had trouble admitting to himself what he was, what he had been since a childhood friend had forced his disease on him before being torn apart by a hail of silver buckshot . . .

Lupo had trouble admitting to himself that the disease had made him into a *werewolf.* That's what society called it, though most didn't believe it was real. But it was all too real to him. He had lived through the fear, the uncertainty, the horror of beholding what he became when the moon called to him.

At first, the Change had been painful. Not like in the movies, with the muscle and bone alteration. But with a soul-burning sensation that seemed to travel through every vein and tendon. The disease had made his youth hellish, and while in college he had sought comfort in the arms of a psychology professor who had become more than just his lover and protector. Caroline Stewart, Martin's sister, had become his own personal scientist, attempting to help him make sense of his Change both physically and psychologically.

It had been Caroline's belief, her theory, that Lupo the man could exert his will on the Creature that lived within him. The Creature had, up until then, exerted itself only during the monthly full-moon phase. But with Caroline's help, they had begun to see some sort of rudimentary influence that Lupo could exert on the Creature, a breakthrough which had indicated to Caroline that perhaps Lupo would one day be able not only to withstand the Creature's influence and even avoid the involuntary Change, but learn to force a Change at will.

Unfortunately, in the testing of her hypothesis, Lupo's Creature side, confused by the mixed signals of control and acquiescence, had reverted to its most bestial and had murdered Caroline as if she'd been a stranger, tearing her apart like helpless prey, and starting Lupo on a crusade to suppress his evil side. Ironically, becoming a cop had helped him channel his rage and turned him into a first-class homicide detective, though prone to monthly disappearances—drives up north to the great Wisconsin woods that Ben Sabatini, his partner, had learned to accept and help cover.

Only in the woods, under the moon and pines, could Lupo's Creature run free, hunt fresh game, and romp like the wild animal—however magical—that it was. And in the last two years, Lupo had proved Caroline's theories almost completely. Indeed, during the worst part of the Martin gang's abduction of Jessie Hawkins, Lupo had learned to call upon the Creature, the wolf, almost at will. Though he still felt its influence, the moon was no longer the enemy. Lupo's occasional involuntary growling and itching (as fur threatened to bloom on his skin) continued to annoy him, but he had made great progress on the heels of the trauma caused by the gang's actions. He had trouble thinking it was *him*, still *him*, when under the Change, but it was and he'd proven it over and over since then.

"Foot hurt today?"

"Huh?" Lupo's thoughts dissipated.

"Humidity's high. Figured your foot would ache like a sonofabitch today. One of the drawbacks of spring—all that rain. Looks like we're in for some," said his partner. " 'Red sky at night, sailor's delight. Red sky at morning, sailor take warning.' Did you see that red sky earlier?"

"I hadn't noticed. I was sleeping." Veiled sarcasm never worked on DiSanto.

"Yeah, it was like a red curtain."

Lupo grunted.

They drove in silence for a while. Lupo knew where they were headed. "Coffee stop?"

"Me coffee, you tea. That okay?"

"Fine." Lupo couldn't figure why younger people had to have coffee every moment. Ben had never been like that.

Dammit. He missed Ben more than he could ever explain. He'd get stuck on a thought and couldn't leave it. Like his dad. And Lupo knew he'd fallen into the same trap again. Thinking of Ben made him think of his father, and there went his mood.

Frank Lupo and his son had honed their differences for years, but they had slowly recovered some semblance of a close friendship, especially when Lupo had finally gone to visit the old man after the Martin Stewart case. A few months of closeness—phone calls, visits—and then brain cancer had eaten up Frank Lupo in little over a year, and now Nick Lupo found himself more easily returned to that blazing hot fall day in the bleak Florida crematorium than in the worst of his experiences as a cop. At night he saw Ben in his casket, and then Ben would morph into his father on a gurney. No funeral for him. He hadn't wanted one, but Nick still felt guilt at not overriding the old man's wishes this one time. Now he suffered in silence, pursued by nightmares and disturbing imagery whenever he closed his eyes.

After coffee and tea purchases, DiSanto drove them to their assignment for the day.

Lupo felt an itch begin on the back of his hands and run up his forearms. If he'd looked, he knew he would have seen dark, wiry hair begin to grow in tufts along his muscles.

He shivered despite the warmth of the spring day.

Something coming.

Jessie

She awoke still hung over from the vivid dream.

It was one of those strange dreams, beginning with a benign, almost pleasant aura of hazy positivity that seemed to caress her brain and stroke her pleasure center while relating to nothing at all. She sensed that she was smiling in her sleep.

Then the background changed, from a music video's gauze-draped room with wind-blown curtains and flickering candles to a dark hollow in the woods, cold and damp and tinged with sepia. It was almost like jumping from one photograph to another. Even while sleeping, Jessie thought she was aware of the change, felt her muscles tighten and her skin tremble as if the weather had suddenly turned freezing. The darkness slid over the woods like a black curtain, and as she shivered she heard a howl squeezing through the tree trunks, which turned black as she looked at them. She heard rustling in the woods and she caught the heavy scent of musk and something else, a strange smell of decay somehow intertwined with a familiar smell of . . . she couldn't quite identify what, but she knew that she was intimately acquainted with it.

Her shivering intensified, and she caught herself wondering whether it was the sleeping Jessie who shivered or the dream Jessie, or if perhaps they weren't both shivering. The rustle in the woods grew louder, closer, more menacing, and she thought back to the safe place, white with its gauze and soft-focus lighting, wishing she could return there, where she knew she would not be afraid. Instead, the dark place surrounding her became more and more vivid, and whatever made the rustling sounds growled—at first softly, but then growing in volume and anger. *Rage.*

Who or what was it?

Nick Lupo. In his wolf form.

Then she had shaken herself awake.

The dream-turned-nightmare left her reluctantly, and she pulled the covers up against the sudden chill.

Why did she have these strange dreams so often? Why were they so similar as to almost be considered recurring? What did they mean? Anything?

The questions zipped through her mind as they had a dozen times before, but in replaying them she found herself relaxing her clenched muscles. Slowly, her limbs warmed up and the chill began to dissipate.

Jessie thanked her lucky stars for Nick's upcoming visit. They had been together long enough now to be comfortable with each other. No longer just his landlord, she had become his lover.

She could shiver herself to death thinking of that cold night Nick rescued her from Martin Stewart. She'd seen Nick shimmer from man to wolf like the bouncy result of an old-fashioned film reel mounted on a shoddy projector. She'd been forced to believe right away, with no doubts. Except maybe for her own sanity; there was always that.

But no, she had seen him magically transform into a gargantuan black wolf—a crippled wolf, but still a formidable enemy, as Martin Stewart had learned.

Jessie had struggled with symptoms of post-traumatic stress afterward, but she hadn't told Nick. She'd found her own way to battle through it, burying herself in her work and—she blushed—in nursing Nick Lupo back to health, which included a healthy dose of intense lovemaking.

She smiled, thinking of the tenderness he had exhibited with her as he healed from the terrible wound she had been forced to inflict. It hadn't kept them from exploring each other's bodies every chance they had.

They had bonded. Old friends who had suddenly become lovers, already comfortable with each other's company, they had enjoyed discovering the whole new aspect of their relationship.

Jessie felt her insides melting at the thought of Nick's hands on her. Nipples tingling under his tongue, gentle nips driving her to near madness. She was wet and ready, and Nick was still hours from arriving. She touched herself, feeling naughty and not caring, knowing she still had time before work.

Fingers caressing her most intimate spots, Jessie allowed herself to imagine they were Nick's, and then she was moving faster, deeper, more pointedly focusing on that one spot where he would have placed his warm and loving tongue . . .

When the phone rang, she snorted with annoyance.

Let the damn thing ring!

But then she heard Arnow's hesitant voice, and the next thing she knew she was leaving her comfortable bed to hear the bad news.

Tannhauser

They had been here a month, laying low, itching to get to work. They had lined up routines that at least appeared legitimate, in case of nosy neighbors. Money wasn't a problem. Boredom was. It ate at them and blunted their edges. Slowed their reflexes. Killed their inner core and reduced them to shells. At least until they had purchased some used bench presses and barbell sets and given themselves an exercise program that would have killed lesser men.

Tannhauser didn't know why they couldn't begin their work as soon as they'd arrived, but he was the leader and even though his word was law, he still felt obligated to mollify them and pen them in.

Until the time came to loose the lightning.

A month of waiting was nothing to someone like him. A month of waiting was an appetizer in front of a meal. And now supper was ready.

He waited for the others, not worried they'd disobeyed their orders. He had been warned about unusual circumstances, and even though they feared nothing and no one, he still acted cautiously.

This quaint northern town in a state they'd never seen was no great shakes, but the sprawling national forest that curled around it was a slice of heaven for him and his kind. The spring weather was so much more complex than what they'd become accustomed to in the last three years. This was so much better. Even if they hadn't been on the payroll, Tannhauser thought he might have liked to settle here.

Why hadn't they ever traveled this far north?

He shook his head. Who knew?

Checked his belt clock. Still nothing.

The woods spread their mantle of pine and fir needles right up to the front door of the rental house. The lot had been carved out of a waterfront copse, but just barely. Evergreens shrouded three sides of the two-story log cabin, a

Cape Cod and Colonial hybrid that said "hunting lodge" to anyone who managed to spot it from the road or the lake.

It was not easy to spot. The trees masking it provided more than adequate screening from the road. A narrow overgrown driveway snaked off the road but was almost invisible.

Suddenly Schwartz seemed to materialize next to him, right at the tree line.

Trees.

What a wonderful thing.

No wonder they had lost their heads a little when first arriving. It had been so long in the sun and the sand that greenery was a welcome novelty.

One second there was only forest—tall pines, wide-armed firs, some spruce and poplar—and then the next second Schwartz stood next to him, grinning his toothy grin, his eyes alight with more than moonbeams.

"Mission accomplished," Schwartz said, grin widening.

He'd grin his way to hell.

Tannhauser didn't smile. You had to keep a certain distance between you and your subordinates.

"Tef?"

"Stopped off for a snack."

Again the grin. Schwartz was a good man, but Tef was a loose cannon. Tannhauser frowned. He would have to reassert. But now wasn't the time.

Schwartz took his silence for approval and asked, "We going out again tomorrow?"

"No, Mr. XYZ said wait, so we wait now."

"What's this Mr. XYZ bullshit? Don't we rate a real name?"

Tannhauser snorted. "We're employees. We rate what our employer wants us to rate."

"Well, that's bullshit anyway."

"Yeah, sure."

Moments later Tef also appeared, stepping out from between the trees, his face glowing with fresh blood.

"All right, we're all here. Time to disappear for a short

while." Tannhauser herded them inside and waited for their grumbling to dissipate.

"Good job, men. My compliments."

They nodded with happiness. They were simple creatures, easy to lead and easy to manipulate.

Mr. XYZ

He had wanted to say, *Call me Deep Throat*, or something melodramatic, but the words had stuck in his throat at the critical moment, and he'd gone with the Mr. XYZ moniker because he wasn't as imaginative as he wanted to be.

Except for some things. He could be very imaginative in some areas.

Though the news hadn't broken big yet, word was spreading slowly about what had happened near the casino, some Indian kid having gotten himself killed, and he had to keep himself from beaming.

That would have been unwise.

He did allow himself a small smile, but to an outsider it might as well have been a smile at the unseasonably warm late spring weather. Or it might have been a smile aimed at the woman who had just passed him on the street. She'd caught his eye and smiled back, tentatively. After all, you never knew when a total stranger would turn out to be some crazed killer.

Word about the Indian who'd been murdered wouldn't have reached here yet. Mr. XYZ was out early, ready to celebrate. He saw the woman with whom he'd shared his smile enter a Walgreen's down the block, one of the old-fashioned storefront ones. He'd seen her feed the meter a half block away, so he ducked into the early-hours pub between the two points, figuring he could stare out the wide window and see her pass again.

He reconstructed her face in his mind. Dirty blonde hair, a bit messy. A long, wide nose. A nice smile. Her eyes—they'd caught his, and he had fallen into them. And he'd trapped her in his eyes, he knew that. She'd smiled because she had to. Because they had connected very deeply. She just didn't know it yet.

In the pub, he was one of only a half dozen customers, each sitting in a pool of his own darkness at the long log-plank bar. He slid into a stool near the window, glanced outside, then ordered a local tap with barely a look at the schlub behind the bar. A long look would connect them, and he didn't want that. He wanted to be forgotten. The bartender would forget him, what he looked like, his features and clothing. But she wouldn't, his new conquest. She could never forget him now, and that was why he had to wait for her.

He sipped the beer, rolling his fingers on the bar like fleshy castanets. He had to stop, or they would look at him. And remember. He forced himself to stop. He sipped more beer.

How long would she—?

Ah, there she was, just walking past, toward her parked silver SUV. Fucking foreign sleek job.

He wasn't in a hurry, but he left a five on the shellacked bar.

He slipped outside in time to see her leave, pulling out of the space and heading for the highway.

He almost waved.

But he didn't. He would see her soon enough.

He had placed a very sharp implement deeply between the treads of her rear tire, and he knew almost exactly how long it would take for it and the highway surface to do their work.

Schwartz

For the first time in a month, Schwartz felt alive.

Two months before, he was also alive and well, earning big money and having the run of the place with his buddies, his muscles vibrating with the smooth hardness of exercise and sun. He had been in his glory, having his fill of food and play and yet fulfilling a job for which he was well paid and eminently qualified. He and his pals were known for their friendship, but few realized how close—or how hierarchical—their relationship really was.

It was glorious.

Baghdad had been the pinnacle of his life.

And then the bottom had fallen out, so to speak, and they'd been shipped home. Not in disgrace or anything like that, but just because the job had finished, or the contract had run out or been terminated, or some high-ranking bastard somewhere had ratted on them or pulled a few strings, or who the fuck knew?

They had been yanked from the best days of their lives, and it was almost a physical pain he and the others felt, once again having to rein themselves in. Having to fit into a system that neither suited nor really wanted them.

This job had come along and they'd been free to take it then, but the job had involved waiting, and Schwartz wasn't one to wait. No, he was one to chase the job, worry at its heels, and gulp it down. In chunks.

He smiled when he thought like that. It was fun.

Fun. That was what Baghdad had been. After learning the ropes, their way around the strange customs, the faces of their allies—after all that, they had learned what their contract allowed them to do, and it was all fun from there. Almost a year of hunting with barely a limit. Schwartz smiled at the thought of the hunts they had organized.

When ordered to "clear" a neighborhood, they had done their work with zeal.

He remembered the first time they took a prisoner "to the alley." Baghdad streets were already narrow, but in the poorer neighborhoods there were constricting alleys behind the squat blocks of flats most of the terrified populace called home. In this case, they were sure their prisoner was a true insurgent, a defiant and somewhat crazy-eyed youth who shouted jihadist epithets at them from the moment they'd kicked in his door. Or his mother's door, if that was the woman who hung just out of sight behind him when they'd first barged in while chasing a pair of thugs who had managed to elude them in the rabbit warren.

Tef had taken some delight in pistol-whipping the boy in front of the mother, to make him talk. But the kid's shouting became shriller, and the mother's joined his until they sounded like stone-deaf banshees. Tannhauser had just up and shot the old woman in the head to shut her up. Her head burst like a melon from the market down the street, and Schwartz couldn't help giggling at the way her neck bone—what the hell was it, a spine?—stuck out of the bloody gore.

Tef said, "Man, why'd you do that? We could have used her to make him talk!"

Tannhauser never pulled rank, but his leadership glowed in the pupils of his eyes. He was Alpha, and there was no one else on the squad who could have led. He'd locked Tef in the glare of his intense eyes and Tef had shut up, though he continued to cuff the crying kid—the insurgent—in the side of the head until his ear was mangled and bloody.

"This kid don't know shit."

That was when Schwartz had the brainstorm. "Take him out back," he said. Tef looked at Tannhauser for guidance. Alpha nodded.

"What you got in mind?" Tann said, as Tef wrestled the screaming kid toward the rear.

"Little contest. Let him go, wait for him to run, then see how long it takes one of us . . ."

"Cool beans, dude," Tef said, interrupting. "Me first?"

Schwartz had frowned. It was his idea. But the kid was Tef's toy from the beginning. "Go for it."

Tef—his name was short for Teflon, the kind of ammunition with which he preferred to load his three 9mm Glocks—kicked the kid to the back door and almost through it. The thin wood splintered under his attack. The alley was narrow, dark, angular. Dusty. They were sick of the dust.

Schwartz said, "Let him go, then hunt. I'll keep watch for flags."

The Wolfpaw Security Services contract called for only Wolfpaw personnel to handle this specific neighborhood, but occasionally "flags"—uniformed US troopers—wandered into the territory and stuck their two cents into Wolfpaw business.

Tef cuffed the kid once more. Blood ran from his scalp down his face. He wasn't going anywhere. His eyes were wide with shock and fear. No, it was hatred. Schwartz could see it in the kid's soul, taking hold. If he wasn't an insurgent or terrorist now, he soon would be.

Kicking the kid in the ass, then pushing him pointedly down the alley, Tef grunted sounds. He pointed down the alley, grunted, kicked, pointed.

The kid finally got it.

He ran.

Raggedly, as if drunk, he bounced off the opposite stucco wall, leaving a bubbly red stain behind. Then he was off and running, arms and legs windmilling like useless chicken wings.

Probably felt the target on his back.

Tef laughed his hyena laugh. He stripped, handing Schwartz and Tannhauser his Kevlar and holsters. Then he shucked his boots and trousers.

Schwartz inhaled deeply and *felt* Tef's Change. It was almost as if his senses exploded right along with Tef's—scents burst into his nostrils and lanced into his brain. It was all he could do to keep from Changing.

The Change was always best when shared by the pack.

Tef now stood on four sturdy paws, his gray coat thick with health and vigor. A male in his prime.

Maybe next year he would challenge Alpha.

With a long, low growl, he was off at a lope. There was no hurry. Schwartz had intended to time the chase, play it like a game, but the beast Tef had become was already snapping at the running kid's ankles, his fangs ripping flesh and tendon and muscle.

The terrified kid screamed and cartwheeled into a wall, missing an open doorway and ending up in a blood-splattered heap.

The wolf leaped onto his back, punched him into the ground with his paws, then lunged in and ripped out his throat with one mighty tear of his jaws. Blood flew in an artistic arc across the alley.

Then the wolf began to feed on the warm, bloody flesh.

Later, back in his clothes, Tef asked, "How long?"

Schwartz made it up. "Forty-three seconds. I'll beat that tomorrow."

Alpha laughed his gravelly chuckle. "Glad you guys are having fun."

It had been fun.

The prey, always there and ready with arteries full of warm Iraqi blood. They had gorged themselves, grateful for the confusion of the war and its aftermath, the executions, the bombings, the suicide attacks, snipers. The disappearances that went unreported. The fearful citizenry behind closed doors, ignoring the growls and howling of the beasts that stalked their narrow streets.

Now, months later, Schwartz smiled as he recalled the hunts they held after that first one. They'd taken turns. By the time they'd rotated out and back to Wolfpaw's Georgia headquarters, the three of them had conducted nearly a hundred arranged hunts. Not to mention those times they had used their advantage in unplanned engagements with their faceless, reckless enemy—an enemy not prepared to face creatures such as they could become, supernatural berserkers covered with fur, their jaws filled with fangs.

Baghdad had been fun.

"Hey, snap out of it," Tannhauser said.

"Sure, Alpha, you got it."

Schwartz waited for Alpha to turn away, then shook his

head. It was a good thing the waiting was over, because they'd been close to biting off each other's heads.

Eagle River my ass. This was Chickenshit River.

The guy who'd hired them was chickenshit, that was for sure. *Mr. XYZ,* he called himself. *How original.* Schwartz remembered a kids' book he'd read in grade school with the protagonists playing at being aliens from the planet XYZ. That was what you named things when you had no imagination.

Well, Mr. XYZ paid well and their leave from Wolfpaw was going to turn out very lucrative indeed.

And fun. *Never forget the fun.*

Mr. XYZ

He pulled up behind the disabled silver SUV. He enjoyed being right, having figured she would drive back toward home. The two-lane highway had recently been repaved, but his implement had done its job within a couple miles.

He flicked on his flashers and waved when he saw her looking at him through his own windshield. He slid out and she recognized him, because their gazes had locked and he had sunk his anchor into her soul.

"Thank you so much for stopping!" she said, breathless. "I don't know what happened. It just went flat all of a sudden. I was going to change it, but I couldn't remember exactly how to do it, and—"

"Never fear, dear lady, I'm an expert at changing tires. I used to do it for a living, way back when I was a kid. Just lead me to your spare. Or do you have one of those mini-tire things?"

Her hair needed brushing, but it was lustrous and full. Her face was just a bit rounded, but her body was still college-age athletic. A former cheerleader, perhaps married early, or career driven in some insurance office.

"I think it's a full-size spare," she said, opening the rear hatch. "It's one of the things I liked about this car when I bought it. I'm really grateful for your help. I'm due in the office in about an hour, and a tow truck would just take too long."

He continued fantasizing about her as she opened the compartment and handed him her tool kit.

She chattered on, but he wasn't listening anymore. His charm had worked. He was inside and trusted, and he now felt the power of his position hardening him down below, where it counted. He hoped she wouldn't note the bulge in his trousers, the dead giveaway that he was not listening to her, but to his own scenario.

"I'll be more than happy to pay for your time—"

Oh, you'll pay, you'll definitely pay.

When she turned away, he swiped the tire iron loosely across the back of her head and grabbed her as she sagged like a sack, to keep her from hitting the ground.

A quick look around. He was alone on the road.

He dragged her to his own SUV and tossed her into the back. If she woke, she'd find no handle on the inside. But there was a thin line of blood now lining the ugly purple bruise rising on the back of her skull, so he doubted she'd wake soon.

No, by then he would be standing before her in all his glory, and she would worship him like his mother had said they would. They *all* would. Then he would show her who had the power, and who didn't.

He drove her foreign SUV into the ditch and into the underbrush, then headed back home in the most roundabout way he knew. He had time, but not that much, and he wanted to enjoy himself.

He smiled when he heard a low moan behind him. This would get him in the mood very quickly. He massaged himself below the steering wheel, hoping he could wait until everything was ready.

He whistled a little tune as he stroked himself and listened for her moans.

Mr. XYZ couldn't help feeling pleased with himself right then.

Arnow

The service road was a slash through the once pristine woodland that snaked around the Eagle River and its chain of lakes. Actually it was only one of many service roads now wending their way through imposing forests of white and jack pines that had been reduced to tiny pockets of groves as development had begun to nibble at the edges.

Arnow drove his sheriff's cruiser carefully through muddy pools from the previous night's quick storm. He'd listened to it stomp its way through with a good book in his hand and a generous tot of B&B on the desk beside him. He was almost ashamed of how he'd lost his taste for scotch and gained an affinity for what was, really, a liqueur—but a sweet, deceptively strong, and hearty one at that, made by the Benedictine monks in one of the most altruistic pursuits known to man. There was not much better in his book than a night like that, a quiet night in which his police radio or cell didn't interrupt. The spring storm was icing on his cake.

But now the aftermath of the storm left a bad taste in his mouth that no amount of mints could remove. He sucked on three Tic-Tacs and hoped for the best. He already thought he could smell death in the air. Maybe it was the undergrowth, maybe the rotting tree trunks that lined the road, deadfall from earlier storms. Who knew? He was still getting used to all the woodcraft people expected him to know.

He pulled up to where Jerry's cruiser was still parked, its strobe light bar rotating uselessly. Exposed dirt and mud all around, with here and there patches of gravel, marked the parking area of the huge construction site. The new casino would be a monster, that was for sure. Arnow always cringed when he figured how much larger the department would have to be, even though the tribal police would have priority jurisdiction. Some places, his sheriff's office would have had no jurisdiction at all, but here some arcane language in the city and county charters gave the sheriff and tribal police force, such as it was, joint jurisdiction. Arnow chuckled mirthlessly—they'd be increasing the size of their department, too. The difference was they would have all the money they needed, thanks to an uninterrupted income stream from the casino and its ancillary hotel and convention center. A tribal police mini-SUV was parked at a skewed angle nearby, no lights.

At first, Arnow couldn't spot anyone.

Where the hell was the crime scene?

He approached the hole in the ground that currently passed for a casino location and looked down. No one there. No laborers, no labor being done. That was good. He squinted, looking around for a clue as to where the victim might have been found. He noticed the silver BMW convertible in the lot, parked well away from workers' F-150 and Ram pickups. The car looked familiar.

Following the perimeter of the foundation depression, he saw that the service road continued past the parking lot.

There. He heard voices, caught flashes of color between the bare, thinned-out tree trunks in the way as the road angled through the woods.

Didn't look as if Dr. Jessie had arrived yet. Her older Pathfinder was nowhere in sight. He felt a slight disappointment. How pathetic was that, glad of the crime so he could flirt? He figured that feeling wouldn't last.

Well, no point delaying. He was about to take ownership of the crime scene. His first murder here. He wondered how it would change things.

As it turned out, it would change things a lot.

The two tribal cops had wrapped some yellow tape around a rather large swath of road, using tree trunks as posts.

He knew them both, having met them shortly after he'd been hired. The unfortunately named John Deer was tall and muscular, while Bill Rogers was shorter and rounder but not fat. He'd only seen them smiling before, but both looked grim now.

"Sheriff," Deer said, "glad you made it out here before any media types."

Arnow nodded at them. "Are there media types nearby?"

"Oh yeah, and they have scanners."

Arnow made a clucking sound. "I've got Doc Jessie on her way. Where's the body?"

"Here." Deer pointed. "And here. And here."

"And there," added Rogers, "and there."

"Jesus Christ!" Arnow said.

"Don't go over there. We barfed up our breakfasts already. It's bad."

Arnow felt the tickle in his throat. He had seen plenty, but there was still a knee-jellying effect whenever you saw a mangled human body. He forced himself to look down and focus, and mangled was not the right word.

This body—or bodies, it was hard to tell—was ripped apart, torn to pieces. Literally. He could see an arm poking out of the underbrush over there. A foot lying in the mud here.

Christ, there was the head, like a deflated football.

He felt his gorge rise, and it was all he could do to swallow hard and keep from spewing up the bottom of his guts.

Then he bent lower and saw something else.

The body had been ripped apart by teeth. He could clearly see the marks, and the torn look of the lardlike flesh was unmistakable.

"Do you know, uh, him?"

Deer responded. He was done stringing yellow tape and just stood back, swaying. "Jimmy Blackthorn."

"Casino guy, right? Investment guru?"

They nodded.

"That his BMW back there?"

"Yup."

Arnow grunted.

This would have some strange repercussions. Blackthorn was a sort of defrocked Indian. That's what somebody at the newspaper had said about him. He'd "gone over to the white man's world," or something like that. He was bringing the investors in, helping the tribe finance the project for a cut, probably a big one. He was hated by whites, disliked by many Indians, and yet he had his hands all over the pie.

Not anymore.

Arnow spit to avoid puking. He still hadn't settled his stomach, dammit. He pulled on latex gloves just to do something. He wasn't going to touch anything.

And now here was the doc.

Jessie Hawkins came into view where the road turned into the taped-off area.

For a moment, Arnow forgot all about the crime scene. She brought an aura with her that seemed to brighten everyone in its light. Damn, she looked good.

She paled, however, as soon as she caught a glimpse of one of the taped-off sections of ground.

He thought he heard her say "Fuck!" before turning away for a couple minutes. He gave her time—even doctors didn't always realize how rough violence could look. And *this*, this was the worst he'd ever seen, bar none.

Well, there had been some close ones. But no, this was worse.

"You okay, Doc?" Arnow had always been a little folksy, but here in this area he played it up. Not quite Andy Griffith, but it didn't hurt for people to think you were a rube sometimes.

"Uh, yeah." She cleared her throat. "Just caught me by surprise. It's not an everyday—"

"No, thank God."

"He was torn apart, wasn't he?" She was looking again now, swallowing carefully. Her eyes didn't miss much, though.

"To pieces." Arnow started to introduce the rez cops, then stopped when they almost broke out laughing.

"Dr. Hawkins almost lives in the clinic, Sheriff," Deer said. "We know her." There were tight smiles all around.

Jessie had pulled on her own latex and was now squatting, examining this portion of the body.

"These are teeth marks!" she said, surprised.

And something else, maybe?

He noticed her eyes seemed hooded, avoiding his.

Hiding something? Almost expecting it?

"My thought, too."

She nodded.

"Where's the rest—? Oh, I see."

She stood and moved on to another taped-off area. A few minutes later, she tracked down the others. Meanwhile, Arnow and the two cops had made a careful search of the general area. He was impressed to see they had followed protocol and wore gloves, too. So now the only clues they had were items that seemed to belong to the dead man. Cell phone, leather jacket. Wallet. *Jimmy Blackthorn.* His ID was intact, and so was his money—in fact, his wallet had been mauled, but left behind full of cash and cards.

"There should be footprints, with all this mud," he said, seeing Jessie looking at the scuffing.

"I'm guessing the murder took place before the heavy rain, when this was mostly dust and dirt."

"Too bad." She still seemed to be looking for print marks. There were some animal tracks nearby.

She spent a few minutes at each major portion of the victim, checking the ground around them.

"Recognize him?" Arnow asked when she had located the head.

She nodded, after turning pale again.

A sawn-off, torn-off human head is not an easy sight. She was trying to keep from heaving, and he was impressed with her control.

"Jimmy Blackthorn. Everyone knows who he is. *Was.* This'll put a damper on the project," she said sarcastically as she waved her hand at the site. "But they'll find a way to go on."

"You don't approve?" This piqued his curiosity.

"I was with the Waters dissenters. The tribe has so many problems already. And now they'll have to learn a slew of new things and new businesses—before they actually attempt to resolve their older issues. I don't believe the benefits of a casino will help them in the short run, no."

"And the long run?"

She smiled. "There are plenty of whites lining up to lose their Social Security money all over the state. I suppose in the long run the casino will manage to soak its share of them. But it'll bring in a lot of outsiders, like Blackthorn here. He was raised in a rez orphanage, but not in this state."

"You didn't trust him?"

"I only met him once. Struck me as a fast talker and a little sleazy, but he brought in the money. My friend Sam Waters, who's on the elders' council, didn't trust him, hence his opposition to the entire project."

"Didn't like it enough to try to stop it by killing?" Arnow realized as soon as he said it that it was the big city talking.

"What? You think old Sam Waters came out here during the storm and tore Blackthorn to pieces because he didn't trust him? Come on! Be serious."

"Be that as it may . . ." Arnow hated to cede any ground. "I'll call Eagleson and tell the Council before they hear it on the news." He pointed at the rez cops. "Looks like we got us a joint investigation."

She nodded, but she seemed to have stepped out for a minute mentally. Her thoughts were not transparent, but the wheels churning in her head were almost obvious.

"Done here, Doc?" The morgue attendants he'd called in from Antigo had just arrived on the scene. He took some pleasure when both heaved their cookies into the mud.

"Wait a while, guys," he said as they wiped their chins. "I've got a deputy coming with a camera. I'll let you know when."

They retreated thankfully, their eyes still crossed.

Jessie Hawkins continued to walk around the crime scenes. His cop's itch, as he called it, said she was keeping some thoughts to herself. Well, that was her right.

"Sheriff, I'll have to defer on the autopsy."

"Tom," he said.

"Sorry, *Tom.* I've never dealt with remains in this kind of condition. And I don't have the facilities. I think you'll get a better result with a full-timer. I'd be glad to assist, though."

"Okay, I'll make some calls." He nodded as Deputy Jonston finally arrived with the photographic kit. The kid lost his breakfast as soon as he saw the first body part.

"Here we go again. Give me the camera. I'll start."

Arnow handled the digital Canon like a professional, starting to layer the first taped-off area with carefully framed photography, missing nothing. When the pale-faced kid came back, looking as if everything he'd eaten in days had been purged, Arnow handed him the camera and gave him directions. Unsteady on his feet, the young deputy went to work.

He took Jessie aside. "He'll learn. Though I'd rather he didn't have to."

Jessie nodded.

He wondered why she had had been so quick to bow out of the investigation. Maybe it was hitting too close to home.

Lupo

The stakeout was low odds.

Sitting in the unmarked squad car down the block from the only mom-and-pop jeweler left in the south side neighborhood, Nick Lupo thought they were just too obvious. A couple of straight-looking guys sipping out of cardboard cups staring at nothing in particular. How effective could they be?

DiSanto played drums on the steering wheel, long rhythmic runs of muffled taps that followed a click track only he could hear.

Lupo wanted to scream. *Does he have to do that?* DiSanto

was no Bill Bruford. He wasn't even a Ringo. It was driving him nuts. The assignment, the partner, the stakeout.

Christ, the appointment he had later today.

He felt the growl building in back of his throat. Involuntary, but the feeling of being trapped had a lot to do with it. *How many hours to go?*

Part of him wanted action, while the other part wanted quiet and a quick end to the shift. No paperwork. Nothing.

"Look at this," DiSanto whispered, nudging Lupo hard enough to make him almost spill his tea. "The fuck is this shit?"

Lupo grunted. DiSanto liked to model his speech on premium cable TV cop and mob shows. At least, that's what it sounded like to Lupo. He'd never heard a cop swear quite as much as his partner, the saintly named one.

"Come to papa, baby," DiSanto said. His hand went for his Glock.

Lupo stared into his visor's rectangular mirror.

Dammit. Looked like DiSanto was right.

A sky blue late-model Kawasaki Ninja ZX had cruised down the line of parked cars like a spider stalking its kill. Now it was almost parallel with their Impala. Two dark forms hunched over the handlebar nacelle, two black helmets.

"Shit, it's going down." Lupo heard the shock in his own voice. The task force's other four cars were wasting their time. He speed-dialed Munson.

"Unit Twenty-nine on National. We've got a bite here. Looks like one of the three bikes. Two riders, black helmets. Black leather gear with red gloves as described. Approaching Manny's Gold and Diamond Exchange. DiSanto and I are engaging . . ."

"Hold up, Lupo," Munson growled in his ear. "We got a strike here, too. Red bike. Same deal, otherwise."

"What the—"

Lupo clicked off Munson and took a call from Glinn. Her voice was excited. "We've got a gold one here!"

He switched to walky-talky mode.

"Looks like they're hitting in threes. We got one, and Munson and Glinn. Rest of you, converge on us. Requesting backup. DiSanto and I are approaching on foot. Use caution. These guys like to hurt people."

He cut out, unholstered his Glock and racked the slide. "Let's do it."

DiSanto nodded.

In the next few seconds, all hell broke loose.

The Ninja's passenger tossed a brick through Manny's plate-glass window, then leaped through the gap, his leather armor taking the brunt of the remaining glass shards. The old-fashioned alarm went off with a blaring horn. Lupo imagined the invader smashing displays, holding the owner at gunpoint, stuffing a trash bag with gold and jewelry. It was brazen daylight work.

He hit the sidewalk and kept low next to the Impala and the other cars parked between them and the idling Ninja now on the sidewalk in front of the store. The driver's black helmet was angled so he could watch for his partner's return. He didn't see Lupo approaching from behind at a fast crouch. DiSanto had disappeared around the building, heading for the side door as arranged.

They'd tried before to ambush the smash-and-grab bandits, but they just weren't quick enough. The bandits used their high-end frat-boy bikes to zip through narrow streets, weave through freeway traffic, and outpace all pursuit. Up to now the gang task force thought they'd been dealing with one bike and two individuals. Now it appeared the gang was at least six.

He reached the last parked car, just behind the antsy rider on the bike. His helmet was still turned, looking for the returning partner. One glance in his mirror and he might spot Lupo.

He considered shooting the guy off the damned bike. But he'd catch hell and an inquest, minimum. Internal Affairs was a looming presence since some improper arrests and confessions had given the department a black eye the previous year. The new chief was trying to appear eager to clean it up. And Lupo was still in IA's crosshairs over the Eagle River deal he'd had to spin when he'd lost his foot.

Now Lupo considered his options. He only had seconds.

Three gunshots in quick succession came from inside the store.

Lupo's quarry, the driver, didn't seem to hear them, due to the helmet perhaps. He was standing up, straddling the bike, craning his neck, oblivious to what was happening behind him.

Two blue and white units squealed around the corner and blocked the road.

At nearly the same time, the second helmeted robber burst from the store and hurled himself onto the bike, which the driver gunned. The passenger must have landed on the seat unbalanced, however, because he slid off the bike when it jumped the curb and headed for the alley. Lupo charged toward the passenger, who rolled and leaped to his feet, following the bike. Four uniforms rushed up, but the bike—now lighter with only the driver on board—maneuvered into the alley mouth before they could block its passage. They converged on the abandoned rider, who tried to evade and bring a pistol to bear, but was tackled by two uniforms.

"Around!" Lupo shouted at the other two uniforms, wondering what had happened to DiSanto. "Check on my partner. He went in the side way."

Lupo raced into the alley. He could see the cyclist picking his way through Dumpsters and bins filled with refuse. Almost without thinking, he holstered his Glock and slid out of his clothes, taking precious seconds to stash them behind a clump of damp cardboard boxes.

As he ran, he visualized himself as the Creature, galloping wildly through the pines . . .

And then, *it's a fact, Jack*, he was over. Four huge paws hit the cracked pavement and propelled the large black wolf's body down the alley.

Confusion rippled momentarily through his brain, a tug of war between the wolf side of his brain and the man side.

And then the war was over. *It was getting easier.*

His senses exploded with the intensity of the trash and rancid food smells of the alley, the exhaust fumes of the bike ahead of him, and the scent of the prey itself. His eyes picked out the prey, whose bike was becoming a hindrance as it stuttered while he attempted to muscle it over some obstacle, strips of wood from a demolished pallet.

The Creature avoided debris, leaping over bins and trash bags with ease. His mind had split into the now-familiar separate consciousness that allowed Lupo the man to give ever-quickening commands to Lupo the Creature with almost complete understanding.

It was Caroline Stewart's theory, finally tested and proven, and put to use since the Martin Stewart case. One more way Caroline had affected his life, though it had taken years to make itself fully known.

The robber managed to free the spokes of his front wheel and turned to check his rear wheel when he saw the giant animal bounding toward him. It was impossible to read his face behind the helmet's blank reflective shield, but his body language showed he was shocked to see the giant wolf. He redoubled his efforts to free his bike.

With a growl deep in his throat, the wolf lunged through the air, paws smacking into the robber's back and hurling him off the motorcycle and onto the alley floor. The motorcycle squirted past them both and toppled, its engine still revving, coming to rest almost upside down against a Dumpster.

The Creature circled the helmeted robber warily, growling. When the robber's hand disappeared under his jacket, the Creature pounced and his jaws clamped down on the biker's wrist right as the hand was coming out with a cheap 9mm in its grip. Simultaneously, the rest of the Creature's body landed on the robber's chest. *Jaws ripping through leather and skin and shaking hard enough to send the pistol flying and tearing the wrist to bloody shreds.*

The robber screamed and tried to roll away from the great wolf's weight. But his struggles were to no avail. The snarling jaws tore into the arm above the useless wrist, once, twice, again.

The Creature's bloodlust had begun to replace Nick Lupo's still-tenuous control. The part of the wolf that was lucid Lupo attempted to rein in the Creature's deadly anger, but it fought against that control, crazed with the taste of prey.

Frightened prey, which was even better.

Lupo tasted the flesh and blood of the robber and found himself giving in, letting the Creature exert his more aggressive control.

Potentially harmful DNA passed from wolf to human, but it was too late for Lupo to worry about that.

The wolf went for the robber's throat.

Protected by his helmet and a thick layer of leather, the robber fended off the wolf's first lunge at his neck, but the wolf changed his angle of attack and snapped, tearing into the jacket's lapels and the skin under them, the taste and smell of blood driving him further even as the robber screeched like a stuck pig.

As the wolf's jaws went for the now unprotected bloody flesh, Lupo tried desperately to induce the Creature's head away from the morsel that would kill the terrified thief.

Lupo tried focusing on a painful image—what he had done to Caroline Stewart in a lust-driven but nearly similar situation decades ago. Caroline's shape and form had been barely recognizable afterward.

The pain he still felt lanced through both Lupo's brain and the Creature's, and, with a whimper, it loosed its grip and leaped off the struggling thief.

The Creature froze the man with its eyes. A warning passed between them.

Then the wolf bounded away, leaving the thief in the stuttering, whimpering shape in which the approaching cops would find him, screaming incoherently about the dog with the satanic stare.

Lupo rejoined the scene a minute later, his clothes soiled and a bruise rising on his face.

One of the cops was reading the thief an abbreviated Miranda warning and cuffing the perp as punctuation.

"Shut up, listen. Anything you say—" *Cuff.* "You're entitled to a lawyer—" *Cuff.* "If you can't afford one—"

"Lupo, where the hell were you?" another cop said upon seeing him arrive.

"Got tangled up in that mess." Lupo pointed at the motorcycle and the remains of the pallet. A huge sliver of two-by-four protruded from one bloody sleeve.

Then they were dragging the blubbering, bleeding thief up on his unsteady feet.

"What happened to him?" Lupo asked.

"Shit if I know. Found 'im like this, screamin' about some dog attacking him." The cop's brow furrowed. "You see anything?"

"Yeah, I was seeing stars. But come to think of it, I did hear some growling." He pointed at the thief's mangled arm. "Looks like maybe a local guard dog got into the action."

The cop grunted. As far as he was concerned, it didn't matter *what* happened to this scum.

When they pulled off the helmet, they saw a tattooed, pierced white male in his midtwenties, his head shaved and a strange mark inked onto the back of his neck. He was crying like a baby now, though.

Jesus, he'd forgotten about his partner! The three shots.

"DiSanto?" he asked the nearest cop.

"Got himself shot inside the store. And his pretty-boy face is all gashed up. Probably from the broken glass. He'll be okay, though."

Lupo nodded. Thankful. This had been almost a fiasco. His control over the Creature had nearly evaporated at the worst possible time. And his partner had nearly been killed.

"Damned frat-boy bikes," one of the cops spit out as he kicked the downed Ninja. "Fuckin' menace on the road!"

"Got that right," somebody agreed.

Sirens approached. Lupo felt his hold on reality slipping.

Was DiSanto doomed to die like Ben?

Suddenly he started to shiver.

Inside his head, he thought he heard the Creature howling.

Mr. XYZ

Later, Mr. XYZ made a call. The cell was a secure, unregistered TracFone. He waited for Tannhauser to pick up, then spat into the invisible mouthpiece.

"You fool! I told you to pick a good place for the first one. I also told you to avoid the site itself. What the hell are you doing? Can't you follow simple directions?"

Tannhauser was silent, as if taken by surprise. Then he recovered. "Who is this?"

"Goddamn it," Mr. XYZ snarled into the voice-changer gizmo, "I wanted the attack to be visible but to lead away from the casino."

"Well, if it isn't Mr. XYZ," Tannhauser said with fake Southern charm. "I didn't recognize your sweet girly voice." Then his tone hardened. "Listen, *boss*, this guy lived at the casino site. We tried for almost a week to grab him somewhere else, but he was always there, making a fool and a nuisance of himself. You want the job done or don't you?"

Mr. XYZ breathed fast, almost hyperventilating. He slowed his words down. "Fine, fine. Just don't make the next one so obvious, and so . . . dramatic."

Tannhauser chuckled, and this time his voice brought shivers to Mr. XYZ's neck. "Once you've loosed the lightning, it will make its own path. *Boss.*"

There was a click, and the TracFone went dead.

Mr. XYZ tried to slow his panting. He'd just heard one of the first detailed reports, and the location of the murder had taken him right out of his wits.

He had growled like a wounded bear, then let the blade slip a bit too far, finishing the woman way too early. The drain had taken care of the blood. Then he had barely touched himself and his orgasm had hit like an earthquake, and he had come all over her silent, bloodless body as he'd pictured in his mind from the moment he'd seen her.

But his anger made it a less than satisfying thrill, and when he massaged the rest of his cum out of his softening penis he'd just made himself angry all over again.

Talking to Tannhauser made his penis go flaccid and shrink, and Mr. XYZ was not pleased about that at all.

Chapter Two

Lupo

Traffic in Oshkosh was thicker than it should have been, but the weekend drew people north and there was no getting away from it. He enjoyed the glint of late afternoon sunlight on Lake Butte de Mort and felt the confines of the city slipping away. The crowds on US 45 thinned out, and he settled in for the rest of the drive. They'd renumbered some highways and county roads in recent years, and they still looked strange on the map and on the new signposts. A short detour took him almost in a circle, but then he was on track again.

He focused on the trees. He'd always loved the subtle shift from mostly deciduous to mostly coniferous. It reminded him of the great woods stretching northward past the border into the Upper Peninsula of Michigan and then Canada. The evergreen smell began driving the Creature crazy—longing for the woods. If he didn't catch himself, Lupo would start panting.

Also in his mind was the image of who would be waiting for him.

He smiled as he thought about Jessie.

He'd tried calling her on her cell and at the clinic but only reached voice mail. No reason to worry, but it was unusual. Still, she'd marked her calendar as he marked his, so she would be waiting. There was time for them, and then the Creature would have his time.

The moon would have him.

Lupo focused on the trees. And on the music. He'd cranked up his iPod shortly after leaving, clicking on his "up North" playlist. Some old acoustic New Age from Narada, giving way to the Alan Parsons Project albums, carefully programmed to culminate with *The Turn of a Friendly Card*, his "arrival music"—driving up Circle Moon Drive to the last strains of Ian Bairnson's guitar solo reiteration of the main theme. It was tradition.

He whisked past some pastoral landscapes and missed his older Genesis albums. Newer Genesis was pleasant enough, but it didn't move him. Maybe it happened when Banks gave up the Mellotron.

He settled in with *Ammonia Avenue* and then *Vulture Culture*, at the end of which Eric Woolfson sang about the same old sun rising in the morning and the same bright eyes welcoming him home. Gave him shivers.

The acerbic but upbeat compositions relaxed him, fitting his mood.

The day had only worsened.

DiSanto was okay, though having a hundred glass slivers tweezed out of his face, arms, and hands was no picnic. Lupo had been forced to repair his clothes as best he could, lest their disheveled appearance lead to questions.

In the washroom, he stared at the mirror and tried to see the Creature in his own dark eyes. Was he there, sulking because he had been thwarted from finishing his prey in the way he was accustomed? Was he biding his time until he could be let out of his pen?

These were questions whose answers changed almost weekly.

Caroline Stewart had written extensively about her theories regarding Nick and the control he could exert over his wolf side. Lupo had managed to keep the journals after her death, hiding their existence from the ensuing investigation. He'd been reading through them recently and once again begun to explore his abilities. And his limitations.

There was a bit of an undercurrent there of his instability. Was he *unstable?* It was hard to judge objectively.

He'd let Munson take the lead interrogations of the two bike robbers, claiming he was shaken up. His limp was more pronounced. The two thugs were clamming up so far, though Lupo's collar kept blubbering about the attack dog. He had been patched up by EMTs and shipped to Froedtert Hospital under guard. Lupo had no sympathy for the thug, but the incident highlighted his problem with using his wolf form on the job. Sometimes it worked, but just as often it caused difficulties.

While the Change enhanced his abilities, it also hampered his movement in the daily world of the street. Lupo was glad the task force didn't need him as lead interrogator—it would be too awkward to face the thug who'd looked into his wolf eyes. The story of the attack dog held up for now. The doctor's report would reflect the animal attack, and he'd have no reason to test DNA further.

Shit, nothing like complicating my life even more.

Then there was Doc Barrett, the police psychologist. The She-Devil of the SS. Considered most qualified to take over for the Wicked Witch of the West. Lupo'd had plenty of run-ins with her, stretching back even further than the damn Stewart case. She despised Lupo, and now he was assigned regular sessions with her since he had lost his foot. Ostensibly taking him through post-traumatic stress, she merely used the time to needle him. The affair she'd carried on with Lieutenant Bowen had ended when Bowen unexpectedly retired, and she blamed Lupo. Of course, she was right—Bowen had been driven to his career's end by a carefully orchestrated meeting with the Creature.

Lupo smiled as he passed slower traffic huddled around the Oshkosh outlet malls. Bowen would have loved a wolf trophy, but his nerve had left him when confronted with a snarling snout clearly more intelligent than he. Last Lupo had heard of him, he'd moved down to Florida. Probably playing canasta in a retirement community.

Doc Barrett was a different animal altogether.

He had knocked on her door and waited for her usual grunt that passed for "come in." When it came, he let himself in, remembering to limp.

Today Barrett had been dressed in a ribbed black suit that showed off her angular, bony figure. Midfifties with gray-streaked hair, her mouth was a purple gash that might have been attractive had it not been so tight-lipped with ill-conceived disdain for him. The ghost of Bowen's aborted relationship with her hung over them and always would.

"How are we doing today, Detective?" she asked, making sure her inflection indicated she couldn't care less.

"Swell. *We* caught two of the motorcycle gang and learned there's more of them. *We'll* probably get nothing out of these dudes, though. Let's see, what else? My partner's face is full of glass, and I ruined my clothes. Not too bad for a shitty Friday."

He could never help being a smart-ass, not since she'd shut him and Ben out when they could have used help with the Martin case.

She smiled. "Sounds like you'll have your hands full. How does that make you feel?"

"Wanted." *Was she serious?*

"How does your foot feel?"

"Fine, for something that's gone."

"Are you still angry about losing it?"

"No, I was tired of having two."

"You *are* angry. You know, if you'd been a uniformed officer, you probably would have been required to retire with disability. You should feel lucky."

"Yeah, luck is my constant companion."

"Detective Lupo, your condescending manner doesn't change the fact that we have to continue with this charade. Frankly, I'm not aware of any change in your attitude or self-loathing."

Self-loathing! What a joke.

He laughed, trying to keep from snorting. "We still have fifty minutes by my watch."

"Hm, yes. Well, let's try this. Why don't you tell me why you're so full of hate?"

And it had gotten worse from there. Sparring over his smart-ass responses to her hackneyed probing questions. They rapidly got on each other's nerves, the sheer joy of hating simply getting old fast, and then going through the motions of the supposedly helpful relationship. By the time the clock hands pointed to the correct hour, Lupo couldn't wait to take his leave. Sadistic as ever, Barrett held him to the last minute, like a delinquent student kept after school. Maybe he could wash the blackboard or serve detention.

"Next week, same time," she said, turning to a file folder on her desk and dismissing him in the same motion. "Remember, Internal Affairs checks my records of your visits." Her tone was just the slightest bit unctuous and slippery with barely repressed disdain.

How could he forget? It was part of the deal that kept him from retirement. He'd been as close to a physical-psychological discharge as anyone could be, and only some adroit string-pulling had kept him on the job.

Damned if he would let a witch like Barrett drive him out of his chosen profession.

It was time for *Pyramid*. He flicked the iPod dial and settled in for the cautionary tale of fame and legacy, and how both are fleeting. Later, *Gaudi*. He related to Eric Woolfson's wistful, metaphorical lyrics.

The music calmed him, and he drove more carefully, navigating through the town of New London. He paused the iPod, gassed up within sight of a picturesque church that dominated the street, then got back on the road feeling better.

By the time he passed through Antigo, *Eye in the Sky* matched his mood perfectly. Inexplicably, the darkest themes always picked up his spirits.

Jessie

It didn't occur to her until after she had almost puked up her Wheaties that the damage done to Mr. Blackthorn might have been caused by a wolf. Though she'd never seen evidence of it before, she knew wolves brought down game much larger than themselves, usually as a pack.

During her session with Sheriff Arnow—

Tom . . .

—she'd started to worry.

What if the DNA evidence showed it was a wolf? What if there was other evidence that muddied the waters? What if the whispers started again?

She remembered how it had been, before Nick Lupo confided in her—had been forced to, really. The people on the rez had started it, but the town had taken it up: a wolf was taking their pets or livestock, leaving only cleaned out fur and carcasses behind.

Nick had explained that there had been another wolf who challenged him for local supremacy. But Nick had battled that outsider and won. And he'd been right, there were no more suspicious attacks. Nick was careful to take only wild game, and as his control had increased, he'd been even more careful. And the loss of his foot had slowed him down.

The citizens of Eagle River and surrounding areas had been so preoccupied with the Martin Stewart "terrorism" crime wave that they'd greatly relaxed their worry about wolves once that was over.

She looked down at the severed head of Jimmy Blackthorn.

The teeth marks were obvious to her practiced eye.

She turned away. *Enough.*

Her stomach was still queasy, but at least she'd held her own in front of the new sheriff. Bunche had been pleasant enough, but here was Tom Arnow, a very nice man indeed.

And the way he looked at her. He had a way of looking from the sides of his eyes, as if he were looking elsewhere and then, just by accident, you'd fall into his field of vision. Not quite askance, but still calculated. She'd noticed that it signaled his intent if he looked at you first from the corners of his eyes.

She shook her head. Why was she concerned with what the sheriff thought of her and how he looked at her? It wasn't the first time a man had looked at her appraisingly. Jessie rarely made a fuss over herself. Except when Nick was coming to visit.

Nick needed to hear about Blackthorn, that was certain. Good thing he was probably on his way. He would hate finding a crime here to worry about, for surely it would steal time away from them, but at least he could keep his senses open while in the woods.

The time he spent indoors, with her—well, that was for *them*. She smiled in anticipation.

There was a strong gust of wind, and the tree line across the dirt road seemed to shimmer.

David Lynch woods, she thought with a sharp little shiver. Her nerves were acting up.

Dammit, she shouldn't have balked at doing the autopsy. Now she would be at the mercy of whatever the lab discovered. It had to be a wolf, didn't it? She recognized the damage, the teeth marks. But this one was extremely savage. Nick was reverent of nature, of what was provided for him in this perfect habitat. Perfect except for the humans who tended to fuck it up. Even before he had learned to bring his wolf side (the Creature, as he referred to it) under control, he managed to avoid taking herd animals and pets.

So then what did Blackthorn's murder mean? Was a man-killer wolf loose in the Nicolet? Was this a fluke? Perhaps a hurt or starving animal, desperate for food, or even cornered?

Her father could have done the autopsy, and he would have kept any secret she shared with him. The old man's career had been partly as coroner, until he had returned to the city to consult . . . but now he was gone, too, killed by a stroke a year before. He'd lived long enough to meet Nick and see his daughter finally happy in a relationship. He'd been indebted to Nick for saving Jessie's life from the Stewart gang—and hadn't known the extent of what Nick had saved her from—but he hadn't been able to enjoy their company for long before . . .

Jessie felt herself tearing up. She could cope with his death intellectually, but occasionally she missed him—missed him fiercely and with a heavy heart she felt aching exquisitely.

She'd edged away from the crime scene and now sat in her Pathfinder, parked near the sheriff's squad car, letting her thoughts run their course. She glanced in the mirror and saw the tear tracks—dammit, she'd have to wash off the mascara.

Tom Arnow approached his car, talking with Deer and Rogers. As least he didn't seem as contemptuous as whites usually were. He was making an effort to give the rez officers the benefit of his experience, while seeming to accept that they might also have experience to share with him. So far, he seemed pretty good.

Who was Tom Arnow? She didn't know much about him but what they'd printed in the paper when he was hired, but her few meetings had been pleasant. Pleasant and . . . something else. Fact was, she hadn't been so involved in police work since the end of the Stewart gang, mostly because she only dealt with occasional fights on the rez and those resulting from continued tension between white sport fishermen and the spearfishing Indians, the perennial source of strife in the county.

Jessie turned the key and started the Pathfinder, but before she could maneuver out of the slick mud, a shiny silver SUV—a Lexus maybe?—nosed past her and headed for the sheriff's car.

Now, what was this? She didn't recognize the vehicle.

Then she saw a large decal on the rear window.

Crap.

Somehow, the press had got wind of this. The decal was the colorful logo of Wausau's WASU-TV, the powerful Fox network affiliate.

This is out of their jurisdiction. What are they doing here?

A brightly colored news van followed the SUV and pulled in next to the Lexus.

Jessie weighed her options. She was an occasional acting coroner but had opted out here. On the other hand, she was at the scene with the sheriff and the rez cops. The casino and convention-center project was big news in the area—protests were still rumored by the project's considerable opponents. A murder at the site was sensational enough, and these details would be explosive.

She made her decision. Sheriff Arnow was experienced enough, but new to the area and its weird dynamics. County, city, and reservation—a volatile mix at best.

She turned the key again, climbed out, and headed for the knot of vehicles. A news team was assembling near the van. From the Lexus, a statuesque blonde woman was approaching the sheriff and the cops.

Jessie angled in and reached them just in time to hear her introduction.

"Heather Wilson, WASU News 9," the woman said as she extended her hand.

Arnow seemed blindsided by the approach—or the woman's camera-perfect beauty. Tall, lithe in a black leather blazer, blonde hair spilling over the jacket's collar. Shapely but somewhat angular, large limpid eyes, a wide glossy pink television mouth full of too-perfect teeth, slightly pointed chin . . . she made quite an impression—certainly on the sheriff. Jessie remembered her not only from newscasts in which she read the news (*while looking great!*), but also some aggressive, middle-of-the-road investigative journalism for a small town television station. Clearly, she was aiming for a network job.

And now here she was.

Jessie felt a sudden jab of fear.

Somehow she sensed things slowly spinning out of their normal orbits.

"Nice to meet you," Arnow said. "Er, how did you hear about . . . this?" He still sounded caught off guard by the news anchor. Maybe it was her looks.

Heather Wilson smiled her TV smile. "I monitor police radio, of course. Reservation, too. This casino has been in the news for months. It's definitely one of my viewers' interest areas. Robbie, Tim, get the camera rolling."

Bearded and long-haired Robbie or buzz-cut Tim maneuvered a hand-held camera on the exchange. Arnow winced, as if he'd realized too late that he had let them get the upper hand.

"Look, this is a crime scene I don't want contaminated. I'll make a statement for the media later today, but right now I'm asking you to put the camera down or I'll have to have you removed." He nodded at the rez cops, and they moved up, ready to enforce his threat.

"Robbie, keep shooting. Sheriff, I must insist you don't put a blackout on this crime. This county's residents deserve to know what's happening. A lot of jobs and a lot of money are on the line. My viewers won't take very kindly to your attitude. Robbie, let's go."

As she started to step past him, Arnow put his hand on the cameraman's chest and held him back. "Okay, you can come forward but the camera stops rolling. Understood?"

Jessie wondered about his strategy. Seeming to give in a little was risky, but might work.

The Wilson woman stared at Arnow for half a minute, her large eyes grabbing his as if she were trying to hypnotize him. Then she turned and nodded. "Okay, Robbie, wait here with the camera off." The long-haired kid nodded. "Tim, call in."

Arnow walked her back to one of the taped-off areas. Jessie wondered if he was trying to make her sick. She figured the Wilson woman was too driven to be affected by mere body parts, and she was right. Arnow pointed, Heather Wilson crouched a bit, looked carefully, and by the time they returned she was still pale, but her color was already returning.

That's one strong career woman, Jessie thought.

"So I will appreciate if you keep some of what I told you to yourself," Arnow was saying as he led her to the van. "I'm going to need your word on that. You can release the victim's name, since we've ascertained there are no living relatives or spouse. But we have to keep back details regarding the nature of the attack to make sure serial confessors don't muddy up the waters with meaningless statements. Got that?"

Wilson was a pro. Jessie had to hand it to her.

"Sheriff, I'll do everything within my power to help with the investigation. Now, you won't mind if I do a remote from here, with the scene in the background but far enough away so you can't see much?"

Jessie swore the reporter was batting her thick eyelashes.

Arnow sighed and caved just a bit. "Fine, do a remote. Make sure she doesn't stray," he told the rez cops. "And keep the details to a minimum, or your access is revoked," he said, making sure she understood his threat. "Now I have to see to having my evidence bagged and removed."

"Thank you, Sheriff."

In less than two minutes, she was set up and the camera rolled as she stood with her back to where the sheriff and his men had begun the tedious removal.

"I'm Heather Wilson, reporting from Eagle River, where a horrific murder that occurred last night is being investigated by Sheriff Thomas Arnow. Sheriff Arnow, who was recently hired here in Vilas County, claims it may be the worst he has ever seen in his long career, and I can attest to how brutal the crime seems to have been. From what has been released so far, the victim is Jimmy Blackthorn, a major force behind the Great Northern Casino and convention-center project, which broke ground here just a few weeks ago. Authorities are requesting the help of anyone who might have information as to what may have occurred here in the late hours last night, during the storm that knocked out power temporarily to nearly a thousand homes in the region."

She broke the videotaping with a gesture, then directed Robbie to pan the area, which Jessie was certain Tom had asked her to avoid doing.

Then Wilson was back with more comments, some background on the project and its controversial nature, and an obvious voice-over to be used later in a follow-up. Heather Wilson covered her bases. So much so, that she finally seemed to notice Jessie and approached her—ran her down was more accurate, Jessie thought. She'd tried to sidle away from the news van, but Wilson caught her before she could make her escape.

Jessie looked for help, but Arnow was off with his cops and the coroner's attendants, probably collecting some of Blackthorn's remains by now.

She was half inside the Pathfinder when Heather Wilson thrust the microphone into her face.

"Dr. Jessie Hawkins, would you care to comment on this brutal crime? Would you care to make a statement?"

Jessie stared into Wilson's eyes, seeing the ambition lying in wait behind the sharp intelligence and the camera-ready smile.

"No comment," she said.

She started the Pathfinder and left the anchorwoman standing in the mud. In the mirror, Jessie saw that Wilson had already turned away to bark orders that her male slaves seemed to be following.

Jessie didn't envy Tom Arnow one bit.

Sam Waters

The council meeting had started.

His mind wandered for a few minutes. He couldn't help it.

The details to be discussed were important, sure, but the major, big-picture decision had been made months ago, over his vehement objections, and now he was nothing more than a hood ornament on a fast-moving race car about to collide with a wall.

A wall of flesh—the good citizens of Vilas County.

Whenever the council met, they did so in this glass-and-chrome conference room at the tip of the four-story glass-and-chrome building they had incongruously planted in the middle of nowhere. It was more than a traditional "big lodge." And decidedly less.

The chairs were sleek leather and chrome, and if you leaned back you could disappear below the table's lip. The conference table would have been worthy of the Round Table knights—thick, rich mahogany with a ceramic inlay portraying tribal life. It *was* striking—a work of great beauty. But its cost could have sent a reservation kid to Harvard.

Whenever Sam sat at council meetings, he inevitably thought back to *Thunderball*, one of his favorite Connery Bond movies. This table was remarkably similar to that at which SPECTRE met. A member to be punished, an electrical jolt, a flash and smoke, and a member executed in his chair, which then dropped through a trap door to be replaced by an identical, corpse-free chair. Meeting continued as if nothing had happened.

A chair sat ominously empty now.

Sam had often wished something would happen. Now, almost a year after the initial vote in favor of building a casino, shit was surely about to hit the fan. The council spent most of its time preening, some members erecting virtual monuments to themselves and their decision to build the Great Northern Casino and Entertainment Center. They hoped the convention facilities would trump other nearby Indian casinos, siphoning business from those older cash cows.

God, he had fought it. He had wheedled, cajoled, begged, intimidated, pleaded, shouted down, and eventually folded after convincing several members to stand with him against this monstrous progress the tribe didn't need. Sam and his group of holdouts had circled the wagons (yes, he was fond of mixing his Native American and White devils metaphors, but who cared when you sat at SPECTRE's table?) against the assault of the money-grubbers.

Led by the aging but not done (*oh no, not done by a long shot*) elder Thomas Eagle Feather, the council had started to believe the hype about the flood of cash that would come pouring down on the tribe. Thomas Eagleson, his name off the rez, had painted a vivid portrait of prosperity and pride, happiness and honor. The old man had made a convincing case and his side embraced it from the beginning. The final vote left Sam and his hold-out enclave in the cold. Defeated, Sam had withdrawn from the council as much as possible. He knew that with big money would come big problems.

The Martin Stewart affair had interrupted his involvement in the casino planning, but he'd been okay with that.

Then they had brought in slick moneyman Jimmy Blackthorn, he of dubious Indian heritage and hazy legal status, and voted him an honorary council member. He had promised much, snake-oil salesman style, and managed to deliver enough investors. Sam was surprised. The project moved forward, breaking ground as soon as winter's hold slipped.

Sam disliked the sleazy Blackthorn on sight, but he had certainly never expected he'd come to such an end. Rumors were already flying, the nature of which had drawn Sam back to the council meetings he had mostly boycotted in the last few months.

But now there would be more to discuss. Jimmy Blackthorn's brutal death would have some effect on the council, even though he had no familial connection to the rez.

Again Thomas Eagle Feather called the meeting to order, but the remaining members continued to whisper and chatter over his reedy voice. He pounded on the conference table, and they quieted down.

"Council will come to order!" His eyes glared at those few

members who had not been cowed by his pounding. Slowly, their voices faded as they realized everyone else was looking at them. The council had grown to fifteen with Blackthorn's membership, based on the tribe's original fourteen clans.

One voice was strong enough to question him. "Thomas, what of this murder? Stop trying to run a meeting with Robert's Rules and give us the information we all need." Bill Grey Hawk was not one to shrink before Eagleson's great ego, or his power.

Others assented. Sam watched with interest as his own group of hold-outs seemed to join this rebellion against the council's most powerful man.

"Bill, everybody, we need to stay calm," Thomas said. "I've spoken with Mayor Malko, and he has assured me that Sheriff Arnow is fully apprised and able to deal with this investigation."

"So he says, but what happened? I've only heard rumors so far." This was Hector Sandy, another of Eagleson's dubious core of supporters. There had been accusations that some "Indian" ringers had been appointed to the council just to get the vote passed. It made for bad blood. In theory, their heritage had been checked by someone at the National Indian Gaming Association, then signed off on by the Bureau of Indian Affairs, which had to approve all new casino gaming projects.

"I heard Jimmy was torn apart," said Alfred Calling.

"Oh, my God." Clara Kee Walters was the only female on the council, easily seventy and generally unflappable. But now she looked sick. She brought her hand to her lips. "The poor man."

"I've heard the same, and it gives me great pain. Jimmy was a good friend."

Sam almost spit. Daniel Bear Smith rarely called anyone a friend. Besides, Blackthorn was so oily-sleazy people said rain bounced off him. Nobody had much liked him. Now Clara, that was different. He half smiled in her direction.

"Thomas, what do you know of the facts?" Rick Davison

was the least native looking, but everyone usually deferred to his superior knowledge of tribal history.

Eagleson steepled his fingers. "I've spoken to the county supervisor and the mayor, as I said. Arnow has opened an investigation, and Dr. Hawkins, whom we all respect and admire,"—he looked at Sam squarely—"will be performing an autopsy on the remains." He paused, leaving the air pregnant with expectation. "I'm told it will not be a normal autopsy."

The murmuring resumed, and Eagleson let it go.

Daniel Bear Smith turned to Sam, his wide features pained. "Has our so-called *defender* gone rogue?" He kept his voice low, but Sam saw that a few heads turned to note his response.

Sam cleared his throat and spoke softly. "I don't believe we have anything to worry about."

"Yes, but how do you know?"

"I guess I don't."

"I'm ready, in case it is him. I've never been convinced having some sort of monster guardian is healthy for our people."

Sam wondered what he meant, being *ready*.

Eagleson interrupted the chatter. "We'll need to vote on ways around Jimmy's loss, and we will have to release a statement that reflects our pain, but reasserts our commitment to finish the project on time."

That's it, Sam thought. About as much pity as Jimmy could expect.

"How long will the site be closed down?" Davison asked.

"It's a crime scene right now. Arnow's got good credentials. I assume he'll do a good job. Our sheriff's department has no great experience. Maybe they'll learn enough to handle their own investigation. But given the, uh, victim's affiliations and the overall sheriff's jurisdiction for the county surrounding a portion of our reservation lands, I'm not making any waves against the sheriff. Let him do his job."

"And Malko seems convinced?"

"Yes, Bill. Mayor Malko expressed full confidence in his new cop on the beat. County Supervisor Burns is away on a trade mission, but I spoke to him on his cell, and he's on board with letting Arnow handle it. Now I suggest we get down to the business at hand. We want construction to resume without delay."

Bill Grey Hawk nodded reluctantly, stroking his beard nervously. His tall, thin frame seemed wedged into the chair, and his usual calm shattered by the events.

Sam allowed his mind to wander. It was as if SPECTRE had burned one of its own, and now the meeting moved on as if Blackthorn'd never been there. Sam hadn't liked Blackthorn, but he expected at least some sort of official mourning period. It appeared there would be no such thing. The empty chair was all the monument the guy would get.

His thoughts rolled around to Nick Lupo. What he'd been asked was bothersome, because it had occurred to him, too. The tribe knew *something* roamed the woods during the full moon, but they'd allowed themselves to be convinced it was benign, if not actually protective of their people. Only he knew the truth. Only he and Dr. Jessie Hawkins.

"Hope you're handling this the right way, Jessie," he muttered under his breath.

Arnow

He threw himself into his leather chair, exhausted. The crime scene was secure, the photos shot, the body—well, the *remains*—carted away, and the lovely Dr. Hawkins had watched him lose to that television anchor. That *very annoying* television anchor.

The office was empty. He'd left Jerry Faber guarding the scene until Morton came on shift, and Arrales was already canvassing other businesses. It was easy given the remote location of the crime. Somebody had questioned Sabin, the head of security for the construction company, but he swore he'd seen and heard nothing—nothing but the storm.

Arnow formed a picture of Jessie in his mind. She reminded him of that model Cindy Crawford with darker hair and minus the mole. But something about her attracted his attention besides her looks. Maybe it was her lack of ego, her unyielding sense of what was right.

For instance, deferring on the autopsy was actually a smart and appropriate move. A larger and better-equipped lab would have to assess the kind of damage done to that Blackthorn guy.

Arnow chuckled. He'd really wanted to be able to work with her, to have to visit her office, her clinic, her lab. As often as possible.

But then there was Heather Wilson.

Arnow shifted in his chair. In the near dark, he pictured the tall television reporter.

She gave Jessie a run in the looks department for sure. And she was spunky, all right. Had outmaneuvered him a little, right there at the scene. By the time he'd put together a statement of sorts, Wilson was looking at him out of the corner of her eye with the same disdain one shows a cockroach that dared the light. He expected her to crush him at any second. In a manner of speaking, she had.

Her live report had been quick and succinct. And his statement had been halting, misconceived, and ultimately hokey-sounding. The usual prattle about "leads being followed," "clues being analyzed," "the department having been placed on full alert," whatever *that* was. His delivery had lacked conviction and confidence. Wilson's look of contempt had swallowed him up but good.

The phone squealed shrilly.

Here goes, he thought.

"Sheriff Arnow, this is Marty Stanton from Green Bay TV-6. Could I have a moment of your time—"

"No," Arnow said, hanging up.

The phone rang again.

"I said no," he snarled into the receiver.

"Sheriff, this is Mayor Malko. You know, your employer,

technically." There was a chuckle on the line. "I guess your phone hasn't stopped ringing, eh?"

"Actually it just started, Mayor. Sorry about that. What can I do for you?"

"Well, I hope you're doing well and all," Malko said, "but this is an official call, I fear."

What did he fear? "Yes, Mayor."

"Call me Ron, Sheriff."

"Sure."

"Sheriff, it's not my way to barge into police work or your job, specifically . . ."

That wasn't what Arnow had heard, but he let it go.

"But in this case, given the situation with the casino project and our status as a vacation getaway . . . Well, you see what I mean."

"No, I don't." Arnow decided to make it harder for him.

"Well, Sheriff, if I have to speak plainly I will. This crime's going to play for all it's worth when television gets hold of it."

"TV already has gotten hold of it," Arnow interjected.

"What? Who?"

Arnow thought he heard the mayor sputtering a little. Probably needed to wipe the phone now.

"Lady from Wausau television, whatever station. She'll be airing anytime now. I gave a statement."

"You gave a statement?" Rage seemed to leak from the headset. "Who gave you permission to make a statement? What did you say?"

"I said very little. And my job gives me the authority to make a statement. It's in the contract and the manual."

Arnow wasn't sure there was a manual, and if it was in the contract, he'd never seen it. But it sounded good.

"Be that as it may, you should have cleared it with me. Or the county board."

"I didn't have you on the line, Burns is gone for a month, and I had a news van full of equipment in my face, messing up my crime scene. I had to say something. Otherwise they make up shit to go along with their pictures."

The mayor grunted.

"Mayor, I may be new here, but I know what I'm doing."

"I know, Sheriff, I know. Just catch our perp and get this over with, as soon as possible. Pretty soon you're going to have the spearfishing problem. You can't handle that and a murder investigation."

"Actually I can," Arnow said quietly.

"No, you can't. Sheriff, a word to the wise. Do you understand?"

"Perfectly." But the mayor had already hung up.

Shit.

Looked like the mayor was going to be a dick about things.

Arnow waited for the night shift guys to come in, then headed home to sort out what the next day would look like.

Jessie

She glanced at her watch. Barely time for a shower before preparing dinner. She felt gritty after walking in the mud of the construction site. Oh yeah, and she felt gritty because she'd just seen the mangled remains of someone who had been—

Just say it, okay?

—someone who had been partially eaten. *Consumed.*

Ultimately, that was what had made her queasy. She'd seen most everything—hunting arrows drilled through skulls, gunshot wounds in which the victim's head resembled a deflated skin balloon, sliced off genitals (rez girls were *tough*, that no one could argue), and even self-mutilation that threatened to haunt her nightmares. And, of course, her own nightmarish flashbacks about being kidnapped by the Stewart gang and what they'd almost done . . .

Anyway, she'd seen a lot, but human flesh as food was new.

She stepped into a hot shower and soaked under its needle spray for a long time, stripping the smell of violent death she imagined clung to her. When she finally stepped out into the steamy bathroom, she wiped the mirror and stepped back. Not to look, but to assess.

In her line of work, she was constantly reminded that the body was a temporary vessel. She remembered seeing her father in his casket, a shell, a mere reflection of what he had been. She tried to avoid the line of thought. Yet it was hard to pretend she would live forever or even look this way forever. She cupped a full breast with her right hand and tried to see herself as Nick Lupo saw her.

For the first time since she'd come home, she managed to smile. For the first time, she felt the thoughts of death slipping away. Her breath came slower, more regular. Suddenly she realized that she'd been as tense as a clenched fist. What was going on with her? She pictured Nick in her arms and instantly felt the arousal build.

I'm a weird chick, she thought, winking at herself. *I must be all about sex and death.*

And rock and roll.

She took a long time dressing and applying her light makeup, keeping a picture of Nick in her mind the whole time.

Nothing like a little naughty thinking to get oneself back from the depths of depression.

In the kitchen she set out two steaks and two potatoes, then tossed a salad and put it in the fridge. A chilled bottle of Chianti came out to breathe. Supposedly it was heresy to chill Chianti, but could she help it that she liked it that way? She set the table in her tiny alcove. The food was ready for the broiler and the microwave. She looked around and decided her everyday clutter was just fine. With a home office taking up most of the living room, she couldn't expect a pristine environment. The space in front of the stone fireplace was, however, nicely empty of clutter and furniture. A deep shag rug gave the wood floor a warm touch. Fresh wood lay in the hearth.

The cottage was one of four in a small double cul-de-sac

her father carved out of pristine pine woods and developed many years ago. These four homes were the only ones left after he had sold tiny parcels of the land piecemeal in order to finance his own schooling and, later, hers. Three of the four cottages fronted on a channel between two sizable lakes that were part of the long chain of waterways, and the fourth was a bit more secluded in the still-wooded environs of Circle Moon Drive.

Her longtime tenant, Nick Lupo, had occupied one of those that faced the water, but after the Stewart case (she made a face even as she thought about it) he had chosen to move to the more secluded structure, a two-room log and clapboard house with a screened porch and a narrow deck overlooking a steep ravine that circled the house proper and led down to the channel in a roundabout way. Her own cottage was a two-story structure built on the hill itself, a natural path joining the ravine and meandering down to the pier. When it was quiet, she could hear the water down in the channel lapping at the pier supports and sliding her boat back and forth in a gentle arc.

Even though she loved the sound, she turned on the stereo and let a little Tingstad, Rumbel and Lanz seep into her life. She'd never really tired of the semi-acoustic New Age that reminded her of the woods surrounding her. Now that the label "New Age" was passé, she felt she enjoyed it even more. Maybe she'd just grown up.

She glanced at her watch.

Nick, she couldn't help thinking, *get here soon.*

Arnow

Restless, he had a quick meal at the local Albanian-owned diner in the center of town, but his heart wasn't in it. The look of Jimmy Blackthorn's mangled body parts had a way of coming back to him just as he was about to rip some chicken meat off the bones. After a few valiant attempts, he gave up on the food and sat back to enjoy the coffee, which was better than it had any right to be. They kept his mug filled, and he was grateful. A chill had crept back into the spring air, and he was already feeling cold.

He sighed.

Word had spread, the TV had been on in many households, and the local populace had had a couple hours to digest the news of a violent death in Eagle River.

Of course it hadn't happened *in* Eagle River, but the proximity made the distinction irrelevant, and he couldn't correct the misperception anyway.

He paid, left a larger than necessary tip to offset his guilt at his lack of appetite, and headed home as light faded from the purple spring sky. As he negotiated the quiet streets of Eagle River proper, his mind whirled with the day's events, and with tomorrow's potential for much worse. The face of Jessie Hawkins came to mind easily, though the face of Heather Wilson seemed to edge it out of focus. There was no denying, the Wilson woman was brassy and attractive, but he knew she was a freshwater barracuda—a muskie—lying in wait. She'd have him for dinner, all for the camera.

He made a halfhearted extra city patrol and then turned into his short driveway and checked his voice mail (too many messages about the day's events, which he noted and saved for the next day), his e-mail (all spam), and flipped through the channels. Sure enough, Wilson's station was running a promo spot for the late news, leading with the savage attack in Eagle River.

Ah, Christ, he thought as he tried turning in.

Too keyed up and tired to give in to sleep easily, Arnow instead wrestled with himself. When he'd taken this job, he expected to lock up drunk locals and the occasional college kid, hand out speeding and parking tickets to Illinois residents, and maybe referee the ongoing dispute over Indian spearfishing. No gruesome murders.

Not *murder, attack*.

He finally gave up wrestling and dressed. He got into his

car quickly as if slowly would allow him time to change his mind.

Something told him it wouldn't hurt to take a look long after the evidence people had finished.

He yawned. *Should be sleeping. Long day tomorrow.*

But the squad car seemed to drive itself to the construction site.

If he hustled, he could be back in bed within forty minutes, his annoying curiosity sated. He didn't know what he was looking for, but his damned instinct insisted it would come up with something.

The county road was dark, but the road to the casino was positively pitch-black. His brights seemed to bounce off the trees and render the woods even darker and more impenetrable. He grunted and flicked on his spot, aware that from a distance he would look like one of those assholes who hunt deer at night.

A breeze had kicked up, swaying the thinner pines. With the searchlight on, he was better able to navigate through the leftover mud and back to where Blackthorn had been attacked.

Murdered, he subconsciously corrected.

Of course, an animal attack was the likely answer. But the way Blackthorn had divested himself of his phone and his jacket seemed to imply a lengthy chase rather than a sudden, unprovoked bear or wolf attack. Not in spring, when there was plenty of food in the woods.

Carefully, he avoided areas piled with construction supplies or cleared lumber. It was a shame, bringing down such mature pines for something as venal as a casino.

His spot found the security office, a trailer parked higher off the road to one side.

Good, Sabin's there, on the job.

He pulled up in front of the trailer and stepped out into the chill air. The pine boughs swayed high above, rustling urgently as if they had somewhere to go but for their captivity. He shivered. *Should have stayed in bed.*

A beefy, balding guy in a tight guard's uniform answered his knock. Sabin's handgun seemed loose in the holster to Arnow.

"Sabin, you remember me? I'm the sheriff here in Vilas County."

Sabin's eyes narrowed. "Sure, sure. But I already talked to one of your cops today."

Arnow nodded. Somewhere in his stack of paperwork he'd seen Faber's notes. "Just following up. Anything strange going on tonight? Hear or see anything suspicious?"

He glanced past Sabin and into the trailer. He saw cheap pressboard furniture and a silent TV.

"Nope, it's quiet now that everyone's gone. Just the wind."

Arnow nodded. "It's kicking up. Hope we don't get another storm. How about telling me what you told my deputy?"

Sabin sighed. "Fine—but I got rounds to do in about five minutes."

"Fair enough."

They stepped inside the trailer, and Sabin pointed at a chair. Arnow shook his head.

"'Kay. You know the site's humongous, right? You got them laying foundations for the casino, a parking ramp, a fucking hotel, and a bunch of outbuildings—condos for snowmobile and ski season, I think. And that pond next door. Anyway, it's a bitch to patrol. They let some guys go and haven't hired new ones yet, so I'm the only guy on the night shift for a while. I'm over at the hotel dig when the storm rolls in—not a lot of warning. One minute it's miles away, and next it's over your head. Really bad. So I ducked into a Port-a-John just to avoid gettin' wet. Thought it would be hilarious if it was a tornado and flattened me in one of those."

Arnow smiled but let him go on.

"Anyhow, the worst of it lasted maybe fifteen minutes. One point, I thought I heard screaming, you know, like somebody's gettin' his eyes gouged out." He swallowed hard.

"Guess it was somethin' like that after all . . . Anyway, I heard the screamin' but didn't have no idea who or where it was until I get back to the main drag and see the construction lot. I see Mr. Blackthorn's car there all the time. The guy almost lives here, right? Anyway, today I go looking for him, and that's when your deputy drives in."

"Why didn't you stay?"

"I told the cop I thought somethin' had happened, but I didn't know shit myself. So he went off looking and so did I. But then my cell went off, and I got ordered to check the casino site 'cause a tree had flattened one of the walls, and I guess that's where I was when he found . . . found Mr. Blackthorn."

Arnow patiently waited. People often race to fill in silence.

"Nice guy, Blackthorn, for a funny little Indi—uh, Native American. Used to bring us smokes and donuts once in a while."

"You never saw his body?"

Sabin nodded. "Saw part of it when that TV chick was around. Don't think you guys had found that chunk yet." He clucked. "Wasn't much to look at."

Arnow agreed. "Thanks for your time. We'll be asking for a statement."

"What the hell was this?"

"Unofficial. I'll call you and you can come in and we'll type it up. Meantime, if you remember anything else . . ."

"Yeah, yeah, I watch TV." He glanced at his watch. "Shit, gotta go. Have to check in halfway through."

Arnow thought about that. "When did you check in last night?"

"Halfway. Oh, you mean where was I? Just getting inside the Port-a-John."

"Thanks." Arnow backed out of the trailer and took a step turned his car, then turned around. "Last thing—you hear anything other than the wind, thunder, and the guy screaming?"

Sabin froze for a second, seemed to be on the verge of complaining.

"Wolves," he said.

"What?"

"Thought I heard wolves howlin'."

Lupo

Even though the lush forest surrounding the town of Eagle River had been trimmed back some, the crisp North Woods air still reminded Lupo and the Creature of total freedom.

And of Jessie.

Windows down in the afternoon chill, the scent of pine and woodsmoke tickling his nostrils, the music hitting just the right spot as he followed the road's zigzags to Circle Moon Drive . . . he couldn't help smiling though things had gone to crap down in the city.

The last notes of Bairnson's guitar and Andrew Powell's symphonic horns faded just as he pulled up to the garage and left the car ticking next to her well-worn Pathfinder.

She met him at the door, her face lit by the huge smile that kept him dreaming of her most nights.

Their lips met before either could speak. That was how their relationship had turned out. So often based on action and thought, so rarely on words alone.

"Nick," she breathed into him. "Nick—"

"Jess—"

Their embrace bore some aspect of the desperate about it. Desperate loneliness as they lived apart, desperate intensity as they drew together. Their scents mingled, and—inside Lupo—the Creature came to life with animal lust and the knowledge that it, too, would soon be sated.

Lupo stifled the Creature's wants and needs as much as possible, but here in the presence of the enveloping forest there was no suppressing the primitive urges.

They embraced long and passionately, their mouths meeting and seeking out those tingly areas that reminded them how much they missed each other while leading their separate lives.

"I'm so glad—" she started.

"I couldn't wait—" he said concurrently.

They laughed.

"We do that a lot."

"Yes," he said, "we do." They parted but still held each other like groping teenagers. Lupo's head and nose were filled with Jessie's strong, lusty scent—it overwhelmed the wolf's olfactory sensitivity.

"Come in." She was almost breathless.

"Let me get my bag. Be right back."

She waited for him in the doorway, her wide smile now gone sad—or perturbed.

"What's wrong?" His neck hairs sprang straight up. The moment of joy and recognition had passed, and now he sensed her worry.

"Come in, and then I'll tell you."

"Okay." He set down the duffel bag and closed the door. Scratches in the woodwork reminded him of the night the Stewart gang had kidnapped her.

He saw Jessie closing the blinds of the windows that overlooked the hill leading down to the channel, then those that looked out onto the rear of the cottage, the garage and parking slab. It made Lupo nervous, as if she were worried about being spied upon. His hair really stood on end now, and he felt an itch work its way down to his palms. The moon was just too close, its influence liable to manifest in various ways.

"Jess?"

She took his hand and led him to the table just off the kitchen, a converted restaurant booth. Two places were set, candles sputtered, a bottle of wine breathed. Her "good" china was matched not by her *silver*, which she had been forced to sell, but by rustic wood and stainless steel.

Lupo still didn't know why silver caused him so much pain. His research pointed to Hollywood screenwriters having invented the werewolf's aversion to silver, but he could attest to the truth of it. It burned his skin much like an open flame. At a distance, the element caused milder symptoms similar to a strong allergy—itching, burning, rashes, and unintentional manifestations of his condition.

Jessie hadn't fretted over the lost silver. "You're much more valuable to me than some stupid knives and forks."

Now he smiled at the spread. Her broiler seemed to be ready to work on a couple steaks, though his would barely grace its inside for a minute.

But when she turned toward him, he realized that he'd been right. She was preoccupied about something.

"There's been a murder," she began.

The seriousness of her tone startled him.

Sam?

She saw the look in his eyes. "Not someone you know, no. And Sheriff Arnow's a good man. I think he'll do a good job. But—"

"But?"

She sighed. "The victim was torn apart, Nick. By a wolf, maybe. Looks like it, right now."

He let out his breath in a continuous stream.

Jesus.

They sat and she told him everything she knew, everything she had seen. Everything she had thought.

Well, no, not everything.

He sensed that she held back a little. However briefly, she must have thought of what he hunted in the woods and how he did it. However briefly, she had doubted him.

"I wasn't here last night, Jess," he whispered. It sounded weak, even to him. He could have been.

Her eyes widened, shocked. "I don't think it was you!" She held out her hand, as if warding off the thought.

He nodded. "But then . . . we have to wonder who, what."

"There are wolves in the North Woods now, you know that. So many now they might sanction a hunt if the farmers get their way."

"I surely do." He had killed one in self-defense. It had challenged him, or the Creature, and there had been a fight to the death.

"I think the sheriff's not sure whether it was an animal attack or a murder. Maybe a murder made to look like an animal attack. It's way too vicious to be just an animal attack. The victim is this casino money guy, and you know how hot-button the casino project has been."

"Was he an Indian?"

"Yeah, I think so, but I'm not sure. Not from here, imported to help smooth things over with investors and stockholders, and to drum up new investors. Apparently not the nicest guy, from what I've heard."

Lupo waited to see if there was more.

"Oh, I forgot the wine!" She reached for the bottle and poured, filling their glasses. "You must be starved."

"I had a long day," he allowed. No need to tell her how long or how stressful. And now there was this. It leached some of his enthusiasm away, that was sure.

They clinked glasses and drank, enjoying their pause from the serious talk.

"Nice," Lupo said after sipping.

"Thanks. I was hoping it wouldn't be too dry."

"No, it's perfect. Nice and fruity. Full."

"I have supper ready to go, Nick. Let's eat. We can talk about this stuff later. I'm selfish. I want you to think about me right now, not the sheriff or his case."

"I'm all for that."

She slapped the meat into the broiler. His would be served nearly raw. She tossed the salad and buttered the potatoes.

Lupo reached down, slipped off his shoe, and slowly peeled down the skin-tone plastic glove that covered his real foot. His friend Mike McCarty, a film special-effects wizard, had created the fake prosthetic for Lupo after his severed foot had inexplicably regenerated. It felt good to get out of the itchy, sweaty latex covering. After scratching absentmindedly, he sat back to watch Jessie move around the kitchen.

He wanted to feel happy here and now—he did feel happy—but the news of the attack had shaken him more than he let on. He wished she'd waited until later to tell him. But Arnow could call anytime.

Lupo already felt drawn into something he knew he would regret.

Right now, the smell of fresh food overwhelmed him, and when all was ready they ate and drank and talked of other things.

But over them hung the thought that some other predator might be stalking their beloved woods.

When they finally pushed their plates away and let the last few sips of Chianti linger on their tongues, they had managed to catch up on all the month's news.

"DiSanto's gonna be all right, but Doc Barnett is out to get me," Lupo said.

"Bitch," she said.

"I love it when you talk like that." He laughed.

"Oh, I can be quite foul-mouthed, Dominic Lupo."

"I bet."

"Want to hear?"

"Want to hear, see, taste, and touch."

They broke some sort of speed record putting things away, dishes in the dishwasher, leftovers in the refrigerator.

Whenever they touched, they both felt electric charges ripple up and down their nerves. Finally his square hands covered hers and drew her toward the blazing fireplace.

"Mr. Lupo, you seem very sure of yourself."

"For once," he muttered, his lips finding hers.

Neither had anything else to say for a long time.

Tef

They had separated right after changing into wolfskin, automatically slipping into their well-practiced routine from Afghanistan and Iraq. They had trained their senses to keep track of time and whereabouts, to navigate desert—or woods—by silver moonlight. To communicate with the howls and cries that came more naturally to them than words. Tef had run through the thinning forest, heading for the construction site. He was disobeying orders.

Hell, if he wanted to follow orders, he'd have joined the military. Not the renegade Wolfpaw security firm that had drawn so much hatred for its disregard of human life.

He grinned. He loved disregarding human life!

Later, they were supposed to meet up and track the new kill, but first they'd stretch their muscles and take in protein. Tef ran a rabbit to ground, played with it a little, and tore out its furry throat, letting the warm blood pour into his mouth, coating his lapping tongue with the gamy taste.

It was like a shorty, he thought. Barely enough for a long sip.

His jaws formed a happy grin as he ripped into the stomach and warm intestines.

He left the emptied carcass behind, but his hunger had increased, so he hoped for a deer rather than another rabbit. Not only would it be more food, but also more of a challenge. In human form, Tef had grown to love shooting humans and watching their riddled bodies bleed out, die. In wolfskin, his preference was for the old-fashioned hunt. The snap of steel-like jaws, the cracking of bones, the gushing of blood.

Tef lived for the hunt.

Tannhauser was an old fogey who tied their paws together. Money was Tannhauser's god. Money and power. For Tef it was all about the blood and twitching flesh.

He caught a scent and analyzed it.

Human.

Armed. He caught a faint whiff of gun oil.

It was the cop, the sheriff. *Arnow or whatever.* They had checked him out at home a while back. So far Mr. XYZ had warned them to avoid Sheriff Arnow, but Tef wanted to play.

Who fuckin' cares what old XYZ says?

He changed course and drew nearer. Among the trees was the bright illumination of the construction site. He'd been drawn to this place again, perhaps to smell what remained of their last victim.

Sheriff Arnow was leaving the security guard's trailer.

Tef smelled the fear on him.

The gray wolf silently approached the tree line. The pines became less dense, and he slipped between them more easily. He kept his eyes on the cop, let them burn into him.

And the cop could sense him, Tef knew. The scent of the cop's fear was as sharp as an arrow.

Tef grinned when the cop's hand went to his holster. He rustled the undergrowth intentionally, just to rattle the old guy's cage.

The sheriff jumped but held his ground. His legs may have wanted to run, but his pride held him. If he ran, Tef would parallel him from within the woods, feeding his quarry's fear with the sounds of pursuit.

Tef would have left him alive. Tannhauser was a boring Alpha, but he was still in charge, and Tef wasn't sure he was strong enough to take him. Not with Schwartz in the way.

Yet.

Tef shadowed the sheriff a while, enjoying the power. Causing fear was his greatest thrill.

The sheriff didn't break and run, and Tef felt disappointment.

He aborted the shadowing and loped off into the thicker portion of this branch of the forest. When he was far enough, he stopped and howled. Tef hoped the cop pissed himself on that one. Tannhauser would scold him. But Tef didn't care. He'd laid off the cop.

For the moment.

Now, on to the night's business.

Jessie

She lay back, naked in the musky, sex-laden air in front of the fireplace and watched Nick as he padded toward the door. She admired his nakedness, feeling a lingering tingle after their heated lovemaking. He'd told her early on that he was in his late forties, but the werewolf gene (he still called it a "curse") apparently slowed normal aging. He looked thirty-five at most. He wore his dark hair longer than average, giving him a rebellious look. His lean muscles rippled in the soft firelight. She imagined what they looked like when he was the wolf. She was awed by the beauty of the image.

"Do you have to go?" She knew the answer.

"I can barely control the Change, keep it from just grabbing me," he said, smiling sadly. "It's because of you I've been able to hold it at bay this long."

He returned from the door and placed a hand on her cheek.

For them, silence was often a conversation. A single word, paragraphs.

He turned away again, restless.

"Be careful," she said, as he slid open the door.

He turned to look at her, and her heart leaped.

His eyes glowed like tongues of fire in the flickering light.

Then he was gone, out into the night.

She stood quickly to watch him run. He was a beautiful human bathed in the silvery moonlight, but before he reached the tree line he had become the huge black wolf she remembered so well. It—*he*—disappeared, swallowed by the darkness between the pines.

The howl, when it came, gave her a shiver.

Staring into the woods, the shiver turned into a full-fledged chill, and she slid the door closed.

Arnow

Sabin's words ringing in his ears, he started back toward his squad car. Why had he parked so far away?

He heard the trailer door get locked and double bolted from the inside. Clearly, Sabin was spooked. And he didn't look the type.

Arnow kept an eye on the trees. The damn trees were too close, an impenetrable thick-marker line that bordered the whole site. Clearing this space had been some job, but the number of trees left standing like silent sentinels was awe inspiring. But he didn't feel awe at the moment.

He was halfway to his vehicle when he heard the rustling behind him. Something moving in the undergrowth.

Something large but stealthy.

Something that wanted to be heard.

Arnow picked up his pace, keeping his head tilted toward the sounds. He would not run, but his legs almost betrayed him.

He unsnapped the holster and kept his hand near the Glock 17. Small comfort.

The rustling paced him, stirring close to the trees but just enough inside the darkness to remain invisible.

With every step, the hair on Arnow's neck and arms stood up straighter. He felt feral eyes raking him from top to bottom, measuring.

Had he racked the Glock's slide?

No, it would cost him precious seconds to chamber a round.

His legs unsteady, he reached his car. Fumbled the keys at first, then climbed in. For some reason, he felt the need to let his watcher know he was unafraid. Once inside, he slid the Glock out and placed it on his lap. He turned the key and stared out at the trees. Not feeling any safer, but slightly more in control.

A long howl split the evening quiet, and his hair stood on end again. The cry receded, moving away into the heart of the pines. Arnow's hands trembled, and he grasped the wheel to steady them.

He nosed the car toward the road, then sped up and headed home. Wondering whether the thing out there—*a wolf?*—was still pacing him. Feeling certain that it was running alongside the car with long, easy strides.

Arnow realized he'd stopped breathing only when the gasp exploded from his mouth. He sucked in air greedily, straightened the wheels, and tried to ignore the feel of eyes boring into his neck.

Prey: Hector Sandy

The front door slammed with the appropriate violent bang.

Dammit, that woman drives me crazy.

Hector had wanted to discuss the crisis faced by the council, but all she wanted to do was talk about her job in the rez clinic. Some complaint that a few days a month her boss just seemed to disappear, leaving her already stretched staff to cover for her while she went off to do whatever it was she did. Ellie was truly on the warpath about it.

Okay, he had finally agreed. *I'll mention it to the council when I get a chance. They'll ask you to fill out a complaint form.*

Everything was a form, a survey, a focus group with the council.

Ellie had been somewhat mollified, but dinner was ruined as far as he was concerned. She complained about *everything* these days. He stalked out of the kitchen, found a jacket in the front closet, and headed out with that satisfying slam.

Let Ellie wonder about that.

He wanted some sympathy once in a while. She always expected sympathy from him, why couldn't he get some from her? The council was fracturing. That damned casino complex. He wished he had voted against it like that idiot Waters begged him. The casino would just bring them different, more complicated problems.

But it was too late to change his vote now.

He had sensed some wavering on the part of the council. The Blackthorn death had sent a shiver through everyone. Was it an animal attack or a murder? Animal attacks were almost unheard of since the turn of the century. So it followed that somebody with a grudge had tailed Blackthorn from the big city and punched his ticket.

Or maybe somebody from *here.*

But who? And why?

The thought angered him. This tiny place had always seemed like paradise, but lately things were spinning out of control.

Hector puffed as he walked, a product of the sedentary life. He had been walking more often lately, leaving his comfortable couch and nice television for some quality nature time. Time away from Ellie and her constant bitching.

Now he found that he enjoyed the brisk walking, the cool evening air coursing in and out of his lungs. Before he knew it, he'd walked a mile from home. The woods seemed to encroach on the cracked asphalt of the roadway, making a narrowing tunnel. He'd never noticed how dark it could get after dusk, with hardly any streetlights and only the occasional hidden-away porch light to mark his way. Houses in this area were all tucked into groves and folded into stands of jack pines until they faded from view.

He'd never noticed how frightening the woods could be.

Ridiculous!

I've lived here most of my life. Never been afraid of the woods.

Not going to start now.

He went over Ellie's complaining tonight and let it make him mad all over again. Maybe she had a good case. The rez doctor shouldn't just disappear every few weeks and leave all the work for her staff, of course, but was Ellie exaggerating? He liked Dr. Hawkins. Hell, they all did. He was willing to cut her some slack.

Maybe because of how great she looked?

Ellie had almost accused him of having a woody for that young doctor.

Well, maybe he did kind of.

He muttered to himself. So what if he found Hawkins attractive? Just because he was getting on in age didn't mean he was no longer aware of beauty.

When he heard the underbrush part behind him, he turned with the hope that he would see a family of deer cross the road.

Instead he uttered a croaking scream.

He had no time for more than that, because the three dark shapes with bared fangs were upon him in a split second.

One went for his throat, the other his belly, and the third ripped into his flailing arms.

Hector died with the image of Ellie screaming at him locked in his head.

She'd probably be screaming at me now, watching me let these animals eat me alive.

Then he thought no more.

Arnow

His Glock in hand and cocked, he edged his way from the relative safety of the squad car to his front door. He fumbled his keys again, trying to keep an eye on his surroundings. His hands still trembled.

He wasn't used to that.

Arnow swore as the keys slid through his grasp like useless tiddlywinks. He heard his breath loudly in his ears.

His back was to the tree line and, suddenly, what had been one of his favorite aspects of the new home became something to fear. The branches rustled high up, but the rustles that frightened him were from down below, making their way through the underbrush. Movement where there shouldn't have been any. A deer? Rabbit?

Something else?

His fingers finally grasped the right key in the correct direction and slid it home, and he was through the door, swinging around and panning the woods with the Glock, convinced he'd been followed.

There was nothing—no one—there. *That he could see.*

The rustling receded.

Was that mocking laughter he heard?

Arnow slammed the door shut, double bolted it, engaged the chain and set the alarm, then wiped sweat off his forehead.

He went to his gun cabinet and methodically loaded the Remington pump shotgun with 12-gauge bear loads and the Ruger Mini-14 with a ten-round clip of military 5.56mm ball ammo.

Only then did he feel safer.

His hands still shook, but he managed to pour himself a drink.

Lupo

He ran on two legs, and the moonlight reached down for him and he was over, *just like that*, thankful for the painless transformation. And for his increasing confidence in his ability to control the realignment of his DNA. The Change that once claimed him without his choice had become a tool to be used with discretion and responsibility. Now he was loping on gigantic lupine paws. His nostrils filled with an infusion of forest smells.

He and Jessie had made long, lingering love in front of the roaring, snapping fire, and their passions had increased until he thought the touch of her flesh enveloping his would consume him. Where they bonded, where he reached deep inside her, it seemed the connection was forged from molten fire. They had devoured each other with their eyes, their mouths, their fingers, and even their toes, wrapped in a shifting embrace, tasting here, nipping there, thrusting, and receiving until the fire had exploded inside them. Then they had rested in each other's arms, nuzzling.

When the second wave of passion swept in and claimed them, it had almost surprised them with its intensity. She had suddenly taken him in her mouth and brought him back to the brink, back to where she needed him to be so that he could mount her and take her from behind as she watched the sparks in the fireplace twirl and sizzle like tiny shooting stars. He was engorged with renewed desire, and she wanted him deep and long. They had found their rhythm and become enslaved by it.

The end had been more explosive than before, drawing loud cries from them both. The fire in the hearth had begun to die then, as if they had robbed its energy and turned the logs into embers too soon.

Now he loped on four strong legs, his giant paws barely touching the forest floor, the scents of the forest exploding in his brain like grenades, and the moon singing its song to him.

The scent of Jessie's sex sweat lingered with him. He was grateful he had finally learned to keep Nick Lupo aware and alert within the Creature, which still tended to be a slave of instinct, but which had increasingly come to obey his human wishes and commands. Thus, Lupo luxuriated in the afterglow of his lovemaking, and the Creature understood and agreed.

But now *it* wanted food.

He tracked the scent of a rabbit, stalked the shocked animal upwind and pounced, soon enjoying his meal with abandon.

Then he ran and felt the night air wrap him in its comfort. It had taken years, but he had finally found the joy of freedom his condition could bring. He slowed to mark his territory, a formality since it had all been his territory, but he stopped when his nose caught a scent that made his hackles rise.

No, it was more than one scent. How many? Two, three?

Not human.

Not quite animal.

They seemed to crisscross the path, heading in different directions.

Inside the Creature, Lupo considered where he was. He

sensed that he had come some miles from Jessie's cottages. In fact, he was now on reservation land, and there were other scents present. Construction site smells, the Port-a-Johns used by the crews, the many lunch buckets, the stale sweat of men involved in hard labor.

And then there were the scents he held in his nostrils now, those that raised an unintentional growl from his throat.

He peered through the trees and saw that he was near the construction site. A trailer stood silent, locked up, its occupant afraid. *Armed.* He smelled gun oil and ammunition.

Then the howling began and went on and on.

A pack celebrating its kill.

A pack.

Stepping cautiously, the Creature held its nose in the air and caught the confusion of scents. It was strong, but could it best a whole pack?

The part of the Creature that was Lupo counseled caution.

He followed the trail of one scent, but soon lost it as if the wolf had ceased to be. A human scent arose in its stead.

The Creature growled. Lupo knew what it meant.

Werewolves.

He was not alone.

The realization shook him to the core.

Schwartz

They met as Tannhauser had instructed and galloped a short distance to where he had been watching the log-cabin home of the new target.

"This one walks at night," he had told them in their usual briefing. "He should be easy."

Schwartz had grinned at the thought of easy prey. Sometimes it was fun to give chase, but an easy meal brought its own rewards.

Tannhauser reiterated their mission.

"We're making this one as messy as the other. The message has to be clear. Fate is stalking these council members, and they are all marked. Our employer assures me the way is clear for us to continue our campaign."

"Cool! Now let's get going!"

Tef's outburst brought a frown from Alpha.

"Please observe protocol. I'm ranking officer and Alpha. I will determine when we 'get going.'"

"Yeah, whatever."

Tef's anti-authority campaign had begun to grate on Schwartz, too. Tannhauser would only tolerate so much insubordination. Schwartz knew he was expected to back up Alpha in such a situation.

They'd finished up the briefing as Alpha wanted it and had separated to limber their muscles, work up their appetites, and just enjoy their wolfskins.

Now together, they stalked the prey, who walked along the darkened road, muttering to himself, unaware of their shadows pacing him from the shelter of the woods.

When they broke cover and pounced, the old man was turning around, a half smile frozen on his face.

There's a lot to be said for easy prey, Schwartz thought. Less fear kept the blood and flesh tastier because there was no injection of bitter adrenaline.

The pack enjoyed its cheap and easy meal.

What they left wouldn't feed a baby coyote.

They howled their pleasure, blood dripping from wet snouts.

Mr. XYZ

The moon was out and it annoyed him, because you never knew when somebody would spot your silhouette from somewhere fuck-all far away.

He parked his dark SUV and doused the lights, then popped the rear door and looked around once before leaning into the cargo space. The long, heavy vinyl bag slid out with a little effort, bending when he swung it over his shoulder. He carried it to the edge of the black pond and lay it none too gently on top of some marsh grasses that flattened under it. The bag was one of those newfangled zippered Christmas tree storage bags, perfect for his purposes.

He stalked back to the open SUV and tossed the chain lengths and padlocks onto the ground. There were four, and he hefted them over his shoulder with a grunt and transferred them to where the bag lay with its silent cargo.

After a few wraps of chain around the vinyl, he secured the chains to the heavy-duty black handles with the padlocks. He worked quickly and efficiently, well practiced and well prepared.

He straightened, wiped a stray bit of sweaty hair from his forehead, then dragged the bag—much heavier now—to the tiny peninsular protrusion into the dark, oily water. He pulled and pushed the bag until it was positioned just right. Then he rolled it over the grassy lip and watched it make a ripple before beginning to sag where the chains weighed it down. Bubbles burst from the slits in the vinyl as it rolled over again, dragged down by the weight, and disappearing with a fartlike sound that put a period to the whole thing.

Mr. XYZ clapped his latex-gloved hands as if he'd gotten dust on them, then stepped gingerly back onto the wider shore of the pond.

Before he climbed into his vehicle, he heard a sound that startled him.

Somewhere a wolf howled. Another joined in. The howling went on and on, never quite fading.

He shivered.

How many wolves were out there?

He wasn't all that unhappy to be heading back home in a few moments, his doors locked.

A good night's work.

Tannhauser

He always enjoyed washing down the taste of blood and raw flesh with good beer, or even an ale. He swished it around and let it trickle down his throat. Dunkel Acker wasn't as tasty bottled, but it was better than being forced to drink that swill Americans called beer.

Schwartz was a good man with good instincts. Tef was a hothead, a loose cannon if ever there was one. He was perfect at watching your back in a fight, but boredom was his greatest enemy. He tended to instigate pointless battles whenever he felt bored. Tannhauser knew that without Schwartz to watch his back, Tef would have challenged his Alpha already. Tannhauser's wolf was a huge, muscular black specimen that would make most humans piss themselves. Tef's was a thin, sleazy-looking gray coat whose shifty eyes spoke volumes about his trustworthiness—or lack of it.

Tannhauser drank more beer. It blended nicely with the taste of his latest meal. So much the flavor of home. He hadn't been home for decades, since he and Schwartz had set off on their adventure.

Wolfburg lay on the tree-covered slopes overlooking the Czech border. Over the generations, it had become a place humans whispered about. To avoid.

By the time Werner Tannhauser and his best friend Hermann Schwartz had eagerly joined the Hitler Youth, the Movement was winding down. The Reich had been sold out, but their youthful enthusiasm led them to offer their lives to the Fuhrer. The Hitler Youth was a start, but when Himmler dispatched a certain Major Stumpfahren to Wolfburg, everything fell into place. The major had been charged with recruiting for a new organization that would be code named Werwolf. Hitler Youth and younger SS members would swell its ranks with patriots willing to sacrifice themselves and anything they held dear to protect the Fatherland. And, if the country should fall into Allied hands, they were to harass and assassinate whoever dared call himself conqueror.

So the Werwolf Brigade was born, in its ruler-straight ranks thousands of keen-eyed Aryan supermen ready to lay down their lives for the Reich. Along with those willing warriors were a few citizens of Wolfsburg, whose secret was that they were *werwolf* when the moon was full and whenever they chose to alter their bodies.

Both Tannhauser and Schwartz survived the war and its aftermath primarily because of their special qualities. Many a traitorous German or American-Soviet-Brit occupier had succumbed to their jaws, and they had learned to hunt together. They combed the ranks of the various squads for fellow werewolves, but no one else carried the wolf inside as they did. Almost every single Werwolf in their unit was felled by machine gun, or hanged, shot, or bayoneted at the side of some road, their sacrifices slowing the Allied enemy advance as a speck of soil hinders the plow's progress.

When their unit was decimated by an advancing American regiment, Tannhauser and Schwartz changed form and melted away like shadows in the forest, slowly finding their way back to Wolfburg. They left behind the remains of a hundred uniformed meals for the forest scavengers to pick clean.

Once home, they alternated between their twin callings: executing interlopers and procreating. Even though the Werwolf Brigade faded from memory, a small cadre of *enhanced* patriots continued to cause the occupation puzzling losses the war's victors chose to cover up, filing them under Mysterious.

Remaining elements of the Werwolf had begun penetrating German business society, and in the seventies the various East and West governments. They continued to flourish in secret, hoping to someday attempt the coup that might result in a Fourth Reich. But some disaffected Werwolf members emigrated, infiltrating the Allied armed forces, eventually finding no shortage of wars in which to amuse themselves.

The grandsons of Tannhauser and Schwartz, both raised in the strict Spartan environment of former SS men—and werewolves—had sought their fortune in the US Special Forces and eventually sought greater freedom. They'd heard of security firms such as Blackwater, code words for mercenary forces. They had connected with a KKK-Aryan militia in Georgia (where they had picked up Tef, a true believer and also a werewolf, to their delight) and had found themselves recruited into the ranks of Wolfpaw, a smaller security subcontractor with sufficient contracts to keep the three happy.

The symbolism of the name Wolfpaw tickled them. They had conducted missions in Azerbaijan, Afghanistan, Kurdistan, and eventually Iraq. And then they had rotated out and one of their KKK contacts had mentioned an indy job in the North Woods.

From the beginning, Mr. XYZ, their secretive employer, had been clear: they were to terrorize the tribal council until the casino project was killed.

Mr. XYZ had gleefully laid out their campaign. A few violent deaths and the council would crumble. The members who remained would seek a different direction and the project would die.

Tannhauser didn't much care *why* their weird employer wanted the project deep-sixed, but he understood well enough the *how.* And so they had waited to be unleashed, and now they, like the lightning, could not be called off.

Schwartz and Tef were still romping outdoors. Tannhauser smiled as he finished his beer.

Time enough for another before the boys came home.

Time enough to develop a hunger for the next target.

He already knew who it was. Who she was.

He popped another beer and toasted the dark woods.

Lupo

By the time his body told him it was day, the smell of bacon and eggs had penetrated the cedar-paneled bedroom. He awoke, fully aware, the scent of Jessie still in his nostrils. He let himself enjoy it before the food called to him. Then he levered himself off the bed to clean up.

The night spent in the forest had replenished his strength. There was a strangely restorative effect from the moon's silvery cold light, from the feel of the forest floor, from the taste of blood in his jaws. He washed it off now, remembering how he'd returned at dawn, tired but aroused, and how Jessie had reacted to the waves of musk he emanated.

She had cornered him and they'd shared mad, passionate love again before seeking sleep in each other's satisfied arms. Now her scent overlay those from the woods, and the memory brought him almost erect again.

He slapped himself gently. "Down, boy."

He remembered all too well what the Creature had discovered out in the woods. Best to keep his thoughts to himself for the moment. He had to learn more while in human form. The Creature was all instinct, but Lupo's intellect would inform its decisions.

He shivered at the thought of other werewolves.

But why should he? If one existed, then others were distinctly possible. Creatures of myth, perhaps, but the scents he had caught were no mere mythology.

"Hungry?" she said when he climbed down to the cozy kitchen.

"Famished." He sat, watching her economic movements. She knew her way around a kitchen and stove. And she knew her way around him by now. She was perfect.

He couldn't help smiling a dopey smile. He pushed his darker thoughts away.

But when she turned to serve him from a large skillet, she seemed grim.

"What's wrong?" His heart sank.

"Tom— Sheriff Arnow called. There's been another attack."

Her eyes held his a second too long. "Another murder, and it looks a lot like the first one." She served herself, but didn't pick up her fork. "Nick?"

"Yeah, I know what you want to ask, but no, it wasn't me."

He ate slowly, methodically. His enthusiasm for the day had leached out of him.

Her eyes were wide, fixing him intently. "No, I didn't mean that—I don't think you—No, Nick, *no!* I was wondering where you'd been, if you had caught a scent or seen or heard anything while you were out."

He could have confessed then, but he didn't.

"Tom?" he said, chewing a bacon strip. He half smiled around the crisp meat to show he was only teasing.

"Sheriff Arnow is kind of a friend now, Nick. He wants me to assist the autopsy."

"Or he just wants you."

"Hey!" She threw her napkin at him. "Well, if you don't want me—"

Lupo remembered the early morning lust. How could he not want her?

"I want you to meet Tom. Maybe you can offer to help with his investigation. Unofficially, of course."

"That's exactly what the sheriff wants, I'll bet, is some hot-shot city cop messing up his tight little world. Where's he from, anyway?"

"Chicago and Daytona Beach, I think. Why?"

"Just wondering how much of a hick he might be."

She put down her fork. "Tom Arnow is not a hick, Nick Lupo. What is it, some kind of cop jealousy?"

"More eggs?" he said, pleading with his plate.

"Yup, cop jealousy."

"No, I'm sure he's not jealous. He's probably eating enough, too."

"Nick Lupo, you're impossible."

"That's what you love about me."

She spooned more eggs onto his plate. "Eat and shut up."

He saluted. "Yeah, can't wait to meet that Tim Arnold—"

"Tom Arnow."

"Whatever."

She sighed.

"What?"

"Nothing. Can we get serious for a minute?"

"Sure, for a minute."

"The second victim is also a member of the elders' council."

"Shit. Any other stuff we should know?"

"Not yet. But we're heading out to the crime scene as soon as you're done stuffing your face."

He pushed the plate away. "Lost my appetite anyway."

"Believe me, from what I saw yesterday, you got that right."

Lupo watched her put dirty dishes in the dishwasher and refill coffee cups, all without looking at him. When she turned back to face him, she tried to hold back tears.

"I think something bad's going on, Nick. Something worse than we can imagine."

He wanted to hope she was wrong but his hope seemed naïve even to him. He steeled himself for the kind of day he hated, a vacation day gone bad.

Part Two

Intermezzo

CHAPTER THREE

Lupo
1977

Nick slapped a mosquito on his forearm and squashed it flat.

Damn bugs. *Vampires.*

He squirmed. Ever since *the incident* with his neighbor Andy and the terrible thing that Andy had passed on to him, he felt new empathy for the movie monsters he once enjoyed hating. Now that he, too, was a monster, he couldn't help pitying himself.

He flattened another mosquito. This one left a blood splatter.

Goddammit-fuck!

He liked to string together obscenities when he could. His few friends found it amusing.

But his biggest *trick* he couldn't share with them, could he? When the moon was full, he could show them a thing or two. But he had no control over himself, and what he became still scared him. Quietly he had abandoned his beloved *Creature Features* on WGN Saturday nights.

The ammunition in Frank Lupo's shotgun still radiated heat and pain from the gun cabinet. After the neighborhood men had "put Andy to rest" (*killed him! they had killed him like a rabid animal!*), Nick's father had kept the handsome Beretta loaded with silver-coated bear slugs. Nick didn't know where they'd come from, and he didn't care. The pain kept him away. The fear kept him wary.

Maybe Frank Lupo suspected Andy Corrazza had passed on his curse to someone in the neighborhood, so he was ready to deal with it.

What would the elder Lupo do if he knew his son had been the one cursed? Nick figured he would have shot the monster no matter who he was.

Nick had suddenly become a *joiner* as far as his parents were concerned. He had sought unusual extracurriculars so he could use once-a-month late meetings or group activities as excuses. His parents believed their son had volunteered to clean up parks or referee evening games. His nighttime romps had gone mostly unnoticed, his bedraggled returns explained away.

But still the shotgun waited for a moment of clarity. Maybe it would be best for everyone if he was put down. But he was a coward and he wanted to live, miserable as he was.

Also he wanted to see Beth Ann as often as possible. A year older, she lived across the street and mostly ignored Nick. But Nick was smitten. All it took was one look at her in her flowered bikini and he was gone . . .

(*sinning in thought, word, and deed—as Sister Louise would say in catechism*)

Beth Ann often sunned in her weedy front yard, but she couldn't know her across-the-street neighbor Nick had developed the delicious habit of hiding in the overgrown arborvitae in front of his house, climbing the springy branches until he was nearly as high as his living room windows and gazing on Beth Ann's sweet flesh through the Montgomery Ward binoculars his father had bought him last Christmas.

Today she was late returning from summer school. His teenager's animal lust had only increased under the curse of the moon. He wondered what exactly he did in the dark woods of the park he frequented. His memories of being a wolf were like snatches of film, strobing imagery that scared him. But there she was, finally returning to her empty house (a latchkey kid like he was), backpack dragging, and then out again in five minutes flat, her pert young breasts poking proudly through the flower print.

If Beth Ann knew she had a spy—

(*an admirer*)

—no, a *stalker*—

—she didn't acknowledge it. She spread suntan lotion in all the right places, turning so the invisible audience could enjoy the whole show, allowing Nick to gaze into the wondrous region of her groin.

The mosquitoes kept feeding on him, but Nick barely felt them.

Beth Ann flipped in the afternoon sun, and he could clearly see the sweat-darkened patch of material covering her *treasure trove*. Nick felt the reaction down below.

Am I a pervert?

He thought about it. Beth Ann wanted to be seen, didn't she? He was secretive because he didn't want her to mock him.

Embraced by the giant hollowed-out arborvitae, Nick watched as the object of his affection rolled over and untied her bikini top. The side swells of her breasts made his breathing more difficult.

Then he almost dropped the binoculars. She flipped again without refastening the bikini string, proudly aiming her bare, stiff nipples at the sky.

Perfect handfuls for some lucky guy! Never Nick Lupo. But at least he could watch.

A short hedge ringed her front lawn, but did not provide cover. He wondered at the brazen, rebellious act committed in view of anyone.

Maybe she knows I'm here. Maybe she's taunting me!

The street was a backwater, adults were still working, and the other kids were elsewhere.

Nick dreamed about crossing the street . . .

But wait, what was this?

Coming down the sidewalk was Leo Sokowski, a barrel-shaped schoolyard bully Nick had learned to avoid years ago. Leo lived way down the street and mostly picked on his own public school mates, but wasn't picky when a neighborhood kid like Nick landed in his sights.

Rumor had it that Leo's father beat him to within an inch of his life at least three times a year, and that was why he had become such a bully. *Shit trickles downward,* they said, and whatever shit he was forced to swallow, it was only natural he would share with those lower on the food chain. Nick was grateful they attended different schools.

He watched as Leo approached the unaware Beth Ann. Her eyes were closed against the scorching mid-July afternoon sun. Her bare breasts seemed to reach for the sunlight like mountain peaks on a poster, or like those *other* posters, the ones Nick had to conceal rolled up in the corner of his closet. Her face was placid in his lenses. But when he swiveled the binoculars and caught Leo, he saw trouble starting to brew.

It was like *Rear Window*, Nick's favorite movie.

Leo stalked the sidewalk as if already bent on some destructive task, and when he caught sight of Beth Ann's lush, supine body only a few feet away, the storm-cloud expression that crossed his face made Nick shiver.

His grin was crooked and evil, and he licked his rubbery lips with his fat tongue.

Leo spoke and Beth Ann's eyes snapped open, blinking in the harsh sunlight.

Instead of covering up, though, she saw who it was and forced a half smile, keeping her nipples pointed right at her new audience.

Nick was astounded.

The two knew each other? This just wasn't *right.*

His hands sweaty on the binoculars, he could no sooner have stopped watching than he could have driven toothpicks into his own eyeballs. Leo and Beth Ann were both in view now, Leo partially obscuring her smooth body.

No tan lines, he thought, forgetting about Leo for a second.

But then Leo stepped over and through the hedge toward Beth Ann. She suddenly got angry, waving him off dismissively. Nick's binoculars were full of a Leo-shaped obstruction, but when he could glimpse Beth Ann's features she seemed more afraid than angry. She scooted away, then gracefully half rose. But Leo had reached her and . . . Nick couldn't see.

Leo was pushing her back down on her knees.

Nick stared at her trembling breasts, mesmerized by their perfect beauty. The bulge in his jeans caused a flash of shame, but he couldn't look away.

Leo's hand came down on Beth Ann's crying face once, twice. Her tears glistened in the sun. Nick's excitement waned quickly. In the binoculars' field, Leo's threatening hand was huge. She flinched, and he backed her up farther, toward a small pine tree in the middle of the lawn.

Still on her knees but awkward because of how he had driven her there, Beth Ann looked up at Leo and her lips formed words Nick couldn't hear. Leo's wide back half hid her from view, and Nick swung his weight slightly to see better.

The bastard had hit her!

Fucking-son of a bitch-bastard!

His hands itched madly, and the hairs on his arms and on the back of his neck stood up in prickly rows. Deep anger built in his lower belly, heating his organs and working its way back up to his head. A growl bubbled in his throat, a sour *animal* taste burst onto his tongue, and it was like on those full-moon nights when the silver disk seemed to reach down and flip a switch in his body, and he would *change* just like that, shedding his clothes . . . and his humanity.

He felt just like that *now*.

In daylight.

He gripped the binoculars harder and swung them, trying to find Beth Ann. Suddenly he had her in focus. He let out a groaning cry of surprise.

Leo wasn't beating her anymore. His meaty hands now grasped the back of her head and held her in place while he drove his groin at her over and over.

Jesus!

Nick's anger turned to confusion. He couldn't see that well, but he was almost sure.

Leo was forcing Beth Ann to give him a *blow job.*

The term was tantalizing in his mind. She was *giving him head, blowing him.*

Whatever.

Nick knew it was sex, and his body started to respond, but he could see that Leo was forcing her, threatening her with one hand, pants bunched down around his knees. Then Nick saw Beth Ann better, her face streaked with tears and disgust, hate and fear. Her eyes were clenched closed.

In her mouth was that . . . *that motherfuckin' ugly dick.*

Leo shoved in and out and in, until suddenly thick white liquid gushed from Beth Ann's mouth and she recoiled, gagging and spitting and Leo was laughing.

Nick's muscles rippled of their own accord and his veins screamed out in pain, his nostrils flaring open and the scent of evergreen suddenly overpowering everything. His hands itched ruthlessly as stiff, coarse hairs grew out in patchy tufts.

What the hell—?

It was all familiar, aspects of the Change . . . but where was the moon? *It was broad daylight.*

His anger swelled, mixed with a strange lust. The growl worked up his throat, coming from deep inside where the Creature waited.

Flash.

Flash.

Images of Leo's lily-white throat parting under his fangs, tearing, ripping, blood spilling out in a thick gush.

Flash.

Nick felt his body beginning to go over, the wolf side pulling him inside out, starting to take control.

Without warning, something grasped his ankle and yanked it off the branch holding his weight. Thrown off balance, he plunged off his perch and crashed onto the dirt below, landing half seated, pain lancing through his tailbone.

The wolf retreated. The scent that now filled Nick's nostrils was familiar. *And feared.*

From the Journals of Caroline Stewart
November 1979

It seems only yesterday I last wrote in these pages, but a glance at the date tells me it was almost three months! I'm not one to wax poetic about love and devotion (though I'm certainly a romantic at heart) because I'm pragmatic and realistic. I've seen enough in my studies to realize that people are selfish and greedy, and terribly self-centered about love and sex, too. So, I've always tended to be cautious in my relationships. But now that Nick and I have become intimate, he's grown into so much more than a pretty former student, a distraction. His need for intimacy is only surpassed by his fear of it, fear that his "condition"—as he calls it—will hurt everyone he loves. Or worse.

I know he worries about me. Ever since he convinced me that his condition is real, we have attempted to understand its nature. After all this time, I still tend to think it's scientifically explainable. Nick doesn't agree. One thing we do agree on is that the condition makes him stronger, improves his physical capabilities, and increases his stamina . . . does it ever! (I'm blushing as I write that.)

Our experiments these last three months led me to the conclusion that scientific or supernatural, or somehow a combination of the two, Nick may well hold the key to its control in his psyche. We have proven the moon's influence on Nick during its full phase, influence he cannot reverse, but it's also certain that traumatic or highly emotional stress triggers partial "events."

We're going with horror movie terminology and calling it "the Change," especially because Nick feels very emotionally tied to those movies that portray his problems with sympathy. When Nick is least in control of his emotions, partial Change occurs no matter what phase of the moon. Whether he is distraught—or aroused!—characteristics of the Change begin to exhibit: sporadic hair growth, involuntary growling, muscular enhancement, and yes, even genital enhancement. All of these occur spontaneously and increase Nick's potential as both person and future police officer. It's my contention that if he (we) can learn to harness his "condition" carefully, Nick will be able to exploit it rather than letting it exploit him.

In the next few pages, I will outline some of the experiments we conducted this summer. Now that classes are about to resume, I'll need to scale down our explorations—except sexually, where I can't help myself! I thought after my father and brother's abuse I would never again be able to enjoy sexual relations, but Nick's so-called condition (and his love, devotion, loyalty, need, defenselessness—all that) makes him a very exciting lover. Since I believe all these elements are connected, I will not exclude them from these private pages. The connection between Nick Lupo and me is real and it can only improve as we set forth to understand this Creature he harbors inside him.

Chapter Four

Arnow

Today his mug was washed and filled. Rita had returned to work despite the cough or cold or whatever. He had pulled rank, gently reminding her she was important to the operation and if she didn't do her work during a crisis, well then, maybe the county would ante up for a replacement.

He wondered if she would spit in his coffee. She didn't seem the type, but you could never tell. She'd been training a night dispatcher, a girl barely out of high school with piercings in her eyebrows.

He sighed and decided to forgo the coffee.

Rubbing his temples, he reviewed his impression of the new crime scene.

Shit. He'd barely gotten over the first one.

The mayor hadn't called yet, but he would.

He looked up and managed a strained smile. At least *this* was pleasant. "Dr. Hawkins, good to see you again."

Who was that, behind her? He limped slightly.

"Tom, I want you to meet Dominic Lupo."

He's a cop, Arnow thought before she could confirm it. Not as tall as Arnow, but more powerfully built, a few years younger. Dark complexion. Italian nose. Hair longer than Chicago PD standards. A wild, haunted look in his eyes, like someone who'd been on the job too long, seen too much.

As he reached out to shake hands, she added, "Nick is a homicide detective from Milwaukee."

"Always good to meet a fellow badge."

"My pleasure," Lupo said. His grip was solid, not a show-off.

"Tom Arnow. What brings you here to God's Country?" He put a smirky spin on the phrase. After all, he had two gutted *and devoured* victims to deal with.

Lupo must have been the taciturn type. Jessie answered for him. "Nick is just up for the weekend. I thought maybe you'd like a fellow cop—a city cop—to bounce off . . ." Her voice faltered as she realized there might be an unintended insult behind her words.

"Sure, sure. Here, sit down." He cleared files off his two guest chairs. "It's messy, I won't lie. Probably could use a second opinion, Jessie."

Did Lupo's guarded look harden at the familiarity?

He described both attacks, crime scenes, and the condition of the bodies. Lupo rarely blinked, didn't interrupt. Arnow sensed the quiet cop was all business. Definitely involved with Jessie. He fought down a stab of envy.

"Torn apart, you said?" Lupo asked finally.

"Bitten, gnawed, ripped open, then torn apart, limb from limb, as they say. Partially consumed." He tented his fingers. "Of course, these are just my observations. First autopsy should be under way by now. The second—well, later. I think there was saliva left on some of the wounds, so we might get a DNA reading but it takes about a week. Fact is, both acts are very similar. Animal attack looked good with the first one, Blackthorn, though I'd say it was excessively savage—even for a hungry animal. The second's a convincing case for murder tricked up to look like an animal, though. Both victims were members of the local tribal council. That doesn't strike me as a likely coincidence."

Lupo met his eyes squarely, but Arnow couldn't read much there besides professional curiosity.

"No, it doesn't."

"I'd like Jessie—Dr. Hawkins—to lend her expertise to the task force."

She blushed. "Task force?"

"Well, so far it's just me and a couple of my deputies. Maybe the rez cops. I'm looking to expand the knowledge base." He looked from one to the other, then settled on Lupo. "Your help might come in handy, too, Detective."

"Nick."

"Okay, Nick. I'm not a territorial guy here. I'm too new. You two are sure as hell more connected locally than I am, and maybe you can cut through some of the bullshit faster than I can. Jessie, you have a lot of pull on the rez, too. And Nick, you're something of a local hero."

Lupo grunted.

Arnow wondered. Pushing the hard sell too much?

"Look, I'm heading out to the scene again in a while. I'm expecting a call in a few minutes. If you'd care to hang out until I'm free and then check it out, I'd be grateful."

Dammit, did he sound like a beggar?

Screw it.

Lupo

A half hour later they followed Arnow's cruiser to the new crime scene. He had waved off their concern about the crime lab folks still being there. He hadn't said a word about his call, but his sour expression was sufficient to give them a clue.

Several taped-off areas indicated pieces of the newest victim. Arnow pulled up and waited for them.

"This guy—uh, Hector Sandy—apparently went for his nightly walk and was ambushed here. Looks like more than one animal got him. He glanced at Jessie. "Bite marks seem to be of different sizes, but we won't know for sure until the autopsy."

"He was a council member?" Lupo asked. "Is this rez land?"

"Yeah, a senior member. And he lives on rez land, but this part of the road is off the rez, by not a whole lot. He walked from the rez into my county. It's one of the things that makes this investigation messy. Both rez and county are involved. Eagleson of the tribal council has officially requested my assistance, given the lack of police resources. I wish I could request someone else's assistance, honestly, given *my* resources. I have a call in to the feds because of the gaming angle to the first killing, but for the moment I'm stuck with this . . . whatever you want to call it."

"Streak?" Jessie offered.

Arnow frowned. "That'd do, I guess. If it's wolves, then it's a pack. And that will bring into question all the reintroduction of wolves that's been going on here and in Minnesota. People will revert to their old instinctive fears. Maybe there's a disease out there messing with their brains."

Jessie nodded.

Lupo felt the Creature stirring inside. It wanted to hit the woods again. But was it also picking up something that might lead him to the truth?

The crime lab people had finished gathering the remains, but the blood splatters now drying on the cracked asphalt road and the undergrowth lining it were disturbingly similar to what the Creature left behind after taking down its prey.

There was no doubt in Lupo's mind that wolves had done the damage here. The photos Arnow had shown them of Blackthorn were clear enough.

Lupo hadn't attacked the two men, but then who had? The Creature had caught their scent, but it was confused. There were several attackers.

Werewolves.

Jessie

She listened to the two cops drone on about the killings. She couldn't help shivering. This brought back memories of Martin Stewart and that psychopath Wilbur Klug. But now she felt as though things were spinning out of control even faster.

She didn't have to read Nick's mind to know what he suspected. He hadn't spoken much of his night's ramble, but if he'd caught the scent of other wolves, then that was bad enough. But if they were humans who carried the werewolf gene, it was a whole other game. Because Nick had always told her he assumed he was the only one of his kind.

Have to call Sam and let him know, she thought. *Tell him to watch his back.*

She felt as if she were drowning. What to do? What could she offer? How to help Nick help Tom? Could the two work together?

"I'll have the crime-scene photos sent over when I get a free deputy," Tom said. "I've got them running around checking on other council members right now."

"Good thought," Lupo said.

"I've deputized the rez cops, too," Tom added. "Not quite sure whether I have the authority, but the mayor's been on my ass already. The county's bound to be soon, too. I figure we need all the help we can get. We're just a resort town."

She broke in. "Mayor Malko is hassling you?"

"Just after you left. I was expecting his call, remember? So far these attacks are limited to Eagle River, his town. Anyway, he chewed my ass for about five minutes straight, then I reassured him we were following up leads, he didn't quite believe me, and we left it at that."

"Nice."

"He's not so nice, Nick," Jessie began. But then she realized that Nick wasn't responding to Tom's description of the call. He was looking at a brilliant Lexus SUV that was just coming to rest behind their vehicles.

Shit, it was that television woman from . . . where? Wausau?

Jessie frowned at Nick. Was he referring to the shiny SUV, or its driver, who was now climbing out? Wearing a tight pair of pants and leather blazer, her golden hair cascading around her like a halo, on her face a big smile.

"Sheriff," Wilson said, nodding as she reached them. She ignored Jessie, but turned right toward Nick. "And you are Detective Lupo from Milwaukee PD, aren't you? I remember you from that terrorist thing a couple years ago. I spoke to you on the phone back then. It's a pleasure to finally meet you."

She extended her violet-nailed hand, and Nick shook it. Jessie thought they clasped a bit longer than necessary.

"Uh, nice meeting you," he said. Nick was usually shy around new people.

Damn her, showing up like this.

Where was her camera crew?

Jessie couldn't help glaring at her in the spring sunlight. This chick had her television face on, lots of perfect makeup, hair perfectly set for a close-up, skin so perfect it almost hurt.

Little Miss Perfect.

Jesus, I'm jealous!

The realization shocked her. Over the years she'd been told repeatedly she was attractive, that she had nothing to fear from other women. Nick certainly seemed committed to her. But the way Tom had reacted to this—what was her name? Watson? Wilson? Heather Wilson. The way he'd let her walk all over him had stuck in Jessie's craw. And now she was set to walk all over Tom *and* Nick. Jessie sensed that all the testosterone present seemed to be heading south. And why not? Wilson looked barely contained in her clothing, as if she'd just stepped from a *Penthouse* photo shoot. What male could resist that kind of star power?

"So are we dealing with a serial killer here, or a wild animal escaped from a nearby zoo?"

Jessie thought Wilson was joking at first, but she appeared dead serious.

"This is off the record," Wilson added. "I'm holding off my crew so I can get some speculation about the killings, Sheriff. Of course, I also hope to film a new report for my remote later on, and assure viewers that the Vilas County Sheriff's

Department is doing its best to capture the animal or whatever it is that's terrorizing the area."

Arnow blanched. "Now, I'm not sure terrorizing is the right word here—" he began, but she interrupted him.

"Two dead, both tribal council members. The rez makes up a large portion of the county. I've spoken to some of the other elders, and I'd say they sound terrorized."

"Well, maybe nervous," Lupo allowed. "But I know some on the council well, and I don't think I'd characterize . . ."

"Sam Waters, for instance," Wilson broke in again, nodding. "Yes, I know him. I remember him from the, uh, terrorist thing." Her smile was enigmatic, hinting at her doubts about the official story. Then her voice turned to honey. "Detective Lupo, your status here is unimpeachable. Your friend Sam Waters was a vocal opponent of the casino project, and by all accounts you two were the heroes of the Martin Stewart mess. Care to share anything you may have discussed with Mr. Waters?"

"No," Lupo said, a bit too quickly. His tone softened. "We haven't spoken yet. I'm here for the weekend, but not officially . . ."

"Yet you're visiting the crime scene. I'd say you have *some* official standing."

"Strictly the sheriff's professional courtesy. Dr. Hawkins may consult on the case."

Wilson turned her high-powered stare on Jessie. "Ah, Doctor, do you have some hypothesis to share?"

Damn you, Nick, she thought. *Nice way to deflect her attention to me.*

"I'm not officially attached either," she said. "I may join a task force, but I'd be representing the reservation's interests more than anything else."

She wondered whether Arnow's look of annoyance was real, whether it was meant for her or for Wilson. This case was too wrapped up in weird jurisdictions, shared concerns, and shared resources—yet there were grave differences in everyone's motives and desires.

"No one here should be talking to the media quite yet," Arnow slipped in. "We have to coordinate our efforts. Then I'll make a further statement."

"On camera?"

"On camera." Arnow sighed.

"Well, that will have to be good enough for me right now, then," she said, smiling coyly at the two men. *Was she smiling longer at Nick?*

Her eyes did seem to hold his a moment longer than necessary, as once again her hand definitely held his longer when they shook. Her violet lips curled seductively.

Or was that just my imagination? Jessie thought.

Nah, the woman's all about manipulation.

Wilson reached into a pocket. "I have some local background work to do for my broadcast, but here's my card. Please call me when you're ready to make a statement. Or call me for anything at all."

She almost seemed to be winking.

After handing out two cards and nodding to Jessie—*I don't rate a handshake*, she mused—Heather Wilson walked back to her SUV with the studied gait of someone completely aware that every man's eye was locked on her shapely rear.

Jessie elbowed Lupo none too gently to bring him back from wherever he had wandered. "Well, Nick, what do you think?"

Lupo shook his head. "I hate reporters."

Arnow nodded. His features had hardened into a grimace.

"I meant about the case," she said, trying to get them back on track. She still blanched at the thought of the Wilson woman butting into police matters. *What a vulture!*

Typical man, she thought, disappointed in Nick's response. Had he fallen under the chick's spell?

Arnow and Lupo were moving away now, finally back to scanning the crime scene. She sensed Nick was uncomfortable with the sheriff's ambivalence. Nick's presence was both helpful and annoying, from a cop's point of view. She hoped she hadn't complicated life by pushing Nick's help.

She hurried to catch up to the two cops, who seemed to be getting along well enough.

Was she the connecting link in that equation? And would it cause trouble later?

Arnow

"The vengeance of the Lord will strike down any who choose to propagate sin," the voice on the radio blared, "and gambling, my friends, is a sin of the worst stripe!"

Arnow frowned as he turned onto the eastern leg of Highway 70. The radio voice droned on, the speaker gathering steam even though the background hiss grew louder. It was the Reverend Bobby Lydell, some transplant from down south—well south of Illinois, by the sound of his accent—who played country music between his hate-mongering speeches on the local low-wattage AM station that unfortunately seemed to be all he could get in his squad car.

Lydell had been on a tear about the casino bringing ruin and damnation to the whole county, and now he was moving into what a wonderful retaliation the Lord was visiting on the Indians' tribal council.

"Yes, indeed, gentle listeners, you know and I know that the Lord won't allow such evil to fester among His people if they be righteous, and I am certain—*certain,* I tell you!—that these animal attacks are an instrument of an angry Lord. Angry at those who would rob and cheat innocents who are too weak to fight the temptation. And I tell you, we must *all* be strong enough to fight off the temptation, or else they will drag us down into the depth of the worst hell we can imagine!"

Lydell stopped for a breath for what seemed like the first time in minutes. When he'd stocked up on oxygen, he returned to his rant, adding a new wrinkle Arnow dreaded.

"My dear friends, as you all know, our neighbors on the reservation have plundered our natural resources for ages, using some shady interpretations of old paperwork to make their case in courts that are way too liberal for your tastes and mine!"

Arnow watched a boat-towing SUV make an illegal turn and let him go unticketed, knowing the tourist would end up beating the rap.

Too many locals sided with the moneyed visitors, as long as they spent their money indiscriminately. Hell, since he'd been here, he had watched several high-brow restaurants open their doors just to cater to those higher-class tastes that preferred wine and champagne over beer, lobster and shellfish over menu mainstays like perch and walleye, and expensive cigars over cheap populist cigarettes. These restaurants attracted those who built the multimillion-dollar homes that now dotted the lakeshores, buying up the cottages and cabins of the olden days and replacing them with elaborate pier and deck complexes to house the multiple motorboats, Jet Skis, and floating toys apparently necessary for true relaxation. Meanwhile, they flouted the no-wake laws whenever they could, eating away at the very frontage for which they lusted. He shook his head, tuning back into Brother Lydell and the middle of his new rant.

"Indian spearfishing depletes our lakes and streams and makes a mockery of our laws and those who follow them religiously. The next time you try fishing in a depleted lake, you can thank your great and wonderful neighbors on the rez, where they'll be eating and tossing into the trash more fish in a month than you're allowed to catch in a season. You want to change that? Then sign up and make your presence known! When the season starts—yeah, they call it a *season,* as if it was even as fair as hunting—then get out there on the docks and the landings and protest! Use your God-given and government-given right to protest and make life miserable for those bastards who want to screw up our industry during the day and suck out our wallets at night in their dens of iniquity. Get yourselves out —"

Arnow switched off the radio with a growl. As if he didn't have enough on his plate, here was some fat-cat jerk sitting in a studio inciting violence. Everyone had told Arnow there hadn't been violence in years, but here they were, stoking the fires for their own self-interest.

He promised himself a stop at the radio station sometime in the next few days. He couldn't keep Lydell from broadcasting, but he could sure make it hotter for him if he caused any violence that could be traced back to hate speech over public air waves.

He pulled off and made a U-turn at Anvil Lake, the outer edge of the county, and headed back toward Eagle River.

Heather Wilson

She looked up at Robbie, her cameraman, and took him in her mouth. She worked her lips over the tip of his crooked penis and swallowed him like a circus sword. He groaned and pulled her closer, driving deeper down her throat. She almost gagged, then pulled back and let him slip out.

"Now!" she commanded, roughly shoving him backward onto the motel bed and climbing over him. She straddled him and rode him like a horse.

She'd always heard the phrase *hung like a horse,* but had never been able to prove there was such a thing until long-haired Robbie came along.

She was coming along nicely, too, her eyes closed and the sensations down below making her toes and nipples tingle.

Heather Wilson took more than she gave, but that was her way. Her conquests eventually understood and either took what they could get, or she moved on quickly. Robbie had stayed longer than most, and she didn't mind, given his apparatus. Though she wasn't exclusive by any means. The evening sports anchor down at the station, for instance, had been "working late" recently as far as his wife was concerned.

She drove her slick body down on Robbie and made him reach deep within her, and when she looked down at him she didn't see his long hair and round face. She saw Nick Lupo's angular planes. The image was so vivid that she came with an explosion that seemed to blind her. Moments later Robbie followed suit, and the ride was over. She slipped off his sweaty body and scooted away, looking for an illicit cigarette, letting the image of the city cop shine pleasantly in her mind.

She was very determined. Everyone said so.

Later, she reached for Robbie again and set to work with lips and tongue. He wasn't going to leave until she was satisfied, and she had plenty of time.

Arnow

He stood facing his daytime deputies in the conference room. Last night's fear had faded, but part of him still felt that eerie sense of being watched, being tracked.

Stalked.

He didn't like it. Not at all.

The Chicago urban jungle had never elicited such a visceral, primal fear in him. Daytona had seemed like one long party with occasional weirdness thrown in for good measure. But last night he had been piss-your-pants afraid. His hands had trembled and his breath had come faster, almost making him hyperventilate.

Now by light of day, he felt less of that strange fear, but its residue still sent an occasional chill down his spine.

Mayor Malko's visit had pissed him off, because he damn well knew his business. The autopsy results were due soon, but until then he had an unfortunate coincidence of animal attacks. Perhaps the same animal, or animals, driven by starvation or disease. Why this should affect tourism that wouldn't pick up for over a month yet, he wasn't sure.

Malko was just throwing his small-town, big-shot weight around, and it was Arnow he could most dump it on, so he had.

Arnow waited for the men to settle down, then grabbed

their attention by raising his hand. They turned in their seats and stared at him, still an outsider, not quite knowing what to expect.

"As you know, we have some sort of situation here. Part of the problem is that we don't know what it is, yet. I haven't heard from the Wausau coroner, so I'm still going by what we first thought, that the first death was due to an animal attack. The second looks like the same, but the victims are connected, which makes things messy."

"Boss, if it's an animal out there, none of us wants to meet up with it." Jerry Faber looked at his fellow deputies and they nodded.

"Never seen anything like that," said Arrales, scraping a finger across his bushy mustache.

Arnow wiped his brow. "I agree. Not exactly sure what we're facing yet, but I want every man here to check out a shotgun and extra ammo. I've got a case of bear loads, so grab some double-ought and slugs, then alternate them in your magazines. You can lay down some pretty wicked fire if something's coming at you . . ."

Morton spoke up for the first time. Rounded and balding, he looked more like the other deputies' father. "Boss, what do you think it is?"

"Well, it ain't Bigfoot," Halloran quipped. Playing the comedian was his role in the squad room. He smoothed his long hair back and waited for the laugh, but this time there was only a snicker.

"Right now I don't want to speculate. Several people have mentioned wolves to me, but I don't have enough experience with wild animals to agree or disagree."

"That's the rumors coming from the rez, Boss," Arrales said. "I hear they're talking about some monster thing they used to call defender of the tribe."

"Can you get me more info on that, please?" Arnow asked.

"Yeah, I have contacts in the rez PD."

"Anyone here have any sane theories?"

They looked at each other blankly. Whatever it was, they'd just shoot it down when they encountered it.

End of story.

Jessie

She bit her lip as long as she could. But then she couldn't stop herself.

"You seem to be taken with the new chick in town," she blurted. "Miss Wausau looked pretty good."

Lupo groaned. "I was just being polite. My folks taught me that. Good manners are important."

She could have let it go. "I hate people like that," she said. "So self-assured. So cocky. She knew you and Tom were drooling over her. It's part of her MO."

"Come on now," he said as he steered back to Circle Moon Drive. "You can't know what her MO's like. You just met her, too."

"I know her type, Nick." God, she hated herself when she got like this. But she couldn't stop. "She got far on her looks and she'll stay there on her devious and cynical use of men who just want to look at her. Or maybe touch her."

Lupo turned sharply. "Jess, I just met the woman. I haven't even formed an opinion yet."

"Bullshit."

Damn, she surprised herself with the uncharacteristic outburst. She wasn't angry, really, but something was stirring.

He was surprised, too. "Jess, I don't have any thoughts of her, believe me."

"But you see, she has thoughts of *you*."

"How do you know?"

"I know her *type*." Did she sound too bitter? Too possessive? She was repeating herself. Geez, this wasn't going well.

"Jess, you know how I feel about you."

"But she's gorgeous, isn't she?"

A well-laid trap.

"I'm sure some men find her irresistible, but right now all I see is a media vulture with more ambition than sense." He glanced at her from the corner of his eye.

"Nicely played, Nick," she said with a smile.

"Can we end on a tie?"

She laughed aloud. Touched his thigh.

"I'm sorry, Jess, if I seemed to be too attentive."

"No, it's me. Really, I'm sorry. I'm not the jealous type."

As she said the words, she wondered if he would believe them. Because all of a sudden she really did feel jealous.

He'd deflected her fears a bit too smoothly.

She was worried now, more than before.

Tef

A thin row of ramrod-straight pines screened the rear of the motel, and he was able to get in close to watch the door to 108 without much chance of being seen. None of the other rooms down this wing of the U-shaped building showed any signs of occupancy. Most of the plastic shades were open to dark interiors, and no light shone under any of the others.

Tef had watched the long-haired camera dude knock, look around nervously, then get ushered in by a shapely female arm.

He could smell that arm, pulsing with blood.

He'd waited a half hour, then wandered closer, slipped into the lengthening shadows of the early spring twilight, and pasted his eye to the narrow crack between the stiff curtain and the paint-flecked windowsill.

She was doing him every which way far as he could see, and skillfully, too. This was one fine chick, came with all the options and a gas-guzzling engine. Needed a certain level of hard-edged TLC and apparently didn't care who provided it. The camera dude was more of a living dildo than a partner, a machine she could pose with. Tef swore she'd probably agree with him.

He grinned.

The boredom had nearly gotten him, after the sweaty intensity of the Iraqi desert, but now he was in his element again, living on the edge and feeding his many *interests.*

He watched for a while, enjoying his own response below as one enjoys the appetizers before a gourmet meal.

The chick was gourmet, that was for damn sure. He couldn't wait to taste her.

An hour passed. He had retreated to the undergrowth beneath the line of sentinel pines when the camera dude stumbled out of 108.

Staggered as if she had wrung him out like a rag.

This chick was a lot of work. *Too much for the poor hairy dude.*

Camera dude was shambling down the cracked walk that paralleled the parking lot, heading for his TV-station van. Tef had followed the colorful van without too much trouble. Camera dude reached it, fumbled for his keys, and dropped them. He bent over and when he straightened Tef was there.

"Man, good thing I found you!"

"Huh?"

Camera dude must have been stoned.

Tef revved it up. "I'm workin' the office, man, and I hear this *scream* comin' out of the woods there. I think something's happened, man. You're with the television folks, right? Get your camera and let's check it out, man! I called the cops already—should be here any minute."

Camera dude must have been ambitious. He turned back to look at the door to 108 for a second, then shrugged. It'd be fun to scoop the boss. He popped the van's side door and reached in for a Steadycam.

"Okay, man, lead the way."

Tef was wearing his working-man's uniform: brown shirt, blue pants, work boots. He was like the maintenance guy on duty anywhere, everywhere. It was a cinch getting people to listen when you *belonged.* He'd learned that lesson early in life.

Tef led the long-hair to the row of pines that had sheltered him just a short while before. "It's right near here, man, just a little farther."

They crashed through the underbrush and when they reached a small clearing, the camera dude almost ran into Tef, who had stopped and whipped around.

"Here it is," he said.

Dude looked around. "Where?"

"Right here."

"I don't see anything."

"It'll just take a minute." Tef dropped his pants, grinning. He *always* enjoyed this part.

"What—whoa, dude . . ." The camera started whirring. Apparently, this guy was so conditioned to record weirdness as news that he couldn't help himself even now.

"No, *you're* the dude," Tef said as he stripped off his shirt. He hated to ruin perfectly good disguises.

"Look, you said you heard screams. You said something happened here."

"So I did. *Something has.*"

Tef's transformation was almost instantaneous. He'd been working on it for decades, after all.

One second he was a muscular white male lowering his briefs, but after an unnatural blur he stood before the stunned cameraman as a wiry gray wolf, eyes blazing and drooling jaws snapping.

His face contorted with terror, the camera dude dropped his Sony and started backpedaling out of the clearing.

But not quickly enough.

The wolf lunged and caught the cameraman with front paws, nearly caving in his chest. His snarling jaws had already closed on his prey's neck, sawing through skin and tendon, tearing it out in a shower of blood and flecks of skin and bone.

The camera dude's scream was strangled and cut off in a gurgle.

Tef stared into the wild eyes as the dude died, his feet scrabbling the forest floor in useless effort. Tef's erection raged as he feasted on the still-hot body below him, savoring the satisfaction in both stomach and genitals.

Snarling, tearing, ripping, swallowing.

Tef took his fill from the carcass, paying special attention first to the withered genitals, then to the entrails. Then he sat to lick his whiskers clean.

You're too much like a cat, Schwartz sometimes mocked him.

Only in the good ways, Tef would respond.

This *was* good.

He finished throwing a few spadefuls of dirt and pine needles over the shallow grave. Then he picked up the camera and returned to the van, which he drove and parked on a side street. This town wasn't very large, so it still stood out, but at least it wasn't prominently on display.

Back behind the motel, he sat in the garish green-and-white-striped Geo Tracker foisted on him by Alpha—

"You must fit in with the locals, and this car is perfect because it almost stands out," Tannhauser said. *"Therefore it's the perfect disguise."*

Tannhauser was an idiot.

—and waited for the news chick to emerge. When she did, clad in an expensive leather jacket and tight jeans, her hair freshly washed and her face made up, he followed discreetly. Keeping her in sight easily, he whistled tunelessly as he drove and felt his desire rise again.

Where the hell was she going?

Abruptly she halted and looked around nervously, then entered a bar festooned with the usual neon beer signs in the window.

He swore, found a parking slot farther up the main drag, and headed for the bar on foot. As he reached it, she surprised him by bursting out the door and brushing past him, her exotic scent lingering in his nostrils.

He could still smell the sex on her.

She had to be working, perhaps pumping the locals for information or background. She entered another tourist bar a few doors down, and he followed. Ten minutes and she was out, heading for the next.

Tef liked this town. Plenty of places to get plastered. And the people here tasted good, too—maybe it was all that fresh pine air. But he was in no mood to keep this up. From across another tourist bar, he watched her. All male eyes were on her. Whether they recognized her or not, she simply absorbed their attention. No other woman in the place could compete with the package—her smile, her perfect features, her lively eyes. She was a tasty one.

His desire grew.

To own her, to be inside her, to pleasure her, and—when the time came—to devour her.

Chapter Five

Lupo
1977

"Che cosa fai?" Frank Lupo's first recourse when angry was always Italian.

What are you doing?

"Stai spiando come un ladro? Ma cosa hai in mente, eh?"

"I wasn't spying—" Nick began.

But he had been.

The first cuff caught him across the face, shocking him into silence. The second was expected, so he rode it. Praying there would be no more.

"Vai in casa e dammi quei binocoli!" Frank Lupo held out his hand and Nick gave up his binoculars. As he headed for the side door, beaten and exposed, he saw from the corner of his eye that both Leo and Beth Ann had disappeared, probably spooked by the ruckus across the street. Or Leo had finished his disgusting business and moved on. There was no way to tell now, but the image of Beth Ann in tears filled his head.

Nick skulked toward the door. His father helped him along with a half kick in the buttocks more designed to humiliate than hurt.

It worked.

Nick escaped inside, his face burning.

No way to tell how much the old man had seen of what occupied his son's attention. Chances were that Frank Lupo would keep silent about this infraction, punishing both Nick and his mother with the silence brought by *her son's* disgusting behavior. Nick had no doubt that he would never see the binoculars again.

But he would see Leo Sokowski again.

Nick was sure about that.

From the Journals of Caroline Stewart
December 1979

Last time I wrote it was like a case study.

I really didn't convey the depth of feeling between Nick, young as he is, and me—wounded as I am. I thought relationships were never going to work for me. Too much baggage, thanks to my screwed-up family. That's the way things were going, until Nick came along. For the first time, here was someone whose tortured soul connected with mine. His baggage was more extraordinary than mine—that's an understatement!—but we were both people who needed to deal with our pasts and with our afflictions. It didn't hurt that he liked sex, and, when we finally reached that level, that he was so good! I'd always had a problem in that area, or at least potential problems that manifested themselves in strange, destructive ways. But taking on Nick's burdens seemed to free me of mine. Oh, and what burdens he carried!

It's a good thing these journals are private, because what I'm writing could get me committed.

After hinting around about a strange "condition" and even pretending it was an acquaintance of his rather than him, Nick blurted out that he thought he was a werewolf. It's strange still to write it! A victim of lycanthropy.

He didn't just think he was, there was no doubt in his mind. He rented a video camera and a huge professional video deck in order to show me. Then he was able to capture the Change on videotape. Just like in the horror movies, Nick Lupo turns into a wolf when the full moon rises.

There, I wrote it, and it doesn't feel too bad.

*I would have been the first to doubt his story, but I had done a fair amount of research into unusual phenomena ever since my own "incident" (more in a later journal), and I was already predisposed to believe in the unusual/bizarre because of my brother and our father's depraved ways (more on this in the journal marked Private)—and their abuse. My study of psychology included some work with multiple personality syndrome (MPS) cases, and I was researching a book on the subject, bolstered by numerous articles I'd authored in my few years in the profession. Nick Lupo may or may not have known I would be receptive, but somehow he sensed it. As he himself has said, the irony of his last name (*lupo = *wolf in Italian) might well be a sort of manifest destiny instead.*

When he showed me his first attempts to record his Change, he made a believer out of me. We'd already become lovers—an inappropriate relationship, but one neither of us could resist. While I might have been predisposed to believing him, his awkward, amateurish videotape attempt was convincing enough. This kid didn't have a George Lucas special effects studio at his disposal, so what I saw was either real or badly faked. I just knew it wasn't faked. His embarrassment, his discomfort—all of it was real. I think he wanted me to throw him out. He expected that kind of reaction. But what he didn't know was that I had already begun to see things—his insatiable appetite for rare meat, sporadic hair growth that seemed based on mood, involuntary growling when angry or excited. And the sex . . . well, there was some level of animal intensity to it, that was for sure. Even as young and inexperienced as he was, and as gentle as he tried to be, his lovemaking often ramped up to increasingly intense, almost dangerous, eroticism. Sometimes, in the heat of our second or third nightly lovemaking session, his strong but gentle hands would guide me to the brink, then urge me to turn over onto my knees, and he would enter me from behind in the most satisfying yet bestial way possible. Yet I was always there with him, ready by then to receive him and sway with him until our sweat-covered bodies united as one and his face would touch the back of my neck, his tongue lapping the salt from my skin even as my own rapture cascaded into a series of explosions, his hardness still large and embedded deep inside me. (Just trying to describe this feeling makes me wet.) Sometimes after all the intensity I'd roll over under him, and I could see the coarse patches of hair suddenly recede and disappear, and his skin would once again look normal. His sweat, musky in nature, seemed to arouse me further and we might then begin again. We were like sex-starved teenagers!

Sometimes, in the dark, I swore I saw him blur a little, as if he straddled both the human and magical worlds he inhabited. I don't know how much was magic and how much was DNA, but there was no doubt in my mind about the truth of what he was.

None of this lessened our love.

And I resolved to understand what Nick is and what he might be capable of, and to see if I can help him overcome this "disability." Not only overcome, but to help him harness it.

Chapter Six

Mr. XYZ

The young woman was one of a dying breed.

He chuckled.

Dying breed.

He'd picked her up that morning, hitchhiking on 45, something her parents must have warned her never to do. Yet there she was. Unzipped ski jacket, tight jeans, maroon cotton sweater showing off her assets, long blond hair tied in a neat ponytail. Not beautiful, with acne scars covered by makeup. Dark-rimmed eyes for that starved-model look. Glossy lips made fuller than they were. But she added up to more than the sum of her parts.

Now she awoke. Her eyes widened when they focused on him.

"Sleep well?" he asked, smiling. He didn't expect much of an answer. He saw her realizing, slowly, that a large rubber ball stretched her lips open and prevented her from speaking. *Or screaming.* Her eyes wanted to jump out of their sockets. She struggled, but the leather bonds held.

He pushed a button on his remote.

"Jennifer. Nice name, though it's a little commonplace, don't you think? Well, can't blame you for your parents' lack of imagination, can we? Jennifer, meet Heather."

He pointed, and Jennifer stopped struggling so she could look. He smiled at that—*a brainwashed consumer.* There was a commercial playing on the flat-screen TV, a clearance on snowmobiles. Then the local news came back on, and Heather Wilson took up the whole frame. She was talking, but the sound was off, so all he could do was look at her lips. He stopped the tape just as they formed a perfect O. Her wide-set eyes shone above her thousand-watt smile. Whatever the news was, it was good. Heather seemed to say so with her face. Her chin was pointed, but not too much. Perfect for her slightly oval face.

Mr. XYZ looked back at his guest. Jennifer paled in comparison.

He sighed. Maybe he could change that.

He leaned over and uncovered a silver serving tray.

"Let's see. Maybe something more subtle today." He selected a long scalpel from a set of a half dozen. It caught the light. Jennifer's eyes bulged. She shook her head, thrashing. Her lips paled on the ball-gag.

Whistling, he went to work.

On the TV, Heather watched, motionless.

He took his time. Jennifer turned out pretty good after all. But messy.

Lupo

Daytime made the North Woods Bar less dingy. Now, at dusk, the light faded from the one small, dusty window, but the bar had already been dim for hours. Dark woodwork complemented the old-fashioned L-shaped bar that spanned the length of the narrow storefront squeezed between a cluttered antique store and a sewing machine repair outfit that had to be a mob front because Lupo had never seen anyone inside. Bare minimum lighting hid the cracked alternating gray and green linoleum tiles that probably covered a once respectable wood floor. The bric-a-brac behind the bar itself was dated, dust-crusted, and generally uninteresting. The bartender, Stu, was dull and uninterested. The taps were mostly local—Rhinelander, Point, Spotted Cow from New Glarus down south Madison way, Leinenkugel Red, and the usual Miller Lite and MGD for the rabble.

The North Woods was the antithesis of a tourist tavern, serving mostly locals in search of less light and no conversation. It had no atmosphere to speak of. The antique bowling game had broken down in the seventies. The one nod to modernity was a darkened Frogger game. The radio played country or sports talk, or sat silently pouting.

What the North Woods Bar did have was the finest Bloody Mary in the North Woods, and the greasiest, tastiest, most fulfilling double cheeseburger ever fried on a griddle, covered with fried onions and dumped in an oily basket piled high with hand-cut spuds.

Right now, two Bloody Marys with their Spotted Cow chasers and two of those heart-stopping cheeseburgers sat in front of Nick Lupo and Sam Waters. Lupo's was barely cooked, smothered in mustard. The drinks were impressive, served in beer mugs, with celery stalks protruding from the thick red liquid, pickles and olives hiding beneath. When Stu could be tricked into conversation, he'd allow that his Bloody Marys were a meal unto themselves.

Lupo and Sam took a break midburger, wiping grease from their hands and faces.

"I like Daniel Craig, don't get me wrong," Sam said after swallowing. "I just don't think he looks like Ian Fleming's Bond as much as others."

"So who looks the best?"

Lupo and Sam never tired of sparring over Bond.

"Maybe an unpopular choice, but I think Lazenby looked right and brought the most human quality to the role. *On Her Majesty's Secret Service* is my favorite, and a lot of the fans think so, too, in retrospect."

"I hear you there," Lupo said. "I like Dalton, too. Way underappreciated." He picked up his burger again, looking for purchase points.

"Sure he was, but he wasn't well served by the scripts. Had he gotten better scripts and another chance, and had Lazenby been given *Diamonds Are Forever*, they might each have done as many Bonds as Connery and Moore."

"We're in the minority, Sam." Lupo grinned around a bite of his burger.

"I'll drink to that." Sam lifted his mug. "Stu should put forks in these."

"Yeah." They clinked.

They shared an amicable quiet for a few minutes, unwilling to broach the serious issues. But the troubles hovered over them.

Finally, Lupo sighed. "Tell me about the council."

Sam inspected their reflection in the dusty mirror behind the bar. "Christ, it's a mess. Two members dead, and we're still arguing about the casino vote."

"Think they're connected?"

"Don't know for sure, but I sense a connection. Both victims were yes votes. I was a no."

"One of the two wasn't really a member, though, was he?"

"No, Blackthorn was like a ringer, brought in to stack the vote and drive the work."

"So what else makes you think they're connected?"

"There was a rash of so-called accidents at the site, early on."

"Accidents?"

"You know, falling lumber. Broken generators. Loose connections. Faulty equipment of all kinds. A few small fires. A couple broken legs. Nothing too serious, except maybe financially." Sam took a long drink and plucked out the pickle spear. "Looks to me like somebody tried easy, less harmful ways of stopping the work, but when it barely caused a slowdown, they graduated to the serious stuff."

"Murder."

"Makes a twisted kind of sense, don't it?"

"Hm." Lupo nodded. Then he fixed Sam with his dark eyes, his eyebrows raised. "Jessie's been avoiding it like the plague, but what about the fact these could be animal attacks? *Wolf* attacks, to be exact."

Sam nodded. "You can imagine the rumors that have started up. Some tribal voices are raising that old chestnut, *defender of the tribe* and so on, and questioning why he'd be turning against his people."

"Shit. You realize, I hope, that it's not me. I'm not working my way through your damn council."

"Well, *I* don't think so, but then I know a lot more than the average person. Or Indian. Plus, I know Jessie Hawkins, and she wouldn't take up with somebody who'd do that."

"Thanks. Any thoughts?" He finished his cold burger in one bite.

"Yeah, I guess. Both the Blackthorn kid and Hector were yes votes on the casino question, but Blackthorn had to be—it's what he was there for. Still, it's the only thing they had in common besides sitting on the council. Oil and water. Those two didn't agree on anything."

"So do we wait for murder number three before deciding we have a trend?"

"What do you mean *we*, Kemo Sabe? You don't have jurisdiction here. What can you do?"

"I met Arnow today."

"Good man." He waved to Stu. "Two more."

"Undoubtedly. Too bad he's got a thing for my girlfriend." Lupo's half smile held no mirth.

"What? You kiddin'? He's sweet on the good doctor?" Sam shook his head.

"Naw. He kept it in check, but I could read him. She's fantastic, so what's for him not to like?"

"Yeah, but . . ."

"But it might complicate things. He wants her to consult. Play coroner, assist, help profile. Anything. He says he needs her help, but maybe he just needs her. Around."

"Like I said, he's a good man."

Lupo sighed. "Yeah, I sense that. Maybe he'll get fascinated by this Wilson woman in from Wausau."

"I've seen her on the tube. She is fascinating, even to an old man like me. What about her? You met her yet?"

Lupo nodded.

"She called me today with a lot of questions about our past. Questions about you and Jessie, too. And questions about the council."

"Crap. What did you say?" Lupo slid the new Bloody Mary Stu had brought closer and hefted it to his mouth.

"I spoke many words and said few things, Nick, but she was very inquisitive."

"Yeah?"

"Yeah." Sam drank, too, smacking his lips. "Watch out for her."

"Indian wisdom?"

"Something like that."

They attacked their new drinks.

"So, you gonna ask?" Lupo finally said.

"Sure. You go out last night?" Sam raised an eyebrow.

"You know I more or less have to with the moon. Yeah, I was out."

"And?"

"There's a bunch of new scents out there. It was confused." *It* was the Creature. Lupo still hated to consider it part of him. "Thing is, I'm not getting the message. Can't tell whether they're just wolves, or . . ." He paused.

"Don't keep me in suspense."

"There's something strange, all right. I think they're all—all *like me.* I've never run into anyone else with my problem."

Sam shifted uncomfortably in his seat. "Hemorrhoids," he muttered, but Lupo knew better.

Sam's son had passed the illness to Nick Lupo's neighbor many years before, and Andy Corrazza had then passed it to Nick. The bond that arose between Sam and Lupo was an awkward combination of blame and responsibility, empathy and resignation. Sam executed his own son to stop the plague from spreading, but then had saved Lupo instead.

Sometimes things worked out opposite of the way one expected.

"If it's true there are others, why would they be hunting down council members? Why not tourists or, even better, some of the more remote locals?"

"Sam, I don't know. Some kind of revenge, maybe. Or maybe they're your people, expressing displeasure with how the council rules. Have you voted on anything controversial?"

Sam frowned. "The casino has been controversial since day one. But why point the finger at my people? Don't we have enough trouble with the poverty and the fishing and the racism?"

"Just theorizing," Lupo said, holding up his hands in surrender. "Nothing meant by it. Anything else?"

"Nothing you'd think would incite violence." Sam set aside his basket of food, an ashen look passing over his features like a curtain. "You think somebody has it in for us because of the casino?"

"You said yourself it's controversial. People who just hate Indians wouldn't go all the way to the top. They'd just beat up or shoot at your average folk."

Stu came by to scoop up their wrecked baskets.

Then Lupo said, "I'll suggest to Arnow that he provide the council with some police protection. Though I don't think he has the manpower."

"Tom doesn't even have enough men to cover the white folks hereabouts."

"Tribal police?"

"A joke still, right now. Proposal's in for a big upgrade, but now you're talking about a six-man force that mostly handles rowdies and D-and-Ds."

"I heard there's unprecedented cooperation with the sheriff on this. If they work together, maybe . . ."

"We're not set up for serious violent crime, and the sheriff's jurisdiction is the land surrounding the rez, so it's not a stretch to see collaboration. Frankly I'm surprised Mayor Malko agreed to share resources."

"Tourism is king. Benefits everybody," Lupo pointed out. "He's just being practical."

"Maybe. But decisions don't usually come this easy to the area. A lot of old prejudices exist, Nick. You haven't got a clue. Pardon an old man's straight talk, but less than ten years ago, I probably wouldn't have been welcome in this bar."

Lupo waved money at Stu. "No need to apologize, Sam, but I do have a clue. This Malko sounds like an agreeable type. You're lucky he's willing to cut through red tape. Usually there'd be bickering, and nothing would get done."

Stu gave up some change. "Come again, fellas."

Outside, daylight's hold was continuing to slip. They stopped at Lupo's car. "I'm heading back to Arnow's office. Can I drop you anywhere?"

"No thanks, I brought my wheels." Sam pointed at a faded tan Land Rover, Cold War vintage, hugging the curb in front of the deserted sewing machine repair outfit.

"Suit yourself," Lupo said. "Watch out for a stiff wind—it'll tear that thing apart!"

"This *thing*'s been to four continents."

"Left some parts behind in each of them."

"Yeah, yeah, you only wish yours would last this long."

"Maybe, Sam, maybe. Just watch your back, okay?"

They parted, and Lupo aimed for Arnow's office.

He cruised Wall Street, the main drag, then turned onto Railroad. He thought he spotted a flash of brilliant blond hair on the sidewalk near the Pirates' Cove Lounge.

Sure enough, it was Heather Wilson. He saw her leave one drinking establishment and step out onto the sidewalk. The traffic light changed and he stopped, anonymous behind tinted glass of his vehicle.

She walked right past him and he couldn't help admiring her sleek lines. A true thoroughbred. Maybe a panther. He stumbled on the animal comparisons, settling for admitting she was a fine figure of a woman. Men on the street turned to stare, unless accompanied by their wives.

Not far behind her ambled a blond man, youngish, who seemed to hesitate, staring at her back.

Was he tailing her?

The light turned green and Lupo was forced to nose forward, but he turned right at the next corner and doubled back a block, making a right onto Wall again. He slowed to a crawl—to the consternation of the driver of a blue sedan behind him, who tapped his horn—and tried to spot either Heather or the blond man. But both had disappeared. The blue and red neon of a beer sign blinked onto the sidewalk. Had she entered?

Dammit, he thought. *Did he follow her?*

He reasoned people must recognize her all the time. Maybe it was just a lovelorn fan who wanted her autograph or to see her up close. She was worth it, that was certain. He'd glanced at those perfect TV features himself, though now Jessie was miffed.

A rusted Bronco of O.J. Simpson vintage left the curb ahead, and Lupo deftly swung the Maxima into the slot. He flipped the mirror until he could see both Buck's Pub and Grub and the Northern Tap.

He waited, his patience seeping away.

The moon wasn't ready to rise yet, but he felt her well enough. The itch drove him crazy. The occasional jolts of clarity through his human nostrils, the Creature picking up scents. He tapped his fingers on the wheel impatiently. His throat was scratchy, and the thirst was already on him. He had a liter bottle of water nestled on the passenger seat. As he drank, he kept an eye on the mirror.

Sure enough, Heather Wilson and the blond man left the tavern together. He moved the mirror to keep them in sight, swirling the water in his mouth.

The blond man's hair reminded Lupo of a lion's mane, long and swirling behind him.

They took a side street and disappeared from his view, so he slipped out of the car, fed the meter, and hustled to the corner. They were a block away, heading toward one of the main highway's offshoots, where a row of motels and motor inns welcomed less-affluent winter and summer visitors.

He ducked into a dingy alley behind the shops on Wall Street, shucked his clothes, and forced a Change.

The Creature was near the surface, for the moon was out there and calling.

Lupo barely had time to prepare for the tingly feeling and then he was suddenly on four paws, his nose leading him.

The two humans had passed merely moments before. The female's scent drove him crazy, for he could smell her sex and its readiness.

The male scent, however, was more complex. It was human and male, yes, but was it also . . . like his own?

Lupo's mind took a minute to wrap itself around the possibility. Even though he thought he'd been prepared, it was shocking.

Like me. Maybe.

Then he's a murderer.

What if he was wrong? What if the scent was someone else?

And was Heather Wilson in danger?

Lupo tracked them to a medium-sized motor court, on the off-street side. He padded down the row of doors, stopping in front of 108. Then he whirled and pounced back to the alley, unaware of the family who stopped short at the sight of a huge black wolf dashing across the parking lot.

"I told you there's still a lot of wildlife here, honey," whined the put-upon husband, who really wanted to find a hunting season rental for Thanksgiving.

His wife nodded dumbly, her mouth open. She held her kids tightly, not quite sure whether to let them go or not.

Across the lot, a rented Altima swung into an open slot.

Schwartz

"Shit."

He sat in the Altima they'd been driving openly as new county residents.

"Shit. Shit!" He banged his hands on the wheel. What was Tef doing? What was he thinking?

Schwartz had been following the younger member of the pack because he'd had a bad feeling, and Schwartzes had been having bad feelings that meant something for centuries.

Seeing Tef openly pursue that television newswoman made his hackles rise. No way to know what Tef's game was, but this wasn't the wilds of Iraq, where an AK-47 and contractor immunity pretty much shielded one from anything. Here was trouble, and now Schwartz would have to report to Alpha that their young friend was jeopardizing the operation. And their safety.

Schwartz and Tannhauser had engaged a Realtor, ostensibly seeking vacation and retirement homes. Tef was assigned the cover of job seeker and had applied for all bits of menial labor advertised in the local paper. Their cover was tenuous, but likely passed muster as far as the locals went, and anyway most residents overlooked strangers in a resort town. Mr. XYZ had been adamant that even this early in the season, no one would question their presence.

Until Tef went and possibly fucked it up. Which he seemed intent on doing.

Schwartz dialed his cell.

"Yeah?"

"We've got a problem, Alpha."

Tannhauser sighed. He just didn't like problems. His strategy was usually to kill and devour problems.

"What now?"

"Tef's been following that TV reporter around town."

Tannhauser was silent.

"They've walked into half a dozen bars. He's hanging

back a little, but she's gonna trip over him sooner or later. What are your orders?"

The phone was silent so long, Schwartz thought it had gone dead.

"Nothing right now," Tannhauser said finally. "We've been given our new targets."

"Plural?"

"Yes, indeed. Tonight we feast!"

A pleasant sensation spread through Schwartz's belly, which was already beginning to rumble in expectation of the moon's call. It was hard to quell the endless hunger during a full moon.

"Oh, shit!"

"What's wrong?" Tannhauser's voice growled in his ear. "What's going on?"

"Tef's leaving the bar. He's *with* the reporter," Schwartz hissed. "Like he picked her up."

"Dammit, I'll have a word with the idiot later tonight. Stay on his ass and as soon as you can, relay the message. If she's too curious, kill her."

Schwartz clicked off and followed. They were walking, heat radiating off them in waves.

Sexual heat.

He could sense it this far away.

That damn kid and his dick was going to get them all in trouble.

Heather Wilson

After the fifth bar, she got tired of the attention. Of course, she knew she'd attract male attention. Usually she sought it and bathed in it, but she could take only so many sweaty blue-collar locals and over-cologned wannabe studs.

All she got for her trouble was nearly asphyxiated by the smoke, cologne, and testosterone. Locals resented the Indians anyway, so a death around the casino didn't bother anyone. But she didn't mind trolling. Often she justified her cruising by couching it in journalistic terms. Now she was just bored and on the make.

Reluctantly she accepted another shot of something clear, bought for her by a meaty tourist ready for a stroke or cardiac arrest. She raised the glass and smiled, wishing him one of each, and down-the-hatched it.

Her eyes roamed farther down the bar, ignoring all those who wanted to catch her glance. Until she reached *him*. He stood out in the small crowd. Late twenties, maybe. Longish blond hair, cherubic lips, strong nose, and the most striking eyes she'd seen since doing that story on elective eye enhancement for which all the movie stars were said to be lining up. He seemed loose, muscled body relaxed and confident. *Powerful.* He was her type.

And he looked familiar.

He smiled directly at her as if he'd read her mind. He gripped a beer mug he wasn't drinking from and smirked at her so fast she almost missed it.

She slid money at the bartender and sent over a shot.

The blond stud turned to acknowledge her kindness and lapped at the golden liquid with an impossibly long tongue.

Lord, she was melting down below.

He smiled again, as if fully aware. Lapped again.

Heather worked her way toward him, but when she got there she was at a loss for words. He watched her all the way in.

"Hi."

"Hello. Thank you for the drink. It's very . . . strong." His tongue slipped into the shot glass again and touched the surface of the liquid, swirling it around like honey, his eyes never leaving hers.

She swallowed. Hard. "Yukon Jack."

"Ah, yes." His eyes were kaleidoscopic, multicolored.

Has to be contact lenses, she thought. *Or transplants. Can't be his own.*

Tingly. She felt tingly, and dripping. She wanted to caress him. He smelled . . . *woodsy.* A lumberjack type, yet pretty.

Face unlined. Young, almost boyish. Yet somehow he seemed experienced beyond his biological years.

Her purpose completely forgotten, she ate him up with her eyes.

She touched his arm while making some comment about the weather. His skin was hot. She felt an electrical charge pass from his skin to hers. She tingled all over.

"I have a room," she whispered hoarsely. She couldn't remember anything else they had said. It was just words.

He nodded.

The rest was a blur. They walked arm in arm, almost ran. The heat enveloped her like a cloud. By the time she got him inside the door, she thought she'd burst. Her panties were soaked. She wondered about her jeans. No matter, they'd be coming off soon.

She kicked the door closed.

He stood before her, blond hair on fire in the dingy lamplight, boyish lips curled up in a smug little smile. Right now his eyes were bluer than any cold water lake she had ever seen, but she could have sworn they'd been dark brown before and green earlier.

She wanted him in her mouth. In her. She just wanted him. Moisture trickled down her inner thigh. Her skin hummed.

"What's your name?" she whispered tentatively, as if she'd forgotten how to speak.

He hadn't said much. Hadn't needed to.

"Tef."

"Hm, sounds foreign." She licked her lips.

"Oh, it is. More than you can imagine."

Was there a slight accent? It was sexy, mysterious.

She was sitting on the edge of the bed. When had she sat? "Where are you from?"

"I have been everywhere. I'm not from any one place anymore."

Her breathing was ragged. "Where were you last?"

"Iraq."

"Jesus," she said, leaning toward him. He stood his ground. "It must have been . . . awful."

"Sometimes. But most often it was . . . glorious."

"I think I know what you mean." She reached up and lay her hand on his chest. It was rock hard. She moved her hand down. *Glorious.* "You must be glad to be home."

"I don't have a home. I'm here."

His voice was dreamy, almost hypnotic.

Her other hand slipped behind him, massaging his sculpted buttocks lightly. Her eyes stared up into his, falling deep within whatever was happening there, the ever-changing colors. Another gush of moisture down below. If she didn't have him soon, she didn't know what she would do. Hand slipping down, she found the bulge with her fingers and her breath caught in her throat. He didn't fight her, enjoying her delighted surprise.

She caressed him—*it*—through his pants. He *did* want her.

"My name is Heather," she whispered, slipping off the bed and onto her knees.

"I know."

When she finally freed him, she almost gasped.

Glorious.

He was a huge, shapely, uncircumcised sculpture. She brought him close and kissed him lightly. He smelled salty, sweet, and peppery, exotic. *Woodsy.* Had he said Iraq?

She took him between her lips and engulfed all of him as if she'd finally run out of time. He groaned, and she gave him her best. She had talent, she knew it, and she watched him enjoy.

She squeezed closer, working him in and out of her lips while staring up into those incredible eyes. Now they were hazel, then sparkling like diamonds. His stare plumbed the depths of her soul, and she swallowed his flesh as far down her throat as she could, willing herself to drink him in.

His erection grew impossibly large, and she could not truly engulf it, but she couldn't bring herself to stop trying.

Then he pulled back, and she knew it was time. She let him slip out, slick with her saliva. She stripped off her wet jeans and panties, panting with lust, while he merely stepped out of his pants. His magnificent chest still hidden, she could only stare at his stupendous penis.

"Please don't wait," she hissed.

She lay back on the messed bed and guided him greedily to her center. He entered her slowly, inexorably, filling her more than she could ever remember, even with Robbie. She gasped as he began his rhythm, lowering himself onto her but resting all his weight on his arms.

Heather forgot about the cameraman, what was his name? Forgot about the dark, sexy city cop; forgot about the last dozen lovers she'd drained. There was only this young, enigmatic foreigner.

Tef?

What sort of name was that?

She didn't care. Her senses were now centered on his erection, her pleasure, his rapid pace. His increasing pace . . .

"Oh God, oh God, oh God—"

Suddenly, he pulled out of her, and she felt as if she'd been gutted.

"*Goddamn it!* What are you doing?"

He flipped her, roughly, and she let him. She needed more, wanted more. He took her from behind for a while, riding her—and she reveled in it. But then he slid out wetly and she felt the tip of his penis push firmly between her buttocks.

"Wait, no —"

Ignoring her, he prodded, and suddenly he was in, his whole length filling her in the forbidden place.

She gasped.

She never let anyone in there!

But he ignored her attempts to squirm away, holding her firmly with steel pincerlike hands. He lowered his head, panting, onto her shoulder, and drove her downward into the bed repeatedly despite her outraged but fading whimpers. The whimpers changed to moans.

He gripped her hips and bore down, reaching deeper and deeper inside her, and her eyes crossed from the combination of pain and pleasure. He was still bearing down, but then she started feeling almost uplifted, as if his pressure drove her upward and she matched his trajectory. She heard her own rhythmic panting match his exactly, and then they were locked in a sort of continuous life-and-death struggle with their own pleasure, unaware of anything else. Without much warning she reached the spot, the mountaintop, the place she needed so many men to help her find.

Her orgasm rocked her to the core, and she knew she had drenched the bedspread below. When he came moments later, he spurted hot and endlessly into her, and the long moment of pleasure left both of them spent, with him lying prone over her back like a living cloak.

When she finally extricated herself from him and felt him slip—still hard—from between her buttocks, she saw that he had shed his shirt sometime while she'd faced away. She'd expected him to be hairless, but he was covered with a fine layer of silvery fur she hadn't noticed in the heat of the sex.

"What's wrong?" he asked roughly.

"No-nothing." And it was nothing, as the hair she thought she'd just seen disappeared as if it had never been there. She wanted to pinch herself or check her eyes. Had there been any hair at all?

His eyes were green again. But they'd been blue earlier. She shook her head, confused. Her curiosity felt like a headache, but she tried to ignore it. That and the pain below, which left her weak and yet sated.

The wet spot under her was cold now, and the heat of their coupling dissipated. She shivered uncontrollably.

When he left, she was still shivering. She no longer knew whether it was the sex or the realization that what she'd seen might have been real. He'd looked at her one last time, his eyes now black as midnight, and she was afraid.

Yes, afraid, but she wanted him again. And she knew she would let him take her whenever he wanted.

Mr. XYZ

The farmhouse was silent, but humming expectantly.

He rubbed his hands with glee, eager to get to work. But there were a few preparations to make. First, he had to step out of his daily clothing. This he did with practiced ease.

Then he needed to find music that would match his feelings for the moment. Although there was always video. He could switch back and forth. But he decided something romantic would fit, and soon strains of a forgettable Michael Bolton album came through his tiny speakers. The video was still set up from last time, but he had TiVoed more newscasts. He fiddled with the remote until Heather Wilson was on again, doing a live report from somewhere, moving her lips while Bolton provided a soundtrack.

He liked irony.

When it was time, he went downstairs to fetch his latest conquest. She was duct-taped to his oversize hand truck. He dragged her up the steps, *thump thump thump,* one steep step after the other.

He liked the way her eyes bugged out of her head as she watched the ceiling slide past. Her lips were bloated around the bright red ball-gag. She wanted to shake her head, but he had pinned her in his custom-built wooden head frame.

She was spunky, though. *She tried.*

He'd found her at the bus station, having just missed the bus to Mankato. Because he made it his business to follow likely women to the counter, he was able to offer her a ride to the next stop on the bus route. She was so happy to get away, runaway or adventurous college student, whatever she was, that he had her seated in his SUV in five minutes, and two minutes after that he had Tasered her and dumped her in back like a sack of pinecones.

Now she was *here*, and she was awake.

"Melissa," he said, "is your name as mellifluous as you look?" He waited for her answer, but none came. "Oh, of course," he said, and loosened the gag. When she opened her mouth to scream, he Tasered her again. "No, no, no." He waited for her to stop convulsing. "Now let's try it again."

This time, she waited until she thought he wouldn't notice, but he always did. As soon as she gathered herself for the scream, he Tasered her. "You really must learn, my mellifluous Melissa."

It was going to be a long night.

While she regained her composure, he flipped on the video of Heather Wilson and began eagerly stroking himself to hardness. When Melissa saw him, her eyes bulged again, but this time he had reset her gag. She scrunched her eyes closed.

Can't have that! One-handed by necessity, he twirled several knobs on her head frame. Small metal appendages reached out and held her eyelids open so she couldn't shut her eyes.

"My Melissa," he said, scolding. "You won't ignore me that easily, silly girl."

Then he went back to work, making sure she knew when he was about to spill his seed by tightening the screws on her head frame. It was the only way he could get a woman to let him come on her face.

As he watched Melissa's eyes start to bleed from the pressure of the metal scoops, he wondered about Heather Wilson.

Now, *she* looked like a woman who enjoyed a sperm bath. He decided he'd find out soon.

"My Melissa, now it's time for the climax of our evening."

The pressure from his genitals relieved, he had all the time in the world to explain his theories to his latest conquest. First he wiped the bloody tears from her face, then set to work with his collection of scalpels.

The duct tape kept her squirming and thrashing to a minimum.

Blood ran in rivulets down the handcart frame and into the handy drain below. He whistled as he worked. Those Michael Bolton songs were hummable indeed, weren't they?

Lupo

The lion-haired youth slammed the door behind him but didn't seem angry. If anything, Lupo could swear he had "smug" all over his face.

Imagine that, Lupo thought. *Never would have figured—*

He spotted the Altima only because it wasn't following the normal tourist driving pattern. It was following the blond man exactly the way Lupo was, hanging back, slowing down and speeding up regardless of the streetlights, slipping into parking spaces and then slipping out moments later.

This guy wasn't a great tail, but he was good enough to not have been noticed except by somebody hanging back even farther. Seeing the bigger picture.

Lupo wondered about the tail. The blond man was clearly uninterested in watching for one, but he'd just been with Heather Wilson, who was connected to the investigation—whether Jessie liked it or not—by virtue of having pushed her way into it. That connected the blond man, too, and therefore anyone interested in *him.*

He followed his hunch and fumbled for his cell.

"Hey," DiSanto said on the second ring as if he'd been waiting for a call. "What's up?"

"How you holding up?"

"Shit, everything hurts. That fucking glass was like shrapnel, man."

"I sympathize," Lupo said. "Look, I need a favor."

DiSanto chuckled. "Sure, I figured you weren't checking on my welfare."

Lupo put a pout in his voice. "I was too! I just happened to hold off calling until I needed the favor so I could kill two—uh, make just one call and save a few cents."

"Yeah, yeah. I hear ya. Just a sec, let me adjust my bandages here."

Lupo whistled an old Pink Floyd tune while DiSanto made rustling sounds, trying to make him feel guilty. He kept an eye on the Altima, which was stopped in front of the theater not far from where the blond man had slipped between buildings.

"Ready. Whattya need?"

"Here's a license number. Looks like a rental. Get me the renter's name? It's a dark blue Altima, late model." He read off the letters and numbers. "Anything else attached to the car, if it's not a rental."

DiSanto read back the license. "Anything else?"

If he'd brought his camera, a shot of the blond man could have been useful, but his cell camera was way too low-res to handle the job unless he stood in front of the guy. "Maybe later. Just following a hunch."

"Uh-oh, every time you do that we get in trouble."

"This is just me, pal," Lupo said.

"Don't worry, I'll be involved by the time it's over. Give it time."

"You may be right. Hang in there."

"I'm here if you need me. Get you that info as soon as I have it. Call you?"

"Great. No, wait. I'll call you."

As he clicked off, the blond man was visible and on the move again. The Altima followed until he reached a small public lot and retrieved his own vehicle, a green and white Geo Tracker with a million miles all over the dented chassis.

The Altima peeled out, apparently now uninterested in the blond man.

Follow the blond man or the Altima?

Lupo weighed the two.

He glanced at his watch. He didn't have much time before the moon would start calling.

He followed the Altima. He could pick up the Tracker again by locating Heather Wilson, provided blondie hadn't been just a one-time fling.

The car wound its way out of town and headed east on US 70, until the road tilted north just past Catfish Lake not far from Lupo's Circle Moon Drive cottage. Tailing the Altima was no longer simple, because there was no other traffic on the road. He hung back, sure, but as the Altima continued past Dollar Lake toward Voyageur Lake, his options thinned out along with the residences. When the Altima turned left onto Hemlock, Lupo just kept going on 70. If his quarry was on Hemlock or nearby, then Lupo could always find him. But it was likely better not to be made by the Altima's driver just yet.

Hemlock, Lupo thought. *Figures.*

He looped around and headed back toward town, heedful of the time.

Prey: Clara Kee Walters

She put the tea on at exactly the same time each night. Snowy was tied up outside, presumably enjoying her evening "poopies" in the backyard.

She glanced at the old-fashioned Regulator clock on her mantel. Ten minutes till her show came on, the one with the cute, quirky English doctor. Enough time to scoop Snowy up off the porch and steep the green tea to just the right point.

To Clara, timing was everything.

That was why three minutes later, she frowned.

By now, Snowy should have been whining at the door, asking to come in for her evening treat, which Clara would dole out in tiny morsels during the first act of the syndicated show.

But Snowy wasn't making a sound.

"That's odd," she muttered. Clara had been alone most of her life, so she talked to herself unabashedly. "Best way for me to get a good conversation," she used to tell her friend Irene, before she died of a heart attack. Now her most social activity was the weekly council meeting. It had been quite the feat, breaking that traditional boys' club.

She glanced at the clock again. Her tea was almost ready, the television was set, but Snowy wasn't begging to come in and have her treat.

"Snowy, are you sick, little girl?" she cooed, opening the door and flipping on the porch light.

Snowy was there, all right. Her body hung limply from the jaws of the huge black wolf that stood at the kitchen door. Blood pooled pathetically below and slipped between the cracks in the porch planks.

Clara's heart almost stopped, and it would have been best for her if it had.

The words *wolf attacks* flashed through her mind even as she began to back up and slam the door on the monstrous image of her loyal Snowy sheared nearly in two by the wolf's jaws.

The wolf was *grinning.*

She paused, staring, as two other wolves, one black with a gray streak and the other mottled gray, materialized beside the one who had killed Snowy—

killed Snowy, she's dead, she's dead

—and then the two lunged through the doorway, knocking her back into the kitchen.

Fangs slashing, the snarling beasts latched on to Clara's throat and face, cutting short her screams.

Tearing and swallowing whole chunks of skin and flesh, they used their clawlike forepaws to bore into her stomach and chest, fighting one another to tug out bloody swirls of intestines.

Clara's eyes were still alive, still registering, as the wolves systematically disemboweled her, then started in on her limbs, cracking through bone and sinew like deboning a floppy chicken.

The larger black wolf dropped the poodle carcass into the pool of gore and watched his pack make short work of their prey. The dog had been an appetizer. He would eat later.

They had a second target, and it was almost time.

Clara Kee Walters, clearly a tenacious woman, finally let go when they started ripping out her vital organs. The two smaller wolves ate their fill while their Alpha looked on with pride.

Lupo

He felt the pull of the moon even before it rose.

His clothes itched maddeningly, his skin hot where the alien Creature within would begin to manifest.

But was it really so alien? He now admitted to himself that when he and the Creature traded places, there was more of himself left in its brain than he liked. And perhaps there was more of the Creature's brain left in him, too, logic dictated.

Perhaps this was why he sometimes acted in a way he thought was out of character, yet found himself unable to alter his own course. He had beaten down the tendencies to overreact and resort to violence all his life, thinking it a hand-me-down from Frank Lupo, but now he had begun to think it had always been there inside him, just waiting for a trigger.

The trigger had been the Corrazza boy, infected by Sam Waters's crazed son.

All that destiny. Was it embodied in the Lupo family name?

Had his father known more about their bloodline than he admitted?

Had the silver-loaded Beretta shotgun been kept handy

in case Nick himself needed to be executed? Was this knowledge the basis of their long estrangement?

Lupo sat in his car a minute longer, the thoughts playing through his head as they had many times before. As always there were no answers, only questions.

He felt the Change arriving. The itch that began in his palms and slowly walked up his forearms to his shoulders and down his back overwhelmed him. When he forced the Change himself, the process was brief and pointed. When the moon exerted its influence and took much of his control from him, he felt the Change slowly seep into each cell until he could no longer delay the inevitable and he would be over, the Creature suddenly up front and aware.

He scrambled out of the car and hastily undressed again, dropping his clothes on the seat.

He spoke to the Creature inside and gave him its instructions.

As he forced his thoughts into the shape they required, he felt the moon reach down and take him in its arms.

And then he was free, running in the woods, his nostrils open to the confusion of scents.

When he howled, it seemed every living thing stopped breathing. When he howled again, nearby humans in their houses felt a shiver of fear.

When he howled, others like him heard and understood.

The challenge was thrown down, a glove to be picked up.

Chapter Seven

Lupo
1977

Nick seethed with anger.

Beth Ann had been more or less missing from his life since the week before. If Nick had been less *gutless*, he would have sought her out and tried to comfort her, but he knew instinctively that if he confessed his knowledge she would push him away.

Gutless, too, because he knew he should call the police and report Leo. Maybe an anonymous call! Later he could testify at Leo's trial and watch him sentenced to hard labor on some Southern chain gang like in *Cool Hand Luke*.

Except Nick knew his word wouldn't count for much. Beth Ann wouldn't testify against Leo. And then Nick would look like a liar. And a pervert.

No, this called for vigilante justice. Like *Death Wish*.

Nick plotted and waited.

He stalked Leo, always aware that the wide-bodied kid could beat him into the ground. He started taking long walks past Leo's house, gauging his family and his life. It wasn't much. The yard was weedy, unkempt, with hulks of rusting or rotting toys dotting its patchy surface like wrecks on the Sargasso Sea. Leo's various siblings all looked like funhouse mirror reflections of him.

Nick considered Beth Ann the love of his life. But now he

rarely saw her. She was quieter, depressed, less colorful. She walked with her head hunched over and eyes downcast.

Nick borrowed a Polaroid camera from a classmate and spent the next two weeks' lunch money on a film packet. He stalked the Sokowski home and managed to snap several acceptable Polaroids of the bastard by riding his bike past, pedaling no-handed, juggling the camera.

Nick stared at those Polaroids daily, stoking his anger, imagining what he would do to Leo given the chance. He had read about mantras in some textbook. He created his own:

Leo Sokowski must be punished.

It was simple and concise, and he repeated it thousands of times as he stared at those pictures until his eyes burned.

Occasionally, he thought he felt something move down in the dark corners of his mind. He liked to imagine the Creature was listening, hearing, absorbing. One day he came home from school, caught sight of one of his Leo pictures, and a growl erupted from his throat.

Over time, the tenderness he had felt toward Beth Ann mutated. Leo had ruined Nick's chances with her, had ruined her, and now it all bounced back as pure white-hot hate for Leo. Nick convinced himself he was just working up the courage to face the kid-crusher Leo without fear. Have it out, man to man. Or mano a mano, as his father would have said.

What Nick didn't know was that Leo Sokowski was incorrigible and could fight as dirty as any adult street brawler.

The day Nick found out had begun like normal summer vacation. His multiple chores done to the old man's grudging satisfaction, Nick embarked on his usual reconnaissance routine. He had elevated it to the level of a ritual, clinging to it with grim determination no matter how ridiculous he felt trying to shoot pictures while on the bike.

Today he rode past the Sokowski household twice, camera in hand, until on the third pass he ran full-tilt into a brick wall.

A brick wall by the name of Leo.

"What the fuck you doin' hangin' out here?" His steel-brace arms had grabbed Nick's handlebars like bull's horns.

"Huh," Nick stammered, flustered. This was not going according to plan.

"I said what the fuck you doin' here, you little fuckwad!"

Leo's tiny pig eyes glowered at Nick from inside rings of fat. Nick's tongue stuck to his palate as he felt the bike vibrate under him, and he couldn't find a single sound to make.

"Shit, who cares?" Leo twisted his body and shook Nick off the bike like a bug flicked off a table.

Nick hit the cracked asphalt and felt the uneven chunks poke him painfully through his T-shirt. He tried to scoot backward, but met resistance there, too.

It was one of the other Leos, a carbon-copy bully in a compact bulldozer body, standing behind him like an immovable object. Before he could manage to scoot away, a booted foot caught his lower spine.

Needle-sharp screaming knives jabbed between his vertebrae. Before he could scream, another jackboot evened out the pain by hitting the opposite side.

The breath wooshed out of Nick.

In front of him, Leo approached. He tossed the bike aside like a balsa wood toy. His body was impossibly wide.

"What the—" *Smash.* "Fucking hell—" *Smash.* "Are you—" *Smash.* "Doing here?" *Smash.*

The camera went flying.

Leo Two picked it up. "Looky here!" He spiked it to the curb like a football.

"No!" Nick shouted, but it was too late. The borrowed Polaroid exploded into a hundred pieces. Something sharp bounced back and gouged a bloody furrow in one cheek. He hardly felt it.

Leo One's open-handed slap rocked him next.

Before he could recover, Leo slapped again with his entire weight behind the blow. Nick went over on his side and landed on the bike. Then he scrabbled, trying to disentangle himself and find enough purchase to get to his feet. But a jackboot kick in the side flattened him. Then both Leos rained kicks on him, mostly missing and scraping, but drawing some blood. The bruises would come later.

Nick retreated into himself. The Creature howled with rage, waiting to be released from its cage. Its paws waited to pounce, its jaws to tear and shred. But it was the human who could unlock the cage.

Had Leo One and Leo Two stopped their fusillade of kicks and looked carefully, they might have seen patches of hair sprout on their victim's hands and arms, on his legs, on his back. They might have seen his eyes change unaccountably from their usual hazel to a clear, bright cold blue—and back again.

Nick no longer felt pain, but he did feel the Creature in there with him. Though the Leos' attack was thuggish and unsophisticated, he'd be sore for a week, and his face would resemble a lump of meat. The Creature gave up its struggle to emerge, and everything was reduced to the painful smashing of boots and fists into flesh and bone.

Leo One and Two soon tired, leaving him on the sidewalk to crawl away painfully.

Later, Frank Lupo would take a belt to Nick's buttocks. Punishment first for stupidly allowing himself to be drawn into a fight, and second for having lost. Then silence reigned for a week in the Lupo household.

From the Journals of Caroline Stewart
October 1979

After Nick showed me the videotape, we devised a way for me to witness an actual Change. Nick was adamant that we provide for my safety, because he said this Creature inside was a monster that would harm me, no matter how important to him I may be.

My theory is that Nick has control over his Change. I hope to prove it to him. First, we decided to do things his way.

We bought a hunter's tree stand at a hunting supply store.

How horrible—killing those beautiful, defenseless animals! Nick reminded me that his wolf side hunts, too.

We drove to Kettle Moraine, where virgin woods cover the glacial hills, and set up the tree stand, knowing the full moon would rise later. Nick's behavior changed as the hour approached. I saw hair grow and bristle along portions of his body. He almost shimmered at times, like a TV picture about to turn fuzzy. His voice broke into soft growls. I saw how frightened he was to finally show me this monstrous side of which he was so afraid.

I reassured him, but his mood darkened. I was no longer sure whether I was dealing with the loving Nick or his Creature.

It occurred to me that I might be dealing with an extreme case of multiple personality syndrome. God knew he fit the profile. Sometimes he reminded me of my brother, who is able to turn off and on various personality traits according to need. I've seen Martin fool a room of experts and beat proven diagnostic tests, so I know it can be done.

But Nick exhibited signs of other, more complex personality disorders—could lycanthropy explain them?

He became afflicted with an all-over itch. I'd retreated to the safety of the tree stand, while he sat in a lawn chair below. Suddenly he stood and began stripping off his clothes. He waited, naked and shivering. The moonlight approached. Shadows passed over his exposed skin. At first I wasn't sure what this was, but then it hit me—it was rapid hair growth, like time-lapse photography.

The air shimmered around Nick's body for a split second, and then, without any horror movie special effects, Nick the human simply ceased—and in his place stood a gigantic black wolf.

I felt so faint I might have slid right off my tree stand if I hadn't hugged the branch.

The wolf turned his snout to the rising moon and howled. Long and tragic and somehow painful. Then he turned to me, his eyes glowing with a ferocious, hellish fire. Long rows of fangs lined his jaws and gleamed in the light. I knew that Nick was not in control.

He was right. If I'd been standing on the forest floor, he would have lunged for my throat.

He—the Creature—howled again, then turned his head as if hearing a voice no one else could hear, and then he was gone, bounding out of the tiny clearing in chase of some rustling animal, prey that he soon brought down.

I heard growling, tearing, and the terrible sound of those huge jaws grinding raw meat and swallowing, lapping at blood, tearing some more. Then he howled, and my blood truly ran cold. For the first time ever, I knew what the phrase meant.

He abandoned the remains of his first prey of the night, scurrying between the pines to hunt and kill again, more raw meat for his insatiable appetite. For hours I listened as he roamed the area, free and happy under the moon's influence, his hunger slowly being sated by the sacrificial offerings of the night forest.

I realized I still grasped the camera with which I'd planned to capture his Change. I had done nothing. I was more afraid than I'd ever expected.

I wondered how we were going to deal with Nick's condition. Fate had already ascribed him a role, and there would be no changing it now.

From the Journals of Caroline Stewart
October 1979 (Additional note)

I'm reluctant to write this, but I feel I must be honest in my assessment of Nick. I have lately started to see a willfulness about him, an immature quality whereby the Creature sometimes comes to the fore, unhappy with being thwarted. Like a temper tantrum, but one much more potentially violent, led by the wolf within. It leads him along until his temper explodes. But later Nick can see that the Creature cannot always have its way. It's a little disturbing, this new personality trait.

Chapter Eight

Prey: Alfred Calling

Contemplating the amount of golden liquid left in the bottle, he decided he could stand another small one. Maybe two.

Dad would have been proud. The bottle chugged merrily as he filled the glass. *Living out your life like a drunken Indian.*

He drank deeply, appreciating the burn and the taste. Certainly the burn.

There were a lot of reasons to drink, he reflected. He'd changed his name to better fit into the white man's world. He'd undermined his own culture, his own people, his own pride. Built a career out of distancing himself from his roots. And then, when that clown Blackthorn tracked him down, the disgraced son of a famed elder, he'd bribed him to return and reclaim his place in the tribe.

We need your vote, Blackthorn said.

And the payment was just too good to resist for a washed-up lawyer recently disbarred after being caught accepting bribes and kickbacks from clients and anyone who needed something.

He turned to stare at the living room, the creamy white leather sectional, the creamy young hooker sprawled on the sofa, where he had just fucked her brains out.

Granted she hadn't shown many signs of brain activity, except for the myriad ways she had taken his dick. She snorted in her sleep, sexy mouth half-open, matted hair a tangled mess.

It was very nice, coming home to this.

He grinned at the pretty young thing. He liked his women attractive, none of that "great body, not much of a face" stuff for him. He had expensive tastes. She was over all the way from Appleton, a convention town, and she liked high rollers even if they were in the boonies. He was willing to pay for her trouble getting here and pay well.

Almost time to wake her up again and make her earn that money.

Alfred Calling swirled the brandy—a Wisconsin thing, drinking brandy—then downed it. Maybe one more after all.

Then more sex. He was Viagra-ready.

He was already naked, unmindful of the floor-to-ceiling glass along two walls of the living room, and the French doors on the third wall. He hadn't bothered to close the vertical blinds. The house was nestled in a deep thicket just barely within reservation land, part of a development still half-empty because hardly anyone who lived on the rez could afford it. But Alfred lived here for free, part of his payment for selling out his vote. The promised percentage he'd rake in from the new casino would keep him in the style to which he was accustomed.

The hooker woke up when he shoved his dick in her slack mouth.

"Time to roll, baby," he growled. She didn't argue. Instead, she purred and started to prove her worth.

As he got busy between her plump lips, Alfred heard ragged knocking coming from one of the glass walls. "What the fuck?"

Before he could pull out to investigate, there was knocking from the *other* glass wall.

"Hey, baby, you hear that?"

She nodded but didn't stop. *Good girl.*

"Well, shit, what's going on?" He didn't have neighbors

who'd come calling at this hour. He stepped away from her—very reluctantly—and turned to look through the glass. Didn't see anyone. Ditto the other wall.

Then there was knocking from the French doors. Loud, irregular knocking.

"This is ridiculous!" he barked. "Wait right here, sweetie. I'll be right back."

She pouted at him but turned to look in the direction of the strange new knocking.

He was only halfway to the desk drawer in which he had stashed a gun when one of the glass walls shattered inward with a shower of jagged shards. Something catapulted inside, a black blur.

Alfred stopped in shock, then dove for the desk just as the other wall burst and a second dark form crashed through.

He gaped at the scene, scrabbling inside the drawer for his SIG.

The woman screamed, covering herself, her eyes bulging.

The French doors blew in and another four-footed shape barreled into the living room.

Alfred aimed at the two wolves who advanced on him, still trying to process what was happening.

Whoever heard of wolves breaking into a house?

He fired over and over, the blasts loud in the house, emptying the magazine. He had always been good with guns (at least one thing for which his father was proud of him), and he knew he had scored with every single 9mm slug.

Yet the beasts approached as if he'd missed entirely.

The SIG's slide locked and the gun fell silent.

The wolves grinned at him, and he threw the useless pistol at them and started to run, his feet sliced to ribbons on the broken glass.

They caught him before he reached the window and brought him down hard, like a deer.

The woman suddenly lunged off the couch and made for the door, but the black wolf who had crashed through the

French doors caught her before she got very far, clamping his jaws on her fleshy thighs and sending her tumbling to the floor.

In less than a minute, the human whimpers were replaced by the sounds of frenzied feeding.

Dickie Klug

The rear of the house was mostly glass. The pines extended almost up to the tiny strip of grass that passed for a backyard.

He settled into his post with a soft groan. The years, the arthritis, the weight—they were all taking their toll.

He sprayed himself carefully, covering his clothes and exposed skin, then dug into the army surplus backpack for the goggles. He fitted the harness over his head and positioned the unit. He was ready for the stakeout.

After slipping a wad of minty tobacco into his cheek, he resprayed his clothes and the air around him, making himself the center of a protective circle.

The tenants were gone, but for how long?

He made himself as comfortable as he could in the slight depression he'd scratched out with his folding shovel.

Then he settled down to wait.

Chapter Nine

Lupo
1977

Psychological wounds always heal more slowly. In Nick's case, when August began he was better physically and back in his father's good graces, but inside he knew he had changed.

He rarely saw Beth Ann, and when he did she seemed to move in a haze. The free spirit who sunbathed nude was gone.

He saw Leo once or twice on his street, but kept his distance. Leo was skulking around Beth Ann.

Fuck. Bastard's probably told all his friends about how he beat me to a pulp.

Nick bided his time, watching the calendar.

Inside, the Creature paced as if locked up behind a gate. As sure as he was of breathing, Nick knew the Creature wanted revenge.

Wanted to rip and tear and devour.

Nick wondered how long the Creature would wait. The next full moon? He also wondered how long he could keep the Creature occupied and muzzled. For the first time, it occurred to him that he might be able to control the Creature and perhaps communicate with it, even though he considered it alien to himself.

Meantime, he spoke to his surviving Polaroids of *the jerk*

after tacking them inside his closet door where his mother wouldn't see them.

It started out simple: "I'll get you for this!"

But in less than a week, he was unleashing a monologue of grievances every time he stared at the blurry photos of Leo.

Inside, the Creature stirred.

But that wasn't possible in the middle of the lunar cycle, was it? Though the gnawing feeling deep in the pit of his stomach was familiar enough—it was how the Creature felt upon its release in the woods, the scent of rabbit in its nostrils.

The gnawing was uncomfortable, but not enough to make him stop raining all his hate and disgust on Leo's picture.

When the full moon finally came, Nick's anger was at high pitch. Leo had cost Nick the fantasy of becoming friendly with Beth Ann.

Now Nick waited to see what the Creature would do.

Chapter Ten

Dickie Klug

The night's chill had settled into his bones by then, but he was dressed for it. His filthy camouflage jumpsuit emulated the shoots of still-bare branches. His night goggles gave everything a greenish glow. He was still waiting for the tenants to make an appearance. He stared down at his notebook, the childish block printing laying out the people's peculiar schedule.

Dickie wondered for the hundredth time if he was wasting his time here. He was an expert housebreaker, used to raiding closed-up houses in the off-season, liberating just enough valuables to keep himself in sausage, donuts, and beer year-round. He'd learned part of the trade from his dear departed cousin, Wilbur Klug. This particular house had been a fat target on his list a long time, but had been rented (rented!) and occupied just when he'd expected to go in and remove the big-screen TV he'd spied through the window, not to mention some stereo components. He knew a fence down in Antigo who specialized in audio crap.

He'd crossed the house off his list, but had returned because he couldn't stop thinking how fat the take was. He'd have rent money for his dump for a year if he hit the place now, even though it went against his number one rule: *never raid an occupied house.* But his number two rule was: *don't let a fuckin' good thing slip through your fingers.* Rule number two overruled rule number one.

The tenants were some kinda rich transients. He'd heard them discuss real estate. He'd kept an eye on the house on and off, waiting to see the three weirdos load up their vehicles and get the fuck outta Dodge.

Any day now.

He was good at his trade. No one suspected him of the careful break-ins that often went unnoticed for months and then unreported.

But this one was different.

He figured the tenants for ex-military. Maybe brothers and a son, or a younger brother. Definitely not gay. He'd been ready to B&E once, but then he saw a bunch of dogs running loose. *Not fuckin' poodles, either.*

Big-ass dogs. Shepherds maybe. He couldn't tell from a distance. He was grateful he always used human scent neutralizer. He bought Ghost by the case and it practically paid for itself.

These dogs could tear him to shreds. Even from afar, they were oversized, muscular, intimidating. They weren't around now.

He wondered if tonight was his night.

No one home. And no dogs.

Fuckin' A.

Jessie

"Tom?" she said tentatively. "What's wrong?"

She'd wanted nothing to do with answering the phone, lying in bed and thinking of letting voice mail pick up. But then she'd glanced at the bright screen and picked up, angry for letting things get to her, but knowing this was more bad news.

She was right.

"Jessie . . ." Tom stopped and sighed. The sound of a man close to . . . to what? Exhaustion? A breakdown?

Just a man at the end of his rope.

"Jessie," he started again, stronger, before she could respond. "Can I speak to Detective Lupo?"

Her heart sank. "Uh, he's asleep, Tom. Wiped out. He caught a bug and turned in to try and beat it. Can he call you back?"

The silence seemed dangerous. "Ah. Okay, sure, have him call me the minute he wakes up. Anytime of the night."

Was that doubt in his voice?

"What's wrong?" Jessie said again. She swallowed a lump the size of a golf ball.

Arnow blew out air. "We had two more attacks. *Killings*. These can't be animals, but they sure look like it. Two more, both council members."

Roaring in her ears, Jessie said, "Sam?"

"No, Walters and, uh, Calling. And somebody who got in the way. Jessie, *these two were attacked in their houses*."

"Christ."

"Exactly."

Now what? She didn't know what to say. Nick was out there in the moonlight, almost captive to it. She sensed Tom Arnow's need—either for her, or Nick, or both of them to bail him out. But she stayed silent too long.

"Just have Detective Lupo give me a call when he can," Arnow said. Maybe not believing her story, but too polite to press it.

Polite? Maybe something else.

"I could sure use a hand on this thing," he added. "Before it blows up on me."

She sensed his embarrassment.

She made a noise and he took it as an affirmative and a good-bye.

Jessie hung up and looked out the window, where moonlight tinted the panes silver-white.

Arnow

Standing on the sprawling deck of Alfred Calling's estate home, as the brochures called it, he stared through the shattered glass panes and into the house proper.

His deputies were getting seasoned, he thought. Hardly anyone had upchucked. Well, there was some gagging. He himself had barely fought off the nausea, thankful he'd had no time to eat anything like a real meal all day. The mess was the worst he'd ever seen. Entrails, feces, chunks of human flesh, limbs.

And the heads.

The heads were the worst.

The two heads had been gnawed, noses and ears bitten off, eyes squished out like grapes.

And then they had been posed. No other way to put it. Whoever or whatever had torn through the people—and he only assumed it was two victims, because he wasn't quite sure—had feasted on the corpses and then taken the time to prop the heads on a soiled cocktail table.

What the fuck was going on in his county?

The mayor was going to go apeshit.

He was still holding the warm phone after calling Jessie Hawkins. Her voice had a tremendously calming effect on him, but he didn't know why. Caused a bit of a belly shake, too—the good kind. Hell, he knew she was spoken for, but a man could dream.

Man could dream.

It rankled him that he'd weakened and given in to his first wave of insecurity and called the city cop. What was wrong with him? Wasn't likely to inspire much interest from the good doctor, using her to whine for help from her boyfriend. But, *shit*, these deaths were getting to him. There were clues, but they didn't add up. Animal attacks? What animal posed its dead prey? Invaded houses?

Tom Arnow was a very conflicted man. And if he'd blown any long-shot chance he might have had with Jessie Hawkins, then so be it. He couldn't enjoy her company if he lost his job, anyway.

Morton and Halloran approached almost apologetically.

"Sheriff, this is the most fucked-up crime scene I ever came across," Morton said.

Halloran said nothing, but he was sallow and his eyes looked stricken.

"Yeah," Arnow said. "Anything we can actually use?"

"Looks a lot like the others. Hair and saliva we got bagged. Then the rest of it looks like it's just these folks, chewed up and spit out, like."

Halloran turned away and walked to the railing. His back was stiff. Moments later, they heard him retching dryly.

So much for that, Arnow thought. "We're going to go over this whole scene again, you and me. Starting now. Nobody leaves." He tipped his head toward where Halloran was still gagging. "Him either."

Morton swallowed and said nothing.

They got back to work.

Lupo

Silvery beams shone through the pines like unearthly flashlights, and the Creature played a game, crossing from beam to beam.

He had brought down a rabbit flushed from its lair and eaten his fill, then chased another rabbit for sport until he bored of it, letting this one flee through his forepaws.

Take only what you need, the human commanded, and the Creature obliged. The synergy between them seemed to increase with every lunar cycle. Or Lupo's ability increased. Either way, he felt more at home in the Creature's body than ever, and the Creature's acceptance of his commands also improved.

Right now, Lupo and Creature were having fun. When he caught the spoor of deer, Lupo coaxed the Creature away—he didn't need the meal. But Lupo registered the scents that played with the Creature's nostrils.

Recalling the blond human who followed the reporter, Heather Wilson, he had the Creature seek and follow.

And now here the scent was again, crossing his nose like a signpost.

It swirled under his nose. Familiar yet not. Pungent. A wolf, reeking of maleness. A human thread, reeking of testosterone. Intertwined.

The Creature growled deep within its throat.

Lupo knew he had found someone exactly like *him*.

The Creature howled an angry challenge.

From far away, miles perhaps, howls answered. More than one.

The Creature howled again, and the response was immediate. A pack of several distinct voices returned the call, raising the hackles along his neck and back.

The challenge was accepted.

The foreign howling crossed the moonlit woods, creeping closer.

Lupo's breathing quickened.

He was not alone.

And now they were coming.

Tannhauser

Senses alive and singing with the joy of being in the moonlight, belly full, nostrils still coated with the blood of prey, Alpha heard the howling—a fellow werewolf.

He and his pack pulled up to listen. He grinned with his fangs. When the Other stopped howling, Alpha and his followers answered with their own joyous calls to glory. He paused to sniff the cold night air for a scent to follow. When he caught it, he led them toward their foe.

He recalled his grandfather's experience in the Werwolf Brigade. Displaced in time, he was his own grandfather, running down Allied troops in the Black Forest, tearing into their bellies and feasting on their intestines.

He blinked and was back in the present. His pack watched him with anticipation, their eyes were alight with bloodlust.

Lupo

He spent the next hour evading the pack, which had split up. His nose told him there were several individuals, but he didn't think he would be able to sniff out the humans based on only these scents. The human thread was just too weak when the person inhabited his wolf form.

Lupo had to learn these things quickly, or the new foes would run him to ground and tear him apart. The Creature was more than a match for a single enemy of any size, but facing down this many was suicide.

The pack sounded fierce and well trained in working together.

Lupo felt the first stirrings of fear. Fear of something other than his own wolf side.

He spurred on the Creature, leading the other wolves in a chase and hoping to reduce their number the only way the Creature knew how. With teeth and claws.

Arnow

There would be no sleep for him tonight. They had finished at the crime scenes as well as they could. He was proud of his deputies. They were holding up well, considering the horrors they had seen in such a short time. Despite their weak stomachs, they did their jobs.

Hell, he wasn't sure *he* was holding up well.

He wondered about his own weakness. He wished he could take back his call to Jessie Hawkins, all that whining about needing that Milwaukee cop, *her boyfriend for Christ's sake,* to help with his difficult case.

Jesus, what was he thinking?

That had been a misstep.

But any way he looked at it, he was nowhere. Lots of stuff out to the crime labs, but nothing concrete he could hang an arrest on, or even some suspicion.

He was cruising South 45 from the rez back to town, his

eyes never still as he scanned the tree line close to the road. Usually you did that to spot and avoid deer as they crossed the highway. But tonight he wasn't sure what he was trying to spot—and avoid—at the side of the road.

What the hell was killing people in his county?

Sure, the killings were technically on the rez, and in most counties the sheriff might not have been drawn into it at all. But Vilas County had more or less married the rez when the casino decision passed. The management had been busy hiring and training not just Indians, but also regular county residents, to fill the hundreds of jobs the casino would create. The economy was bad, and people needed jobs. The rez was proving to be a good neighbor. Only those hold-out racists or so-called sport fishermen still pissed about spearfishing treaty rights refused to get with the realities.

Arnow steered around a mound of fur in the middle of his lane. The asphalt was streaked bloody and still slick.

Some nights there seemed to be more roadkill than live animals around here. Those semis headed up to Watersmeet in the U.P. mowed down anything in their path.

He glanced back at the lump of meat and sighed.

But then he slowed down.

There was another mound of fur in his lane, this one with bones sticking through its skin. The blood around it wasn't pooled, it was splattered.

Jesus.

He slowed to a crawl and edged onto the shoulder, flashers and brights on, aware that he still took up too much space in the lane. People regularly barreled through here in their 4x4 pickups and souped-up muscle cars, completely ignoring posted limits. He could have raked in a ton of cash for the county just setting up speed traps. But that wasn't his style, and he'd not been instructed to crack down on speeding—only fighting and race baiting.

All too aware of his exposed body on the narrow highway, Arnow stepped out. The ribbon of road behind him was hidden by a long, gentle curve. Oncoming traffic would be nearly invisible until they were almost upon him. Grimly, he walked back to where the roadkill lay, bulky Maglite flashlight in hand. A breeze ruffled the fur on the dead animal, a badger.

The state symbol, he thought. He was from Illinois originally, but he knew badgers were sacred in Wisconsin.

Blood splatters all around the animal indicated a fierce struggle. He shone the light farther down the dark asphalt. *More splatters.* There was a trail of them, spread out on both sides of an invisible line.

Damned if it didn't look as though the dead animal had been carried and shaken, maybe still thrashing for its life, until it was dumped. Badgers were ferocious in a fight—this was some predator's work, not a semi. A *large* predator.

He touched the fur with the toe of his boot, half expecting the dead badger to rear up and attack. *Geez, you're touchy!*

Skin still pliable. If he put his hand on it, he knew it would still be warm. He did it anyway, feeling the stiffness setting in. The nearby blood glittered in his light, barely beginning to dry.

He stood and swirled the light around, seeing nothing between the trees tilted over the road. Grunting, he flipped over the carcass with his boot.

Christ.

He couldn't keep from grimacing.

The underside of the badger had been cracked open like an egg and hollowed out. No organs or entrails remained, as if it'd been sucked clean. None lay nearby. The flesh was torn, though. No tools, no metal had done this. Ragged tears.

Teeth.

The dark woods all around threatened to swallow him alive. He thumbed his radio and visualized the patrol schedule.

"Jerry, you there?" Being informal with his deputies was one of the perks of a job away from a red-tape-bound big-city force. "Jerry, come in."

After a crackle or two, Faber clicked in. "Boss, I'm just past Phelps, cruising south on 17. Need somethin'?"

"Uh, good. Swing around onto 45 and come at me. Got some weird roadkill here I want you to see." He gave his location and waited.

"Roadkill? What's so strange about that?"

"You can tell me when you get here."

"Copy."

Arnow chuckled to himself nervously. You could hear the doubt in Faber's voice, even over the radio. Since when was roadkill any kind of news? Logging trucks flattened critters out here all the time.

But this one hadn't been flattened.

Crouching, he studied the ground around the carcass. No footprints or tracks of any kind. The splattering seemed to indicate the badger had been flung to where it now rested.

Wind rustled the white pine branches all around him. But was that wind? The lower branches rustled, but not the higher. The pines suddenly seemed eerily still.

Except for the rustling that slowly came even with him.

Blood drained from Arnow's head and he felt the light-headedness that always came before a bust or a confrontation.

The undergrowth rustled once more, roughly, then was still.

Hair stood up on Arnow's neck.

He drew his Glock and racked the slide.

Schwartz

The moon rolled in his eyes and filled him with the power that made him feel invulnerable.

He followed Alpha for a while, fixing their prey in his head like a target in the crosshairs. But he saw Tef break off and start a flanking motion, and he wanted to do the same, feeling the pull of the moon breaking him away from Alpha.

The pack was not as together as Alpha wanted. Lately, it seemed as though the old man's hold on them was slipping, with Tef going off for hours to do his own thing. Schwartz had smelled *woman* on him again. Wherever he went, Tef seemed to find himself some cooze, somebody to boink until he felt hungry enough to take her apart piece by piece. Schwartz envied the kid's good looks, almost frozen in time as they were and helpful in getting him human ass he could sniff and lick to his heart's content.

Schwartz ran through the pines with abandon, pulling away from Alpha and Tef, feeling as if he was the only wolf caressed by the moon's silky hands. He heard them crashing through the woods, glorying in the sounds that would frighten their prey. But then he got stealthy, figuring the enemy wolf would do the same. Sometimes Alpha and Tef thought they owned the world, but Schwartz knew their confidence was more arrogance than intelligence. Their prey could hear and sense three opponents stalking him, but why would he keep making noise when it was more likely he'd slip between them and force them to overrun him, then disappear behind them?

Only Schwartz understood that their prey considered himself the hunter, not the hunted. He was sure of it.

He grinned widely in the moonlight. By slinking behind the others, he'd set himself up to catch their prey when he made his slick move to flank them from behind.

Alpha would have to recognize his superior intellect in outsmarting their opponent, whoever he was.

Schwartz wanted to feel the Other's flesh between his jaws, taste his blood on his tongue.

He knew they were retracing their steps from earlier that night, where the moon had led them in their search for sport and easy food.

Appetizers.

They'd left the carcasses on the road like signposts, and now he could sense he was drawing even with the spot they'd painted with the badger blood.

He pulled up short. The others were too far ahead, too moon-wed, too blood-wild to notice that a human stood out on the highway, right where they'd left their mark.

Schwartz doubled back and sniffed the night air. It was the cop, the sheriff, the guy they'd toyed with before. He smelled the cop's fear, the stink of his adrenaline souring as he sensed Schwartz's presence. He grinned again and stalked closer, seeing the cop through the trunks. He was crouched over the badger Tef had flung down the road. Schwartz crawled on his belly through the pines, rustling the undergrowth.

Suddenly the cop stood and drew his gun.

Schwartz's saliva pooled in his snout, the thought of the cop's flesh and bone mangled in his jaws making him hungry again. The scent of prey filled his senses until he could think of nothing else.

A growl behind him brought him up short and made his bladder loosen.

Chapter Eleven

Arnow

Whatever the hell was crashing through the brush was toying with him.

Arnow knew it, because there was silence—absolute silence—for a minute or two and then the sounds of *something* bullying its way through the close underbrush resumed, farther away. Whatever it was, it was trying to psyche him out.

He kept his back to the car, its flashers still on and reflecting crazily in the ground fog that had suddenly sprung up and started swirling over the road. He hoped some semi carrying a load of logs didn't come speeding through the fog and flatten him and his car like the roadkill at his feet.

Jesus, it was a clear night just a few minutes ago.

The fog seemed to suck into itself any light it touched. His car's flashers were so cocooned he could barely see them, and he was only yards away. The silence was eerie, and he imagined that even oncoming cars would be silent until they were thrust upon him inside the cocoon. White tendrils eddied like soapsuds over the roadway, down the shoulder, and through the first rank of pines, disappearing into the black-edged darkness beyond.

Arnow had never seen anything like it.

In the distance, he heard a rumble that was either one of those monstrous trucks rolling along up 45 or a thunderstorm brewing up somewhere in the county. Seconds later, a second rolling boom sounded more like thunder. He heaved a short sigh of relief. The gun in his hand seemed peculiarly like overkill right then, and he started to holster it. But before he could, he heard a loud growl erupt from somewhere within the trees, a growl that sent icicles down his back. He kept the Glock up and ready, his mind going numb with terror.

The growling was closer, only feet away, but the swirling ground fog obstructed his view, and all he could do was aim the squared-off muzzle toward whatever seemed to be ready to burst through the brush any second.

Then he heard a second growl, lower pitched and farther away, and the sounds of branches and brush being crushed by something large. Heading his way.

Sweat broke out on his forehead. Arnow waved the pistol in a short arc, wondering at what point firing any of his precious rounds would be too late.

Mr. XYZ

Rubbing his hands with glee, he stepped from room to room, his excitement building.

He was talking to himself. "Ashley, my darling dear, I'm coming!"

He wasn't yet, not really, but the leather harness he wore around and over his genitals kept him erect. The built-in cock ring helped keep him rock hard. The black studded strap that tightly ringed his testicles alternately tickled and strangled him, reducing his scrotum to a tiny, stretched ball sack. The tip of his penis glistened with his anticipation.

He'd known in his head that this was what Ashley wanted from the first moment he'd seen her, shuttling back from town to some resort rental on her Vespa scooter. She was underdressed in a tight sweatshirt and Brewers ball cap through the back of which she'd fed her honey-blond ponytail. She had a small Trig's bag of groceries tied down behind her. Mr. XYZ might have ignored her, but she had zigged around his slow-moving SUV and grinned at him with a glance that indicated she'd noticed his good looks, appreciated them, and wanted to get to know him.

Ah yes, yes indeed! He grinned back.

They'd played tag through several stop signs. She surged around him only to lose her lead to his much larger engine, and then vice versa when her acceleration sent the tiny machine speeding past him with a bumblebee buzz that seemed to caress his brain right at the stem.

Then they were on open road, a stretch with no traffic at all.

He paced her, enjoying when she turned occasionally to glance at him with interest. Her eyes were wide and grew wider as he raced to approach her from the rear, enjoying the innocence of the game she found as exhilarating as he did.

He grinned at her, then tapped the accelerator and nudged her off the road with his bumper, knocking the Vespa into the ditch just off the shoulder and tossing the girl in one direction and the grocery bag in another. The Vespa buzzed loudly one last, long moment, then was suddenly still.

He pulled over and went through the motions of seeming concerned, a Good Samaritan helping out a poor accident victim. No one drove by, so when he reached the limp blonde girl, he deftly lifted her onto his shoulder and climbed the slight incline back to his SUV. He tossed her into the back row of seats like a sack of cornmeal, slipped a ball gag between her lips, and slid her wrists into small handcuffs already secured to the seat back.

He shoved the dented Vespa down the incline, where it sank into a stand of tall weeds growing out of a scum-covered pond barely visible from the road.

He was soon back at his secure base of operations, and in minutes he was ready to entertain his new guest.

Now he stood over her expectantly, waiting for her to awaken, his erection ready to bring her pleasure and joy.

"Ashley, my darling dear, I'm waiting for you." He had checked her vitals and she was fine, just a little bruised and battered. He considered waking her with a nudge, but decided to wait and let nature take its course. If he called her name enough, she'd awaken eventually.

When she finally did, the duct-tape bindings and the rubber ball in her mouth kept her quiet and motionless, and Mr. XYZ flicked on the TiVo to help put her in the mood.

The girl closed her eyes when she saw him "looking" at Heather Wilson on the screen, and he slapped her to make her watch and participate. Tears and mascara dribbled over her distended cheeks.

"You're so lucky to be here," he whispered in her ear, sliding the straight-razor along the outer ridge of the ear an inch from his mouth. He flicked his tongue at her, touching her tingly flesh and blade both, electrifying himself all the way down to his penis. He was dripping now and he grabbed himself, wiping his sticky wetness on her glistening skin. She struggled against her bindings, but she could barely manage to shiver the red hand truck.

"Ashley, darling, I know you can't wait," he said, "but give me a minute."

By the time he loosened his own bindings, she had fainted. The moment had been too much for her. He understood. He was patient. He'd wait for her.

Anyway, he had a phone call to make.

Lupo

Slinking around the oldest, widest pines, the Creature approached the other wolf, who was too busy with his own stalking to smell him. The scent of prey had clouded his judgment and he'd become careless, letting Lupo maneuver the Creature closer and closer by sticking to his blind side.

Lupo used the Creature's eyes to examine his opponent. He was a good bit smaller than Lupo, covered in a thick black pelt like his own, but with a gray streak across his chest. Muscular but not as massive. He looked fast and savage. Blood flecked his snout and paws.

The Creature snuck up on the other wolf with the infinite cunning born of many years of practice.

But his practice had never involved another just like him.

He broke a branch under one paw and froze, standing stock-still, ready to pounce.

Incredibly, the other wolf seemed oblivious, his attention fixed on something or someone past the tree line.

Lupo forced the Creature to follow the other wolf's line of sight, even though the Creature wanted to press his advantage and attack.

Between the pines, Lupo saw movement out on the road. Fog covered the ground, but the police car was visible with its flashers and light bar bouncing red and blue off the mist. Somewhere out there was a cop, probably Arnow, thought Lupo. The other wolf was stalking *him*.

No more howling, so he sensed the rest of the pack had moved on to wherever they were headed. The slim black wolf had fallen behind, entranced by the unexpected prey.

Lupo's ears pricked up at the sound of another police car pulling up near the first.

It's a convention. But the Creature was focused on the other wolf, invader of his territory. He dribbled a mark where he stood, making it official.

The Creature took charge. He growled a challenge and bared his fangs. The moment had arrived, whether Lupo was ready or not.

The intruder turned to him and the two black wolves stared at each other across the few yards that separated them. The intruder growled his response, and they approached each other menacingly. Now the other wolf caught his scent and acknowledged one of his kind. His jaws snapped, saliva looping out from his snout. Cold gray eyes fixed on his and flicked a warning a bare moment before he pounced.

The Creature leaped and the two wolves clashed, jaws snapping, the nearby humans temporarily forgotten.

The battle had begun.

Arnow

"Christ, what the hell is that?"

Faber had pulled up silently behind him, climbed out of his cruiser, and approached his boss.

Arnow turned, feeling a rush of gratitude to see Faber's angular, ex-Marine profile, gun in hand. The semi-auto drooped downward, though, as if he'd forgotten about it. The deputy stared at the mess of fur and bone scattered over the asphalt. "Jesus!"

Arnow said nothing, scanning the tree line and wishing he could see into the thicket.

"That wasn't done by no semi," Faber said between his teeth. "I seen plenty of those in my time." He crouched. "Are these teeth marks?"

Arnow nodded. "Think so."

"Shit."

Suddenly there was a commotion of breaking branches and flattening of undergrowth just a few yards away, and both Arnow and Faber brought up their gun muzzles. Arnow's bladder seemed suddenly quite full, and he prayed he wouldn't wet himself.

The two stood warily side by side, with nervous feelings and twitchy hands, facing the woods and half expecting something to come hurtling at them.

Now they heard the sound of breaking boughs from off to their left as well and something moving slowly through the woods toward the right. Growls, deep and frightening, torn from fearsome throats, raised the hair on the men's necks.

Out of sight behind the tree line, but seemingly only yards from the road, two great hunters came at each other, growling, roaring like movie monsters.

Faber and Arnow exchanged looks, watching the woods as if the fighters might crash out at anytime and turn their attention on them.

"Christ!" Faber said as the combatants clashed, invisible, but all the more frightening because of it.

The growls and yelps moved farther away, deeper into the woods, and Arnow started to call for backup.

Faber turned his wide eyes on his boss. "What? We're going in there? No way!"

Arnow's feet wanted to take flight. He fought it, swallowing his own fear so his deputy wouldn't see it.

"We're . . . waiting to see who comes out."

"Boss, they're getting farther away. I say let 'em. It's nothing to do with us. It's a forest thing."

"It's a forest thing that's been killing our people," Arnow noted.

"Not *our* people."

"Shit, not you too, Jerry?"

"Well, they ain't. They already got all the treaty rights they want."

In the dark woods the battle still raged, but it seemed to be inching farther and farther away. Arnow wrestled with himself, his own fear, and Jerry's lack of commitment. By the time somebody got their ass out here to back them up, the animals would be a mile into the woods. And maybe by then they'd have become food themselves.

Arnow opened his trunk and hefted out the pump shotgun cradled in the rack. But by now he knew it was just for show, to not let Faber off the hook so easily. He couldn't admit it, but his knees were still jelly at the sounds of the fight. Even far enough away to be muffled by the thick woods, it still sounded ferocious and painful. The sound was further muffled by the ground mist, which acted like a reflector and confused directions.

He pumped a round into the chamber and hoped they didn't become dessert for whatever lurked out there.

In the distance, thunder rumbled and lightning strobed

over the forest. The sounds of the fight were fading fast now. Had it really been so fierce?

"Fuck it," Arnow growled. "We're too late. Let's go in."

He was pissed at the racist asshole at his side, pissed because he'd thought Faber was one of the good ones.

Let his true colors show. They all do, eventually.

Faber looked at him funny and turned away without a word. Arnow figured he looked like he wanted to use the shotgun on anyone too close.

When he was alone in his cruiser, he felt a telltale warm-cold wetness along the inside of one pant leg.

Sonofabitch.

He smacked the steering wheel hard.

Jessie

She awoke with a start, her eyes suddenly as wide open as if they'd been pried with a crowbar.

The echo of something loud faded quickly.

Thunder?

Lightning flared over the treetops.

It was thunder.

But for a second, she couldn't help thinking she'd heard a scream, or continuous screaming, and maybe growls and howling.

And what she thought was thunder at first could have been a gunshot.

She shook her head. *Nightmare.*

Thunder rolled and boomed, coming closer.

No, it was a gunshot.

And another.

Lupo

Lupo steered the Creature away from the road, away from the cop. His jaws snapping, he dragged the black-and-gray wolf with him, disorienting his opponent and giving him nothing else on which to focus, only himself.

And survival.

Lupo knew this Other was a sworn enemy, whether in human or wolf form. There would be no quarter, no respite. There could only be a victor, and Lupo's faith in the Creature and his strength had increased a hundredfold in the last couple of years, but there had been no opponents like this one.

And he is only one of a pack, Lupo thought as he fought for his life.

The advantage of his surprise attack was fading fast, and the balance now swung toward the other wolf. Its supernatural origins made a difference, canceling Lupo's inherent advantage over his usual pray.

The black-and-gray wolf was cunning, fearless, and ruthless.

He came in, jaws snapping, taking every opportunity to draw blood and tear flesh from Lupo's larger body.

But Lupo worried his enemy with the same tactics, knowing that the blinding pain of each wound would be only temporary. He surmised that the Other was no different, but that meant they were on equal footing.

They traded bites and clawings one for one, bleeding from each gash and tear, rolling through the mist from tree to tree and taking a bloody bruising from the sharply angled branches that protruded from the mature pines.

And then suddenly Lupo felt his back shoved up against a giant pine trunk. He was shackled to the unyielding wood, his movements limited.

Now fear tinged the edges of the Creature's brain.

The Creature half howled, half growled its fear and tried a counterattack with tooth and claw.

Seizing its advantage, the other wolf fended off the worst of Lupo's attack with its own muscular body, taking most of the wounds in less vital areas. But it still managed to sharpen its fearful combinations of deadly snaps, its snout a snarling blur of raging fangs.

Lupo felt the Creature tiring, felt himself slowing in response, felt the pain of each sharp bite or claw hurt more, bleed more, and sap his energy more.

Now the Creature's body bled from too many painful wounds. His life seeped into the ground below them, disappearing into the mantle of mist hugging the forest floor.

The black-and-gray wolf paused to let out a single loud howl, the howl of a victor.

And that was when a shotgun blast took him square in the side and flung him like a rag doll away from Lupo's struggling. He yelped and whimpered like a car-hit dog in intense pain.

A second shotgun blast took one eye and most of an ear and flayed the skin and pelt as if with a rusty razor.

The wolf shuddered, shook itself back to its unsteady feet, and turned to locate its attacker. Blood glistened in the black hole where the left eye had been. The wolf shook itself again, splattering the pine trunks and forest floor. But there was something wrong.

Lupo watched as the wolf listed sideways like a ship about to slip under the waves, unsure what he was seeing. Smoke curled from some of the Other's wounds, the monster's remaining eye turning glassy and rolling as if he were about to lose consciousness.

Sam Waters stood to the side of the tiny clearing, calmly breaking open his old double-barreled shotgun and ejecting the spent shells. Two new shells appeared in his hand and slid into the chambers.

But before he could complete his reloading, the black-and-gray wolf snarled, its lone eye blazing at both enemies. It lunged into the underbrush, crashing through and finding its legs, making its escape with a crooked lope into the woods.

Sam Waters

"Dammit!" Sam cried, bringing the gun up to his shoulder and firing again, his shot shredding the brush where the wolf had just been.

He turned to where Lupo's Creature had been a moment before, but now it was Lupo. His hairy pelt disappeared rapidly as if it had never been, and suddenly it was just a naked human lying against the huge pine that had almost been its undoing. He screamed as Sam approached, putting his hands up to cover his face.

"Oh, sorry, Nick," Sam said, lowering the shotgun. "Silver buckshot."

"Sam," Lupo croaked, "I can't stand it, it's too much in one place."

"I'll stay back. Can't take the chance he'll come back and attack us when we let our guard down."

"He's done, believe me," whispered Lupo. "Those two shots would have finished me. I can't believe he survived them."

"I didn't have time to aim, dammit. I should have hit his head."

"Oh, you did," Lupo grinned past the pain. "You sure as hell did."

Sam grimaced. "You're a mess."

"Tell me about it."

He set the shotgun against a tree far enough away, then helped Lupo unsteadily to his feet.

"How did you happen to be wandering around in here? This is miles from your place."

"Call it destiny maybe," Sam said. "I couldn't sleep, so I figured I might as well make myself useful. Went huntin'. Figured one of these monsters might show up where I happened to be."

"Yeah, well, you're lucky because I think I had three of them on my tail all night."

"Three?" He blinked. "Jesus. So it's true—there are more of you out there?"

"Yeah, it's true, dammit. And we better move—the other two might show up anytime."

Sam stepped back and grabbed up the shotgun, keeping it away from Lupo but at the ready.

"Your old shaman friend wasn't the only one to mess with the unknown. Or maybe these guys are a result of his experiments too. Where did you get that silver buckshot?"

"You didn't think I would have some silver shells left?"

"You didn't trust me, did you?"

"Let's just say I was playing it safe. Looks like I was right, thinking that way. Now let's get you home to the good doctor."

Lupo

They limped from the clearing and picked their way through the closely set pines until they reached the highway where Lupo had seen the police cruiser parked. The car was gone.

Good man, he thought. *Nothing for you to see here.*

He wanted to lean on the older man, but as long as Sam held the shotgun, Lupo needed to keep clear. The silver in the shot radiated heat that stung and burned the closer he came. He could barely imagine the pain the black wolf would have felt ripping through his tissue, burning through his veins like molten fire mixed with acid. He shuddered at the thought.

The black wolf had exuded an air of . . . Lupo hesitated to label it, but it felt like *confidence* or the kind of arrogance born of a snobbish sense of entitlement. Maybe experience. Lupo had nothing to compare it with, but the other wolf had seemed old and well practiced. Even though he'd been startled by Lupo's attack, he had taken the initiative easily and almost won. If Sam hadn't shown up when he did . . .

Lupo's wounds stung, but they were already healing,

cuts and scrapes closing themselves as if by invisible zippers. It was one small benefit of the "curse." Today he was grateful.

The roadway was still covered with eddying mist. Lumps of flattened fur and bone marked what had probably stopped Arnow while on patrol.

Sam had brought clothes in a small knapsack, which he retrieved and gave Lupo. "Jessie called. We figured I might run into you."

Lupo shook his head. He never tired of relearning how logical Jessie Hawkins could be. He'd almost forgotten he was naked, his usual state during the moon-influenced runs. He slipped on the jeans and sweatshirt.

"We'd better talk," Sam said. "Two more council members were murdered."

"Christ. Who?"

"Alfred Calling and Clara."

"Clara was the only woman, right?"

Sam nodded in sadness. "The nicest member, too, though we disagreed on some issues. Calling was . . . less nice. He was a *player,* barely interested in the true issues facing the tribe. He was brought in by Blackthorn. Everyone knew he was just there to sway the vote. His loyalty was paid for with luxuries most other Indians can't even imagine. Still, he was another human wiped out by this . . . gang, whatever you want to call them."

"Pack. I think they fit the definition. They were after me tonight. I was acting as bait, hoping to catch one unawares. Problem is, he turned out to be more than I could handle. Faster, meaner, more ruthless."

Lupo thought Sam might have been sweet on Clara. He would always be faithful to his dead wife, Sarah, but it didn't mean he couldn't be attracted to someone. He put his hand on Sam's shoulder. "I'm sorry about Clara, man."

Sam nodded, his lip trembling. "What are we gonna do, Nick? I feel like this is more than just the usual anti-Indian sentiment, even though I hear there's some group now pushing for demonstrations about the damn spearfishing again."

"You have to talk to Eagleson. He's still okay, right?"

"Yeah, so far. But . . . well, I'll see to it. Now what?"

"I guess I'm heading home, Sam. And you should, too. You have more of that silver ammo?"

"Can't you feel it?"

"Oh, yeah. My whole body's tingling and not in a good way. That wolf is in a whole lot worse shape than I am, I'll tell you that."

"Good."

"You bet. But why do you have silver ammo?"

Sam cleared his throat. "Uh, it was just some leftover shells from when I was hunting my . . . my son."

"And you kept some in case I needed to be put down someday, right?"

Sam's eyes sparked with sudden anger. "What would you have done? Would you have taken the word of, of—"

"A monster?" Lupo prodded.

"Well, at the time—"

"Just let it go—"

"*You* let it go, Nick! Without the silver ammo, you'd be roadkill like that." He pointed.

Lupo sighed. He hated being mistrusted, but it came with the whole werewolf territory, didn't it? How often had he reverted to his monstrous nature and proven himself unworthy of trust? How often had he hurt someone he loved, or worse?

He nodded. "Fine, I agree. Hope you have more, 'cause we're gonna need it."

He checked his torso, pulling up the sweatshirt. Most of his wounds were already fading scars, healing impossibly fast.

He stripped. "I'm gonna run home. I need to give the Creature some of its night back. I was in charge too long. It makes him cranky."

"Nobody wants that."

"Yeah. Here." He handed Sam the clothes. "Thanks again."

"You'll do the same for me before this is over. I'm sure of it." He'd become accustomed to seeing Lupo naked, but what came next he was never quite used to.

"Call Eagleson," Lupo said. Then he began a lope down the asphalt highway.

Before he could disappear in the mist, he was over and came down on four paws, knowing Sam could still see him. He knew it because he sensed the old man's fear.

Lupo took charge of the Creature and headed him home, with a short detour for protein. He knew a place where deer congregated and headed there now.

He howled his love of the night and the waning moon.

He hoped it was a warning to the pack that nothing was finished, nothing was done.

There was no response. But that didn't mean they weren't listening.

Mr. XYZ

The night air had been filled with portents.

Strange sounds, whisperings, voices, and screams. It made him feel alive, though he couldn't have explained it.

He wrestled the Christmas tree bag out of his SUV and dragged it down to the water's edge. This one rolled easily. It wasn't all in one piece, so it was easier to handle. He repeated his usual ritual with the chains and padlocks, then hefted the bag and pushed it a few yards farther out, where it hit the black scummy water with hardly a splash and began to bubble up and out of sight immediately.

She hadn't lasted all that long, this one.

His disappointment caused him to feel unfulfilled.

He listened to the night. Something was out there in the woods, something loud and frightening.

But he wasn't frightened. He recognized other creatures of the night. Knew he wasn't the only predator. Knew he wasn't the only one following a predestined path.

He picked his way over gravel and clumps of wild grass back to his SUV and climbed in.

He sighed.

His needs were greater these days. He sensed that everything was driving toward some kind of end crisis. And then he would deal with that, too. He had been here too long anyway. Maybe it was time to scout a new territory. But this location and its perfect combination of tourism, dead-end service jobs, two-year community colleges, and an overall acceptance of underachievers had been perfect for so long.

He had to see what the end result of his plans would be. He had plenty of wiggle room.

And he still had needs.

Arnow

He went in to change, but the next thing he knew he had been in the bathroom an hour, his wet trousers now dry and nearly forgotten.

The shakes. He'd had them once or twice in his career. After a shooting he'd thought was his fault. After seeing a particularly vile crime committed on a young child. One time, when he'd hesitated and another cop had been wounded. But in a long career, he'd never felt quite the same way he felt now. Powerless. Fearful. Completely unable to process what he had seen, yet unable to let go. He'd set his Glock on the vanity, sat on the covered toilet, and put his head in his hands and cried.

Cried.

The tears were just relief, he decided later. A reaction, completely physiological and not related to his own strength or lack of it. He'd heard of cops who ate their guns when they felt fear so strong they couldn't go out on patrol anymore. In his case, he was just glad to get home without having seen what was in the woods. The relief at *not knowing* was what made him forget his fear.

Whatever, he thought. *I pissed my pants. Christ.*

What would Laura think if she knew? She'd been supportive of him through all his emotions, all his fears, until he had conquered them. They'd been good together, he and Laura. But then he had felt some emotion for a fellow cop, a vice detective in Chicago, and when Laura had caught him, somehow reading him like the proverbial book even though he hadn't acted on any of his feelings—might never have acted on any of his feelings—she had needed less than two days to make her decision. She had taken the kids and disappeared, later to resurface at her parents' house where he was no longer welcome. The divorce papers had come in two weeks, and he let his family go without a fight, because he knew the trust was broken and he had been the one to break it.

Jesus, I haven't thought about them in weeks.

No, that wasn't right. He hadn't thought about Laura in weeks, but he always thought of his kids, Freddie and Jill, and he thought about them now. He thought of them without a father, but he knew they had one—a stepfather—and didn't need him. Who'd miss him, if he ate his gun? Who would have missed him if he'd encountered the thing in the woods? Whatever had happened, he knew it had spooked him badly. Here he was, huddled in his bathroom as if a tornado was raging outside, knowing the tornado raged inside now. His hands shook when he held them up to his eyes.

He had double locked the front door, set the alarm, and even locked the bathroom.

His tears were dry now. His pants were dry. He held up his hands again. They were steady now. Steady enough.

Whatever he would have to do required strength. Did he have the strength?

He picked up the Glock and his grip was steady.

He came out of the bathroom.

He stripped and threw the clothes in the hamper.

He showered the fear off himself, out of his pores. He hoped the stink of that fear left, too, because he wanted those *things* that were ripping people apart in his county to know that he was no longer afraid.

He dressed in much fresher clothes, strapped on an ankle holster and slipped in his backup, a Glock 26 subcompact semi. At least he was changing the odds, he thought, as he checked his Taser and Mace, items he hadn't carried since Chicago. He felt weighed down, but if that's what it took to feel slightly safer, then so be it.

It was well past dawn by now, and he was famished, his empty stomach complaining, even though his mind thought he would never want to eat again.

There would be time later. Right now, he wanted to check in and talk to Faber.

And see about getting some of those lab reports, even if he had to light fires under somebody's ass. Malko and his cronies on the county board were bound to request *his* report today. Or his resignation.

He wished he could take them out to where he and Faber had heard those things in the woods. He wished he could leave them there.

Heather Wilson

The door was locked and bolted, but she heard him slip through her defenses in every possible way.

She smelled him as he approached in the dark, the musk almost intoxicating, something else in there giving him the aura of danger she craved. She smelled his sex as if he held it under her nostrils, and when she reached toward his shadow and touched him, she realized that he was holding it toward her.

What an arrogant son of a bitch.

She felt him with hungry fingers, caressed the length of him down to his testicles and cradled them in their gnarled sack, thrilled by the feel of his hairless engorged flesh.

Fuck, he was irresistible. Arrogant but delicious.

She guided him to her mouth and took him as he stood at

the side of the bed, silent, demanding and yet strangely submissive. His smell was strong and feral, a sharp tang of something she couldn't quite identify, but she didn't care. All she knew was that she wanted him. She hadn't been able to find Robbie all day. Maybe he'd bolted out of jealousy. Didn't matter what his excuse was, she'd have him fired.

"Tef," she muttered.

"Don't speak with your mouth full," he said.

He shoved hard and she gagged but kept working him, feeling her saliva pool under her tongue and gush out in ropes, making the way slick for him. He grunted, and she took that as a good sign and continued to swallow him until he pulled out and reached for her, flipping her in the dark so he would have the access he wanted. She wondered how he could see so well in the darkened room, but then she didn't really care as he parted her thighs and buttocks and drove in from behind.

His grunts became more rapid, more violent, and she swore his manhood swelled inside her, reaching her depths and stroking her to some kind of cataclysm she barely understood.

All she knew was that she wanted more. She reached back, groaning from the pain and pleasure he provided with each stroke, and grabbed his arms to lever him deeper and faster.

To her shock, his arms were much hairier than she remembered, almost peltlike, which was a contrast to his beautiful hairless groin. She almost let go in disgust at first, but the heat was on her—and apparently on him, because he did not stop his rhythm but instead increased it until she thought the bed would crash under her. Was that a cheap motel bed leg cracking?

Behind her, his long hands held her bent legs like handlebars, and he drove her faster and longer than anyone before. She screamed when the liquid heat of his orgasm rocketed inside her. It seemed never ending, and his hardness never faltered, but rather he continued to pump into her until finally she begged him to stop, never mind the neighbors and the late hour. When he finally complied, he was as large as ever. She rolled over on the creaky bed and took him in her mouth again, tasting herself and him mingling on his skin. When he came again, only minutes later, she jerked back and let him bathe her with his thick cum.

All men like that, she thought. But then he insistently pried her lips open with his tip and fed her the last of his seed.

Demanding bastard. For someone so young.

No matter what, she was hooked. She couldn't help it. Something inside her melted at the thought of coupling with this . . . She struggled for a second. . . . with this creature.

There, she had said it. To herself, but she had said it.

He slid down onto the bed and lay beside her. She smelled his musky sweat and something else.

Blood, she thought crazily. *He smells like blood.*

When she reached out for him, his skin seemed smooth again. And she swore she saw his eyes blazing at her in the dark.

Instead of screaming or leaping out of bed, she smiled and took his manhood between her fingers again, holding him as if he were a lever she needed to control.

"Tef," she whispered, nuzzling him. "Tef, my amazing young boy."

He snickered, his teeth glistening in the thin slice of dawn that reached them through the plastic curtain.

"Let's go again," he said.

"Okay." She didn't care that her genitals felt raw and abused.

She just didn't care.

Chapter Twelve

Jessie

She lay next to Nick Lupo, once again wondering at the burden of his dual life and considering herself lucky to have found him, to be able to hold him.

They had made love, hard and passionate, and she noticed the lines that indicated new, healing wounds. She had been with him long enough to know his injuries healed quickly, closing up and almost disappearing with magical ease. But *almost* was the operative word—for the lines that remained seemed to be permanent. She could read the worst times of his life in the scars crisscrossing his body. These new lines would join the others in mapping out his existence.

He had given her a quick rundown of the night's happenings as they lay entwined and sweaty on her bed.

"So there are others," she whispered in awe. "You were right." She traced the lines of his newest wounds, gently and with reverence for the unknown workings of his condition.

"I think I interrupted this one from attacking Sheriff Arnow."

"Thank God you were there then."

"He was a straggler, or he'd turned aside to follow the scent. But Christ, he was a tough one. He almost had me, Jess. He had me backed up, and if not for Sam, good old sleep-deprived Sam . . . well, I think I wouldn't be here right now." He shook his head. "If the others are anything like him, I think I'm better off tracking them down as humans."

"But they'll just change right on the spot, won't they?"

He grimaced. "If they get the chance. May have to be sure about them, then take them out without giving them anything like a sporting chance."

"You're talking assassination, Nick."

"Yeah, I am. If I have to face three of them as wolves, or even two, I wouldn't put your money on me. He was . . . something else. Like he'd been bred for battle. Like he'd been *trained.* A werewolf soldier."

His eyes were hard in the soft light of dawn.

"But if you're wrong—"

"Then I'll be a murderer."

The words hung between them a long while. Then he said, "Did you know Sam still had silver ammo?"

She wished she could deny it. Her silence said it all.

Lupo

The sudden sting of realization hit hard—his friend, and even his lover—had never quite trusted him, never quite let go of the knowledge that he was both Nick Lupo and some other Creature.

He wanted to be hurt. He wanted to protest, to complain that at least Jessie should have trusted him, after all they'd been through. He wanted to pout and let her know how much she had wounded him, perhaps more even than that other wolf, but he held his tongue. He swallowed the hurt feelings and swore to himself he wouldn't hold them against her.

Deep down, he knew he wouldn't have trusted Nick Lupo either.

Sam Waters

Two old men, he thought. We were young once, full of life's promise. Now we're both alone and old as dirt.

He stood in front of the door five, ten minutes before finally ringing the doorbell with regret he could almost taste. He had left the shotgun down the driveway, leaning on a crooked sapling.

Wild-haired Thomas Eagle Feather threw open the door and seemed about to slam it closed again when Sam reached out a hand and stopped its arc.

"Have to talk to you, old friend."

"I haven't been your friend in years."

"Clara and Alfred, Thomas, they're dead."

Thomas stood still and his eyes widened a fraction. "You telling me this officially? You working with the cops suddenly?" The pain was etched on his face, though he chose to pretend otherwise.

"Not exactly, no, but the information comes to me through Jessie. You trust *her*, I take it."

"Usually. She's half-white, remember."

"That's a low comment, even for you."

"Clara's dead?"

"And Alfred."

"I don't give a shit about Alfred. *But . . . Clara*." Sudden tears coursed down his cheeks. "Is it really true? What the hell's going on? How did it happen?"

"Like the others, more or less. And yes, I'm afraid it's true."

Thomas Eagle Feather stepped aside, sighing. "Come in." His eyes roved the street out front, but the early morning traffic consisted only of an occasional rusty pickup, laborers heading off to their rez jobs.

Sam didn't feel comfortable sitting, so he stood in the foyer. Thomas seemed shrunken now, no longer the huge presence he'd cultivated on the council. They faced each other over a huge chasm.

"Well, friends or not, here's the thing," Sam said. "I believe you're in danger. Anybody on the council who voted for the casino project may be in the same danger."

Thomas looked far away.

"We lost our friendship because of your son. Your son

and that charlatan shaman he took up with. Whatever no good they got up to, it was enough to almost get you banned, Samuel Waters."

"I wasn't in agreement with him or what he was doing, but I couldn't—he was still my son . . ."

Silence blossomed briefly. Sam looked down.

"I don't know what happened to him and you wouldn't talk about it, but your sorrow speaks volumes. Now we bury two more friends." Thomas shook his head.

"Council members."

"Friends first. Council members second."

"Alfred wasn't much of a friend to anyone," Sam pointed out.

"Nor was he much of an Indian, but he didn't deserve to die. It's the whites. They hate the casino. They're jealous of prosperity, and they fear we'll take all their money."

"They're right."

"You're just like them. Can't let go of old prejudices. The old ways don't work anymore. Many tribes flourish with casinos, bettering the lives of their people. Why not ours?"

"Because it curses us, Thomas. Look at what's happening to us now."

"That's no curse," Thomas spit. "It's pure racism in action."

"I don't think so."

"What do you think it is? You know how people feel about *Injuns*. You've felt it yourself, even if you won't admit it."

Sam ignored him. "Go somewhere safe, Thomas. There's reason to believe you and everyone else who voted yes on the casino project is on the list."

"You're not on that list, then, are you?"

"I didn't vote yes, if that's what you mean."

"So you'd be safe. Why bother to stick your neck out for us?"

"I can't explain it, if you don't get it." Sam waved his hand, searching for words. "I don't care what the reason is, I don't want this killer getting any more of us."

"So then you think it's related to the council vote? Somebody's killing the yes votes? It's as simple as that?"

"I suspect, but I don't know."

"But why?"

"Again, I don't know. If you go somewhere safe, and make some calls to the others so they'll come too, we'll cheat him of any more victims."

Thomas Eagle Feather drew himself up, marshaling his pride. "I'm not going to run screaming like a woman at the first sign of danger."

Sam had been afraid of this knee-jerk response.

"Thomas," he said, "if you don't come with me, any more deaths will be on your head."

"I'm head of the council. Way I see it, I'm already responsible for everyone, including the deaths. I ain't leaving my house without a fight."

Jesus, Sam thought. *Now what?* He wondered if he should pick up his shotgun from outside and just force Eagle Feather into leaving. But what would that prove?

He settled in for a long argument. Outside, the sun rose anemically over the spring day.

Heather Wilson

She carefully applied her makeup while Tim waited outside, checking his camera equipment. She was bummed about Robbie, but he chose to bolt and no one had seen him since.

"Fuck him," she muttered. He was far less interesting than her new boy toy, Tef, who was most definitely worthy of her attention. She smoothed mauve on her lips and then her trademark, a striking violet gloss, thinking of *him*. How could she not? She still tingled all over from his attentions.

His eyes, though. His eyes were what drew her in. And made her want to know more.

She had begun asking questions about him, but had little response. He was new in town, he came into a couple of the bars for beer but didn't seem to enjoy it, and he looked harshly at anyone who wanted to talk to him. That was all she had. Of course, it wasn't the way she saw him. He had picked her out of a crowd and made her his with a look; she didn't doubt the chemistry. But what about the rest?

Go on, say it.

What about . . . ?

Go on, say it!

Fine then, she scolded herself, putting away the makeup and taking a good long appraising look, patting down her hair where the cheap motel dryer had failed.

What about the murders? Was Tef the mysterious Indian killer?

She thought she might be able to find out something about him today.

Messages about the two murders the night before had filled her voice mail overnight, and she'd gotten up to speed with her laptop and the motel's wi-fi, e-mailing her assistant producer back and forth for an hour after Tef had left. She knew the sheriff might be a dry well today. He was probably under fire from the town and county officials, and chances were very good he'd been told to shut up when a camera rolled. There'd be no information there. But she was good at what she did, and she had infallible instincts when it came to investigating weird crimes. Now she began to wonder if the story had come to her.

The way he had sought her out bothered her. Not what they'd done after that, but just how he had set his sights on her and zoomed in to the target without even a side glance. Last night he could have killed the two and then come to her. She remembered his blood smell.

She sprayed the hair that rebelled against her brush. It was a windy day, and she would do at least one live remote and a couple of taped updates.

Some murderers lusted for attention and media coverage almost as much as they lusted for the kill. It was definitely possible Tef was one of those, maybe one who wanted her to cover his story.

Maybe one who wanted to make *her* part of his story.

While he slept, she had slipped out of the sweat-soaked bedclothes and snapped a picture of him with her trusty Sony set on Night Shot. The picture was a grainy black-and-white and lit eerily like an alien portrait, but she'd e-mailed it to Deb and then printed it on her portable Epson. Inquiries might be more fruitful with a photograph and a twenty to hold up. Maybe Deb could match him with any of their wanted and "person of interest" databases, using some of her Madison law-enforcement connections.

Until she heard something from Deb, Heather was going to spend the day checking up on her new lover and digging into the new murders.

She pushed away from the chipped vanity and hoped this story would lead her to a big city, preferably New York—where she could stay in hotels near Central Park and do follow-up reports from the Village or on Wall Street. Hell, even Newark was better than this.

There was a knock at her door. Tim must have been getting impatient. She swept up her purse and keys and headed out to see how this story could help her escape these nowhere burgs.

Lupo

Arnow was in the middle of a greasy burger he didn't seem to want. When he looked up and saw them approaching, a shadow passed over his weary features. He put the food down on his desk. *Maybe he's glad for the excuse,* Lupo thought. *Maybe he has a sour stomach. Not much chance of helping him feel better.*

"Detective." Arnow nodded at him before his gaze lingered on Jessie. "Dr. Hawkins."

Arnow pointed at the chairs. Pushed the burger aside with a bitter look. "They told me I should eat, but they can't make me call that food." He half smiled. "Thanks for coming in. I'm glad to get your advice. I respect your expertise."

Lupo could see the cop's brain spinning behind his quiet eyes, beneath his relaxed look. He sensed the relaxation was a well-practiced front. And the intense eyes were hooded, not quiet.

Frightened?

He gave little away, this big-town cop trying to squash himself into a little pond. But the pond had gotten a whole lot deeper, and now he felt the lack of land under his feet. Lupo didn't want to extend the metaphor, but he couldn't help thinking the cop had realized he would soon be over his head. Something had broken, and he'd missed it. Missed the chance to stop it, and now it was growing and would swallow him up. He looked lost, and he must have been, to call for Lupo to come down.

A strange series of looks washed over the sheriff's face. He was embarrassed to have called Jessie the night before, Lupo realized. Ambivalent. Didn't quite want to admit it, but felt trapped.

The new murders had probably ratcheted up the pressure. The city council was likely in special session. The media was hovering. He remembered the luscious but predatory Heather Wilson. She was just the first, the quickest out of the gate. It was a weekend in the off-season. Soon the Milwaukee and Madison and Green Bay trucks would show up, bristling with antennas and perfectly turned-out reporters. Arnow was seeing all this in his head, already measuring the size of the media circus. He had been desperate late last night, feeling his own weakness and flailing about for help.

Lupo and Jessie had discussed it.

With no real choice, Lupo jumped in. "Sheriff, I think we can help you, but not quite the way you're expecting."

"Oh?"

"Let me just get to the point. We might have information you'll find useful in your investigation of these murders."

Arnow leaned back and twined his fingers, wincing as if the motion hurt. "Might have? Information?"

"Jessie said you called asking for advice last night. By now I'd bet you're more in need of information."

Arnow looked lost for a moment, but then he chose to process Lupo's words as an insult. Lupo saw it happen, wished he could have rephrased. He had misread Arnow, thinking blunt would be the best approach.

Arnow's eyes turned cold, his demeanor defensive. "And what would this information consist of?"

Lupo looked at Jessie, made a micro-shrug, but didn't get any words out.

"There's more going on here than a crime wave. Look, I'm not in the best of moods, so *I'll* be blunt. Information? When I called last night, I was asking for help, I guess. Not information. I used to get that from snitches." He squared his gaze at Lupo. "Care to confess?"

Lupo dismissed the awkward question. A mite too condescendingly, he realized. "No confessions. But we have some inside knowledge we'd share with you. Call it a professional courtesy."

Arnow squinted at each of them in turn. The look on his face seemed to waver between anger and amusement, curiosity and disbelief. "Look, I appreciate the gesture from a fellow cop. And I respect the hell out of you, Doctor."

"Tom, I know how you feel, but—"

He held up a hand. "My perspective changed overnight. But I'm trying. This is still my case until somebody takes it away. I have all my men, every shift working on this, even though we're stretched thin. I've got calls in to the state police, but so far they've been slow in responding."

"What about the feds?" Lupo asked.

Arnow grimaced. "Not yet, but I may be forced to make that call if something doesn't break by tomorrow, or if another victim lands on my doorstep." His irritation was showing now, though he covered it with smiles. Strained smiles. "So then please feel free to inform me about my murders."

Lupo saw through the bluster. Arnow was floundering,

but unwilling to let it show. Who could blame him? A man in his position, new and with an impressive résumé, yet here he was, completely baffled by what was happening and insulted by the whispers that probably followed him into each doorway. The mayor breathing down his neck, the city council fighting over whether to fire him and bring in the cavalry. But who was the cavalry?

Arnow wanted the cavalry, but he wanted to resolve his own problems, too. Lupo understood him, but he wasn't sure Arnow wanted to be understood. And he clearly didn't want to be understanding. He was impatient to hear his visitors and then usher them out and get back to chewing his nails, waiting for inspiration. Maybe driving around, hoping a clue would land on the road in front of him.

Well, Lupo thought, *here's your clue.*

"Listen, Arnow, we're here to offer help, but there's information we have to give you first, and it's not gonna sound terribly sane."

Jessie cut in before Arnow could respond. "Tom, you saw for yourself how the victims looked. No sane person would do that. No sane human."

"Yeah, so you're selling me an insane perp?" He laughed, a little too hysterically. He was on edge. "That's not a stretch. So, who's doing this and why?"

"We don't know why," Jessie said, "though we think the tribal council is the key. So far, all the victims are connected by being Indians, being on the council, and one other thing that wouldn't be as obvious."

"Something that would be private, privileged information and not accessible to the general public," Lupo said. "They all voted in favor of the casino project. It wasn't unanimous."

"So there were two groups? For and against?" Now Arnow looked interested. He reached for a legal pad and scrawled something too quick to be legible to anyone else. "Who else was on the yes side?"

Lupo nodded. "We thought of that and have calls in to them all. I'm going to sequester them."

"I'm the law here. I'll do whatever sequestering needs to be done." He didn't like his feet stepped on quite so openly. "I need that list."

Jessie spoke up. "Tom, your plate is full. Believe me, we're only trying to help. There's a couple things we can do for you, uh, unofficially, that no one else can." Her level voice, her perfect face delivering the words, kept the sheriff from exploding.

It had been a clear tactic, bringing Jessie to help the medicine go down. Arnow was so smitten, he'd fight the urge to get ugly in front of her. Lupo was sure he had him pegged.

Lupo directed a half smile at Jessie while Arnow fixed his gaze on her, unsure how to respond.

"Sheriff, I guarantee you need to listen to us. We're not grandstanding or trying to hog the spotlight or whatever you might think."

"That might convince me of *your* motives, Doctor, but I'm not sure about other people's."

Lupo smiled crookedly. "Your employers are breathing down your neck, right? You're not at all sure you'll still have this job next week. Might have to sell that cozy condo you bought, thinking you'd be here twenty years. Believe me, we don't have an axe to grind, but we do have an opportunity to help you and keep some people from getting killed."

Lupo knew it had backfired as soon as he'd said it.

"Look, Detective, I'm not sure I like the way this is going. You have information, then lay it out. If not, I *am* busy." He shifted in his seat. "I'm sorry, Jessie, but I'm not in a good position here. You turned down the autopsy, and now . . ." He waved at them. "You two are in here talking about information. I wanted a consultant, not a snitch. Sorry, that's how I feel right now."

Lupo said, "A half hour of your time. Just what you need to help you digest that burger from Joy's Diner. Not the best place in town, by the way. The Lifeson Café is a lot better."

Arnow grimaced. "That's what I get for taking some people's advice. Why's yours any better?"

"Because we live here, Tom. We care about the place."

He sighed, exhaustion written on the lines in his face. "All right, tell me what you have. Insane or not, I'll listen."

They looked at each other sheepishly for a moment. Lupo spoke up. "Follow us to where we can talk privately. My car's outside."

"What?" Sudden anger flared up and colored Arnow's face. "All that talk about caring and then I'm supposed to *follow* you somewhere? You can't talk here? What the hell're you saying about my people?"

Lupo tried to soften the words. "We just need you to follow us, Tom. Just out of town, away from prying eyes. It's better if people don't see us talking to you."

"You're here and people see you."

"Please, Tom, trust us," Jessie implored.

"Son of a bitch, Doctor, I don't like being manipulated."

She nodded. "I know it looks like that. But you really should set aside the notion and just go with your gut."

Arnow smirked. "My gut tells me I'm being played."

"I wouldn't do that," she said with sadness in her voice.

"Nevertheless, I'd rather have help that makes sense to me. Insanity I can understand. But following you somewhere, you being coy about your connection to this case, it all makes me very uncomfortable."

Lupo stood. "All right, then, Sheriff. We'll be on our way. But I think you'll be calling us again."

Arnow shook his head. "I don't know what came over me. I apologize, Doctor. I think that crime scene last night affected my judgment." He shuffled some papers, the universal gesture of dismissal.

Lupo's fuse was short, but he snuffed it, heading for the door instead. Jessie followed reluctantly. "Good day, Sheriff."

Arnow grunted.

The main entrance of the sheriff's department was snuggled between the rear of the remodeled courthouse and the new jail they'd built after the Stewart case, a redbrick cube with long glass-block windows up high.

Hot anger rippled off Jessie's body. She was going to let him have it for the way he'd handled things. He ignored her piercing stare.

"Time for plan B," he said.

"Oh, and what's that?"

"You got me. I'm not sure." He grinned at her, hoping to disarm her anger. She'd obviously gotten to like Sheriff Arnow. *Tom*. He'd have to be careful.

He looked at her across the roof of his car. The cool wind rippled her hair just right. "I've got DiSanto running a plate for me. That might lead to something. A strange guy, probably just a tourist, but he was following that reporter. And somebody was following *him*."

"Oh, yeah? And what were you doing, following her, too?"

He started to protest, then noticed she was grinning.

Was it a real grin? Hell, he didn't know fake from real with women. He hadn't had the best luck with them. He'd lost a few along the way, most to violent deaths. One he had killed himself. Caroline Stewart, his first great love. The professor who understood him, who knew about him and his secret, and whom he'd savagely murdered. No, the *Creature* had savagely murdered her, but it was Lupo, too. Bound up in his destiny, maybe. *But still.*

"Check in with Sam?"

"He was gonna talk to Eagleson, Eagle Feather, whatever's his name."

"Eagleson's his white name, what he uses in the white man's world. White people frown on names like Eagle Feather. The Indian people are proud, but they'd rather have two names than be ridiculed for one. It's one of the many compromises they make."

Lupo nodded. Sam had explained once. He dialed his cell and waited. "Voice mail," he said, frowning. "Sam, call me back. We're coming to meet you, but I need directions."

"Hope he was able to convince them."

"Yeah. They don't strike me as very open-minded."

"No worse than any of the whites around here," she pointed out.

He ceded the point and drove north, heading for reservation land. The highway wound in a sweeping curve to the right, past the tiny Eagle River Union airport, and he opened up to match the highway limit.

He dialed up "Ammonia Avenue," more of his Alan Parsons Project "up north" music. The high-hat intro and bass line of "Prime Time" always put him in mind of driving.

They sat in companionable silence listening to the music they both enjoyed until the signs alerted them they were entering tribal reservation lands. Lupo followed the highway to the main drag, where a row of newer shops and boutiques seemed deserted. The post office was a new log building, and there was a community center, Jessie's clinic, and a grocery store. Children rode rusty bikes across the empty streets.

"See, we need the casino to bring in people," Jessie said. "At least, that's how it was sold."

"What about the new buildings?"

"All recent, built on the promise of bigger crowds. The stores are barely staying above water, though."

Lupo nodded. Sam had mentioned it. The tribe was in a sort of limbo. Maybe good times would come, or maybe they wouldn't. It all rested on the casino project, and right now the casino project seemed cursed.

"I need gas," Lupo said.

"Pull in there."

Lupo pumped, noticing the prices were lower than outside the rez. The station had a dingy convenience store shoehorned into it. Children and teenagers came and bought candy and soda, like kids anywhere.

"I'll pay with my tribal ID," Jessie said, flashing a photo badge. "Discount," she explained. He mouthed a *thank you.*

When she returned he said, "That's a nice perk."

"We're all about perks here on the glamorous rez."

"The casino should kick it into gear."

"Yeah, but now somebody doesn't want it completed. You think it's about that?"

"The pattern seems obvious, but not the reason. The tribe'll get rich. Everybody wins."

"Except the whites," she muttered.

"Maybe, but they love to gamble. And the jobs will be top-notch. I still think it's a win-win. Who isn't it a win for? That's what we should figure out."

"And what the wolves have to do with it."

"My guess is hired guns. Like in the Old West."

"Nick, I'm scared." Her voice was fragile. "I don't want to lose you. I think I almost did at least once today already."

He grinned to reassure her. "Takes more than a few scratches to stop me."

She touched his leg, her warm hand comforting. "They weren't just scratches when they happened. And you even admitted that without Sam . . ." Her voice hitched, her eyes welled up.

He watched her from the corner of his eye. "Hey, Jess, don't bet against us. We make a good team. You and me and Sam."

She nodded, not convinced.

Lupo's cell buzzed, and he flipped it open. "Speak of the devil. Yeah, Sam." He paused. "We'll be right there."

"What's wrong?" Jessie said, seeing his frown.

"Half the remaining council won't listen. Eagleson called them, but he's refusing to go anywhere. He's still got some sway over a couple of the others. They're doing their own thing."

"Don't they understand it's dangerous?"

"They're being stupid," he said, with a wave.

"Nick, they're intelligent people. They need convincing. I don't think calling them names will help."

He glanced at her briefly. "Why the defense? They're part of a dwindling group. They should feel the crosshairs on their backs."

"They're my people, Nick. Half my people, anyway."

"All the more reason you should convince them to listen. Your buddy Arnow's a good guy, I can tell, but he doesn't have a clue what he's up against. He's never going to understand the real danger, and so he can't offer any real solutions. Even if he gets the state police here soon, they're all helpless. Jess, *it's us.* We're the last line of defense for these elders of yours. Before there aren't any left." He chose to not tell her Arnow might have ended up a half-devoured carcass just hours before.

Jessie sat quietly. Lupo sensed she was seething. Maybe he'd been too blunt about the old folks. But dammit, was he wrong?

They headed for Sam's hideaway in chilly silence.

Tannhauser

He watched Schwartz convulse for the hundredth time, his skin mottled with bruises that looked inflamed. He knew they hurt like liquid fire in Schwartz's veins. He knew he'd almost lost one of the pack overnight, and it was his fault. As Alpha, he should have made sure the others were with him.

He and Tef had swept across the woods after the rogue wolf, whoever he was, but Schwartz had decided to hang back. Clearly, Schwartz had deciphered the rogue's plan—the bastard must have let them sweep by and faded back behind them. *An old partisan trick.* His grandfather would have approved. If Schwartz hadn't figured it out, they never would have had a chance at him.

Schwartz could hold his own against any wolf out there, with the possible exception of Alpha himself.

And he had, apparently, backed the other wolf into a corner.

But no one had expected somebody out there, some human, wielding a silver-loaded shotgun.

Alpha sat in an armchair and watched his friend suffer,

his body contorting and his skin seeming to melt off in strips where the silver shot had penetrated. His eye socket was a nightmare of grue. Inside, he would be feeling as if hellfire had taken hold of his guts and was twisting them in super-heated furnaces.

Alpha heard the groaning, and he didn't envy Schwartz one bit. The lesser wounds inflicted by the rogue wolf, serious as they were, had already begun to heal. They would vanish in a day or so. But the silver shot had to be removed, and Tannhauser had spent several hours digging with a long scalpel and probe, the skin on his hands sizzling at the proximity of the element.

No one knew exactly why silver was so toxic to werewolves. It was one of the few myths that had turned out to be accurate. It represented purity and sensitivity to it had evolved through the European strain of lycanthropy, his grandfather had once explained, when he was aged and no longer basking in the enjoyment of his powers. The younger Tannhauser was in the full of his, and the arrogance that came with them, so he had shrugged off the implied warning. He had learned his lessons later, while employed by various shady companies tied to the international intelligence community.

Now he watched Schwartz fight off the effects of the *pure* metal with bitterness.

Where was Tef?

The young pup was a great asset in a fight, but his free spirit was likely to be the death of him—and all of them—if he wasn't reined in.

Alpha blamed himself. Right after they'd gotten Schwartz home, Tef had stalked about their house with some mysterious purpose. He had spent time in their den, the most secret of their rooms, and had looked smug when Tannhauser asked him what he was up to. By then Tannhauser was up to his elbows in Schwartz's blood, trying to remove the silver shot without causing himself serious pain. His request for help had fallen on deaf ears.

"Got business to attend to," Tef said over Schwartz's groans and Alpha's protests. "I'll be back later."

His eyes burned with a fire all his own. Schwartz had reported on some of Tef's behavior during his liberty, and Alpha supposed Tef was off for some human cunt.

As if on cue, the phone rang.

"Crap," he muttered.

He knew exactly who this would be.

He closed the door on Schwartz and his throbbing, burning pain, taking the call with his most businesslike tone.

"It's nice to see you answer your phone so quickly," Mr. XYZ said, oozing sarcasm.

"What do you want?"

"Ooh, so short with the hand that signs your checks."

"I have a team member down right now," Tannhauser said tersely. "I'm shorthanded."

"Not my problem, is it?" The voice chuckled. "Run into the unexpected, did he?"

"Yes, someone who may oppose us."

"Hm, the sheriff?"

"No, an outsider. Somebody with, er, experience."

"Look, I don't know what you're doing exactly, but so far you're doing it well enough. I want the campaign stepped up, but I hear through a source that the targets are holing up in some kind of a safe house. If you find it you'll have more than one victim all lined up for you, even without the manpower."

"Anything else you know?"

But the other end of the line clicked off. The caller ID function showed *Unavailable*, as it always did with XYZ's calls.

Shit.

With Schwartz down and Tef off to follow his dick, Alpha's chances for an assault on any compound didn't look good.

In the bedroom he watched his friend writhe on the bedclothes, his blood still sizzling even as it oozed out of the silver-lined holes in his tortured flesh.

Tannhauser held up his own bandaged hands and hoped they would heal quickly.

Sam Waters

Eagle Feather had listened enough to make the calls, but then he put his stamp of disapproval on Sam's effort and managed to keep a couple members on his side.

Daniel Bear Smith and Rick Davison agreed with the elder that they could not show weakness, and retreating to a safe compound with police protection (as Sam had spun it) was likely to look bad to the tribe when the details were made public. Eagle Feather stood against showing the white world any weakness, and so Smith and Davison had turned down the opportunity of huddling together for comfort, as Eagle Feather had scoffingly described it.

Bill Grey Hawk had readily accepted the offer of protection and made sure his family could be included. Grey Hawk was a realist.

Sam planned on stashing them in his old fishing cottage. It was located deep in the woods once, but new homes crept closer every year. He had taken Sarah there on their honeymoon, and since her death he could barely stand to be there alone. Her touch was everywhere, in the curtains and the way the bookshelves were arranged, in the way the tiny kitchen was organized, and the way the furniture caved comfortably around you. He missed her more there, so he avoided it. But Lupo had agreed it sounded like a remote enough safe house.

After collecting Bill Grey Hawk and his wife and three young children, Sam headed for the cottage. He gave Lupo and Jessie directions.

In his trunk, Sam had a stash of silver ammo and several long guns. Lupo would have to steer clear of it.

He figured the wolf out there—the pack, if Lupo was right—would at least be deprived of Grey Hawk's family as a kill. But that meant they could find Eagle Feather and his two holdouts. Sam stared at the woods that surrounded his cabin. The pines were still so thick here that from the forest floor you almost couldn't say it was day.

A shiver slid down his back. He once feared Lupo's Creature. But this time it was worse, because of what those monsters had done to his colleagues. His *friends.*

Lupo

The silence of the latter part of the ride left him feeling snarky. He greeted Sam warmly enough and tried to reassure Bill Grey Hawk.

"What exactly are we being protected from?" Grey Hawk asked. He had sent his wife and children to the loft to play games. Their tinny voices filtered down to them, and Grey Hawk looked up occasionally, worry etching his long, scholarly face.

Sam reintroduced Lupo. Grey Hawk remembered him from the infamous Stewart case, but they'd only met briefly.

"That's the thing," Lupo explained. "We're really not sure." The lie sounded hollow even to him. "We think it's related to the casino."

"Townies?" He meant *whites.*

"Not that simple," Lupo said.

"Have you heard Lydell? He'd bring it down to its simple roots. Kill Indians because they're taking all the fish and soon they'll take all the money."

Lupo had heard about the radio preacher. Pouring gasoline on the long-damped fire of racism and hate.

Scumbag.

"Sheriff Arnow's doing his best," Lupo said, changing the subject. "But he's shorthanded. We're helping out as unofficial deputies."

"Dr. Hawkins, too?"

Jessie nodded. When Grey Hawk had climbed to the loft to see his family, she said, "What can I do, really?"

"Might be good to have you here with the wife and the kids."

"Woman's work?"

"Gee, Jess, I didn't mean it that way. With all the guns, they're probably spooked."

"I'll have to get an overnight bag."

"And some weapons. Like what Sam's got in the trunk."

Sam spoke up. "You knew?"

"I've been itching since I got here. It's starting to burn."

"I don't have any silver ammo," Jessie said.

"Not even at the clinic?"

She didn't respond.

"I knew there was a reason you kept me from seeing you there," Lupo said. He'd guessed, but the look on her face was a confession. "Hey, it's okay. I'm a freak."

He laughed to let them both off the hook.

But it hurt.

With a promise that Jessie would return as soon as she could, they left the family under Sam's protection again. Lupo would have bet they were safe in the daytime. Later, that was anyone's guess. The other council members would not be safe tonight. How to keep them alive?

Jessie put her hand on his knee, and he let her warmth dispel the chill between them. When she leaned her head on his shoulder, fragrant hair tickling him, he could almost forget the sense of betrayal he felt.

After dropping off Jessie at home with a kiss and a wistful wave, he headed back to town. He dialed his cell and waited for DiSanto to pick up.

"Jesus, Nick, I'm at home with my family."

"Hello to you, too. Of course you're with your family, it's a weekend."

"No, you don't understand. I'm *with* my family. Sundays Louise makes sure I don't do any work stuff . . ."

Lupo made a face. Through the windshield, on the left, pine trees. On the right, an occasional strip mall announced the arrival of the town proper.

"DiSanto, I want you to go to your car and give me this information now, before I drive down there and extract it with a pair of pliers and an awl. Got it?"

"You just don't understand," DiSanto grumbled. He spoke through his hand, heard some kind of low-volume argument, and then his voice came back.

"I forgot you were gonna call," he said apologetically. "Shouldn't have promised to leave work at the office."

"I got quite the situation here."

"Word's trickling down about some shit going on with the Indians. You involved?"

"Yeah. What you got?"

"Nice side step. That Altima, you were right, it's a Hertz. Rented out to a D. W. Schwartz, paid for with a credit card. Get this, the rental's a long-term. Three months, starting about five weeks ago."

"Phew," Lupo whistled. "Expense account."

"I'm bettin'." There was hesitation in the voice. "Something else, Nick."

"What? Anything on this Schwartz?"

"Didn't get much. Ran his license, came up clean. Almost too clean, like it was swept by somebody. Homeland Security maybe, since those bastards have all the weight these days. But there's no complaint department yet that I know of. Nah, it's something else. Maybe not related to your thing, but I found it . . . and it's . . . curious."

"*Curious?* That a fancy way to say fucked up?"

"Maybe. Nick, didya know there's been a bunch of women and girls disappeared near you?"

Lupo pulled into a hardware store lot and turned off the engine. "What do you mean, *near* me?"

"That's the thing. Saw a missing-persons report come over the wire. Then I remembered there was one about a month ago. I asked around, and it looks like there've been a bunch more over the last couple of years. Some may be runaways. Others are just plain old disappearances. Fact is, they're all over a large area—Minocqua, St. Germain, Rhinelander,

Woodruff, Manitowish. And on. I started to stick some pins in a map—"

"Pins? In a map?"

DiSanto huffed. "Virtual pins in a virtual map. You know, Google Maps or whatever. Listen to me, Nick. These disappearances have nothing to do with Eagle River."

"So?"

"So that's the point, they're all around Eagle River, but never in, so it sticks out like a sore thumb when you put all these separate reports together."

"Like somebody not shitting in his own backyard?"

"Exactly what I was gonna say."

"Sure, if there's a cliché for it, you'll use it."

"L-O-L, buddy. R-O-F-L-M-A-O."

Lupo chuckled, but his thoughts were whirring.

DiSanto came back on. "Shit, wait. Louise, it's important! Nick's got trouble. Yeah, I know what day it is, but he's my partner . . . Look, Nick, I better go. I've gotta talk to you tomorrow 'bout some crazy shit going on at the county jail—the dude we collared is . . . ah, tell you later. Wish I could have helped more with the Altima."

"No sweat. Thanks, Rich. Give your wife a kiss for me."

There was slightly bitter laughter, cut off by the connection breaking up.

Disappearances. Now, what the hell was *that* all about—and how did it connect to the council killings?

And their frat-boy bike collar was acting up?

He tapped the wheel in a rhythm from memory.

Tef

He watched her coming out of the courthouse with her camera crew—one of them a new guy to replace the hippie. She wouldn't fuck this guy; he was ugly and fat. She stopped and consulted with the two drones, then pointed at the news van. They nodded and hauled off on a mission.

Heather was left alone in front of the art deco main entrance, checking her phone.

He admired her sleek lines. Wanted to layer himself on her, fill her holes, spill his seed in her. Eat her. *Devour* her.

The old guys didn't understand him. He was all about sensation. They were living in the past, following some kind of pseudo-military code. He'd done his share of the shit work in the military. And then again in the Wolfpaw brigade. He wanted more. He wanted this woman right now, as he'd had her earlier.

He was far enough away in the shade of a couple of drab houses that she hadn't noticed him. She barked into her phone, clearly perturbed by something. Her nostrils flared when she was angry or sexually aroused. He felt the growth inside his trousers.

She set off in the opposite direction, and before he knew it, he was tailing her as she headed straight for Railroad Street, which marked the beginning of the tourist drag.

What's her mission today? He had to wonder what a star TV reporter would be doing here in town other than working on the murder story. What angle was she working?

He chuckled.

He knew what angle *he* wanted to work.

Lupo

He was planning to see Arnow again, to check on those disappearances DiSanto had mentioned. Maybe nobody up here had noticed the pattern. Maybe they had a lot of runaways from these towns, places that seemed awfully dead-end to kids sick of working tourist traps for tourist bucks, but wanted to be tourists themselves.

He thought about that Altima driver.

But then he spotted the beautiful Wausau reporter coming out the door. Heather Wilson grabbed your attention for sure.

And, not far away, the blond guy again.

If Lupo hadn't nosed his car around the fancy new restaurant on River he might never have spotted the guy, but there he was, on foot, clearly hanging back to tail Wilson.

It was a weird situation. The blond guy was apparently fucking her. Yet here he was, following her like a pervert.

Fuck this, Lupo thought, flooring the accelerator. The Maxima, old but with a well-maintained engine, roared as he twisted the wheel and steered straight for the guy. If he'd jumped the curb, the Maxima would have pinned the blond under its grille.

The guy turned and stared at him through the windshield. Lupo squealed to a halt barely a foot from the guy. Blondie stood his ground calmly. Unconcerned.

"Hold it right there," Lupo called, flashing his badge.

"Not going anywhere," the guy said, amused. "You're not a local cop, are you? Their badges look different."

Lupo closed the distance fast, imposing his muscular body on the guy's wiry physique, invading his space.

"What are you doing, tailing that woman?"

Blondie smiled infuriatingly. "That woman is Heather Wilson, the news anchor. I'm a fan. I want her autograph. Is there some law against that?"

Lupo hated to be physical, but he crowded the smaller man further, the distance between them short enough to grab him. "You're acting like a stalker."

"I'm shy."

"You're behaving suspiciously."

"There's no law—"

Lupo felt the Creature gurgling up into his throat. His hands reached out before he could stop himself and grabbed Blondie's lapels, dragging his face closer. "You're starting to make me mad."

A look flashed over Blondie's features, like a brilliant flash of insight followed by an ingratiating smirk. "Hands off me, bro. I'm warning you." He smiled, but his eyes changed colors under the weak sunlight.

Lupo felt the connection below the surface. Felt the

similarity. Or the Creature felt it. Either way, the look passed between them, and Lupo's Change almost bubbled up, unbidden, the Creature taking control.

Until a voice broke through the haze of the moment.

"Boys. *Boys!*" Heather Wilson had spotted them and crossed the street while they grappled. Her presence was like a pin bursting a balloon, and the air blew out in a rush.

"What's going on? Detective?" Then she turned to Blondie. "Tef?"

Tef. What kind of name was that?

"Nothing," Tef said, crossing his arms and smirking. "Least, not yet."

Lupo noted some tats peeking from under his sleeves.

"You harassing my friends?" she said, aiming at Lupo, frowning. Her eyes flashed anger and surprise, but curiosity too.

He backed off. No point getting all of them arrested. Blondie smiled widely, smarmy and condescending, like a bully who'd been given a free pass.

Tef is one of them. He's one of the pack.

Lupo knew it without a doubt.

And he had to let him go. For now.

Heather Wilson

The testosterone level was intoxicating. Standing near these two men, she wished she could bed them both right then. Not that she'd ever shied away from such things. She had left a long trail of broken and used-up men in every town, and more than one had been forced to perform in a duo or trio in order to satisfy her.

She smiled to herself. The anger hovering over the two splendid males was still there, but so was something else underneath it all.

Tef was smug. Sarcastic. Lupo was—well, Lupo was a cop. He'd got his back up, wanted to beat Tef senseless, but she sensed something stronger there, something more savage. She thrived on the sensation of danger.

And there it was, in front of her.

Tef was a cipher, but Lupo she could read.

"What are you doing here?"

Tef said, "I was coming to meet you."

Did he smirk while saying *coming?*

"Were we supposed to meet?"

"I thought a late lunch. If you're free."

His photograph was in her pocket. What better way to keep an eye on him than to be with him?

"And you, what were you doing here, Detective Lupo?"

Tef started at the cop's name.

"Police business," he said. Almost *growled.*

He was adorable when his anger was aroused. She smiled widely, one of her best weapons. "I was here on business, too. The murders are keeping me busy. I have a remote update to tape, but then I'm available." She batted her lids at Lupo, though she spoke to Tef. This was her favorite game. Pitting two men against each other and seeing who fought the hardest.

True, Lupo had his little doctor girlfriend to keep him busy, but she couldn't possibly offer as much as Heather Wilson. She'd found him attractive way back when, and now she'd be making a play for him if it weren't for this strange Tef kid who really rang her bell.

And who just might be a murderer.

She couldn't buy it, really. Strange yes, but murderous?

Then again, she'd seen some bizarre things in her career.

No doubt about it, Lupo was the safer one to pursue.

She batted her eyes at Tef now and gave him the big smile. Grabbed his arm and started to lead him away.

Who needs safety, anyway?

"I have a few minutes for coffee. Want some?"

Tef nodded uncertainly, as if control had shifted too quickly for him.

She pulled him away, and they left Lupo standing there, his car askew on the street.

Lupo

Arnow was in his office, under assault from the jerk they called a mayor. The door was closed, but the tone of their voices said plenty even if Lupo didn't hear the words. He waited, watching the hectic doings of the deputies as they prepared to head out. They glared at him, knowing he was a cop, but somehow on the outside. He wasn't one of them, a local.

The mayor—wasn't his name Malko?—exited Arnow's office and frowned at Lupo as he walked to the door.

Arnow waved him inside and into a chair.

"Jesus, you have to put up with that a lot?"

Arnow grinned with no humor. "You can't imagine. That guy's my biggest headache. Listen, Lupo, I apologize for being a jerk earlier."

"Nah, I get it. We're interfering."

"Well, I asked for help, you know. So then I can't go ballistic when people try. It's just, you know, the way you came in here."

Lupo made a gesture. "No problem. Forget about it. I've got a couple things for you, though. The lady reporter has a stalker. He calls himself a fan, and she's letting him puppy-dog her, but he's a strange one. Name of Tef. Drives a striped Geo Tracker."

"Tef? Weird name." He jotted some notes on a pad. "I'll see what I can find out. What else?"

"Yesterday somebody in a rented Altima was following the Tef kid."

"Really? Interesting. You ran the plate?"

Lupo grinned. "Yeah. Figured I'd save you the time. D. W. Schwartz. Hertz long-term rental."

"No bells ringing." He added the name to his pad. "Anything else?"

Lupo wondered if there was sarcasm in the sheriff's voice. Couldn't quite tell.

"One more thing. May be nothing to do with this, but my partner down in MPD actually caught it. I gather there've been some disappearances?"

Arnow nodded. "I've got a small stack of reports from around the tri-county area, but—"

One of the deputies leaned in the door. "Sheriff, we got a riot brewing over at River Park." *Halloran, maybe,* Lupo thought.

"What's the deal?"

"That Lydell guy on the radio's callin' 'em out to protest the casino and shit."

"Christ. I don't need this! Hal, grab everybody available, call in the patrols. Then go disperse the idiots before they get out of hand. Use some judgment, okay? I'm going to Lydell's. Care to join me, Lupo?"

"Lead on."

They took Arnow's cruiser. Lupo squished his bulk into the passenger seat, crowded with the laptop station, the camera and recording gear, the radar gun, and the Remington shotgun in its cradle. Lupo spotted the short, squat shape strapped to Arnow's ankle. "Extra Glock?"

Arnow nodded. "Whatever's out there, I want to have enough rounds."

Not good enough, Lupo thought. But he nodded in understanding.

They swung past the park, where about a hundred people were scattered around a group of picnic tables. Somebody with a megaphone had climbed a table. A couple of signs waved limply overhead. As they raced past, sirens came up from behind.

Arnow growled. "Just what we need, shit like this."

Lydell's station was a converted Quonset hut with a clapboard addition and a huge garage shed erected behind it. A rusted transmission tower was the only clue the building housed a radio station.

Arnow burst into the front door, Lupo trailing him, curious.

"I need to see Lydell," he snapped at the pimply kid sitting behind a computer. He tapped his badge.

"Brother Lydell's on the air!" The kid jumped up halfway but stopped, intimidated. "You need an appointment!"

"Official business," Arnow said. "I'm making one."

They invaded the rear room and saw Lydell at the microphone behind a glass partition. His voice rattled a wall-mounted speaker on their side of the glass. His round body was slouched as he shouted into the microphone. When he heard them, he stopped in midsentence, and his eyes widened.

"Brothers, it looks as if the forces of fascism have broken the sacred seal of the First Amendment and entered to wave their weapons in my face."

Arnow made a face. "This guy's full of shit. I can't believe anybody listens."

"The masses need jerks like this to give them purpose." Lupo shook his head. "He's right, though. You can't shut him down."

Arnow nodded. "Sure, but it's my duty to remind him that if his little science project blows up and somebody on either side gets hurt, it'll be his ass in both civil and state court. Chances are he doesn't realize he can be held responsible for inciting that riot."

"But I do, Sheriff," said Lydell, who had stepped out of his booth. On the speaker, a recorded rant played.

"Then consider yourself warned, Lydell. Keep up the hate speech, and we'll be seeing a judge. I'll have your license pulled."

The round body shook with laughter. "You think so, Sheriff? You'll find it's not that easy."

"No? Try me."

"I don't have to. We're supported in part by a city fund. I believe there are also county interests, due to our public-service programming. Check with the mayor if you don't believe me." His chins shook as he wagged his head. "I bet Mayor Malko doesn't know you burst in here. But he will!"

"I don't give a shit about the mayor," Arnow growled. But his anger had been tempered. "Just lay off the hate speech, or we'll find out in court who wins this one. It'll cost you in some way, I promise."

Lydell turned on Lupo. "I know who you are. You're that Indian-lover cop from the heathen city. You'll get yours."

Arnow put a hand on his arm. Lupo waved him off. He wasn't taking the bait. But the Creature inside him threatened to erupt in an angry growl.

They left with Lydell's mocking cackle still in their ears.

"Fuckin' Malko," Arnow said when they were back in the cruiser. "The fucker's rapidly dropping off my Christmas card list."

"Doesn't sound like he should be helping fund that jerk," Lupo said.

"You wouldn't think so."

"Maybe he's our guy?"

"Faking animal attacks? I don't see it. He's just a fat racist hate-monger."

Lupo nodded.

They headed back to the sheriff's office. Meanwhile Halloran reached the sheriff by radio to report the crowd had been dispersed without incident, at least this time.

Arnow pinched the tip of his nose and wiped his eyes.

"We've got one council member and his family in a safe house," Lupo said, explaining Sam's location. "The others are resisting."

"I was pissed about you doing that, but I gotta admit, my hands are tied. The county and the tribe have an unusual relationship. The mayor wasn't thrilled to hear you and Doc Hawkins are offering to help by sequestering surviving council members. Said we can protect our own."

"Point is they're not really your own, right?"

"Yes and no. Gray area. I never expected so many gray areas, dammit."

"Me either, Arnow. Me either. Life's a shitload of 'em."

Heather Wilson

They had coffee in the Internet café on Railroad Street. She used the wi-fi to check her e-mail, while Tef made eyes at her and lapped at his drink with the same tongue that set her genitals to melting. His mocking look annoyed her, but she couldn't help lusting for him anyway.

Lupo looked good, too. She would have made a move on him if this kid hadn't got under her skin. *Damn him!* He was insufferable. Quietly mocking, superior, demanding, damn near abusive of her body—if she hadn't liked it rough, she might have had him arrested. But he seemed to have her number from the first moment they spotted each other.

"What have you learned about the . . . killings?" he asked when she'd shut her laptop.

"I'm only covering the crimes for the station," she explained. "Not investigating."

"You are being disingenuous, no?"

Big word! she thought. "Well, yes, if I learn something that'll help solve the case, I'd pass it on. It would be a—a coup, for sure." She dazzled him with her best smile. "Do you have any information for me? You seem to be here on some kind of mission."

Did his eyes harden at that? She smiled again and under the table set her bare right foot between his feet. She worked her way up his leg, then caressed his bulge with her toes.

"Maybe I'm your mission?" she said playfully.

"Maybe you are," he whispered, his look betraying the fact that her caresses were working. "Maybe we now have a mission together."

"Again?" she mocked. "So soon?"

"You'll pay for that," he said, smiling tightly.

"I hope so," she said, withdrawing her foot.

Another blur, almost as if she'd passed out and awakened, and she was back in her motel room, riding his sinewy body beneath her, but in no way feeling that she was in control.

He was in her to the hilt. She faced away from him and lowered herself onto his penis again. They'd started the usual way, and then he had indicated she should straddle him, and she had complied, and now he was huge inside her, driving upward between her buttocks. Her pain was exquisite and she thought she could never leave him. He had found a key to her she had never known existed, and he exploited it from the beginning. His fingers manipulated her as if his other attentions weren't enough. She groaned with the pleasure, felt her wetness wash over him below her. Their rhythm increased as they approached the peak they sought.

In the dim room, she could barely see his legs in front of her. She bucked wildly on his throbbing hardness, and suddenly she felt something change beneath her—*no, it was inside her, as if his penis had changed inside her, become longer and more insistent—*

But that was crazy, wasn't it?

And then she was rocked by her orgasm and lost all sense of time and place. Her waves kept rolling as his hot seed filled her in one sudden gush after another.

She nearly screamed with the pleasure as she fell backward onto him, but it turned to pain as she felt his teeth on her shoulder and bicep.

He was biting her!

Biting and tearing, growling like a—

Jesus! He was ripping into her flesh like a carnivore!

She leaped off his still-engorged penis and felt hot wetness flowing from her shoulder and arm, wounds that began screaming with their own pain.

She rolled off the bed and lunged for the bathroom, hearing him gathering behind her, trying to grab her and bring her back, but she was healthy and fast and made her target before he could, slamming the door onto his face—

It wasn't a face anymore!

Her mind screamed its confusion and terror, but she still managed to bar the door with the flimsy lock, and he smacked onto the wood with a yelp.

Jesus, he had turned into *something.*

Something else. Something *not human.*

Naked, sobbing, bleeding, his thick ejaculation still running cold down her inner thighs, Heather Wilson threw her weight onto the door, praying she could hold him off until . . .

Until something or someone came to help.

There was silence from outside the bathroom for a few minutes, and she relaxed. Had he left? Her terror drained, but she felt the spiking jabs of pain from the wounds he had inflicted.

Suddenly he renewed his assault on the door, growling like a monster as he threw himself against the wood, which began to splinter under her hands.

She yelped now, trying to keep away from where the door might split. To keep it from splitting.

Then she heard a ringtone from the outer room, an insistent tune that caused him to pause.

She put her ear to the door, but heard nothing.

Was he on the phone? What had he become? What would he do after he was finished with the call, if that was what it was? Did she hear him whispering furiously out there, or was that her imagination?

The answer came when suddenly the outer room door was whipped open and slammed shut, causing the walls and bathroom door to vibrate.

She was alone.

She was bleeding. In the mirror, the wounds looked like miniature shark bites. *Bites.* He had bitten her and torn off several chunks of flesh.

Sudden, sharp pain came with the sight of her mangled flesh. She tried to close the wounds with her hands, to no effect.

The reaction hit her. She broke into bitter tears.

Chapter Thirteen

Jessie

He had stopped by to fill her in on what happened outside the courthouse. Later they'd separate and she would head back to Sam's hideout cottage.

She wondered how safe it really was.

And now she was being a bitch.

She couldn't stop it. She knew she was wrong to keep hammering at him, but after he had told her about today's encounter with Heather Wilson, she couldn't help herself.

"Strange how you and her keep ending up near each other," she said cattily. Even she couldn't believe they were her words.

"Jess, I think she's in danger. This guy she's seeing, Tef or something, he gives me the creeps. I can't tell whether she's stupid or whether she's working him. He could be involved in the murders, and she might be following the lead herself. If so, she could be in his sights."

"She's a big girl. She doesn't need you to older-brother her."

"True. But if he's the guy . . . I don't want her blood on my hands. I have enough blood on my hands, Jess."

She knew he was right. And she knew she could trust him. But she'd been so rattled. By the murders, by Tom Arnow's manner around her. She'd been possessed by some sort of avenging spirit since Nick had arrived. And he seemed to have noticed. There was a distance opening between them, despite the lovemaking, that she wanted to just wipe away. But every chance she got, she found some nasty comment bubbling to her own lips. It was amazing she'd repressed half of them. But for how long?

Now he was colder than she had ever known him. His Italian blood should have made him the more passionate one, and he usually was, but he was withdrawing.

And as he withdrew, she couldn't help thinking of that television slut and how she threw her figure and her hair and her ass around and men came running.

Jessie knew it was self-destructive, but she let the thoughts rattle around anyway.

He's angry about the silver. After the Martin Stewart case, when she had been harshly introduced to Nick's very real lycanthropy, Sam had convinced her they should be ready, just in case. He'd been right, but with the wrong werewolf. She'd backed the wrong horse.

"Jess?"

She looked at him and kicked herself mentally. How could she not trust him? He'd been the only good thing in her life since even before those dark days of Wilbur Klug. Well, her practice on the rez was good, but Nick's love *completed* her.

Sounded like one of those Dr. Phil clichés.

But it was true. So why was she giving him a hard time? He hadn't brought the Wilson woman to town. And it wasn't his fault the reporter lusted for him. Jessie herself had felt the same way when he was just her tenant. Now that he was her lover, she'd become possessive.

"Jess?" he said again. "You can come back now."

"I'm waiting to make sure they can cover for me at the clinic," she said by way of explanation. "Otherwise I would have left already."

"Good thing I caught you," he said, smiling. He put his hand on hers and the warm touch reassured her. At least for the moment.

Her cell phone rang and in a minute she was clear for the

evening, her shift covered. Ellie wasn't thrilled again, but there were favors to exchange.

She watched him from the kitchen doorway and saw his face harden when he thought she wasn't looking.

They parted with a cool kiss, the good moment somehow lost in their separate missions and disparate dark thoughts.

Mr. XYZ

"Ah, Courtney," he said with a wide smile. "You look lovely."

And she did. She'd needed a bath when he found her, but now she was fragrant. He had gently wiped her down with soapy water and then scrubbed under her perky breasts and carefully washed her genitals inside and out. Her feet had been black, but now they glowed.

She'd been slouching on the highway south of Three Lakes, trying to bum a ride and looking too ragged to get one. Ratty hair, smudged face. Only he could see the beauty under all that road dirt.

He'd pulled up and opened the passenger door. "Heading north?"

She nodded, amazement all over her features. But suddenly she shook her head and stepped back, away from the door. As if she'd seen his soul, his black soul behind the bright eyes.

"Okay then, how about some money for food?" His ready hand held out a ten.

She wanted to say no. She wanted to get as far away from him as possible. He could see it on her face. But she was weak.

They were *all* weak.

When she reached for the money, he was faster and grabbed her wrist. She squeaked like a mouse when he yanked her within range and his other hand swung the leather-covered sap once across her head and she sagged into the seat. He pulled away, the door closing on its own.

Now she was awake and twisting her naked body against his leather restraints. He knew her name from her cracked Illinois state ID—*perfect.*

She stopped struggling when he ran his tongue between her breasts, down to her navel, and lower into her folds. He watched his saliva dry on her skin.

She began to shiver, and then her eyes rolled up, and she sagged back onto his hand truck.

He had plenty of time.

Lupo

Maybe he should have let it go. So she had silver ammunition. *Just in case.* What was wrong with playing it safe?

He smacked the wheel.

Dammit, she was supposed to trust him.

He caught sight of the green-and-white Tracker crossing Railroad Street. Where had the kid been all this time? With Heather? He swung in behind another car and followed at a safe distance on 45 until it turned onto 70. Fortunately the other sedan stayed between them, and Lupo hung back to see where the kid went.

The Tracker kept on 70 to where it curved up and around Dollar Lake, and then turned onto Hemlock.

Alarm bells rang in Lupo's head.

This time he followed slowly until he passed several driveway entrances camouflaged by overgrown bushes and tightly packed tree trunks. He spotted a flash of metallic green between the pines of the second-to-last one so he slowed, backed up, and waited a minute before nosing his Maxima past the mailbox, down an overgrown path leading away from the house, and shutting off the engine.

Silently, he eased his door open and swung out, shucking his clothes. This was the best way for a quick recon, and it granted him more protection than going in as a cop with only a gun for defense if he found the wolf pack.

He visualized himself as the Creature and *went over* in a

flash, now padding on the needle-strewn driveway and heading for the house on his four paws.

The structure was set perpendicular to Voyageur Lake's shore, with a wall of glass on one side and a deck on the other, lots of wood between. Pines hugged all sides like a blanket. The Tracker stood hunched on the driveway. Next to it, the rented Altima.

Lupo's mind gears turned as he directed the Creature closer. Why would someone who knew the Tef kid follow him?

The Creature caught scents now, strong and full, and growled involuntarily, hackles rising.

This had to be the wolf pack's base then. Lupo caught the scent of the black wolf he had faced down. Now it was a diseased silvery smell, due to the serious silver-caused wounds. *They'll be a bitch to heal,* Lupo thought. There were confusing scents, human and wolf, human only, and even something reminiscent of the past. Whatever it was, it reminded him of the Martin gang. The thug Wilbur Klug, to be specific. But different somehow.

The Creature whimpered softly.

He wondered if the pack's military tendencies extended to its hierarchy.

He padded closer to the house, checking for perimeter security. If there were silent alarms, Lupo wasn't aware of them, although he saw motion-sensor floodlights mounted around the house proper. He was nowhere near those and it was daylight, so he didn't worry about them.

He made his way around to the rear of the house and stayed within the darkness of the tree line. Here the disturbingly familiar scent from the past wafted past once, then shut down as if magically dissipated.

Keeping upwind, he stalked nearer but still within the protective pines. He crawled on his belly, half human and half wolf, until he reached a corner where the glass pane stretched from ceiling to floor and the incline to the water's edge was still gentle.

His nose touched the pane, but the Creature fought his human commands. This style of stalking ran counter to the wolf, but Lupo the human won the fight and the wolf had to comply.

Inside, two men were gesticulating at each other animatedly. One, tall and broad. Angular. Military bearing complete with crew cut and pumped-up biceps. The other was the Tef kid, on the defensive, though he clearly wanted to get into it with the older, higher ranking man. No third man visible—the Altima driver?

Through the wolf's eyes, they appeared less human and more like fellow werewolves. Lupo wondered whether they'd catch his scent.

Outgunned, he had no choice but to retreat. He had no interest in having them run him to ground like a pack of hounds catches the fox.

He forced the Creature to back away toward the cover of pines.

Tef

He tuned out Tannhauser's lecture. Yeah, the old guy was Alpha, but he'd become a true square wheel since they'd debriefed on the Iraq gig. A rudderless ship—that's what they had become. Tannhauser was obsessed with pleasing the dickhead Mr. XYZ, and Schwartz played salivating lapdog to Alpha when not getting himself nearly whacked.

Tef nodded and offered a halfhearted defense. But he didn't give a shit. Hated the way he'd been summoned, right during playtime. Wasn't his fault old Schwartz was doing the silver jitterbug now. Tannhauser's bandaged hands looked like hams in the late afternoon sunlight.

"Yeah, whatever. You about done?" He set off another lecture on rank and duty.

Tef was sure the hothead cop was a werewolf. He hadn't been able to provoke a reaction yet, but the guy was tightly wound, what with the girlfriend and the hots he had for

Heather Wilson. He chuckled. The girlfriend was pretty hot herself—maybe now that Heather was broken he could learn to play with a new toy.

And an enemy werewolf spiced things up. Their instructions were to avoid killing cops, but temptation was strong. Tef was sick of old, frail Indians. Who gave a shit?

Tannhauser was still at it. He was livid. "You are sacrificing the mission to spend time with your whore."

"Rather spend time with a whore than a bore."

Tannhauser held back his gnarled fist. "Have you left behind our discipline? Our training?"

"That's fuckin'-A right. I'm sick of your orders."

"I'm Alpha!"

"Not necessarily forever, old man." He muttered, because he was still afraid of Alpha in a fair fight. The old wolf was a survivor, a fighter, a true soldier and also the wiliest wolf Tef had ever seen. But Tannhauser was losing his edge.

And Tef was right there.

"You didn't even pick up the scent, old man. Your nose is failing."

"What? What are you talking about?"

"We've been reconned, that's what. You're so wrapped up in your buddy back there, you haven't realized we're gonna get raided."

Alpha blurred suddenly, and the huge black wolf stood before him, his nostrils tasting the air.

His subsequent growl amused Tef. He visualized the cop who had the hots for the reporter woman. He was sure they'd come to blows soon. And he lusted for the chance. But first he had to be rid of the old man.

The odds were better. The time was nearing.

Arnow

He tried to wipe the sand from his eyes. There was too much grit there, too much sleeplessness. He sighed.

Bad enough he had the murders or animal attacks.

Whatever the fuck. The pressure from Malko and the county supervisors. The idiot Lydell inciting riots for the first time in a decade. And now Nick Lupo mentioned those damn disappearances.

Wasn't this too much for the quiet job he thought he'd taken? Would anybody blame him if he bolted? Ran back to the Sunbelt?

He watched the deputies change shifts. They looked exhausted, too.

Then there was Heather Wilson. Looked like a million bucks, and definitely interested. But she had this weird kid hanging over her, Lupo had said. Come to think of it, Arnow had seen that Tracker. What was that all about?

He remembered how he'd felt on the road not that long ago.

"Jerry? Can you step in here for a minute?"

"Boss? You need me?"

Arnow stifled a smartass remark and nodded. "There have been some disappearances in the outlying area the last few months."

Faber nodded. "I remember we briefed on them a while back. Basically not located in our area, so we just agreed to keep our eyes open and our phones handy in case it spread here."

"Hm," muttered Arnow. "Get me whatever you can find on them."

Soon he had a folder. As Lupo had said, they happened all over, but not Eagle River. *Weird.*

Jessie

They'd all met at Sam's again after Nick's recon.

Lupo took her out to the back porch, where they could talk. She left the shotgun inside, so Sam could watch the front and try to keep the Grey Hawk clan calm.

"I've got them, Jess. They're in a house at the end of Hemlock."

"You tracked them there? That's pretty remote."

He explained everything up to spying through the windows. "I wounded one of them and so did Sam, but I don't know how badly. I couldn't see him. There may be others we don't know about."

"What about . . . the Creature's instincts?" No matter how long they had been together, she still felt funny referring to the other side of Nick as a monster. But he was a masochist and insisted on it.

"Don't extend to sniffing out others of my kind, far as I know. I never knew there were others."

"Okay, so assuming you're right, why are they doing this?"

"To stop the casino. That's a guess but I don't know why they're doing it, or who wants it done. Not even sure it would work, unless they hope those opposed would just naturally halt the project in the face of a crisis."

"That's pretty twisted."

"Jess, none of this sounds rational. But people do irrational things all the time. They don't see themselves as irrational, that's the point. Convince yourself you're right and you don't back down."

She bristled. "I don't think that way."

"I'm a cop, Jess. I've seen three-time losers figure the same old behavior—like an armed bank heist—will result in some new outcome, like being able to retire on a tropical island. They're a dime a dozen, the self-deluded."

"So now what?"

"If we could get Eagleson and Smith and Davison and their families here, we could protect them. But if we can't, then I think we need to hit these bastards hard." His eyes were cold, as cold as she'd ever seen them.

She opened her mouth, but nothing came out at first. Then she said, "What about Tom? Can't we bring him into it?"

"Sure, he'd believe the whole werewolf thing."

"I did."

"You *saw*. You had no choice but to believe. You needed

to believe to survive, Jess." He softened his tone. "It wasn't my choice to share it with you. None of it was my choice."

She avoided his tender trap. "You want to go it alone? Even as a group, we'd be nothing but vigilantes. There's another word for us then. Murderers."

"Judge, jury, and executioners, maybe. But with good reason."

"Everybody who does bad things thinks they have a good reason."

"Shit, Jess, you saying I'm one of the bad guys here? These rogue wolves are killing your people. Something's going on beyond our understanding. I'm just trying to be practical."

"Practical? That's what you call it?" Her lips formed words without her brain's collaboration. "Is that what your friend Heather Wilson would call it?"

He appeared genuinely hurt at the jab. "What does she have to do with it? She's just a careerist out for a boost. Nothing to do with this. Maybe she's in too deep herself, come to think of it."

"Can't have that."

"Jess, be rational."

"Rational!" she snapped. "Rational? You just said it's irrational. What part of this is *rational?* Are you calling murder rational?"

"Putting down rabid dogs is not murder. It's a favor to all their victims, past and future. I doubt we can drag these guys into court, let alone whoever's pulling the strings. Plus they're very good. Got to be trained, probably by the military. It was a miracle I caught the one with his guard down, and he still almost had me."

"I don't agree with you." Sadness swelled in her breast. They'd never seen things so differently. This was more than a fight, it was a philosophical difference she'd never expected. She was no vigilante.

"If we explained it to Arnow," Nick said, "I bet he'd agree with me."

"I don't believe it. Tom's a man who upholds the law."

"The law never expected to deal with monsters."

"Again you want to label yourself a monster!"

"I have to go, Jess. No one else can keep an eye on these guys. They might go for us here, or try to get the others." He began to strip.

"Then why not stay?"

"I know when I'm not wanted," he said coldly. Moments later, he was bounding for the woods.

She let the tears roll down her face untouched.

Tannhauser

They found him on his back porch, puffing a long pipe like an Indian cliché.

Stalking him, they had both caught the scent of fragrant woodsmoke and followed the swirling clouds that bobbed and weaved through the railing. He seemed to be offering himself up.

Tannhauser approached from one side of the porch while Tef came at him from the other. Both wolves snarled and leaped up and over the railing simultaneously.

Daniel must have been named "Bear" because of his size. He was not intimidated by the two beasts that approached him with their fangs bared.

Tannhauser's inner alarm jangled even as he stared the human in the eye. There was a wild determination there he hadn't expected. Was he off his game since seeing Schwartz maimed?

The human growled like his namesake. Instead of backing off, he ignored Tef behind him and attacked the larger wolf.

"I'll have your pelt, you fucking piece of wolfshit," the human screamed before lunging like a drug-crazed berserker.

Tannhauser had overcommitted.

His paws scrabbled for purchase on the slick planks.

He was closer than he expected to be to this not-so-helpless prey and—too late—he saw the glint of metal in the man's hambone grip.

Some kind of knife . . .

The blade scraped through Tannhauser's top layer of skin and raked fire along the cut's edge. His flesh parted like warm lard under the blade, causing his blood to gush, boiling, from the slit. The wound was screaming agony.

The knife—treated with silver?

Daniel Bear Smith was a formidable opponent. To humans. He was extraordinary even to a werewolf, but he was no match for two. Tannhauser retreated to nurse his wounds, but Tef lunged from behind, caught the big man by the scruff of the neck and dragged him down before he could do any more damage.

The knife skittered away into the bushes.

Snarling savagely, Tef tore through the thick cords of the human neck and bathed in the great gush of hot blood that met his snout. The human's fists beat uselessly at his nose, then grasped his neck and squeezed. But the strength was going out of him, and Tef's jaws closed on one wrist and ripped it to pieces.

By now Tannhauser had recovered.

The human could no longer keep the two wolves from tearing him apart piece by piece. He went down on one knee and tried to fend them off with one hand. Tef's jaws took the Indian's fingers off and swallowed them like dog biscuits.

Prey: Daniel Bear Smith

His veins grew cold in a rush as the blood drained from his shredded neck.

His last thoughts were of the great arrogance Eagle Feather had shown in giving *him* the sacred knife, requesting that he attempt to stop the beast plaguing their tribe.

"You're the only one of us able-bodied enough to get this bastard," Eagle Feather said. "And to think we used to think of him as a defender. What romantic crap. The knife has been in its place since that so-called *shaman* loosed the disease on us."

Daniel Bear might have laughed his booming laugh now. This beast was *not* the defender of the tribe.

In all his wisdom, Eagle Feather had not figured on more than one monster. And Daniel Bear Smith had sacrificed his life for absolutely nothing.

His dying scream was cut off by his attackers' jaws and teeth.

CHAPTER FOURTEEN

Lupo

"Goddamn it!" He swore vehemently and the Creature growled in response, affected by his tone, not the words. He steered the Creature back, hoping to catch the three suspects at home.

Were they *suspects?*

No, the cop in him agreed, they *had* to be the wolves who'd come to town to kill elders. No more evidence needed, no juries, no legal system. Execution was the only answer.

He crept through the woods near the house at the far end of Hemlock. Water lapped at the piers below the slight rise that hugged the house's foundation.

Maybe he could do it tonight, himself.

But no, first they had to be home, and second they had to have their guard down. There was no way he could take on three experienced wolves and survive. He needed the silver slugs, and he didn't think he could wield them himself, no matter how much he wanted to.

The house was dark. Lupo directed the Creature to follow his earlier footsteps. Inside, he couldn't see much that looked different, but he sensed a presence. It wasn't exactly a scent, but he would have been hard-pressed to say what it was. A scent, a feeling, a hunch, some instinct—all rolled into one.

A light went on in a back room, and the Creature shrank back into the shadows. His nose twitched. He caught a faint trace of disease, the sickening smell of burned skin and flesh.

The wolf he and Sam had cornered. And gravely wounded. It had to be. Was it the Altima driver?

Perhaps the others were probably out stalking the safe house even now. Divide and conquer, sure, but how to be certain they were divided?

He faded into the woods. Quiet on his paws, treading on the pine needle forest floor, he nearly backed into a human who faced the house and had not heard the wolf approaching.

Now, what's this?

The beefy guy wore ragged camouflage and emitted no scent the Creature could discern. He wore what Lupo recognized as a slightly outdated night-vision unit on his head, and seemed to be intently training his gaze on the house Lupo had just stalked.

Lupo avoided a loud scuffle. He pulled the reins on the Creature, with difficulty, and they soft-footed past the distracted human.

He ran the Creature through the woods, giving it the chance to expend pent-up energy after feeling the chafing harness of Lupo's will.

Later, when he checked his cell, there was a message from Arnow telling him that Heather Wilson's camera crew was looking for her. Had he seen her since earlier? He reversed the call and left a message saying no. Why would Arnow call him about Heather? He shook his head. Lupo's head was spinning. Arnow seemed to be interested in Jessie, and Jessie seemed to think Lupo was interested in Heather. Heather was mired in some kind of relationship with the weird kid, whom Lupo suspected of being a wolf.

He sighed. Maybe Jessie was right. Maybe they needed Arnow to legitimize the vigilante action.

The moon's influence grew and the thirst hit first, then the lust. He drove back to the safe house.

Jessie

He woke her gently and gestured at the door. Groggy, she shook her head. He nodded, smiling, bringing a finger to his lips and gestured more insistently. She rolled out of the hallway bunk and made her way to him without creaking any floorboards. In the tiny bedrooms and in the loft, the Grey Hawk clan slept. Sam was on watch in the living room.

"What?" she whispered breathlessly in his ear.

"Let's take a walk," he whispered back. "Talked to Sam already, so he won't shoot us."

"That's good to hear." She reached out for his hand and found something else. "Hm, Nick Lupo, you're a beast!"

He cleared his throat comically.

"Leave the silver behind, okay?"

Her hand left him. "Dammit, Nick!"

"Kidding," he said. But the mood was slightly broken.

He led her outside past her minor resistance, and they climbed into his car.

"Sorry," he muttered, while he nuzzled her neck. "I'm not being a jerk on purpose. There's a case back at home that's causing me trouble, and I expected to come here to get away. Not find myself in the middle of some sort of war. And I didn't expect to run into others . . . like me . . . ever."

She caressed his face, hoping he wouldn't sense the tears forming in her eyes. When his lips found hers, she felt his loneliness and the desperate need. She felt the lust the Creature so often brought with it. And she felt her own body responding.

"Nick," she muttered, and then she was climbing on top of him and they were ripping cloth strategically, exposing flesh here and skin there. He took her breasts in his mouth one at a time, licking her stiff nipples, and then they maneuvered patiently until he could take her from below as she straddled him, the steering wheel digging into her back.

Pent-up passions, conflicts, and fears fed their lovemaking until their rhythm hit a fever pitch, exploded, and then slowed as they melted together in a comforting afterglow.

Later, he told her about the camouflaged and night-vision equipped watcher at the Hemlock house.

"His scent was familiar?" she asked.

"That's just it, he didn't have a scent."

"Neutralizer. Hunters use it."

"That's what I thought. But earlier I caught a familiar scent. Brought to mind the whole Stewart thing again. I think it reminded me of that thug, Wilbur—"

"Klug?"

"Yeah. He have any relatives?"

She thought, then snapped her fingers. "A cousin, I think. Maybe other family. You think a relative's scent would be similar to your memory?"

"Not so much mine, but the Creature's." He started rearranging his clothes. "Why would Klug's cousin be watching the wolves' house?"

"Nothing makes sense anymore."

"We'd better get inside before Sam sends out a search party."

They kissed once more, and she tasted the night on him. She both feared and adored the way he made her feel.

Part Three

Toccata (Con Fuoco)

Chapter Fifteen

Julia Barrett

When the few, more imposing redbrick cubes of downtown New London disappeared from her mirror, she admitted to herself finally that her obsession had taken over.

She was taking the scenic route, following the twisty state highway through town. Fortunately, the weekday traffic was light and she didn't have to grip the wheel with her usual sense of imminent doom. Which was a good thing, because she was distracted, ruminating about her dear Detective Lupo and putting puzzle pieces together over and over in her mind.

The detective was a thorn in her side.

She had been treating him long enough to have formed some sort of bond, but instead she had come to despise him even more. She didn't even kid herself. It had been a sort of benign antipathy from the beginning. His quiet, serious demeanor had angered her for some reason. Then something had happened between him and Don Bowen, something she still hadn't figured out, but it had led to Bowen's escape from his life. *From her.* She would figure it out someday, she swore.

Then there had been Lupo's "lost weekends," days during which—even in the middle of a case—Lupo would simply disappear. His partner always covered for him. Old Sabatini did it for years. Now Lupo was her case file, and DiSanto was covering for him. She'd mapped it out, spending long hours with payroll records and squad room assignment logs. Lupo dropped off the face of the earth for something like a weekend a month. *Like he's done since the very beginning.*

It was odd. Her first guess had been a girlfriend, of course. A logical guess.

The highway outside the city opened up in front of her, and she nudged her Lexus to the speed limit, watching the farmland slowly start to turn to forest in patches.

She had tried to get to the bottom of the whole strange terrorism case in which Lupo had been involved up to his neck, but somehow he had been able to pull strings and throw a blanket over the whole thing. What CNN and other news outlets eventually reported smelled like dog shit to her. She knew a cover-up when she saw one, and her low-key efforts to get at the truth had been stymied.

Lupo did have a girlfriend, the reservation doctor, but by all accounts, they had not been so close before the suspicious events. His trips up north went back as far as his earliest police work, long before he'd paid the Hawkins woman rent money.

Barrett wondered what his scam was. She had tried to worm it out of him during their sessions, but he resisted deftly. She watched him. She watched him *very* closely. She had seen him limp, and then not limp, on his prosthetic foot. She knew he was connected with the tribe up there, but wasn't sure how. All her inquiries met with silence or flat refusals.

She had tried the Vilas County Sheriff's Office, but they had been in disarray following the death of Sheriff Bunche and the new man, Arnow, had apparently moved her requests from a "maybe" pile to the round file.

Now there was something else going on in Vilas County. Word was just filtering south about a series of violent murders. Was it a coincidence that Nick Lupo was also there?

This was just too much. Barrett decided to learn something for herself. She couldn't have Don Bowen back, that was a given. He had retired and moved away, leaving no forwarding address. She couldn't reignite the flame she had only shared with one man. But she could have revenge on the one who had cheated her out of everything good in her life. If he was into something else up here, she wanted to catch him at it.

She heard the quiet roar of the Lexus engine under the hood and would have been surprised to see that she was smiling widely, a little crazily. She glanced at the passenger seat, where her purse sagged with the weight of her Glock. Don had made her an expert, and she was grateful.

Speeding up to pass slower traffic, she felt the wheels dragging her closer to the secret at the heart of Dominic Lupo's life.

Chapter Sixteen

Lupo
1977

The Creature hit the road but didn't follow its usual path of side streets to the expansive park it considered its own territory. This time the Creature was motivated by feelings beyond itself, beyond its simple needs of flesh and blood for sustenance.

Its four paws followed a certain road it remembered from somewhere. A certain street. The scents were familiar. The houses dark, the streetlights progressively less reliable, broken, simply dead, but the Creature felt no fear. Dogs barked and whined as it passed, but it paid no heed. Occasionally it raised a leg and marked, knowing his domesticated cousins would cower at the scent. He howled once and the others fell silent, afraid.

Suddenly a hated scent filled its nostrils. Hate exploded in its brain and threatened to consume it from within.

It padded softly behind the structure in front of which it had halted. There was no mistaking this scent. The Creature growled. It reached the flat, grassy area behind the structure and saw:

A wide, wooden table used as a bench by two humans huddled so close together they might have been one.

A female, fear and hate radiating from her in waves. A male—the Hated One—dipping a spadelike hand beneath the female's clothing and inside her birth canal.

Lust radiated from the Hated One, lust and malicious glee. The female pushed him away, but he was too strong.

"Come on, Beth Ann," he whined, "you got no reason to put me off like this. We been here before."

The Creature heard the words, but understood only their tone. It growled softly.

"Goddammit, let me in there, you slut!" the male said, his wheedling tone turning to anger. "You given it up plenty with other guys. Don't think I ain't heard all about it."

"Ow, you're hurting me!"

"Serves you right, bitch."

"I'm gonna scream . . ."

"No, you won't, 'cause you'll get a reputation. I'll make fuckin' sure of that, you cunt. Now, open them knees."

As the two humans struggled on the table, neither noticed the Creature stalking them.

The anger, the hate, the scent, what the male was trying to do, all exploded simultaneously within the Creature. He growled deeply and leaped.

The girl human screamed and fell off the table. She ran and the Creature let her.

The Hated One stood his ground. Though surprised and suddenly afraid, he scrabbled for something inside his clothes.

But the Creature reached him first, his jaws open and tearing even as their bodies made contact.

The human first grunted, then screamed as the Creature sank his teeth into the white flesh of his neck, tearing repeatedly at the tissue, raising a cloud of blood and meat.

His mouth open in a silenced scream, Leo stared into the wolf's eyes.

The blood smell maddened the wolf even more, and it snapped downward, ripping off a chunk of fleshy neck that included Leo's Adam's apple and much of the throat. Then the Creature shook the human's body like a twig before burying its snout in the flabby abdomen, seeking out the organs.

Leo's screams dwindled to croaking, and then they died along with him.

The Creature fed, unhurried, a strange pleasure overlaying its appetite fulfillment mechanism. It did not dwell on this new development, but a small portion of its brain seemed to understand.

House lights came on and the Creature bolted after ripping off one more great bite. It disappeared into the night.

When Nick awoke, naked, stretched out in his backyard, the first thing he felt after the cold on his skin was the remains of bloody flesh in his mouth. He knew immediately that it wasn't the usual taste of rabbit on his tongue.

Shivering in the late August night chill, he checked for pain. *No pain.*

But the taste in his mouth sickened him, and he fell to his knees retching. In a great gush he vomited up bits of bloody bone and meat.

The memory was hazy, but it was there in flashes.

Leo's horrified features.

Blood gushing from a torn neck.

All seen through alien eyes.

His eyes.

Nick knew *he* was the alien.

Thunder crashed overhead, then a steady rain began to wash over him as he brought up more of the contents of his stomach.

The rain would wash the gore into the summer grass. He hoped.

Nick coughed and gagged until he thought his chest would split. Then he stretched his head back and let the warm rain wash his face like never-ending tears.

He was disgusted, but for the wrong reason. He felt happy for the first time in weeks. Spitting the taste of Leo out of his system, a strange sense of pride overwhelmed him from some dark place in his soul.

He grinned, the rain cleansing his bloody mouth and teeth.

Leo's death was blamed on the rabid dog described by a shaken Beth Ann. The animal was never found, though nearby homes were relieved of their larger canines for testing. By the end of the summer, no one remembered Leo all that clearly. And his daily victims felt free to breathe fresh air again without fear of his bullying.

A much quieter Beth Ann ignored all her old friends, met a new boyfriend, and died when his old Norton motorcycle wiped out on a wet autumn day and slid under an out-of-state semitrailer. It was said the two young people were decapitated, but no one ever confirmed the fact.

Nick's grief was all-encompassing, but he shared it with no one. He let it eat away at him, like so many other things.

CHAPTER SEVENTEEN

Lupo

They drove to Jessie's early, after making sure Sam and his charges were all right. During the drive, Arnow reached them on Lupo's cell.

"Got another one," he said. His voice sounded as if he'd gargled with gravel. Exhaustion poured from each inflection. "We've already secured the crime scene. It's like the others, except at the end they were, uh, more creative." He went on to explain.

"Jesus, who was it?"

Jessie stiffened beside him.

"Uh, Smith. Daniel Bear Smith. He put up a hell of a fight, but they made him pay for it."

"Any evidence we can use?"

"Same stuff. I made sure the boys were careful, but frankly, I don't know if it'll ever help us. I still don't have anything from the labs. Well, they called and said they'd have to do more tests. Sounded a little flummoxed. You guys don't get so much crime up here, eh?"

"Might be more than that, Arnow."

"How do you mean?"

Lupo glanced at Jessie as he drove. He shrugged as if Arnow could see him. "Hard to say." *The labs didn't know what to make of the evidence.*

"You know something? Out with it, man. I've got a death toll here."

Lupo glanced at Jessie. "Maybe we can help, after all. You've got to trust me. *Us*. Dr. Hawkins, too. It's not something you can do over the phone."

Arnow swore. "There's always a price."

"Something like that."

"What are you planning, Nick?" Jessie asked after he'd clicked off.

"What we talked about originally, but I want to bring Arnow into it. Completely."

They argued heatedly for the next twenty miles of winding roads.

Finally, he said, "There's no choice! It could take me days to track them all down. I don't know what the Altima driver looks like. He may be wounded, but I'm not sure. I know who the Alpha must be. Wilson's boyfriend may be the other, but there could be more than three. I just don't know."

"So then we go the vigilante route? Are you prepared for the consequences?"

"We—*I* don't have any experience with others of my kind. Hell, I didn't know there were any." He made a face. "They clearly do. They have the advantage here. If we're not careful, we could attack the wrong humans. Do we want to take the risk? So the answer is to take them down as wolves. But when they're wolves, they're incredibly efficient. And brutally sadistic." He told her what they'd done to Smith and she paled.

"There are three of us," she pointed out. "We could ambush them somehow, without involving Tom."

He was thoughtful. "Three against three. Sounds good at first. But even with the silver, their odds are better. They're like a military unit. In fact, I think they are ex-military."

"What can Tom do? If we bring him in, I mean."

"First, not arrest us for multiple murder. Second, he may be able to sneak some silver ammo into his men's guns even if they don't know it. Could mean the difference between life and death. Ours. And it'll protect the cops. They haven't attacked cops yet, but they could start if we get too close.

And Arnow says something's holding up the samples. They're dead in the water, Jess. And if the feds or state cops show, we'll never get them to silver up or listen to anything we say."

Silence enveloped them for a while.

Then Jessie said, with resignation, "I can't believe all those good people are dead. We have to stop them before there's no council left."

Lupo could see she was conflicted, but he had thought it through. He hated his solution more than she could ever know.

"Call Sam and give him the news," he said. "Then tell him we'll set it up with Arnow and swing by later on to pick him up. He'll have to leave Grey Hawk a silver-loaded shotgun and instructions to shoot at anything that moves."

She started to shake her head. "But—"

"Jess, we're running out of choices. And time."

He turned onto Circle Moon Drive, and for a second the idyllic cottages in their placid pine groves calmed his nerves.

Sam Waters

He could barely believe what Jessie told him. Lupo was willing to go public. And with a cop? Was he crazy? He sensed from her tone that they'd wrangled over it and he had won.

Jesus, sometimes he wished he could call in James Bond.

Then again, maybe Lupo *was* Bond. Sort of.

"Listen, Bill," he said. "Let me show you how the shotgun works."

He spent the next half hour instructing, trying to calm their fears. He wanted to tell them he and his friends knew what they were doing.

But did they really?

Julia Barrett

Lupo's black Maxima pulled out of Circle Moon Drive just minutes after she arrived.

She had barely taken the time to check into her Days Inn motel, fix her makeup, peer at her chamber of commerce city map and figure out where his place was, and then she had headed straight over.

No illusions. *Maybe he is just here to bang his girlfriend.*

She winced. That was how Don would have put it, the old cop coming out in him. But really, she expected that's what she would find, despite the strange happenings just beginning to hit the news down south. Lupo had connections with the tribe up here. He'd not likely be killing anybody on the rez.

Would he?

She followed, keeping just to the other side of the narrow lane's winding curves so he'd get only an occasional glimpse. She was a psychiatrist first, then a cop, but she knew a few tricks.

Lupo's windows were tinted, but she thought his chick was in there with him. They seemed to be headed to town, turning onto moderately busy Highway 70.

Barrett had no idea what she'd accomplish or how long it would take, but she'd signed out for a week's vacation and figured in a day or two she might catch Lupo at something.

She swore as he suddenly crossed lanes and pulled into Bill's Bait and Booze. Figures, she thought. Only up here in redneck-land would they sell bait in a liquor store. Or vice versa. Oh, and fireworks, the sign also promised.

She had no choice but to keep driving, since there was some dimwit riding her bumper. She'd noticed here they all tailgated constantly. She sped up and tried to put some space between her and her idiot. She spotted a gas station a ways up to the left. She could pretend to gas up and wait for Lupo there, catch him as he went past.

She pulled into the station and up to a rusty pump and swore again. The idiot tailgater pulled up behind her, his dark SUV filling up her mirror. Now she had to pump some gas, or he'd make a fuss.

Shit.

She jumped out and grabbed the nearest nozzle, keeping an eye on the highway.

"Nice day for early spring, isn't it?"

She whirled. It was the idiot, trying to make conversation. Just what she needed!

"This is nice?" she said, frowning. "It's cold."

"January—now that's cold," said the guy.

He was tallish and big-boned, reminding her of Don, though Don's hair had been salt-and-pepper while this guy's was almost red and thinning rapidly. His watery eyes lingered on her face. He smiled at her self-consciously.

"Whatever," she muttered.

"You from far away?" he said amiably.

"Uh, yeah, just passing through."

Her tank was almost full, so the pump made a *thunk* and stopped before hitting her wallet too hard. She wished he'd get the message and leave her alone. She turned away pointedly, slid her credit card into an iffy-looking slot, completed the transaction, grateful it worked, then nodded at the guy who still stood by, looking hopeful.

Pathetic, more like.

"Have a nice day!" he called as she lunged into her car just in time to see the black Maxima draw even with the station. Seconds later, she was pulling onto the highway behind Lupo, barely the worse for wear.

"Lead on, Nick Lupo and chick," she mumbled.

Lupo

"We've got a silver Lexus on our tail, I think," Lupo said. "If this guy doesn't get off my ass soon, I'm going to have to take evasive maneuvers."

"And you hate that," Jessie said. She glanced back without turning her head too much. "Recognize the car at all?"

"I do hate it. Driving is DiSanto's thing. He went to school for police driving. He's much better at it than I am." He looked in the mirror. "It looks familiar, I guess. Can't think where I might have seen it."

The car seemed to stick to them closely for about a mile, and kept coming.

"I think it's been with us since around Circle Moon. Not one of your neighbors, is it?

"Don't think so."

Suddenly Lupo pulled across the oncoming lane and turned into a half-circle driveway with an island of pines making up the center.

"We're stopping at Bill's? Need some worms?"

"There's enough worms in the county to last me a lifetime," he said, pulling up to the door of the long, narrow clapboard store and parking. "How do you know I don't need booze?"

Jessie turned and squinted, laughing. "Oh, it's going straight."

Lupo grinned. "Guess we're getting a little paranoid."

She agreed.

He gave it about five minutes, then pulled back onto the road.

Julia Barrett

There was something wrong with the car.

The vibration caught her by surprise. She had the damn thing serviced on schedule, obsessively. But now it rode rough and next thing she knew she heard the tire pop and had to steer hard for the shoulder, hearing the gravel crunch underneath.

"Goddammit!" she shouted, watching Lupo's Maxima turn with the road and disappear. She'd never catch him now. "Goddamn, goddamn, *goddamn.*" She usually tended toward a physical temper tantrum that would damage any man within punching range. So she made fists now, but beat them uselessly in the air.

Then she saw a dark shape pull up behind her.

Great! Somebody stopping to help.

Maybe she could still catch up to Lupo.

She leaped out, but her heart sank when she saw it was the red-haired idiot tailgater. The breeze lifted his thin red hair, and she figured it was a piece.

"Goddamn," she whispered but then forced a fake smile.

"Need some help?" the big lug called out, approaching.

No, I'm going to fucking sit here in my goddamn car all day and night with a flat goddamn tire. These people were *idiots.*

"Yes, thanks! My tire blew out."

"I can see that."

Guy was a genius. *Save me from these yokels.*

He was even with her now. "Got a jack and a spare? I'll get you on the road again in a minute. Well, maybe five minutes."

She almost swore. "Uh, yeah, here in the trunk." She popped it and reached inside to where, unlike many people, she knew exactly where her jack was stored in its hidden compartment. "Here it is," she said.

And then a loud noise exploded in her ear.

Except it wasn't a noise, it was something very hard smacking solidly into the side of her head.

The pain shot through her in a blinding jab, and she sagged to the ground.

A half-formed thought about helpful yokels died along with her consciousness.

CHAPTER EIGHTEEN

From the Journals of Caroline Stewart
April 1981

Nick has been accepted to the police academy, and I hope that will turn out to be a good thing.

I hope so, because his will to find ways to "make amends" for his condition is touching. We've proven that his physical abilities are greatly affected by his lycanthropic powers, though control is still elusive. However, I expect he will be an outstanding cadet and probably a very good officer. He has great will to do the right thing.

But I'm frightened by the possibility that he will be unable to control his urges.

Nick Lupo is certainly NOT a monster, but the Creature he carries inside is wild and unpredictable—even savage. His memories of hunting in wolf form are harrowing for an animal lover like me. When the wolf "romps" (Nick's word), his prey consists of rabbits, deer, etc. If there were elk in these woods, he'd go for that, too. Nick says the wolf occasionally wants farm animals and domestic pets. He's not sure whether he was able to thwart the wolf, or if that side of him just prefers wild food . . . but clearly this topic is very troublesome to Nick, and he changes the subject whenever I bring it up. He becomes defensive and uncomfortable, and though he wants to be trusted, he can't quite be sure he can be, so he seeks classic avoidance. I've let it go, but planted the seeds of (what

I hope) will be some techniques for control. He'll have to try them on his own.

Having brought up "techniques," I should mention here that I've started to try convincing him to undergo regression therapy. A friend and colleague of mine here at the U whose work in that field is notable, is willing to take the case. So far, Nick refuses. I'll continue trying to convince him. I believe the therapy could be the breakthrough he needs to learn more about himself.

Chapter Nineteen

Lupo

Arnow pulled up next to the Maxima in the wayside parking lot and glared at the three of them as if they had morphed into space aliens. The lot was screened from the main road by a thick stand of pines, and they were alone.

"Look," he growled through his open window. "I've got dead people everywhere and very little time for games. I thought you could lend a hand, Lupo, but so far you've just shown up at a crime scene looking thoughtful. You gave me some runaround about weird shit that's supposed to help. If you know something about that kid, or any other possible suspects, give it the fuck up. My apologies, Dr. Hawkins." He glanced at Sam and said nothing.

Lupo hesitated. This was his baby. Jessie had given in, but Sam had argued against it all the way.

"How can you be sure he won't hunt you down, like I once tried to do?" Sam had protested.

"I can't," Lupo admitted. "But if we help him stop the bastards, he'll be too grateful."

"You hope," Jessie added.

"I could say some crap about hope, but I won't. I'm too much a pessimist." Nick winked at them. "Don't worry, he'll be all right."

"It's not *him* we're worried about," Sam muttered.

Lupo's hands and scalp tingled unpleasantly. But it wasn't

as painful as the deep scratches in his back where the other wolf had caught him. No, that was a lot worse, and he sensed how close he'd been to a broken back. The wounds had closed, but they still ached sharply deep inside, like arthritis. He'd never tangled with another werewolf before, and now he would have to do so again.

Of course, his early morning session with Jessie in the confined space of the Maxima hadn't helped. Not his back, anyway.

"Arnow, I know it sounds kooky, but bear with me. You know deep down these murders don't look right. They're not normal. So you've got to start looking for the abnormal. Reason I have the doctor and Mr. Waters here is to be my witnesses that I'm trying to tell you the truth."

Arnow tapped his hands on his steering wheel, anger etched on his tired face. "Okay, fine, I'll grant that nothing looks right. The victims are torn up, there's no usable evidence at the scene, there's some kind of motive built into the casino project, but I can't put my finger on it. And the damned lab's not getting back to me. I'm in some kind of weird limbo. So when you gonna show me something that'll start setting me straight?"

"Right now." Lupo got out of the Maxima and waited for Jessie and Sam to join him. Sam went for the trunk, which he had popped. Lupo could feel the heat radiating from there and stepped away hastily.

Arnow climbed out and stretched his entire length. The weariness lay on him like a blanket. He looked like a man haunted by circumstances. His red-rimmed eyes indicated there had been no sleep within recent memory.

"Fine, now what?" the sheriff said as he watched Sam lift a shotgun from the Maxima's trunk. The thought was clear as it passed across his features—were they planning to kill him and bury his body near the wayside?

Lupo kept away from Sam and also mostly out of sight of Arnow. "Sheriff, we tried to tell you something about the nature of your murderers. We're not profilers, but in a minute you'll see why this case has to be handled differently from what you're used to. My friend Sam is here to make sure nothing happens to you or anyone else during this little demonstration." He started to strip, keeping behind the car so the cop couldn't see him clearly. "Even though I thought it would be the last thing I'd ever do, now I think it's the only way to convince you."

"Whatever it is, get it done so I can get back in time to mop up another crime scene." Arnow looked at his watch pointedly, though it was obvious the trio was beginning to pique his interest.

Lupo gave Sam and Jessie the signal and they stepped closer to Arnow. Sam cradled the shotgun expertly. He was the pistol in the lion-tamer's belt, ready to take down the beast if necessary.

This was new to Lupo. He'd never had an audience, except for Caroline. He cleared his mind as much as he could, eventually leaving behind human thought. He summoned the Creature from the depths, wherever it hid, visualizing himself on four legs.

At first he thought he couldn't do it with people watching, but then he felt the mushy invisible wall he crossed from one form to another, and in a few seconds he was running as a human—

The Creature answered the unusual call . . .

—and then he loped off on four paws toward the woods opposite of the highway.

The sensory blast cleared his nostrils and brought the multitude of smells into his brain. He sensed and remembered the silver in the long gun held by the old man—

Sam, a friend . . .

—and he could smell the sex of the woman, his mate, and the suddenly frightened presence of the stranger near the cars.

He snarled once, over his shoulder. Normally he avoided humans, but the union of Lupo and Creature was slowly beginning to favor Lupo.

He reached for the woods and leaped into the underbrush, a howl of joy torn from his throat.

Julia Barrett

Jabbing pain in her head awoke her.

She groaned, but the sound was swallowed by the duct tape stretched across her lips.

Her crusted eyelids opened slowly, but as her eyes focused, they bulged at what she saw.

She was immobile, her head facing sideways. A few feet away, a girl—*what used to be a girl*—lay duct taped to a red hand truck, flaps of skin folded down, slashes across her body at irregular intervals, and wounds too grotesque to even contemplate. Barrett's breath hitched in her throat, and she almost choked.

Breathe through your nose!

Breathe!

She recovered, snatched some air through her nostrils, then continued to check her fellow prisoner.

She had to be dead.

Barrett no sooner thought this than the girl's eyes popped open in a monstrous blink, like something out of a horror movie.

Barrett jumped, startled, and felt a trickle between her legs.

Apparently you really could piss yourself, she observed in her professional mode. In her personal mode, she started to thrash around, realizing soon enough that she, too, was duct taped to what was probably a hand truck. The rigid metal bars that cradled her were cold and harsh on her bony frame. They were frighteningly unyielding. Like the one nearby, her hand truck was angled about forty-five degrees by being hooked to a kind of sawhorse bar.

She sagged, giving up the thrashing to conserve strength. She looked around. Long fluorescents above gave everything in the cone of light a harsh greenish tone. It was a typical farmhouse basement, bare walls and a dirt floor. The walls were painted with spattered blood that had dried black. A cart held a small flat-screen television, which now showed silent gray snow. A TV tray held grimy implements of a surgical nature.

Tears squeezed from between Barrett's lids.

This was an experienced torturer.

Christ, whatever Lupo was into up here, she sure wished she could see him now, bursting through the door and rescuing her and the poor wretch nearby.

But he didn't even know she was here, spying on him, and if he did, he loathed her enough that he would probably have let her die.

She prided herself on her toughness. But now she cried like a helpless child.

In essence, that's what I've become. Complete reversion.

The girl taped to the next hand truck stared through her. The eyes might as well not have been open at all. Her facial muscles seemed to have been severed. She was a living corpse.

I must have showed up just when he was trolling for his next victim. He probably used to space them apart by long periods, but now he's given in to his urges and has started to overlap them. He can't help himself.

Maybe she could use that knowledge.

She fixed his features in her memory. The reddish hair, an obvious hairpiece. Large frame, tallish. Thin legs. Very average. A typical American. He'd slide under most radar screens as if he wasn't there. The perfect serial killer.

And here he had an assembly-line torture factory.

Barrett circled her eyes to their widest angle, ignoring the thrusting pain in her head. Whatever he'd hit her with had laid her open and scrambled something in the side of her face, but she could still use her brain.

Dear God, was that her purse lying on the dirt floor near her feet?

If he hadn't opened it, her Glock was still there.

She slowly rolled her legs and body in order to loosen the duct tape. If he bought cheap, she might loosen enough to squirm out from under it. Her clothing was loose, so there was a chance to slip out of the garments and leave them behind. She set her mind to working toward that goal and had been doing it a half hour when a shaft of light fell on her from behind, and she sensed a door opening.

She went limp, pretending unconsciousness.

"I'm back, Courtney and guest!" His voice sent shivers down her back. If only she hadn't stopped for gas. She should have ignored the tailgating asshole!

He was babbling now, mostly to the other girl, whose eyes and body no longer acknowledged anything. Her beating heart seemed a mere formality.

He likes to know their names. If he goes into my purse, I'm done for.

She felt him sidle near. He breathed over her for a few minutes, watching. She faked being out, and he must have bought it, because he started to undo her tape job. As tape fell off, she felt metal touch her skin. He was using shears to cut through both tape and clothing.

Careless idiot!

A mouth-breather, too.

Perhaps he'd been in a hurry and had intended his tape job on her to be temporary. He wanted her nude while still knocked out. Then he would retape her, and the torture would begin. She prepared for the right moment.

As soon as he'd removed most of her skirt and the tape, she sprang off the hand truck, naked but motivated by an adrenaline rush of fear and determination.

Arnow

Later he would feel embarrassed. He was shocked seeing the naked cop running, and instinctively he turned to make a lame joke about living in the city too long.

But then the air rippled around the running man, and *just*

like that! he disappeared and in his place was an animal on four paws, a black wolf larger than any he had ever seen.

Arnow sat down on his ass hard enough to feel the cracked asphalt dig into his buttocks through his uniform pants. It felt weird, as if moving in slow-motion.

"Jesus Christ!" he blurted. "What the fuck?"

He looked around for some sort of CGI rig. What kind of smoke-and-mirrors gag was at work here? But the grim faces discouraged him.

"What—what was that?" His voice was a croak. "What the hell was that?"

Jessie Hawkins turned her lovely face toward him, and he tried to focus on what she said. She seemed very uncomfortable. He couldn't shake the sight of the man he knew as Nick Lupo blurring and then turning into a wolf. Jesus, this was more than he could handle.

Jessie was still talking, trying to get his attention. "Tom. Tom, that's what you're up against, except that Detective Lupo is not the enemy. He's not one of *them*. But there is a group—*a pack*—and they're killing the tribal council one by one."

"What—what is he?"

Sam still cradled the shotgun as he scanned the trees. "I'm sorry, but we call that a werewolf, Sheriff, and it's not something any of us wanted to acknowledge, either." Sam's eyes welled up. "The story's long and tragic, and I won't bore you with it now. My son was infected with a disease many years ago, and it eventually passed on to an innocent youth—Nick. I had to put my son down with my own hands, Sheriff. I know how this must look, but we really haven't got time to tell you everything."

Arnow shook his head to clear it. He rolled himself slowly, painfully, to his feet. "What—How the fuck am I supposed to fight *that?*" he growled. "Assuming I accept any of what you're saying?"

Sam tilted up the shotgun. "Silver buckshot in my shells, Sheriff. That's how, just like all the B movies. But there's no shooting at Detective Lupo, even when he looks like *that.* He's one of the good guys. I hope we can convince you."

Arnow reflected that perhaps the only two people in the entire county who might were standing in front of him.

"When is he coming back?" he asked.

"He's going to hunt and work on tracking the other werewolves, Tom. We're leaving him be for a while."

"Can he control that *thing?*" He waved a hand. "That thing he turns into."

"Not always," Sam said. "Hence the shotgun."

"Jesus," said Arnow again, staring at the trees where the wolf had disappeared. "All right, fill me in."

"Let's get back to town first," Jessie said. "We have to try to keep the remaining council members alive. Eagle Feather and Davison, and the Grey Hawk family. We've got Grey Hawk covered. He doesn't know it, but he's got just the right ammo." She handed him two boxes of Remington shells. "Take these now. Twelve-gauge. Maybe you can issue these to your men, or sneak them into their guns. Tell them to use their riot guns. Otherwise they'll never kill the wolves."

Stunned, Arnow took them. "You're telling me regular ammo won't—"

"Nope," Sam said.

"Why is this shit happening? Why in *my* county?"

"We don't know," Jessie said. "Something to do with the casino?"

"Not sure what's slated to happen after the council is gone," Sam added. "There's got to be a motive for all this death, but—"

"Yeah," Arnow said, "you don't know it."

Jessie had Lupo's keys. "Let's get back, Tom."

Arnow looked at the two of them, hysteria rising in his throat like a bitter column of bile. He was shaken, his world tilted, his understanding of reality was now warped forever. He wasn't sure he'd ever recover.

But he couldn't deny the evidence seen with his own eyes. He brushed off his uniform pants and headed for his cruiser, feeling somehow diminished in the face of the universe.

Now *anything* was possible.

Julia Barrett

Hampered by the angle, she fell off the cart sideways—but under his desperate grasp.

She rolled away, her cart moving backward and striking the other hand truck. The implement tray went flying in a shower of clanging metal. Her captor was tangled up in the metallic mess, but already gathering himself for pursuit.

She faked him out by rolling back toward him, and he overshot her naked body just as she snatched up her purse and felt the weight of the Glock still inside.

After fumbling with the zipper, she reached in while her attacker grasped a metal bar. He swung it, and its long reach caught her a glancing blow on the shoulder. The gun, barely clutched, flew into the shadows, and she growled in frustrated pain and anger.

They faced each other briefly, his eyes crazed, and then he attacked with the bar and feinted, this time catching her across the side of the head when she fell for it.

She felt her skin rip open and hot blood rush down her face like a warm caress.

He pressed his advantage and backed her toward the wall, where bare cinder block ground into her shoulder blades. Keenly aware of the bloodstains behind her, she realized she was adding to the grotesque art gallery with her own life's blood.

His rancid breath and bulging eyes came closer as he pressed the bar two-handed into her throat.

She kneed upward and caught his groin hard enough to throw him off, grabbing the bar from him and giving him a backhand stroke across the side of the head that sidelined him into the wall headfirst. She barely noticed her feet being slit open by the spilled scalpels and sundry blades that littered the floor.

The Glock lay behind him, and he was already recovering. He grasped the bar before she could swing it again and tore it from her grip. Assessing the situation, Barrett let the Glock go and made for the doorway he'd come from, slipping through only seconds before him. She turned and kicked him with a bleeding foot, sending him flying backward into the basement.

Regretfully, she reached ground level and followed the hallway to the front door and out, stumbling down off the porch and into the woods.

Regretful because she wanted to recover her Glock and empty it into him.

But out was out, and she wasn't going back until she had the local cops with her. If she found her way through these damned trees.

Her feet throbbing, sliding, leaving bloody chunks behind on the forest floor, she ran blind, letting whiplike branches slit her skin further. Ragged breathing flew behind her, and she realized it was hers.

Unmindful of the slashing undergrowth, she ran on into the woods.

Lupo

From his cover in the trees, Lupo watched them go. It had gone better than he expected. After racing nearly a mile in the Creature's body, he had pulled the reins and returned to the wayside, Changed again, and waited to see what would happen. The Creature was confused, questioning, but it accepted. His clothes would go home with Jessie, so he would head back out into the forest to seek out the enemy.

Jessie's jealousy of Heather Wilson aside, would he be able to save the reporter from the bastard? She seemed in control of whatever was happening between them. Maybe she was a part of it. But her ambition was narcissistic—she wanted television fame, not the tabloid kind.

For now, Lupo accepted that they were still at a disadvantage. No evidence, no chance of a judge granting warrants against the Altima driver or the kid. Or the anonymous older man he'd seen lecturing the kid. No way to legally search their house on Hemlock, if that was their base. No, even with Arnow marginally on board, they were now vigilantes. Nothing else. There was no other way to deal with this situation, and now was the time. If Arnow's reinforcements suddenly arrived in the form of state police or even feds, they'd get in the way and nothing would get done, and everybody on the death list would die. Lupo was sure there'd be no chance of subjecting these killers to regular justice. He and Jessie had gone back and forth on this, but even though she was right—his approach was risky and not constitutional—he couldn't come up with a better way. Would feds and state cops ever be convinced to use silver ammunition? Would they acknowledge the obvious when it threatened to rattle their rational outlook?

Doubtful.

In fact, it was fucking unlikely.

Lupo's method was the only way left.

And Lupo's method was to ambush the bastards and kill them all. *No quarter.*

He wondered if Jessie would ever look at him in the same way again.

Chapter Twenty

From the Journals of Caroline Stewart
September 23, 1981

I'm almost at a loss for words. Today Nick's first regression session was a disaster. Dr. Jerry Boone is a colleague I trust implicitly, so I had great hopes for Nick's therapy. Unfortunately, bringing Nick back to when he was bitten by the neighbor boy who carried the illness and spread it to Nick before being killed, turned out to be just too traumatic.

November 19, 1981

True, I pressured Nick into the regression, and I swore Boone to secrecy regarding what Nick might reveal. Afterward, Boone seemed frightened—no, terrified. I tried to ask him what had happened in the session, what Nick said that caused Boone—usually the most unflappable guy in the room—to react with such fear. But he stuttered that he couldn't tell me due to his confidentiality concerns. Which was the right answer, but still not what I wanted to hear. He was a bit of a stiff, Jerry Boone, but his integrity was solid.

Of course, I suspected what might have caused this reaction. Knowing Nick's secret, I could imagine what he might have blurted out. For some reason, it didn't occur to me until much later that maybe the session had triggered a change, right there in Boone's office.

I'd guess that would have torn a large rift in Boone's view of the world.

I'm so smitten with Nick that I didn't press him when he refused to tell me. I wasn't always thinking straight. Our love had blossomed, and our bond had strengthened to the point where I trusted Nick's word—or his silence—as much as I would have trusted my own. Maybe naively, I believed that Nick's one session had been a failed experiment and his reluctance to talk about it was ultimately of no concern.

Now, two months later, I understand how foolish I was and how blinded I had become.

Today I learned that Dr. Jerry Boone was found in his East Side office, shot with his own handgun in an apparent suicide. That office was the very same place Nick visited in September for his one and only session. Boone left no note, no clue as to what caused him to take his own life, except that he had pulled every single book off his office shelves. Dozens of books, all flung to the floor as if in anger.

The police will investigate Boone's patient list, but the trail won't lead to Nick because his session was kept strictly off the books. Boone had a crush on me, and I used him ruthlessly.

Nick was sincerely distraught when I told him, but I can't deny that he also appeared relieved.

Only now with hindsight do I wish I had thought through my bright-eyed theory. As much as I love Nick, I don't know that I can trust the Creature he harbors within. I don't know that Nick himself trusts that Creature.

Did Nick drive Dr. Boone to suicide?

I may never know, but I suspect I'll always have the niggling thought at the back of my mind.

Maybe I didn't pull the trigger, but I might have loaded the gun.

And I'll always feel guilty.

Chapter Twenty-one

Tannhauser

He was nearly done stitching the wound where the Indian bastard had sliced him with that silver-bladed knife.

The pain was exquisite, but it reminded him that they took too much for granted.

Just how many people in this place knew about werewolves? He'd taken the job figuring they had a natural advantage, but suddenly the field was crowded with enemies.

His skin had sizzled under the silver blade. He held the last bit of blackened edges together and made one more stitch, then knotted it.

Where was Tef? Half day's liberty, probably carousing. He hadn't been right in the head since they'd left Iraq. Tannhauser knew he should watch his back. The kid was sniffing around for an opportunity to challenge.

Now he needed Schwartz more than ever.

Julia Barrett

Darkness advancing. The forest floor nothing but clumps of long shadows.

A light in the sky indicated moonrise. It meant nothing to her.

No idea how long she'd been running. No idea what direction or how many directions.

Naked, bleeding, sweating.

Barrett realized she'd reverted to some sort of primal version of herself. She'd bared her teeth at the motherfucker like an animal.

But *he* was the animal.

He was a predator, and she refused to be his victim. She was nobody's victim. Damn them all, including the coward Bowen, and Lupo and his enabler partners.

She'd been running so long, afraid to hear his tread behind her, that she didn't even realize her feet were a mess of open wounds and slashes. She was weakening, the blood loss finally getting to her. A bony frame didn't help. She'd been strong, stronger than the bastard expected, but now she wished she had some reserves of stamina to draw from, but she didn't.

Had she been able to consult a map, she would have realized that she'd run in a chain of tiny little circles on a roughly southeasterly course between Dollar Lake and Eagle Lake, which would have pegged where her attacker plied his trade. Now she spotted moonlight glinting off water on her left. She followed it as best she could. These yokel fishing-type bastards always built on the water, so she'd run into some kind of habitation sometime.

A phone and then a police raid. They had a sheriff here. She'd lead him right to the predator.

Suddenly she broke through the tree line and stumbled forward into a clearing, startled by the lack of obstacles. A dark house stood before her.

Weeping with joy, she dragged herself to the back door and started pounding with weakened, bloody fists.

Jessie

She drove Lupo's Maxima back to town, following Arnow to the courthouse and leaving him there before heading back to Sam's.

Arnow was shell-shocked. The term dated back to World War One, but it fit Arnow's glazed look perfectly. She'd left him with a warning to remember that Nick Lupo was one of the good guys. He agreed, but his distant look spoke to how hard they'd rocked his worldview.

There was a desperate quality to the way he looked at her when she left him. She knew he'd been attracted to her from the beginning. Maybe it would have worked out if she hadn't had Nick.

She followed the side roads that led around the lakes and channels, past the resorts, toward Circle Moon Drive. She wasn't sure when she became aware of the shadow pacing her, but every time she glanced out the window, she sensed rather than saw a shape loping along with the car.

Nick?

Or . . . ?

She wished the shotgun was in the car with her rather than in the trunk.

The shadow paced her for a few more minutes, then faded deeper into the woods.

She breathed out in a rush, suddenly aware that she'd been holding her breath.

Arnow

The bottom drawer of his desk called to him. There was brandy there. Brandy was his drink of choice. He resisted, switching his interest to the shotgun shells Jessie had given him. He set them down.

Jesus, what was he supposed to do, believe that crap they were selling?

He sat and put his hands on his head.

No, he shouldn't believe it. But he'd seen it with his eyes. No drinking. *But no sleep, either.* Had he been dreaming, hallucinating?

A man turning into a wolf? Something out of kids' books.

And there were more of them?

But he'd seen it clearly enough. Dammit, his eyes didn't lie.

And in a crazy sort of way, it explained the crime scenes better than any of the logical, practical, realistic theories he had constructed.

He stood so suddenly that his head spun for a second. He couldn't be seen like this by his men. He emptied half a box of Sam Waters's special shells and filled the loops on his old-fashioned gun belt, then spilled a few more into his pocket. He'd figure out a way to spread them around later.

First he had to make a call. The mayor had left a message looking for an update.

Jesus!

Death, death, and more death.

How's that for a report?

There wasn't a lot more he could say. A couple of the surviving council members were under protection of sorts. Sam's cottage was remote, according to Jessie. There was a family huddled there. And a couple of the others were together, watching each other's back. Arnow didn't have the manpower to patrol and also protect. He accepted that now. It was time for action; no more cleaning up crime scenes. He had to get ahead of the game.

He thought a few things through, made a mental inventory, then made his phone call.

Out in the squad room, he saw Faber and Arrales, both so weary they seemed to sway. Or maybe he was swaying. Phone in hand, he waved them in. Now to get them to switch the ammo in their riot guns.

Meanwhile, he spoke into the phone.

Tannhauser

Running, running, running through the woods. He felt the wound healing. It was his mind-set, his age, his experience. Wounds healed faster when in wolfskin, so he'd gone out running in the hope of finding Tef and leading him in. And sure enough, he'd found the kid playing with that car, shadowing it and taking a huge risk. Tannhauser caught a slight scent of silver from the rear of that car. Did everyone around here carry a stash?

He nosed Tef's gray wolf away from the road and led him back to the Hemlock house.

Julia Barrett

In the middle of scrabbling for a rock large enough to break into the house, she heard the door whip open behind her.

"Oh Jesus God!" she shrieked uncharacteristically, as she dropped the rock and dashed for the dark rectangle a skeletal hand held open.

"Thank God you're home," she blurted as she stumbled inside, naked and scratched, bruised and bleeding. She knew she must have looked hideous, but the thought of the depraved killer possibly only a few steps behind her propelled her into the darkness of the house. "Please, I need to call the police!"

She tried catching her breath, which came in ragged bursts.

A strange odor permeated the air. She tried to cover her genitals with her torn-up hands. And she turned her attention to the man who had opened the door. He still stood next to it, and she wished he would close it. Close it and bolt it, in case the maniac arrived. She paused and looked him up and down quickly.

He was gaunt, anemic looking. His skin was patchy with some sort of disease or bruises. His hair was thin and oily, sticking up in tufts, the sign of having just awakened.

She spoke fast. "I'm sorry to bother you, but thank you for opening your door. I'm not crazy or anything like that. I'm a police officer." She'd found that using her police status over her medical status worked wonders for people's cooperation. Of course, she was usually dressed and made up like a professional at those times, while right now she looked like an escaped lunatic. A *naked* lunatic. "Someone's following me, chasing me, trying to kill me," she blurted out. "I got away, ran through the woods. Ended up here, but I don't know where I am . . ."

Her voice faded, and her hands shifted nervously before dropping.

The man at the door was smiling.

Smiling!

He did not look convinced. Or interested. He only looked . . . What did he remind her of?

Hunger. He looked hungry. As she watched, he licked dry lips with a very long tongue.

"Of course I can help," he said in a whisper.

What was wrong with his voice?

Why did he look so close to death?

He started to close the door and, for a moment, she contemplated—*insanely!*—making a run for it and taking her chances outside, where *he* was most likely still on her trail. But suddenly she felt more threatened here, in this house. It was too late—the door was closing. She gathered her breath, made sure her hands were still covering her strategically, and then her mouth just fell open.

And what was left of her sanity deserted her, this time for good.

Two huge dogs loped in through the door, but as soon as they were inside, the air blurred around them and impossibly—for it *was* impossible!—they stood there as men, staring at her.

Naked men, she noticed.

One older, distinguished even in his nudity. An ugly black wound stretched across his chest. The other was much younger, punky, godlike . . .

And *oh so aroused.*

"Wha—" she blubbered, simply lacking words.

The older man turned to the one who had opened the door and spoke. Was it German? It sounded so military, so guttural. The sickly man responded in the same tongue. The younger man smiled at her, his huge gleaming erection drawing her eyes downward.

In a part of her mind, she forgot her own nakedness. She almost forgot her predicament. Her thoughts whirled. Nick Lupo was the reason she had come here, some vague sense of revenge, payback, in her angered mind. Now she understood that something else was happening, *happening to her.* All in a rush, she understood that she was looking at the cause of it all.

She was in the lion's mouth.

"An appropriate image," said the older man, switching to English. She must have spoken her thought aloud. He smiled too, and she couldn't help noticing that his gnarled penis was now engorged as well. Now they were all smiling at her, and new tears broke out on her streaked, bloody face.

The air blurred again and the men were gone, replaced by the savage dogs. Smiles turned into toothy grins on long snouts.

Julia Barrett's highly advanced mind recognized them as wolves and made numerous connections, numerous conclusions.

But it was too late.

The three wolves lunged, their jaws snapping.

They were no longer smiling.

Arnow

"Get your Remingtons."

He stared at their confused faces, letting them get uncomfortable.

"Remember the bad ammo I told you about last week? I got the replacement shipment."

Sure enough, neither wanted to admit he didn't know what the boss was talking about.

"Oh, yeah," said Arrales.

"Right, right," muttered Faber.

They hauled ass and returned with their shotguns, ejecting the shells from their magazines.

"Good job. Make sure you spread the word." He handed out the new shells and watched them jacked into the guns.

There was no need for further explanation when you were the boss. One of the few perks.

"I'm leaving these here on my desk. Make sure everybody else loads up."

"That all we have, boss?" Faber nodded at the yellow and green boxes.

"Uh, for now. It's just a demo batch. We'll get more."

"We planning a war, boss?"

"You've seen the crime scenes. We get lucky, you may get to use it when it counts."

They smiled through their fatigue, clearly excited.

Fools.

Tannhauser

Their employer's voice boomed into his ear. If not for the rather sizable secret payments, he might not have taken the call. "Yes."

"Two rings this time. Congratulations."

"Aim to please," he growled.

"Not always, in my experience. Nonetheless, I am calling because I, uh—well, I hesitate to speak of it, but—"

"But?"

"I have had a slight problem with, shall I say, a friend and playmate who wandered off. Sad to say, she was a bit bloody the last time I saw her, the result of an . . . accident that left her confused and disoriented."

Tannhauser laughed into the phone. "Ah, yes, the naked lady who appeared to have been *played* with?"

Pause. "Perhaps it's her," Mr. XYZ said cautiously. "I would have to see her."

"You'll have to settle for parts of her. Your problem has been resolved by our *efficiency.*"

And to the great good luck of her stumbling onto our doorstep.

Breath exploded on the other end, and tangible relief. "Excellent news! Was she, er, alone and unencumbered?"

"Very much so." Tannhauser grinned. "Perhaps now we know a little about you, our generous employer . . ."

"You best forget anything you may think you know. Much better for everyone. I have it on good authority that two remaining council members are sheltering in a house on the reservation. Here's the address. You can't miss it—it's the only Cape Cod around."

Tannhauser swallowed his retort. There were payments yet to be made—no need to poison the well. The woman had briefly entertained and then fed them. She was Mr. XYZ's business, and Tannhauser had been taught to follow orders without question.

"We'll get right on it," he promised.

"See that you do. I'll be in touch."

"Use the secure line," Tannhauser said.

"Of course. Now go earn my money."

Tannhauser threw the phone across the room, where it shattered into fragments.

"Gentlemen, the endgame is upon us."

Chapter Twenty-Two

Arnow

Fatigue made him light-headed, after an hour in his basement. He remembered Jessie telling him about Lupo's recon of the house on Hemlock. It was one of the Timber Shores timeshares on a channel between two lakes. Fancy vacation houses, usually rented by the week or month. During business hours, Arnow would have asked for the company records. But it was late, and he had no time to observe the niceties. He could barge in there and claim probable cause. Ending the killings would erase any improprieties he might rack up meantime.

He wanted to talk to Lupo about the Hemlock house, but he was getting antsy. Why not just go in blazing?

Arnow knew he was slipping the bounds of good sense. What if they were innocent timeshare buddies? Then it would be his ass strung up for everybody to kick. Lupo would be irrelevant. It was his job he'd fuck up.

The Remington lay on the desk like a coiled scorpion with its military folding polymer stock and pistol grip. He jacked in silver rounds, wishing he could feel the power. Wishing he could prove to himself it was all true.

"Rita, patch calls through to my cell," he instructed. He plucked his Kevlar vest from its hook and shrugged into it.

"Knock knock," came from the door. "Heading somewhere?"

Arnow looked at his watch.

"Hello, Mayor." Infinite patience in his voice. "Do for you?"

"You look like a man on a mission, Sheriff. I like that. I'd like to go along. I'm good with a scattergun, if I say so myself."

Great, Arnow thought. *Just what I need—a cowboy for a boss.*

Heather Wilson

Curled up in a ball on her bed in a dark hotel room.

That was where she was.

Her crew called and knocked, her cell had vibrated itself off the nightstand, and she had ignored the hotel phone bleating at her like a lamb to the slaughter.

She was in a dark place within a dark place, and she thought she'd climb out when she felt like it.

Unfortunately, Heather Wilson the television anchorwoman and reporter couldn't disappear for long. Somebody would come looking. She worried Tef would be back. He'd been interrupted once, but soon his focus might return to her.

She breathed heavily, quickly, almost panting.

Fear made her heart flutter.

Who could she rely on?

The sheriff was a cute enough guy, but as a cop he didn't have a clue. And now she needed a cop. Or somebody who'd act like one.

That left her with the enigmatic Nick Lupo. He seemed both taken with her and totally uninterested, which made *him* interesting. She pictured him, dark hair settling on the collar of his black leather jacket, light stubble giving him a roguish look, boyish face just now beginning to show his age but gracefully. She pictured him with a gun in his hand.

He was what she needed. He was the only one she could count on in a struggle with that Tef kid and his weird eyes. And—*whatever else.*

She uncurled, freshened up, and snuck out into the hall.

It was time to find the man who could help her. She wasn't sure why Nick Lupo was the one, but she sensed his ability.

Heather Wilson was finally past her self-pity. Now she was back on the path of ownership, looking to buy back something she'd lost.

Tannhauser

Driving his men to the edge was routine. He'd done it in Iraq and on a dozen other "security" assignments, many only borderline legal. Schwartz was a good man, a great wolf.

He was *old school.*

Tannhauser liked that phrase.

Old school.

They were both old school, like their grandfathers who wore the Fatherland's uniform when in humanskin. In wolfskin, they had been throwbacks too, to something even older school.

Tannhauser led his pack to where Mr. XYZ had instructed.

It was a neat Cape Cod, at odds with most of the log-built and clapboard homes on and near the reservation. Here two survivors of the elders' council were holed up.

And they would both be food soon enough. At this point, there was no telling yes votes from no votes—they were all *meat* for the taking.

They circled the house, and Alpha howled his orders. One-eyed Schwartz still smarted from the damage done by the silver buckshot. Had the humans gotten together and coordinated their defense? He didn't think so. His one long howl signaled he was in position. The others responded.

Tannhauser reserved the best part for himself. He stood on a crooked concrete slab in front of the glass patio door along the rear of the house. Tef and Schwartz were on front door and driveway watch.

Their howling would shake loose the humans' fear.

But then the nearby undergrowth parted and another wolf lunged at him. Before Tannhauser could sidestep, the heavily muscled black wolf was upon him. Powerful jaws closed on Tannhauser's shoulder and tore flesh and fur in a bloody cloud.

Tannhauser yelped.

Enraged by the attack and his own weak response, he whirled, his jaws ready to tear into his assailant.

But the black wolf was already disappearing into the spaces between the pines on the other side of the tiny backyard.

Alpha howled for his pack to follow his lead.

They could run down mere humans with their eyes closed, no hurry there, but an enemy wolf must be terminated with extreme prejudice.

This *verdammte* wolf had already caused them enough trouble!

He heard his pack howling behind him and led the chase, the chill night tasting like heaven in the back of his throat, bloodlust filling his nostrils.

Prey: Eagle Feather and Davison

Inside the house, the loyal Rick Davison stood locked in his study with the elder, Eagle Feather. *Eagleson.* Both cradled shotguns.

Eagleson held his shotgun loosely, defending the door.

Davison had heard the legends, the rumors, but he hadn't believed.

Until now.

Sweat poured from his forehead. No matter how much he wiped it, there was more. The shotgun stock was clammy.

The howling outside had begun to recede. Whatever they were, perhaps they'd been called off.

"Are they gone?"

The tribe's unofficial historian stared at the elder, who stood arrogantly surveying the room.

"Sounds like it. There, you hear it? The howling's moving away. But they'll be back."

"How do you know?" Davison looked at his hands. They shook as if he had Parkinson's.

"We're in the way. I think my old friend Sam Waters was right."

"I thought you and he were no longer friends."

"Don't be a fool, Davison. Tribal blood outlasts mere friendship. I half believed him. Gave Daniel Bear our sacred dagger."

"Fat lot of good it did him."

"Do you have something to say to me, *Davison?* Do you even remember your given name?"

"Your stubbornness led us to this mess. Your lack of real leadership, your interest only in enriching yourself and your investors. You made a pact with the devil, old man, and *he's here to collect!*"

"What the hell are you babbling, idiot? I'm the only one here with vision enough to bring our tribe the riches it deserves. The destiny it must meet."

Davison hefted the shotgun, his anger and fear colliding. "You call *this* destiny? At the point of a gun? Defending ourselves against—what, *monsters?* You're pathetic. No one on the council should have listened to you, no one!"

Hysteria was taking hold, but Davison no longer cared. "Our friends and colleagues are gone, butchered to fulfill some bullshit destiny you convinced yourself you could bring about. You have no sense of history, old man. No sense of decency." He broke down. "Our friends. All gone. Thanks to you and your precious project."

"Davison, *you're* pathetic. You're losing your marbles. We're fine here, protected. The others were fools. The new council will be bolder, more efficient—"

"Get out of my house." He trained the shotgun on the old man's chest.

"What?"

"You heard me. Get the fuck out of my house. And don't come back."

"What about the wolves?" Eagleson whined. His eyes

swiveled from side to side. Stared at the gun barrel in his face.

Davison grinned without humor, gesturing with the shotgun. "Take your chances, you bastard. You always liked gambling.

"But leave the gun," he added.

Arnow

Malko's cell phone had trilled at just the right time. Arnow took the opportunity to sidle toward the door, collecting several riot guns and straightening his Kevlar. The mayor's voice rose as he spoke into his phone, the sheriff and his mission apparently forgotten.

But before he could leave the building, Malko caught up to him. "Sheriff, Tom, wait for me. I'm going on a ride-along. You seem to be heading for trouble. I'm not afraid of a little trouble."

"Thanks, Mayor, I appreciate it, but I'll have my deputies waiting for me when I get there."

There was no way Arnow would tell the mayor he was about to raid a vacation property. Fuckin' headlines!

At the door, Arnow stiffened. Somebody with a long gun approached out of the shadows.

"Uh, who is that?" His hand went for his pistol.

"Sheriff, it's Rick Davison, from the reservation. We met last year." He was panting.

Arnow turned to Malko, shrugging. The mayor seemed curious. "Yeah," Arnow said. "I remember, but—"

"There's something terrible happening, Sheriff. Eagleson and I were just attacked in my house. Attacked by wolves!"

Malko laughed loudly. "Surely, Mr. Davison, you're mistaken."

"No, Mayor, we both heard them." His intensity floored them.

"Where's Eagleson now?" Arnow asked.

Davison hesitated. "I kicked him out."

"Into the woods? By himself?"

"Yes. He's an evil man whose ego dragged our tribe into some kind of hell. I blame him for all this killing."

"Not personally?"

"No, I don't think so. But I think he called up some kind of demon. He thought so too. Gave a sacred dagger to Daniel Bear. Poor Daniel, butchered like a—"

Arnow stopped him from blubbering. "Give me the shotgun. I'll have some deputies meet us at your house. We'll look for Eagleson."

Shit, now he'd have to postpone raiding the Hemlock house.

Malko nodded. "Sounds logical, Sheriff. I'll stick here and direct your deputies in your absence."

Arnow started to object. But then the idea of Malko staying behind suddenly appealed and he agreed.

"Let's go, Davison."

Arnow planned to switch the elder's shells. *Why not?*

Lupo

They were close on his trail, confident they could track and run him to ground.

They've done this a thousand times before, he thought inside the Creature's head. Trained military style. Small comfort—they could probably outrun, outflank, outfight, and outgun his Creature.

The chill air froze his breath as it puffed from his snout, and he felt ice chips in his whiskers. The ground grew harder beneath his paws. The North Woods liked to remind they weren't ready to grant spring quite yet.

The aches of fatigue began clamoring for his attention. Legs and paws burning, shoulders straining, neck shooting painful jabs throughout his body. His nose tasted the air again, and he suddenly realized the Creature was slowly leading the pack toward Sam's safe house.

Jesus, no!

Once again, he had to wrestle the Creature for control.

Confusion rippled through his brain, the usual tug of war between the wolf and human sides.

Finally, with the three seemingly only yards behind him, he veered away from the familiar track and started leading them in a circle.

One of them, the wounded wolf, guessed Lupo's intended direction. Suddenly he came straight at Lupo, somehow cutting a secant path straight through the thick stand of jack and white pines. Heading him off and leading him into the others' jaws in a classic flanking action.

The darker swath to Lupo's right was the narrow channel between two lakes. In one quick motion the Creature lunged through the trees and into the frigid water, submerging completely and being swept away by the mild current.

Ears aching with the cold, his head reaching for the night sky, he broke the surface. The wounded wolf teetered on the shore, hesitating.

Bastard'll probably catch hell from the others, Lupo thought. He swam toward the opposite shoreline. The Creature growled. He hated swimming.

Tannhauser

"We had him!" he raged at his friend Schwartz. "You fool, you forced him into the water. Now we're back at square one."

The pack had doubled back to the Cape Cod, but the house was empty, and scents indicated the occupants had split up. They had tracked one, but lost the spoor in a confusion of trails left by others, including the enemy wolf.

He led them back to the Hemlock house to regroup.

His stitched-up wound throbbed.

Aching from the missed opportunity, they had a snack from the freezer, tearing into the still soft flesh there.

Tannhauser roared at them until the phone interrupted his tirade.

Tef

He heard Alpha take the call and grinned. More action was definitely better than less. Their employer was ordering them out again.

Tef glared at Schwartz, who lay in his bunk moaning.

Bastard was weak. To think he'd once thought the old fuck had his back. But now he was like half a man. Less than half a wolf.

The way Schwartz had let the enemy wolf slip through his fingers was unforgivable. Tannhauser had about busted a gut. But Schwartz didn't seem to care, wrapped up in his own pain, the pack be damned.

It was almost time to challenge Alpha's authority. But no Schwartz to watch his back.

There was much unfinished business here tonight.

And when it was over and done, Tef would be holding the reins. Tannhauser would either submit, or he would be dead. Only then would Tef be free to recruit his own pack.

Dreams floated above him as he awaited his orders.

"Some real-estate records seem to have given up the location of a certain safe house," Alpha announced. "Saddle up."

"Rock and roll," Tef whispered.

Schwartz just groaned.

Tef suddenly wished he had the Wilson woman here. She was unfinished business. He wondered where she was. But there would be time for her later.

"Rock and roll!" he shrieked. *About bloody time.*

Chapter Twenty-Three

Jessie

The silver-loaded shotgun was in the Maxima's trunk, where she hoped it wouldn't bother Nick too much. But she had wished she could hold it in her hands when she felt the presence nearby.

They'd agreed to meet at his place on Circle Moon Drive, so she'd parked in his driveway. Her place was at the far end of the long drive, a circuitous route away.

She watched the tree line anxiously, hoping he would arrive soon. They would decide how to arrange the ambush he suggested. She agreed now, but reluctantly. It went against her principles.

One second it was dark and lonely on the gravel drive, and the next she heard rustling. Her breath hitched—*was it him?* She caught the blur of his wolf form leaving the woods, and then he was beside the car, leaning in to kiss her behind the ear.

She shivered slightly, from relief and—something else, too. She wasn't afraid of him, but afraid for him. She wondered if this latest crime wave would take him away from her. Maybe it already had.

"How're things?" he asked. His muscles stood out in the twilight, glistening with beaded water. His dark eyes sought hers. Then his lips found her mouth.

"Mmmm, better now," she muttered, kissing back with heat.

Once in the car, dressed again in the clothes she had brought, he described his run-in with the wolves at the Davison house.

"We'd better head out there and see if they're all right," he suggested. "Then Sam."

"I have a silver shotgun in the trunk."

"I know," he said, grimacing.

She looked pained. "Thought you could handle it that far away."

"I can." He added, "Maybe give the elders some shells."

"Sure." She hated admitting she and Sam had stockpiled so much silver ammo.

"You drive," he said. "I'll call Sam."

Sam didn't answer his phone.

Sam Waters

He was on patrol around his cottage—*checking the perimeter*, Lupo would have said—when Eagleson showed up.

After almost shooting him, Sam invited him in.

"What were you doing out there? You know our enemies are on the path . . ."

"There's evil about," Eagleson agreed, shaking with cold and something more. "Davison threw me out of his house. What have we done to deserve this hatred?"

"You know, maybe you should look within." Sam felt bold, probably because there was no fancy conference table between them. "Maybe some of it is hatred bouncing back at you."

He herded the elderly man inside. The Grey Hawk family gaped at the elder, perhaps noting that his trademark bluster was missing.

"Please join us," Bill Grey Hawk said. His sarcasm was subtle, and Eagleson didn't catch on.

"Thank you, thank you. At least there's one left with a bit of civility."

There was a tap at the front door. When everyone whirled

to face the door, two living room windows burst inward in showers of glass and wood. A large black wolf and a smaller gray wolf leaped through the jagged openings.

Sam let loose with the shotgun and a partial load of buckshot burned off part of one wolf's head.

The black wolf's skin sizzled and smoked, and he screamed like a gut-shot hyena. The smell was sickening.

Sam tried to bring the shotgun to bear on the other wolf, but the front door exploded and sent sharp wood slivers flying in a wide radius. Sam took a large strip of door frame across the head and landed in a heap. The shotgun flew out of his grasp and skittered behind the other wolves. The gray wolf approached the defenseless humans menacingly. The wounded black wolf whimpered, trying to bite off his own head.

"Hold up," said the tall man who now stood in the doorway. The gray wolf stared like a stone sentry at the terrified Grey Hawk family.

Bill Grey Hawk looked desperately for the shotgun, but the gray wolf advanced, fangs exposed. Grey Hawk retreated, hugging his children. His diminutive wife hid behind him.

"What do you want?" he asked the man in the doorway, who seemed to control the beasts.

"You," the man said. "All of you."

He smiled, and his wolf's fangs made the children cry.

Schwartz

The silver should have killed him, but his wolfskin was tough. His grandfather had passed down good genes, forged in the Fatherland and nurtured with patriotism and ruthlessness.

Instead, the silver ate into his flesh and killed everything in its path. Schwartz swore he could feel each organ shut down in the onslaught of the silver cancer from the humans' buckshot. How, how was it that they knew the ways of the wolf? How did they know what they faced? Why were they not impotent in the face of Tannhauser's pack, as they should have been?

The pain kept him from speculating. The pain kept his flesh a constant miasma of hallucinogenic reveries interrupted only to drag the screams from his raw, bloody throat.

Schwartz struggled to rise and reach Alpha, for he knew Tef had become ambitious and materialistic. He recognized the signs in Tef and would have warned his old friend, the other descendant of the old order. Tef was a scrappy little mongrel they had thought they could shape into a great future Alpha male, but he had seen the false light of indulgence and instant gratification, and he baldly rejected their notions of the military code crossed with the rule of Alpha and the way of the wolfskin.

No, Schwartz knew he was done. He half expected Tef to finish him right now, but the young one had been distracted by a bright object once again. This time a woman, of all things. *A disgusting human.* Tef had the right to challenge Alpha and take over, start his own pack, but Schwartz and Tannhauser once thought he would learn at their side.

Now Schwartz knew better. From his single eye he shed bitter silver-acid tears that stung and burned and sizzled the external skin as well as the internal.

He still felt his noble grandfather living through him and his experiences, but now the connection faded. It was time to step aside. Schwartz awaited his fate, grasped by the blinding torturous pain of being eaten alive from the inside out.

Tef

After helping One-Eye Schwartz back down to his bunk, he went into the den to get away from the crybaby's whimpering.

Christ, you'd think the bastard hadn't spent all the same months in Iraq.

Yeah, he'd been wounded a couple times. Silver was a bitch. But as a hardened combat veteran, he should have been able to handle it without crying like a girl. Alpha had been hurt, too, by the enemy wolf, but he hadn't whimpered about it.

Still, that had been a lapse in Alpha's judgment, hadn't it? Tef shook his head in disgust.

Now was almost time for breaking Alpha's hold. He was hampered by the current financial arrangement. Their employer made payments to Tannhauser's private Cayman Islands account, which they verified through a secure Web site. For Tef to claim his pay for this and other missions, he needed the account number and password only two people had: Tannhauser and their employer. Tef could torture it out of their employer, but he'd been stymied by all the secrecy.

They had tied up their terrified prisoners, and then they'd tortured the old man, Eagleson, asking him about Cranberry Island until he led them to his leaky old boat. The island idea had come from Mr. XYZ, who decided they could more easily lure their enemies to a remote location. Tannhauser had taken the group of prisoners to the island, and Tef was to lure the other wolf and anyone else who came along into their jaws.

Tef loved missions like this.

Gave him a big old boner, they did.

He conjured up the sexpot Heather Wilson and the hold he'd had on her. Sometimes the werewolf gene affected humans who came in touch with it in bizarre ways, but Tef had had the same effect on humans his entire life.

He grinned, approaching the freezer for another snack.

And went rigid.

The freezer door had been opened. He could tell because it hadn't closed right.

He Changed and stood on four legs, sniffing the air. He'd tasted the same scent, crossed with that of the wolf who had reconned them. Having another wolf in the area was akin to a challenge for Tef, but there were various threads here in this supposedly sleepy community. The radio preacher seemed ready and willing to incite a riot over the fishing rights. The casino project caused a problem for their employer. And presumably for others in the community. Tef loved strife of all kinds.

But somebody had breached their base.

He left the wounded Schwartz, barely able to control his disgust.

It was almost time to bug out. Every wolf for himself.

Mr. XYZ

Ground mist ebbed and flowed like an ocean tide off the road and down onto the shoulder. Visibility had decreased steadily, but he knew the landmarks well.

He steered off the main road and bumped along through the claustrophobia-inducing pine trunks until he reached the spot. *His spot.* When he climbed out of his SUV, he displaced the mist around his legs and sent it swirling away into eddies.

He dragged the usual vinyl Christmas tree bundle, unmindful of the sickening crunch heard each time the sagging end thumped over a rock or tree root. The black pond beckoned.

Had things played out differently, he might have had *two* bundles to mess with. He was suddenly glad for the less work. His head still throbbed from where the other bitch had smacked him. That was a lapse in judgment. He'd gotten greedy, careless, too wrapped up in his other business. He'd learned a lesson!

Plus she'd been older than his usual preference, even if well preserved enough. She'd looked a lot better behind the wheel of that Lexus than after he spread her out on his hand truck.

No, he'd been lucky there. He knew it.

He threaded the chain through the loops in the bag. He locked the padlock and stood, sighing with fatigue. Then he lifted his heavy burden.

Somewhere, a wolf howled and another answered. He shivered.

A sudden voice startled him, and he dropped the bag at his feet.

The flashlight beam blinded him when he whirled. A burly shape stood behind it.

"Oh, it's you!"

Mr. XYZ said nothing.

"I was wonderin' what all the commotion was. The fog's got me a little spooked, I guess. And those damn wolves. What are you doin—"

The voice faded to a whisper and the light wobbled.

Mr. XYZ looked down and saw that a long strand of bloody hair had somehow poked out through an unzipped portion of the bag. The flashlight beam made the blood glitter black.

"What—But that's—"

"This is unfortunate, Sabin," he whispered. "Very unfortunate."

The light flicked upward.

"Wait! Wait!"

The Taser shot who knew how many thousands of volts into Sabin and turned him into a dancing marionette, then dropped him like a sack of shit.

"Shit!" Mr. XYZ muttered.

He stepped on the flashlight and ground it under his boot. Then he swiftly deployed his Gerber folding knife and, a little sadly, slit Sabin's throat before he could recover from the Taser's effects.

He watched the big security guard bleed out, most of the blood hitting the pond. All the while, he wondered how the whole fucking thing had spun out of his control.

Now he had two sacks of trash to dispose of after all.

He set to it. He had other commitments to keep.

The howling intensified and gave him the creeps.

Chapter Twenty-Four

Lupo

Arnow's call found Lupo and Jessie on their way to Sam's.

"Listen, I got a council member here. A Mr. Davison. Says he and Eagleson were hunkered down at his place when they were surrounded by wolves. Then there was some sort of scuffle and the things backed off."

"Yeah, I was *kind of* there." Lupo grinned despite his fear for Sam.

"You or *it?*" Arnow's voice was crushed gravel.

"Both of us, Tom. Both of us. But I got them away from the house and hurt one of 'em. But what's worse is that no one at Sam's safe house is answering. We're heading there now, but it looks bad."

"What the hell's going on, Lupo? What are these guys—these *monsters*—doing?"

"Somebody's pulling their strings, maybe getting revenge for past wrongs. Something like that. Fact is, we're always a step behind. Reacting instead of acting."

"What the fuck am I supposed to do about it? How can I stop something that doesn't even make sense? I'm stranded here—no feds, no lab reports yet, and butchered bodies everywhere."

"You get some of that silver ammo distributed?"

"A couple of my deputies have it, maybe more by now. But how are we gonna catch these bastards in one place?"

Lupo looked at Jessie, grimly driving. "We have to ambush them and wipe them out, Tom. No trial, no evidence, no jury. What we showed you today should make it clear that this is no typical crime wave. We don't know the motive, but it doesn't matter. They'll never pay if we don't take care of it ourselves. Think of it as a disease." There was a blip in his ear. "Hold it, I got another call."

He cut off Arnow's voice and looked at Jessie. "Sam," he said, clicking in.

"Nicholas, it's Sam."

"Hey, Sam," he said, wary.

"My old friend Eagle Feather stumbled into our safe house," Sam said. "He told us we weren't very safe there, that Davison and he had run into the enemy. He convinced me we should move on from my cottage, to let him take us to a safer hideout."

"Shit," Lupo mouthed. *"They've got them all."* In the phone, he said, "Sam, where did Eagle Feather take you and the Grey Hawks? We can meet you there."

Jessie's face was ghostly pale in the dark car. One hand was on Lupo's knee, gripping hard.

"Turns out there's a perfect hiding place on Cranberry Island," Sam said. "You know it, Nicholas?"

"I know of it. Never been there."

"Eagle Feather has a boat. We're at the north end of the island. There's a construction site here."

"How the hell are we supposed to get out to you there?"

"You don't have to come here at all, Nicholas."

There was some commotion, a sound that might have been a slap, and then Sam hurriedly said, "If you want to meet us here, you can find a boat. Jessie has one."

She nodded.

"All right, hang on. I'll see what we can do. Call you back?"

"Sure, Nicholas, anytime."

The line was cut. Lupo clicked back to Arnow. "Shit, man,

they've been grabbed—Sam, Eagle Feather, Bill Grey Hawk and his family."

"How do you know?"

"Sam called me Nicholas, but he knows my given name is Dominic. They've got them stashed on Cranberry Island. The fuckers're using them as bait. Probably they want to get rid of us because we know what they are. They figure there are too many of us clued in. This is their chance to finish the job and take out the witnesses, too. Of course, they don't know we told you about the werewolf thing."

The werewolf thing.

Jessie's hand was scalding.

"The disease? But *you* have the disease."

"Don't I know it."

He added, "Jessie does have a boat. We'll wait for you."

"Davison tells me he has a boat here at the marina. Go in separately and meet on the island? Wait." There was silence for a minute. "They're developing the island. The north end has piers for the construction site, but the south end has an old one too. Meet at the south pier and go in together, or squeeze them? I have two of the special shotguns here. No time to clue in my deputies, except I can tell them to follow us in and mop up."

Lupo thought hard. An obvious trap, but if they showed up in greater strength and from two directions, they might turn it into a trap's trap. "Hell of a gambit, Arnow."

"This whole thing's fucked, far as I'm concerned."

Prey: Halloran and Morton

The patrol almost over, they swung out toward the marina. Last stop before turning over the shift to Faber and Arrales. They'd been doubled up since the killings began, but Halloran kept complaining.

"All we do is drive around and around, and then we clean up a crime scene."

"You want to be there when it goes down?" Morton was close to retirement. He preferred cleanup duty than getting involved in some kind of weirdo killing.

" 'To protect and to serve,' " Halloran quoted. "It'd be nice to actually manage that sometime."

"You're a good cop, Hal. I'd rather be a live cop."

"At your age."

Morton laughed, but he was serious. "Damn right at my age. I've earned some free time. I like fishing."

"You fish every weekend."

"Yeah, but I'd fish every day if I was done."

"You're done, old man." Halloran liked Morton, but he was beginning to tire of this retirement talk. Got in the way of the job.

"By the way," Morton said, "Jerry said something about switching our 12-gauge slugs for some new stuff at the station."

"What?"

"Don't know what it's about. The boss said we've got defective ammo, I guess."

"Figures! We'll be back in about fifteen minutes. Do it then, I guess."

"Hey, look at that," Morton whispered.

Halloran squinted where Morton was pointing. At the water's edge on the ramp, a figure was wrestling one of the marina boats into the channel. He had it half in, almost floating, and soon he'd start winching it off the trailer.

"Christ, he's stealing the boat," Halloran said. His hand went for the radio, calling it in.

"We better grab him."

They slid to a stop near the top of the ramp, and Halloran hit the lights. "Police!" Morton blared out over the PA. "Hold it right there, next to the boat! Hands where we can see 'em!"

The figure froze and held up his hands.

"Keep them high up!" Halloran said. They popped the

doors and stepped out, Halloran with his Glock in hand and Morton with the pump gun.

It was a young guy, blond, wiry looking. He was smiling.

"What's he smiling about?" Morton muttered. They approached cautiously.

The air rippled around the guy, and then a wolf stood in his place. He growled and lunged.

The deputies let loose with their guns, but the wolf didn't seem to feel the bullets at all.

The wolf was upon them, his jaws tearing Halloran's throat out before the cop could bring his hands up. Morton turned and lumbered up the concrete ramp, puffing and blubbering in panic, dropping the shotgun. But the wolf caught him and brought him down in seconds, ripping out his jugular. He sampled the hot blood and howled.

A distant siren seemed to answer.

Moments later Tef floated the boat, climbed aboard, then headed for the middle of the dark lake.

Heather Wilson

She'd been driving around, ready to give up and go to the courthouse to grab Arnow when Lupo's black Maxima roared past, screeching around a slow-moving pickup.

Jesus, what the hell was he doing?

She turned behind him and started laying on the horn.

Her skin was flaming hot, but she felt cold as she negotiated the curvy road, trying to catch up to him and make him pull over.

Suddenly his brake lights flashed, and the car slewed to the side, rocking to a stop.

Lupo leaped from the passenger seat, Glock in hand and pointed at the Lexus. "What? What's the deal? Hands in sight!"

She slid her window down and smiled grimly. "Is that an official police greeting, Detective?"

"What the fuck are *you* doing?" The gun barrel didn't waver.

She felt irritation coloring her cheeks. "Hey, I'm trying to tell you. That guy I was, uh, *seeing*. I think he's the killer."

"Helluva reporter," he muttered. "So, why tell me?"

"Look, I don't know what's going on, but it looks to me like things are fucked up around here. I was going to tell the sheriff, but frankly I'm not sure he's the right person."

They stared at each other.

A car drove by and swerved, seeing the gun in his hand.

"Shit," he said. The Glock disappeared. "What's your interest? Journalistic?"

"Hell no, not anymore. Personal. I can't prove it, but I think he killed my camera guy. Almost killed me."

"Look, we don't have time to discuss this. We're helping Arnow with this thing, but unofficially. It's dangerous. People are dead."

"I can handle a gun." She held up the Beretta 92F she'd kept in the glove box.

He leaned into the Maxima and spoke to the driver. Then he said, "Follow us. We're taking a boat ride. Keep that gun handy."

She gulped. Had she hoped he'd laugh at her, tell her everything was normal? When she got in behind them, it was all she could do to keep up.

She tried to ignore her hot and cold flashes.

Lupo

Getting the boat uncovered and gassed up took longer than he expected. Damn good thing it was already in the water. Heather seemed to shiver and shake the whole time he and Jessie worked. Jessie was clearly not happy with Heather's presence. But there was too much at stake.

At Sam's cottage they had found blood and a mess, the results of a struggle. Lupo felt the silver pellets embedded in the wood and had to wait outside.

"Looks like they tortured somebody in the bedroom," Jessie said grimly.

So they'd torn out of there and driven like demons until the sleek silver Lexus pulled up, honking like mad.

Now Jessie handed Heather the silver-loaded shotgun, explaining curtly that it was not to come close to Nick. They loaded up with extra shells—did she have a never-ending supply?

Jessie piloted the aged tri-hull expertly through the narrow channels and along the darkened shores of Lakes Catfish and Cranberry. Dark huddled shapes indicated where the historic Eagle River boathouses rose out of the lake surface. One boathouse had hosted T.S. Eliot himself in its second-floor apartment. It was a story Lupo had found fascinating, but now the characteristic buildings were nothing but hiding places for the enemy.

Without Jessie's knowledge of the night-shrouded landmarks, they never could have found their way to their twin targets.

First they swung out north to Voyageur Lake, where Lupo jumped off and waded to shore. Inside the tree line, he shed his clothes and Changed. The Hemlock house was quiet, but lights were on. The Creature caught the scent—the wounded black-and-gray wolf, with silver sizzling away inside his many festering wounds.

The Creature reconned. It was as if the enemy wolf had given up—wounded twice, he had lost all heart. Lupo knew silver had that effect. It ate you up from the inside, consuming your organs and your brain, tunneling through healthy tissue and leaving behind disease and death. This wolf had been around, but its heart had been ripped out.

Once inside the house, the Creature found the helpless enemy wolf and lunged, jaws closing around the muscular neck.

The black-and-gray wolf's remaining diseased eye seemed to plead for death, and the Creature dealt it out without mercy. The wolf died, gratitude written in its last expression.

The air blurred, and then a middle-aged man lay where the wolf had been, his body crisscrossed with horrific wounds and slashes.

The silver buckshot in the corpse scalded Lupo, too, and he backed off. He felt no pride at the killing.

By the time he waded back out to the boat, Jessie was visibly worried. "Nick! What happened? We heard—"

"Nothing!" he snapped. "Nothing." Then his voice softened. "It had to be done. Just get us to the island before Sam and the others pay for our slow response."

Heather huddled behind them in the stern. Her face was flushed.

Jessie turned away and started the motor. Dark shoreline fell astern as they ate up the miles back through the northern lobe of Catfish and then up a channel to the wider Cranberry. A night wind whipped up whitecaps. If there hadn't been clouds, they might have seen the Northern Lights. Even so a weird glow seemed to light the water from below.

Cranberry Island was a thickly wooded pear-shaped mass bisecting the middle of Cranberry Lake, one of the larger bodies in the Chain of Lakes. The north shore flowed into an elongated spit of land like a finger. A privacy-seeking Hollywood movie star had purchased a portion of the north side and had begun to build, literally, a green mansion. Speculation had run rampant about whether the celebrity was named Pitt, Costner, or Affleck. The money just rolled in.

Heather told them she had covered the early days of the construction, which was now about half complete in the middle of a large clearing near the northern beach. The first-floor beams and fireplace rose up from the gentle hillside, looking more like the hulk of a destroyed mansion than one on the rise.

They circled around the north side quietly, then found the pier on the southern side.

"We'd better wait for Arnow," said Lupo.

Barely minutes later a low rumble marked the arrival of

Davison and Arnow in a narrow vintage speedboat. As it nosed toward them from the darkening waters, Lupo spotted a third figure.

One of the deputies?

He took the hawser and tied up the fifties "woody" behind Jessie's boat.

Christ, what was Mayor Malko doing here?

Arnow climbed onto the pier awkwardly, with Davison and Malko following much more gracefully.

"The mayor insisted on a ride-along. Claims he's good with a gun. I, uh, deputized him."

Lupo stepped back hastily, the silver in their loads scalding him. "Whatever, it's your show."

"That's right, Detective. Sheriff Arnow is the ranking law enforcement official present, so he's in charge. Dr. Hawkins, it's nice to see you. The sheriff filled me in on what's going on—"

"*My* show?" Arnow snorted. "You're making vigilantes out of us and you give me command?"

Lupo took him aside and asked how much he had filled in the mayor. "I left out some bits he wouldn't believe."

Lupo rubbed his tingling arms. He quietly explained what he'd done to the wounded wolf. "Regardless of what you think, we're in it now to the end. Or the hostages will die. And we still don't know what the fuck they want, really. Got any better ideas?"

"No."

Heather and Jessie's silence was chillier than the cold night air.

This is it, Lupo thought. *We're risking it all.*

They distributed their weapons, making sure all the shotguns carried silver loads. Lupo, Jessie, and Heather followed the eastern shore, while Davison led Arnow and Malko in a straight traverse of the island following a roughly overgrown service road.

Sam had indicated they were inside the construction site.

Arnow's group would reach the site from the south, while Lupo's would come in from the northern beach. They hustled over sandy dunes and piney clearings, aiming north to swing back down. Heather and Jessie tripped over exposed roots and were slashed by branches whipping them mercilessly. Lupo instinctively navigated the woods as the Creature might have. Suddenly the site was upon them, set amidst a wide clearing bordered by pines on the southern edge and beach on the northern.

Chill wind whistled through the bare rafters and wall skeletons huddled around a massive chimney. Neither the bad guys nor the hostages were visible.

When they were in position, Lupo took Jessie's hand and kissed it. "Watch out for her," he said, nodding at Heather.

Before she could agree, he willed the Change and after the air blurred around him he stood as the wolf. Then he bounded toward the enemy's camp.

Chapter Twenty-five

Jessie

When Lupo Changed, Heather's mouth opened wide to scream, but Jessie clapped her hand over it.

"Easy," she hissed, "he's with us."

Heather's eyes bulged, and she sagged into Jessie's embrace. "Gee, what a wimp," Jessie muttered. But then she checked Heather's pulse. It was racing, her skin clammy. *Great time to get sick.*

Jessie grabbed up both shotguns.

Arnow

The road on which Davison led them bisected the island and ended at the mansion site. They hunkered down and waited for Lupo's group to arrive—a vibrating cell phone gave them the message.

Arnow had avoided filling in Malko on what Lupo and Jessie had shown him, but he made sure the mayor wielded a silver-loaded shotgun. He seemed to know his way around it. Now that he knew Lupo would recon the site, Arnow led Davison and Malko closer. He could see heads now, people seated on a fieldstone wall surrounding a wide patio.

The hostages.

"Let's move up on them," he whispered. "Lupo and his group will come around and flank them."

"Yes, let's move up," Malko said, jabbing the shotgun muzzle painfully into Arnow's back. "Drop the guns."

Arnow whirled, but the shotgun dug into his side, throwing him off balance.

"Drop them," Malko ordered again.

Davison looked confused, but he dropped the Remington.

"What the hell are you doing, Mayor?" Arnow lay his gun down near his feet.

"Step away from them." They did so. "You threw a monkey wrench into my plan, Sheriff, you and that fucking city cop." He stood up and called out, "Tannhauser, it's XYZ coming in with prisoners." He prodded Arnow and Davison toward the patio.

"About time, XYZ," a whispered voice responded.

Arnow felt the rage boiling up inside. All the time the mayor gave him hell for doing his job, *he* was part of it. He wanted to kick himself. They approached and he recognized Sam Waters and Bill Grey Hawk and his family, but not the tall, distinguished military type called Tannhauser, who held an HK submachine gun on them.

Christ!

Lupo

Wearing the Creature's skin, he made a half circuit of the site and caught sight of the hostages and the lone gunman. Where was the other one, the young blond guy? He hated making a move while a piece like that, a bishop at least, was invisible on the board.

Now he watched as the fucking mayor led Arnow and Davison into the camp at gunpoint, and he forced the Creature to slink closer silently. He had to hear what sort of game the mayor was playing.

The one called Tannhauser turned his nose up and sniffed the night air.

He knows I'm close.

Where was the young one?

Now the mayor conferred with the Alpha man, pointing at the opposite side of the site.

Then the underbrush broke suddenly and Jessie and Heather stumbled out, also at gunpoint. The blond guy, the bishop, walked behind them.

Fuck! Lupo swore and the Creature stifled a growl.

Better to hold out and wait. He was their only hope now.

He slinked even closer.

Mr. XYZ

It was exhilarating! Much more than he'd thought. He always loved control over others: his town, his cops, his women. He loved this gun pointing and having *henchmen* to do his bidding. Tannhauser and the weird kid. Where was the third one? *Didn't matter.* He had two henchmen, hostages, the council was nearly decimated, and—he looked at Jessie Hawkins and imagined her spread out on his hand truck. The Wilson chick, too, but there was something off about her. She was green in the gills. But the doctor, she was a feisty one. She'd struggle nicely with the duct tape. She'd be worth the wait. Maybe Heather Wilson would make a good appetizer, and Jessie Hawkins could be the main meal.

Jessie and the Wilson chick stood desultorily near old Sam Waters and the sheriff. Davison and the Grey Hawk family made a tight little knot. They'd all have to die, of course.

The sheriff had a whipped look about him. He'd been shocked all right. Malko luxuriated in the way his game plan had come together. Even if the last quarter was mostly improvisation, it had worked out all right.

"So what was it, Malko? Religion? Hated the gambling? What's your beef with the casino?" Arnow flinched when the young guy went to cuff him with a gun barrel, but Malko waved him off.

"Nothing quite so *moral*, I'm afraid, Sheriff." He was turning positively garrulous now. "No, I was being preemptive. You see, if the construction continued on schedule they'd be draining the pond next to the site soon. They were supposed to leave it alone, but then they added the parking structure and that was it. When they drained that bowl full of scum, they'd find too many things that would have affected me. I couldn't let them do it. Shutting down the project seemed the only way."

"The disappearances!" Arnow snapped his fingers. "I should have—" His voice faded, full of failure and regret.

"I hired these highly recommended gentlemen to cause a little chaos. They were spectacular, weren't they? Now it's time to bring it on home. Looks like we're only missing your cop friend. We'll drag him in here. His lady friend, his buddy, you. He'll have to show up, won't he?"

"Don't count on it," muttered Jessie.

He stalked over, took her lovely chin in his hands and squeezed until she whimpered.

He liked that. *Liked it a lot.*

Tannhauser stepped up and removed his hand with a vise grip. "There's something you don't know about that cop," he said.

"I don't care. I'm in command, Tannhauser. *You* work for *me*."

Tannhauser smiled. "Yes, we do. Did you make the last payment as agreed?"

"Of course."

"Great," Tef said, and he shot Malko twice in the head with his HK.

"I guess it's a transfer of command," Tef added.

Arnow

He hadn't expected the quick justice. But he wasn't all that shocked.

These fucking criminals always eat their own.

He sidled closer to Sam Waters and whispered, "What about Eagleson?"

Waters shook his head sadly. "They tortured him and then dumped him over the side in Cranberry Lake. He was dead by then."

"Christ, it's all on your buddy Lupo now."

"He'll show. He's here already, I assume."

"Oh yeah." Arnow tilted his head. "Malko was an idiot. Dangerous but an idiot. I have a backup piece in an ankle rig. If I get the chance . . ."

"But you know they're—"

Arnow cut him off. Tannhauser was coming closer. The air rippled around him, and he Changed.

Suddenly a black wolf leaped out of the woods with a roar and landed on the other—Tannhauser's—wolf, jaws biting and slashing.

Lupo!

Arnow didn't hesitate, going for the tiny Glock 26 in his ankle holster and coming up with the two black wolves in his sights. He tracked them both for a second, whispering a quick prayer to choose well, then squeezed the trigger three times quickly.

Three fountains of blood spurted from the larger wolf's head.

It roared in pain and surprise, and Lupo's smaller black wolf backed off a few steps.

Arnow had coated his 9mm slugs with molten silver earlier that day, and now he saw what they did to Tannhauser. The old wolf died screaming, bleeding, and smoking, and changed back to his human form.

Sam Waters pushed Bill Grey Hawk and his family over the fieldstone wall, shouting at them to run for the beach. Davison herded them, looking back in horror at what was happening before his eyes.

Where's the young bastard? Arnow turned, gun following, but he was too late and out of balance, because a muscular gray wolf was in midleap and headed for his throat.

Sam Waters moved much faster than his years and met Tef's wolf, knocking him aside and out of his trajectory. As he fell sideways, the gray wolf snapped and his jaws took a huge jagged bite out of Sam's neck.

Sam staggered and fell to his knees, his hands up around his neck covered with blood. When he rose again, he scooped up the shotgun dropped by Malko, planted the stock in the sand and took a last look at his friends Jessie and Lupo, who was now circling the gray wolf. He smiled sadly at Arnow, then rested his chin on the Remington's barrel and pushed the trigger downward with his extended hand.

"Noooooooooooooo!" screamed Jessie, as the blast destroyed the top of his head in a bloody cloud. She turned and hugged a shell-shocked Heather, desperate with grief and disbelief.

Arnow wanted to repeat his trick-shooting, but by now Tef and Lupo were snarling and snapping at each other, both their fur blood streaked. It seemed the gray wolf was getting the worst of it, but the black wolf wasn't making enough headway. Suddenly Lupo yelped and fell aside, his side badly slashed.

The gray wolf headed for Jessie and Heather, and Arnow brought up the Glock again, but before he could take a shot the air rippled and now it was Tef, the blond guy, grabbing Jessie by the hair and pulling her out of the clearing and into the woods.

"Goddammit!" he shouted, starting to give chase.

"Hold it, Arnow!"

It was Lupo, standing next to him and holding him back, his side bleeding profusely.

"That's one crafty fucker," he said, breathlessly. "Let him go."

"He's got Jessie!"

"He won't hurt her—yet. She's his ticket out of this. There's no boat left. Davison got the Grey Hawks to the beach. There aren't many moves he can make."

Lupo turned and saw Sam Waters lying in the sand. His dark eyes filled with hurt and sadness.

"He saved my life," Arnow said.

"I know," Lupo snarled. "He didn't want to be like me." His eyes were wild, nearly no longer human. "Look, we have to finish this." He nodded at Heather Wilson. "She can help us."

He told Arnow what she'd told him about Tef.

CHAPTER TWENTY-SIX

Lupo

They tracked Tef and Jessie down to the beach, where they now stood at the end of the pier. The boat was gone.

Lupo held his sadness at Sam's death off with his fear for Jessie's life. If he'd managed to neutralize the gray wolf, she'd be safe now. But he wasn't prepared for the kid's toughness and tenacity. Now he would have to outplay him.

Heather Wilson had agreed to help, though her hooded eyes showed clearly that she'd been damaged by this night. But she'd been fucking this Tef character, and there was no other option to play. Jessie was his human shield, and trying to shoot Tef would kill her, too.

"Ahoy there, Tef!" he said. Arnow was armed with a riot gun, and Heather was down to bra and panties. She should have been shivering, but her skin seemed inflamed, and she was sweating. "Want to propose a trade."

"Speak up," said Tef from behind Jessie at the end of the pier. "You've got a lot to learn about your wolfskin."

"That may be. But if you want to get past us, we want Dr. Hawkins. Your girlfriend here wants to join you. She says she's attached to you. We're willing to make a trade. You give us the doctor, and we'll give you Heather. We don't want either of them dead. They die, you die. Simple as that."

Tef worked it out in his head, the thoughts written on his face. There weren't many choices with his back to the water. Even if he leaped in, they'd pick him off from shore.

Lupo knew well enough Tef would think he had the queen in his hands. But there was a chance he'd make his play during the trade. Tef *had* to kill them all, or they'd track him down now that they knew everything about him. And he wanted to live to spend his money.

"Are you set?" Lupo whispered to Heather.

"I'm set," she said, grimacing.

"He's going for it. He'll make a move during the trade, but he thinks he has to."

"Send her across to me. I'll send the doctor."

Jessie's eyes said it all.

Tef

He'd grab them both. They were naïve if they thought he'd go so easily. But he did feel a weird kinship with Heather Wilson. He'd ridden her so much, so well, and she'd been so *giving* . . . it was fitting that he use her to his advantage now that options were few. These humans weren't thinking like an Alpha male, and now *he* was Alpha. He would use Tannhauser's contacts to build his own pack, and he'd return here and make this backwater his own private kingdom.

The bastards had done him a favor, ridding him of Tannhauser. He had the bank codes, he had the hostages, he would maneuver his way past these hicks. He'd eat their guts before this cold night was over.

Heather was almost naked. He felt a boner coming on.

The doctor felt it too, through her clothes. She squealed, and he ground himself into her, enjoying her disgust.

"Send her across to me," he barked.

Heather Wilson

She stepped across the wide pier, aiming right for the doctor. Her gaze grabbed Jessie's tear-bloated eyes and blinked, blinked, then signaled left.

She should have been freezing, but instead felt heat glowing from inside. It was strange, but she didn't care.

She saw Tef watching her from behind Jessie's hair as it flew in the cold breeze.

Just a few more steps.

He smiled at her. *Were those fangs in his mouth?*

Tef gave Jessie a shove forward, but kept behind her.

But Jessie had understood. She dropped to the left, surprising him.

At exactly the right moment, Heather pulled Arnow's small cocked Glock from where she'd had it tucked into the back of her panties, and put four quick rounds into Tef's chest.

A snarl came from behind her and Lupo had done *whatever the fuck he did* and now the black wolf lunged and tore at Tef, who also changed, but whose wolf was mortally wounded by the silver slugs.

The two wolves grappled, air blurring around them as they changed from wolf to human and back again over and over, to gain the advantage, arms to paws and back again.

Muscles tearing, bruising, blood pulsing from jagged wounds, both screaming as humans and yelping as wolves.

But finally it was over.

Tef was under the black wolf, the man, the wolf, and it was the black wolf whose jaws tore out the weakening wolf's throat.

Arnow was putting his vest and shirt around her, and hugging her to warm her cold skin. *Except her skin was scalding.* He whispered in her ear and put his arms around her while Jessie and Lupo met in a huge hug a few feet away.

Lupo's side was a ruined mess of slashes and open wounds, blood coating his pelvis and legs.

Heather looked into Arnow's eyes and saw something there.

Respect.

Interest.

Caring.

She shrieked, then tore out of his embrace and jumped into the black depths of Cranberry Lake.

His shouts were dulled by the cold water, which seemed to boil around her.

Jessie

Safe in Lupo's arms, barely able to comprehend what had just happened, she saw his wounds and immediately went into doctor mode. He smiled at her gratefully, then kissed her and she thought he would never let her go.

Behind them, Arnow was still splashing in the frigid water, looking for Heather. But she was gone.

They heard a rumble, and a boat materialized through the mist.

It was DiSanto, Faber, and Arrales, wearing SWAT gear and bristling with firepower. DiSanto's face was covered in bandages, but to Jessie he'd never looked better.

She squeezed Lupo with joy she could barely have described. But tears of grief ran freely again. *Sam was gone.*

"About time you got here," Lupo said, taking the rope they tossed. "Cavalry's late, as usual."

DiSanto frowned. "Had to drive like the dickens to get here, man. Traffic was a bitch."

Lupo groaned.

Dickie Klug

He wiped the fever sweat from his brow and felt the goose bumps rise on his arms like a dread disease.

His heart wanted to burst through his chest cavity.

He was filthy with gore.

He'd checked himself, desperate to make sure it wasn't his blood. It wasn't, but he could barely keep from screaming.

His hands shook like an addict's.

He had finally gone into the house. He lusted for the

take—it would keep him in rent and beer for a good long time, and away from the shit-ass jobs. Too many folks knew who he was, who his lazy fuckin' cousin had been. They hated him on principle, and he hated the fuck out of them, too.

He broke into the back door, easy as fuck, and he was in a large kitchen open to the front. A weak stove light dispelled the gloom. He knew where the top-notch stereo and the big-screen television and high-priced DVD player were. But he opened a side door thinking, *second television.* Instead it was a freak show full of fuck-all weirdness.

Three battered military footlockers with stenciled names he could barely see because they'd been partially sandblasted off lay in one corner. But that wasn't what made his head spin. No, there was something else. It was out of place, which was why he looked.

A wide coffin-shaped freezer plugged into the wall and softly humming. Out of place. In the kitchen, he'd never have looked at it twice. Here, it beckoned to him like a hypnotist.

He stood in front of it, not sure whose hand it was he saw reaching out.

He opened it and held the cover up and peered down into the cold fog, plastic trays, and a deeper space below.

And backed away as soon as he had a good look.

There was a stack of butcher-paper wrapped bundles in the trays. An incongruous ice cream bucket. He read the label. *Butter Brickle.* But then his eyes slowly focused on the center of the main compartment. The image resolved into something . . .

It was a human torso.

A *female* human torso. The breasts stuck up at him like tiny mountain peaks, their nipples dark and full. A few curly hairs sprouted from the aureolas, and he giggled like a madman when he saw those, because then he knew beyond any doubt that it was indeed a real human torso and not a latex sex doll kept in cold storage.

He saw the jagged edges of bones and frozen arteries or whatever the hell they were sticking out of the holes at the ends, flecked with dark red just beginning to crystallize.

The cover snapped closed with a crash to wake the dead.

He couldn't stop giggling. He snorted and broke out into a guffaw.

Fuckin'-A.

Jesus Christ.

He must have passed out, because when he thought he heard sounds from outside he couldn't quite remember what the hell he'd been doing before he opened the freezer.

Sounds from outside.

The dogs? The tenants?

He scrambled to his feet, all thought of thievery wiped from his mind.

He retraced his steps, stumbling out of the grotesque den, back into the kitchen and out the back door he had cracked. How long ago? *No fuckin' idea.*

Rustling in the trees made his blood run cold. He dove for cover, barely making the tree line and hitting the dirt with his face and chest.

Grateful he used that spray so religiously.

His night-vision goggles flipped down and turned on.

A huge dog broke through the brush near the back door. Then came a naked man who could barely walk. He was covered in blood, streaked with it as if he'd been in a war. The door opened. Another naked man came out and helped the bloody one inside. Then the guy stopped and stared at the cracked door, scanned the trees, and let out a growl Dickie would never forget.

The door closed and Dickie resumed breathing. He squirmed his way back to his stakeout spot, realizing too late that it was exactly where they had emerged. He felt and smelled the wetness. He had rolled in a pool of blood and—*and some kind of thick, disgusting pus.*

Jesus, it stank!

He scrambled up and took off through the trees, hoping

the dogs or men or whatever he had seen didn't decide to track him down, because he knew he could never outrun them.

He ran until he thought his heart and lungs would burst.

Later, safe in his shoddy one-room walk-up, he tried to put the whole thing out of his mind. But he couldn't. The goose bumps wouldn't go away. His clothes were in a reeking trash bag ready for the dump.

Dickie Klug crossed himself.

He hadn't done that since the nuns made him.

He couldn't erase the image: that woman's torso, breasts thrusting up at him. No matter how much he tried. Or how much cheap brandy he guzzled.

As he slipped under a haze of artificial comfort, his memory cleared.

The dogs had turned into the men. The wounded man had been a blood-covered dog.

Dogs?

No. He'd seen wolves before. These were wolves.

And yet they were men.

Dickie drank himself into a stupor trying to erase all the fucked-up images.

In the morning, he went fishing to help him forget.

When he saw the woman's corpse floating in the middle of Cranberry Lake, he put his hands to his mouth.

Jesus!

He pulled his boat alongside. And when he lifted her out of the water, her eyes popped open and stared at him.

He screamed.

"Take me to shore," she said. "And stop that yelling, for Christ's sake."

He clapped his mouth shut and followed her orders.

She looked *familiar.*

Chapter Twenty-seven

Arnow

Reports, bodies, explanations, investigations. It would all take a long time to sort out.

But the worst was knowing what he knew, and what he couldn't tell anyone about the perps. Sure made things difficult, he pondered. But draining the pond helped divert attention from the bizarre island raid. Malko's crimes were of a huge magnitude and stretched back over a decade. The feds and state police would be on it for years, matching DNA and remains with missing girl reports.

Bobby Lydell's show and his hold on the local populace faded fast once Malko's secret funding dried up. It was yet another case in which privately Malko undermined his own city. With no one to incite them, locals lost interest in the meager Indian spear harvest.

Arnow shook his head.

He wondered about Heather Wilson.

He'd really taken her death hard, only to tune in to her Wausau station two weeks later to see her filing a report about her experiences during that weekend.

He picked up the phone and made two calls.

Lupo

They sat quietly in Jessie's cottage, listening to their "up north" music, murmuring into each other's ears.

He had mourned Sam Waters privately. Davison had been voted to head the council, now that Eagleson was dead. The casino project was on hold, perhaps temporarily. But the void Sam left in Nick's heart would remain forever.

No one expected to find Doc Barrett's remains in a freezer inside the perps' rented house, least of all Nick Lupo. Why had she followed him here?

What kind of obsession would lead her to stalk Lupo, an officer she was sworn to help? What kind of luck would lead her to cross paths with the killers? Her funeral would paint her a hero, a dedicated law enforcement officer and doctor who risked her life to carry a warning to her patient Detective Lupo. They would award her a posthumous medal, of course.

Lupo snickered. When Jessie slapped him lightly, she avoided the multitude of bandages that crossed his bruised body.

He reached for her and drew her down to the rug in front of the blazing fire. For a while it was just the two of them, the flames, and the music.

Jessie

She held him close, and they kissed as if it were the first and last time. She thought briefly of how jealous she'd been and how stupid, but as he lowered himself gently on her waiting body, she couldn't help crying. From joy. And from sadness, too.

She'd put *Eye in the Sky* on repeat. "Silence and I" was just starting.

In the back of her mind, she saw an image of Heather Wilson on her television, looking radiant. She flicked it off and lost herself in Nick and the special music.

Still, her tears flowed and fell on Nick's shoulder.

She hoped his shoulder would always be available.

And she let a smile replace the tears for a while. A long while.

CODA

The candy-apple red low-rider Chevy had been sitting in the same spot for at least fifteen minutes when the driver's door of the silver Mazda 6 parked two spots behind it swung open.

The Mazda's window glass was tinted and license plates were mud spattered.

After climbing out, the Mazda's driver walked around to the sidewalk and checked the meter. The liquid crystal numerals indicated there was still time. He checked his watch, then headed west on National, his head angled toward the grimy shop windows and dingy doorways. His gait was long but unhurried, a man with a destination and perhaps an appointment, but early.

By the time he drew even with the low-slung Chevy, his eyes were locked on the Chevy's lone passenger, who was waiting with the car. His hand slipped under the ripped denim jacket and came out with an unregistered Taurus Millennium Pro 9mm. He veered toward the Chevy suddenly and with an economy of motion eased the barrel onto the glass. The startled passenger started to whirl, and the first two slugs took him squarely in the face as he turned. The third entered the top of his skull, and the fourth took him high in the chest just before he slumped into his seat, jiggling and convulsing, his mouth open and filled with blood and worse. His head was a burst balloon and his body had begun to smoke as if on fire.

A small cagelike brass catcher held the spent cartridges after they were ejected.

The Mazda's driver glanced around, slipped the clean Taurus back under his jacket, and sauntered back to his car. He slid in, started up, and nosed out onto the deserted street.

After three quick turns he pulled into a used car lot. Groaning, he stripped himself of the holster and pistol, tossing them as far away from his body as possible. His hands were on fire, fingertips and palms sizzling as if pressed onto a hot griddle. His chest was seared where the Taurus had rested.

He slipped out of his seat, leaving the keys, slapped a car-lot sticker on the Mazda and let himself into the black Maxima parked in the next slot. Already the skin of his hands and fingers felt cooler. He tore off the crinkled piece of latex that had covered his features and tossed it on the passenger seat. He started up and backed out slowly, reaching Mitchell just as a lone siren began converging.

Later, the car would disappear and resurface sporting a new paint job. A favor called in. *Playing with the devil.*

Dominic Lupo struggled to breathe normally. It was difficult with his hands and chest burning as if dipped in lava. But his pain would eventually diminish. The silver-coated slugs he had used in the clean Taurus would keep the thug dead. Nobody would notice the unusual slugs, not in an obvious south side gangland hush killing.

He couldn't allow a hardened criminal to *turn wolf.*

Lupo sighed through the tears.

Welcome to the Dark Side.

Welcome to hell.

In Rib Mountain State Park, west of Wausau, the moon glazed the treetops with liquid silver.

A howl split the darkening night. It frightened every furred animal within earshot.

She howled again, declaring her delight at the explosion of senses that had caught her for the third time. She felt each of her muscles tighten and relax in a sort of internal inventory. A cool breeze ruffled the thick fur on her back and made her skin tingle. She started to run on four paws, alive and excited and free for the first time ever.

She wanted to mate. She *lusted* for a mate.

But first she lusted for fresh meat.

The possibilities were endless.

SARAH PINBOROUGH

Author of *Breeding Ground* and *Tower Hill*

London streets that were once filled with pedestrians, tourists and shoppers are now clogged with thick webs and dead bodies. Spidery creatures straight out of a nightmare have infested the city, skittering after their human prey, spinning sticky traps to catch their food . . .

"I loved it! The tension explodes on the first page and climbs steadily. Take a look, one and all, at an original!"
—Horror Web on *The Hidden*

A few desperate survivors have banded together, realizing their only hope for survival is to flee the dying city. Their route will take them through wrecked streets, into an underground train station. Only too late will they discover their deadly mistake: their chosen tunnel is home to the hungry creatures' food cache, filled with cocooned but still living victims. Instead of escape, the group has run straight into the heart of a . . .

FEEDING GROUND

ISBN 13: 978-0-8439-6293-2